GLORY REVEALED

Also by Paula K. Parker

Sisters of Lazarus
Beauty Unveiled
Glory Revealed
Grace Extended
Slow Love
An Unlikely Evangelist
The Carpenter and His Bride

with G.P. Taylor
YHWH: The Flood the Fish and the Giant
YESHUA: The King, The Demon & The Traitor

Stage plays
The Sam Jones Story
Bloodlines
Jane Austen's Pride & Prejudice
Jane Austen's Sense & Sensibility
Jane Austen's Emma

GLORY REVEALED

Sisters of *Lazarus*
Book Two

PAULA K. PARKER

WordCrafts Press

Glory Revealed
Copyright © 2019
Paula K. Parker

ISBN: 978-0-9909761-8-9

Cover concept and design by David Warren

Published by WordCrafts Press
Cody, Wyoming 82414
www.wordcrafts.net

ACKNOWLEDGEMENTS

I have a confession. I have been guilty of flipping past the acknowledgements page in a book, not truly caring about people I did not know, and simply wanting to get to the heart of the story. Now that I am on the other side of the book creation process, I realize that while the story might be birthed in the author's imagination, it takes a team of behind-the-scene people to take it through to the published state. And then there is the author's family, who selflessly sacrificed so that he or she could craft the story.

Please take a moment to allow me to publicly acknowledge and thank these people.

Thank you to everyone who read *Sisters of Lazarus: Beauty Unveiled* and then encouraged me to write this sequel. Your enthusiasm, your kind comments and readers' reviews were a blessing and balm to my heart. I wish I could list each of you by name, but alas, there is not sufficient space.

Thank you, Malcolm Down. Even though we no longer work together professionally, your belief in my writing and your comments made me realize that it was possible to finish the story that began in that first book.

Thank you, Rick Larson, for sharing information from your research about the Star of Bethlehem and the Christ Quake.

Thank you, Helen Jones and Ximena Lindsey. Your eagle eyes caught the typos and grammatical faux pas, and your creative suggestions helped to polish this story until is gleamed.

Thank you, David and Dee Warren, for friendship, immense talent and generous nature. My new head shot is amazing and the book cover is simply breathtaking.

Thank you to Fred and Jean Parker, for your encouragement and for being the best in-laws ever. To my mother, Helen Jones, thank you for always believing in me and for being one of my biggest fans.

To my children, Rachael, Anna, Joshua, Bethany and Mary; my three sons-in-law, Nathan, Billy and John; and my grandchildren, Isabella, Penelope, Aubrey and Harrison. You are everything I've ever prayed for and one of the reasons that I do what I do.

To Mike, my best friend, the father of my children, the best husband a woman could ever have and now my publisher. Thank you for the love, support, encouragement and courage to pursue our dreams and chart a course into untested waters.

Of course, I cannot end an acknowledgment page without thanking the One who loves me more than anyone in the world, Who sacrificed everything for me, and Who daily reminds me that I am worth so much more; my Lord and Savior, Jesus Christ.

PROLOGUE

10 Nisan 3793
Bethany

T he door *whacked* under the force of Judas' palm, chipping off edges of stone where the wood slammed against the house's exterior. Unconcerned that he might have damaged the expensive hand-cut stone, he stomped down the front path and turned onto the street that led towards the marketplace of Bethany.

Located two miles southeast of Jerusalem, the village was a convenient stopping place for those traveling to the City of David. Despite its small size, by day it bustled with local residents going about their daily lives; people gossiping and bartering in the marketplace, priests traveling to and from the Holy Temple, Roman soldiers assigned to the Antonia Fortress in Jerusalem, or people from around the world visiting the heart of the Jewish world.

With the setting sun, Bethany's dusty streets emptied. Travelers moved on or sought lodging in the local inn while, here and there, lamplight flickered in windows as the town's residents retired to their homes to enjoy the evening meal and their beds.

Judas was doing none of it. Slender, with a black beard edging his chin and hair that fell straight to his shoulders, wearing a simple white tunic and sleeveless brown robe, his appearance would not give anyone pause or concern. This had always been of value to him, both when running from the Romans and later when hiding for darker reasons.

He glanced skyward. The full moon—a creamy orb hanging low in a clear sky—poured its soft light over Bethany's quiet streets.

His frown lifted briefly. As a child, his father had pointed out the *mazzaloth*, the pictures formed by the arrangement of the stars. Judas could still name them. His eyes roamed the sky as he located his childhood favorites: The Great Bear leading its cubs to the north; the Hunter and his two dogs chasing the Bull; and the Ram. Beyond marveling at the pictures in the night sky, his father taught him that the positions of these particular star arrangements announced to every Jew that Passover was nearly upon them.

Passover. His frown returned. *It was to be* this *Passover,* this *year,* Judas' thoughts raged. *Not just the traditional celebration to remember Israel's freedom from Egyptian bondage long ago. But freedom* now. Now! *All of their plans were in place, everything was coming together. Everyone was ready, everyone relying on* me *to bring in the last piece. In a few weeks, a few months, life would be different. This Passover would be remembered throughout history; and I would have wealth and power.*

Now all of that may fall apart—all because of a woman! *Because of Mary*! In frustration, he kicked a low growing nabk bush and yelped a curse when a long thorn pierced his foot. Hopping to the village well, he held on to its stony edge for balance, wincing as he removed the thorn.

Beer—lots of beer—that's what he needed to ease the pain and the memory of the humiliation he endured. *At the hands of a woman!* He turned around and headed towards the tavern, the sound of his sandals slapping against the hard packed dirt echoing the cadence of crickets and frogs.

He had taken only a few steps when his skin prickled. He was certain he was being watched. Glancing around, he scanned the moon-drenched street. *There…* A man was standing in the shadow of a house and—from the way he pressed against the mud wall—it was obvious he did not wish to be seen.

Judas turned and continued down the street until he came to an ancient olive tree, and slipped behind its gnarled trunk. Reaching beneath his robe, he grasped the handle of the dagger tucked into the girdle wrapped around his waist. Silently drawing the knife from its scabbard, he waited.

Soon, the sound of rocks crunching quietly underfoot reached his ears. When the man passed the tree, Judas leapt out and grabbed him, threw him against the tree's trunk and held the blade against his throat.

The man struggled. Judas pressed the blade in a little deeper. "Move once more," Judas snarled, "and I'll slice your throat like a sacrificial lamb."

The man stilled.

"That's right," Judas said. "Now, who you are and why are you following me?"

The man drew a ragged breath and whispered one word. "Judas."

Frowning, Judas lowered the blade and pulled the man into the moonlight. A little taller than himself, the other man was muscular with dark wavy hair and beard edging his face. He was dressed in the white tunic and black robe of a priest.

"Abel ben Joktan?" Judas released his grasp on the other man's arm and slipped the blade back into its scabbard.

"You held a knife to my throat," Abel rasped in wonder. He rubbed a hand across the skin below his beard and lifted it to peer at it in the moonlight. "There's no blood," he breathed in relief.

"Afraid of blood?" Judas sneered. "You are training to be a priest. Priests sacrifice animals every day in the Temple."

"I'm not afraid of blood," Abel straightened his garments. "Passover is but days away. If you had cut me, I would be ceremonially unclean and would have to wait a month to celebrate it."

Judas laughed. "A man nearly slices your throat and all you can think of is whether or not you can eat the Passover meal next week?"

Abel sniffed, frowning at Judas. "Why are you carrying a dagger? Is violence one of Jesus ben Joseph's teachings?"

"If you ever truly listened to him, instead of criticizing him, you would know what the Teacher's thoughts on violence are." Before Abel could reply, Judas continued, "I ask again; why were you following me?"

Abel paused before answering. "I was sent to watch Jesus ben Joseph."

"To watch the Teacher? Why? Who sent you?"

"Some men in authority are interested in him."

"You mean the Temple Leaders."

"I did not say—how do you—"

"Your father is a Pharisee as was his father. The High Priest and his father-in-law are Sadducees. Aside from them, you wouldn't do this for anyone else."

"They want to talk with Jesus bar Joseph."

"About what?"

Abel frowned. "Who are *you* to question the Temple Leaders?"

"I have no allegiance to them. They worry about angering their Roman friends."

"They have no friendship with Rome," Abel spat. "Roman dominion is a punishment from Yahweh. When all Israel once again walks in the way of the Law given to Moses, then Yahweh will intervene and free us. Wait," he narrowed his eyes. "Now I understand."

"Understand what?"

Abel pointed at Judas' robe, where the handle of the dagger was still visible behind his robe. "You carry a dagger." He lifted his hand to his throat. "You threatened to harm me." You are a *Sicarii.*"

Judas' laugh held more threat than mirth. "What do you know of *Sicarii*?"

"Everyone knows of *Sicarii.* They are Zealots who call themselves *Sicarii* because it means 'daggers.' It is rumored that they use their daggers to kill anyone who opposes war with Rome." He looked around and dropped his voice to whisper, "Some even say they kill Roman soldiers. The *Sicarii* leader Jesus Barabbas, along with two of his brigands, were arrested last month for trying to stir up a rebellion against Rome. It is said Barabbas killed a man." His eyes widened as if a sudden thought occurred to him and he stepped away from Judas. "Are you going to kill me?"

"No," Judas grinned at the fear in Abel's eyes. "Unless you give me reason. Now, let us go back to my question. Why are the Temple Leaders interested in the Teacher?"

Abel looked around the darkened streets—lamplight flickered in a few windows—and stepped closer to Judas. "All have heard Jesus ben Joseph speak of the Kingdom of Yahweh. Many people. . .*believe*—" his tone stated that he was not one of these believers,

4

"that Jesus might be the *Messiah*, the next King of Israel. The Temple Leaders would like to meet him—to learn what his intentions are—in order to determine whether or not to align themselves with him. You can help arrange this meeting."

"Why me? Why not ask Lazarus? He is your cousin."

"It is known that you are one of Jesus' disciples. Moments ago, I saw you leave the house of Simon *the Leper*," Abel's emphasis was derisive, "where it is known Jesus was supping."

"You mean Simon and *Martha's* house? She's your cousin as well."

Abel's brow lowered. "I will not speak of her. Her decision to disobey my father's command and marry that *sinner* caused irreparable damage to our family."

"I also heard that her sister Mary announced that she would rather choose a life of poverty over marriage to you."

Even in the moonlight, Judas saw Abel's eyes blaze with anger. "What do you know of this?"

"I was there that day."

Abel looked away. "Mary has proven she is not worthy to be a wife to one who will be a priest."

"Mary has proven she is not interested in being wife to just *anyone*," Judas murmured, adding a profane description about women who mislead men. He looked at Abel and grinned. "Everyone in that family harmed you that day, did they not?"

Abel's gaze shot back to Judas. "What do you mean?"

Judas laughed. "Lazarus."

"I was—pleased—to hear my cousin was not really dead."

"Oh, is that how your father explained it to you?" Judas' grin was not pleasant. "That Lazarus was not really dead?"

"What else could it have been?"

"The Teacher resurrected him."

Abel snorted, "When Jesus ben Joseph arrived, it had been *four* days since Martha and Mary announced Lazarus' death. If he had truly been dead, by that time his spirit would have left the area and ascended to Abraham's bosom. There would have been no possibility of his returning to the land of the living."

"How do you explain all who saw him dead?"

Abel waved away the weight of the witnesses. "They wanted everyone to follow Jesus. The rumor he had performed a miracle like the prophets of old would only increase his popularity."

"Lazarus was dead." Judas' tone was flat. "Deny it all you like, but that is the truth. If he had remained dead, your father would have had possession of his wealth and you would have had a beautiful wife. Now you have neither."

"Enough!" Abel's hand sliced through Judas' words. "The Temple Leaders would like to speak with Jesus ben Joseph. I do not wish to approach Lazarus, so I came to you. Will you help or not?"

"I do not know whether Jesus would want—" Judas started to turn away.

"The Temple Leaders are most anxious to speak with him," Abel interrupted. "I was told to inform you they would be happy to *reward* the man who helped."

Judas' foot froze in mid-stride. "A reward? How much?"

"It would depend," Abel shrugged. "For mere information they would pay little; for arranging an *actual meeting*, they would pay more." Abel's smile was slow and not at all pleasant. "Much more."

CHAPTER ONE

Mary bat Jacob, just what did you think you were doing?" Martha crossed her arms under her breasts, wrinkling the moss green linen robe and copper tunic. The coins edging of narrow gold ribbon threaded over her black hair reflected the flames dancing from the lamps around the room.

Mary smoothed her clothing and bent over to pick up her head cloth from where it had been discarded beneath the table. The dark rose length was scattered with stains; lifting it sent a waft of perfume into the air.

She didn't need to ask her sister to what she was referring; it was the same question Judas Iscariot had asked earlier in the evening. *It was probably the same question everyone present was thinking,* Mary thought. *He was just the only one to give it voice.* Whereas Judas—who was neither her kinsman nor her husband—had no right to criticize or demand an explanation of her actions—her older sister did.

Mary sighed. How could she explain to Martha, or to anyone, what she had been thinking when she herself didn't understand why—instead of giving the alabastron to Jesus ben Joseph—she had poured the spikenard over his feet.

She bent and lifted the jar from the floor where she had set it. Carved from white alabaster, it was about the length of her hand, flaring from a long, delicate neck into a wider base. Sealed inside the alabastron had been a pint of pure spikenard. The warm musky perfumed oil was so treasured that a pint of it was worth more than 300 denarii.

Most Jewish families did not have the funds for a treasure that cost more than most people earned in a single year. But for young women whose family could afford it, an alabastron filled with spikenard represented more than an expensive perfume. It was given by parents as part of their daughter's dowry and was to be saved for her wedding.

Mary ran a finger along the cool length of the jar. Less than a year ago, she had valued it more than any other possession in the world. In her bed chamber here in Bethany, her alabastron was placed in a protective niche, where she could see it every day. Whenever she had traveled, she carried it with her in a wooden box, padded with thick wool and secured with a latch.

She had treasured the pure white jar, not because of its monetary worth, nor for its fragrant oil, but because it was the last gift from her father before his death. Whenever she had looked at the alabastron, she had seen what she missed most: her parent's love.

But all that had changed less than a year ago when Lazarus announced to her and their older sister Martha that he had invited Judas Iscariot, a childhood friend—along with the twelve men Judas was traveling with—to their house the next day. One of these men was Jesus ben Joseph, the Teacher from Nazareth everyone was talking about.

From the first day, Jesus changed the siblings' lives forever. Some of his actions were considered great miracles. Simon—Martha's betrothed husband—was healed of leprosy and, even greater, Jesus had raised Lazarus from the dead. Although not considered miracles, Jesus touched her family in other life-changing ways. Martha—who for years had considered herself ugly—was now a wife and soon to be a mother. Lazarus had married Abigail bat Nicodemus and was soon to be a father. And as for herself, Jesus had revealed to her that value was not found in beauty or accomplishments. He showed her that her true value was that *she was created and loved by Yahweh.*

All of this—and more—had come to those she loved because of Jesus ben Joseph's teaching, love and miracles. Every day she offered praise to Yahweh for sending him into their lives.

Whenever her family had an opportunity to bless Jesus, they

responded without hesitation. When they had received word that he and his disciples were coming to Jerusalem to celebrate Passover, Lazarus and Simon had sent word inviting the thirteen men to stay at their homes in Bethany.

Within moments of the messenger leaving with their letter of invitation, she—along with Martha and Abigail—began planning a feast to honor and thank the Teacher for raising Lazarus from the dead. Martha and Simon's house was always clean, but this was going to be the first time since their marriage that Jesus would come to their home. The three women spent days washing walls, scrubbing floors, beating rugs and polishing the furniture. The meal was to be a simple one—due to the tenderness of the two pregnant women's stomachs—but was served on their best dishes and goblets, including delicate *terra sigilata*, the glossy red serving ware that Lazarus had brought back from Rome.

Including the Teacher and his twelve disciples, less than thirty guests had gathered for that feast, among them Abigail's father, Rabbi Nicodemus ben Melech. In addition to being one of the seventy members of the Sanhedrin, the highest religious council of the Jewish people, he was also one of the wealthiest men in the land. Abigail's brother Michael was present, along with her younger sister Ruth—who was a close friend of Mary—and her older sister Joanna, as was Joanna's husband Matthias and their young son David and baby daughter Deborah. Mary and Ruth's friend Leah had been invited along with her mother Susanna and her father, Samuel ben Efraim, who had acted as Simon's near kinsman when—over seven years ago—he had approached Martha's father to ask permission to marry Martha.

With Abigail, Mary and Martha serving, the meal had gone smoothly.

Mary had been standing by the door, holding a platter of oatmeal raisin cakes, when Simon and Lazarus had presented the Teacher with a small wooden chest filled with 200 denarii. Her brother had explained the coins were a gift of thanks for Jesus' touch on their families' lives and their desire to help the Teacher spread the message of Yahweh's coming kingdom.

She remembered thinking, *I want to thank Jesus,* but she didn't have anything to give him. That was when she inhaled the fragrant oil rising from the lamps set around the room; in that instant, she knew what her gift would be.

Setting the platter down, she had walked down the hall and up the stairs to her bed chamber. Under the light of the full moon streaming through the windows, she had crossed to the corner niche and lifted her alabastron.

The delicate alabaster jar, along with the spikenard inside, were worth more than the box of coins Simon and Lazarus had given the Teacher. It was the only thing of value that belonged to her, but that did not matter.

I want to help Jesus tell other women that Yahweh loves them too.

She remembered her heart pounding as she had hurried back to the front room and crossed the tiled floor to stand behind Jesus. Looking around, she had seen all those she loved; all those whose lives had been changed because of Jesus ben Joseph. Including herself. Jesus, who had looked at *her* and saw Mary bat Jacob, not the beautiful daughter of a wealthy family. Jesus, who had shown her that she was worth so much more. Jesus, who had helped her forgive her mother's hurtful words, forget the past and look forward to the future with hope. Jesus, who *loved* her.

Without hesitation, without thought, she had grasped the lid of the alabastron and twisted, snapping the seal. The fragrance—heavy and dense, sweet and musky—had filled the room. Tipping the bottle, she had poured a trickle of the precious oil onto Jesus' head; it had run through his hair and down his beard. Her only thought had been, *He loves me.*

Somewhere in the back of her conscious mind she had heard the shocked gasps rippling through the room; but they had not come from the man in front of her. Jesus had closed his eyes and breathed deeply.

Kneeling in front of him, she had tipped the alabastron over his feet. The spikenard ran over his skin, between his toes, and soaked the cushion beneath him. *He loves me.* Setting aside the jar, she had grasped the rose-colored cloth wrapped around her hair to wipe first one and then the other of Jesus' feet. Her hair had gotten in the way, but she had not cared. *He loves me.*

When she had finished wiping his feet, she had sat back on her heels and looked at Jesus. He had opened his eyes and looked at her, smiling.

I love him.

"What were you thinking?"

Mary remembered looking over her shoulder to see Judas standing, shock and outrage painting his features. He had glanced at those around the room; they were staring from her—kneeling at the Teacher's feet—to him. "Her act was a horrible waste," he had sputtered. "That perfume was worth a whole year's wages." He had pointed a finger at her. "If you didn't want it, you should have at least sold it and given the money to the poor."

"Leave her alone," Jesus' voice had echoed around the room. Mary remembered his gaze as he looked at her. "What she has done for me is *beautiful.*" He looked at Judas. "You wish to *help* the poor? That is a good thing, for there will always be poor to help.

"But you will not always have me. My Father intended for her to save this perfume for the day of my burial.

"I tell you the truth that, whenever the gospel of the Kingdom of Yahweh is preached," he looked down at her, smiling, "what she did will be told, in her memory."

All of that flashed through Mary's mind in the time it took to place the alabastron and her head cloth in a basket and turn to face her sister

They were alone in the room; after bidding farewell to their other guests, Simon had escorted Jesus and the remaining eleven of his disciples to the guest chamber where the women had arranged sleeping pallets. Normally, Martha would be busy clearing away the dishes but, from her stance, it was obvious that she refused to be ignored.

Mary gave herself another moment by straightening her garments again. The tunic, girdle and the spikenard-soaked head cloth were colored a slightly deeper rose than was her robe and reflected the spots of color in her cheeks. Finally, she turned to look up at her sister.

Taller than most women, Martha was even taller than some men. Her pregnancy gave her curves she normally did not possess. Martha and Lazarus had their father's jaw; on Lazarus, it looked strong while on Martha it looked manly. Her hair was straight and heavy and—until Jesus came into their lives—had always been worn in a braid.

Mary was shorter than her siblings and had inherited their mother's womanly curves, thick wavy hair, delicate features, silky skin and almond shaped eyes. She closed her eyes for a moment and took a deep breath.

"You want to know why I poured an expensive perfume over the Teacher's feet?"

Martha nodded.

Mary opened her eyes and lifted her shoulders in a delicate shrug. "I do not know."

Martha's frown deepened. "What do you mean?"

"Just what I said," Mary replied. "When Simon and Lazarus presented the coins to Jesus, I realized I also wanted to thank the Teacher and help him spread the message of Yahweh's coming kingdom. However, I had nothing to give. I know, I know—" She lifted her hand when Martha would have spoken. "—you will say that the gift was from our *family* and, in essence, you are right. But, none of that money came from me." She paused. "Do you remember what our parents taught us about King David buying the threshing floor from Araunah?"

"Of course I do," Martha said. "King David wanted to build an altar to Yahweh."

"And when Araunah offered to *give* him the threshing floor," Mary said, "King David insisted upon paying for it, stating, 'I will not give to Yahweh something that costs me nothing.'

"I know this is not the same; I was not building an altar to Yahweh. But Jesus ben Joseph has shown me that Yahweh *loves* me," she laid her palm on her chest, "and that I am valuable to Him. I am certain there are others who feel unloved and unworthy and I wanted to help them hear his message. All I had to give was the spikenard in my alabastron."

"But you didn't *give* it to him; you *poured* it over his feet."

"I know." Mary filled her lungs. "I don't know what happened but when I stood behind Jesus," she spread her hands—palms lifted—in front of her waist, "*something came over me.*"

Martha stared at her for a long moment. "'*Something came over you?*' That is your explanation?"

Mary nodded. "I felt *compelled.*"

"Compelled." Martha sighed, uncrossing her arms. "Since a child, you've always acted without thought." She picked up a tray from the table and began loading the dishes filled with leftover food onto it. "Mary, you are old enough for marriage." Color bloomed in her cheeks. "You know what an alabastron is intended for."

Mary's cheeks echoed her sister's blush. A gift from a girl's parents, the alabastron was to be saved until her wedding night. After she had physically joined with her husband for the first time, the bride was to rise from their marriage bed and take the alabastron. Then, kneeling before her bridegroom, she would break the seal and pour the spikenard over his feet, acknowledging him as her husband and her beloved.

"Can you see why some might have been shocked at what you did? Your actions might have been interpreted as . . . intimate."

Mary gasped. "Are you suggesting that Jesus and I—"

"No, no, no," Martha waved her hands as she straightened up. "I know better than that." She took a deep breath. "But others do not know you nor do they know the Teacher. If word of this gets out, they might think—something—has occurred between the two of you. Or, at the very least, that you two are betrothed." Martha frowned. "Although I do not understand why Judas Iscariot openly chastised you. He has been with the Teacher; he knows nothing has happened."

Mary sighed. "Perhaps because he thought one day to be my husband."

"What? Lazarus never told me of this."

"I do not think Judas spoke to Lazarus," Mary said. She picked up another basket from the table and began walking around the room to place soiled dishes in it. "Judas spoke privately to me. It was during the feast we gave to celebrate Simon's healing."

"I heard what he said to you," Martha lifted a hand this time, "Since that night, I have wanted to tell you that I was looking for you, when I saw Judas stop you in the hall leading to the cooking area." She took a deep breath, "He is one of the Teacher's disciples and a guest, but there is something about him that leaves me… unsettled." Her brow furrowed. "I recall him saying something about the Teacher's plans."

"He said that it won't be long before Jesus—as the *Messiah*—will drive out the Romans and return Israel to the glory of King David's reign." Mary shuddered at the memory of Judas' predatory gaze. "He said that if I were to marry him, then our family would have a position of power in Jesus' kingdom."

Martha frowned. "That was most improper of him—"

"—as you heard me tell him," Mary interrupted. "I said that he should have approached Lazarus first." She shook her head. "Perhaps he intended to speak with Lazarus." She paused. "I can see how what I did might have shocked him."

"I can see it too; he was furious when he left the house. Thankfully, Jesus did not appear to have been shocked by your actions. He called them *beautiful*." Martha paused. "What do you think he meant when he said that his father wanted you to save the spikenard for his burial?"

"I do not know. I wondered whether I had mis-heard him." Mary shook her head. "I confess I often do not understand the Teacher's words."

"I as well. Perhaps as we get to know him better, we will understand more when he speaks." Martha covered her mouth to hide a yawn. "For now, it is late and I must rest." She placed a hand on her swelling abdomen. "Passover is days away and there is much to prepare." She looked at her sister. "As for Judas, I will tell Simon and Lazarus; they will know what to do. I am sure they will speak to Jesus—"

"Oh no! Must they?"

"Your actions reflect on more than yourself. At the very least, Lazarus and Simon need to assure the Teacher that you were acting without thought. I am sure they will also speak with Judas. But I do not *think* he will do anything rash. I remember him from our childhood. To speak truthfully, he always reminded me of something Father—may his memory be blessed—used to say; 'Empty vessels make the most noise'." She indicated the alabastron. "What should I do with this?"

Mary shrugged her shoulders. "Whatever you want. It has no value to me now."

Chapter Two

"Abigail, are you certain you wish to host Passover this year?" Nicodemus asked.

Although the two young couples lived only a few streets apart, the elderly rabbi had insisted his daughter and Lazarus ride in his carriage from Martha and Simon's house to their home. At first Abigail had resisted, stating that walking was good for an expectant mother. However, when Lazarus saw the baskets filled with serving ware she had lent to Martha to use during the evening meal, he readily accepted his father-in-law's offer.

"Otherwise, I will be spending most of tomorrow bringing all of these dishes home. As it is the day we must select our sacrificial lambs at the Temple, I would prefer to leave for Jerusalem early."

The trip across the village of Bethany took little time, and soon Michael and Lazarus were helping Abigail and her younger sister Ruth out of the carriage. While Lazarus and Michael carried the baskets into the house, the sisters stood next to the carriage speaking with their father.

"Only Joanna and Matthias—along with his family—will be celebrating Passover with us. We have plenty of room for more." Nicodemus smiled. "It would be wonderful to have all my children together for the festival."

"I want to do this, Father," Abigail said. "It is my first Passover as a married woman."

"At the least allow me to send some of our servants to help you," Nicodemus said. "When your mother—may her memory be blessed—was expecting, preparing food was a challenge for her. She turned over the cooking to the servant girls."

"I appreciate your offer, Father," Abigail said. "Tomorrow we move to the building in Jerusalem that Lazarus' family uses for Passover. Should I need help, I won't be far from you. Besides," she draped an arm around her younger sister's shoulders, "with Ruth staying with us until my stomach eases, I should be fine."

Standing side-by-side, it was obvious the two girls were related. Ruth was slightly taller than Abigail, but the sisters were petite, with delicate features, smooth skin, full red lips and dark, almond shaped eyes inherited from their mother. While Abigail's waist-length hair had auburn tints and waves, Ruth's raven-colored hair fell thick and straight to her waist.

"Do not worry Father," Ruth said. "Even if Abigail feels too unwell to cook, I will help Martha and Mary prepare the meal."

"Ahhh…" he smiled, "King David wrote, *It is good and pleasant when brothers live together in peace and unity.* I am certain that, if he had met my daughters, the King would have included 'sisters' in that psalm."

"I quoted that psalm to Martha once," Lazarus grinned as he lifted a basket of *amphorae*, "when she and Mary had gone for several days without quarreling."

Abigail placed a hand on his forearm. "That was *before* Jesus ben Joseph came into all our lives. Now Mary and Martha set a standard for all of sisterly love."

Lazarus looked at her, his gaze softening. "My wife is as wise as she is compassionate. I am blessed."

"As I am blessed in husbands."

"Yes, yes, we are all blessed and it is all due to Jesus ben Joseph," Michael said, hefting another basket. "But as the Teacher is not here to help with these *baskets*, perhaps we can delay this offering of thanksgiving until after the carriage is empty?"

Lazarus and Michael were both tall and muscular with dark eyes and beards. Michael looked like a younger version of his father with black curly hair and beard while Lazarus' sprung mane-like around his face. Nicodemus had been a close friend of Lazarus' father Jacob and, as such, the two younger men grew up treating each other as blood kin rather than friends. Within the last year, they had become brothers-in-law.

"I am sorry, Michael, but I cannot help that I am enamored of my wife." Lazarus lifted a basket and followed his brother-in-law up the short rocky path into the house. "When Yahweh blesses you with a wife, then you will understand."

"Lazarus ben Jacob is a good man and godly husband," Ruth said.

"Yes, he is," Abigail placed a hand on her abdomen. "And he will be a good father," she smiled at Nicodemus, "just like you."

"Thank you, my daughter," he patted her shoulder. "Now about Passover; will Jesus ben Joseph and his disciples join you this year?"

Abigail lifted her shoulders. "I do not know. We did not have an opportunity tonight to ask him, so we do not know if he has already made plans. I am certain that Martha or Simon will extend our invitation. Having the Teacher and his disciples celebrate Passover with us would be wonderful."

"I hope he comes. I welcome any opportunity to speak further with him. For one who was not Temple trained, he has a deep understanding of the Holy Scriptures."

"That is all of the baskets," Michael said as he and Lazarus came back to the carriage.

"Father, are you certain you and Michael do not wish to stay the night with us?" Abigail asked. "The guest chambers are ready."

"Thank you, Daughter, but no," Nicodemus smiled. "I find as I grow older that, no matter how elegant and comfortable the guest chamber may be, I prefer my own bed. Michael and I are serving at the Temple tomorrow. With such a large number of people expected, we need to arrive early. In fact, had tonight not been such an important celebration, I would have sent my regrets and sought my bed early."

"Besides," Michael added, "the full moon provides sufficient light for the trip to our home."

After bidding farewell, Michael climbed up next to his father. Gathering the reins, he turned the horses and drove down the streets of Bethany and onto the road leading to Jerusalem.

Nicodemus glanced up at the starry sky. "While Passover is always a joyous occasion, this year's festival will certainly be happier for our family than most years. A life restored. New marriages.

The promise of grandchildren. The celebration of the miracle of resurrected life."

"It will certainly be a memorable one," Michael agreed. "And although I made light of it, I do realize that much of our family's happiness is due to Jesus ben Joseph." He laughed. "To think that we count a prophet of Yahweh among our friends."

"We do," his father nodded and then frowned. "Although I confess that I am concerned for him."

"Concerned? Why?"

"Some of the Council members are concerned that Jesus' growing popularity poses a threat to their own authority. Since he was first acknowledged as a teacher and—some claim—a prophet, there have been several meetings of the Sanhedrin concerning Jesus. As you recall, just days after Jesus raised Lazarus from death, I was called to a meeting of the Temple Leaders. I have tried speak calmness and wisdom into the proceedings, trying to remind the Council that the Law given to Moses does not condemn a man without first hearing him. Sadly, my words were rejected."

"I have never heard the Teacher speak of usurping the place of any member of the Sanhedrin or of taking any position of power."

"Neither have I, but there are those who are worried nevertheless. Some of the Council members are concerned that Rome will interpret Jesus' popularity as a threat to the Empire. They fear that Pilate will remove their power."

"Father, if the Roman consul, Lucius Aelius Sejanus, was alive and still held the position of Tiberius' regent and the *friend of Caesar*, I could understand the Temple Leaders' concern. Sejanus hated our people, and when he appointed Pontius Pilate as Governor of Judea, Pilate followed Sejanus' example."

Nicodemus shook his head. "Those were sad days indeed. I remember Pilate seizing the Temple offerings to pay for the work projects authorized by Rome. Even worse, he brought images of Caesar Tiberius into the Holy Temple. When a vast number of our people gathered in protest," he shuddered, "the governor ordered his soldiers to draw their swords and hack them into pieces."

"But Father, it has not even been two years since the emperor learned that Sejanus was killing all of his successors and had Sejanus—and anyone allied with him—executed."

"That is true. I do not know why Pilate—who is also called a *friend of Caesar*—was spared. Thankfully, since that time, the governor's actions towards our people have changed. He leaves the rule of the Temple to the priests."

"But, to go back to your concern about the Teacher," Michael said. "It is no secret that many of the Temple Leaders hate him. I know, I know," he lifted a hand to stop his father's words, "you will say that is a harsh judgment to make. But Father, we all know Caiaphas was appointed High Priest by Valerius Gratus, and he is but a puppet of Rome. Is it not obvious that anyone who speaks of a new kingdom might appear as a threat to Rome and the High Priest?"

The older man nodded. "You are correct, my son. That is why, after the meeting with the Sanhedrin, I sent word to the Teacher urging him to leave the area for a while. It would not surprise me if members of the Council have met without me or Rabbi Joseph, as we are known to be associated with Jesus. I can only pray that the Teacher will use the peace of this holy festival to settle some of the concerns of the Temple Leaders." He smiled, laying a hand on his son's forearm. "Your studies have sharpened your understanding not only of the Holy Scriptures, my son, but also of the world. Rabbi Gamaliel ben Simon has spoken well of you. That is an honor; he is known as one who is careful with his praise."

Michael placed a palm against his chest. "I am honored by Rabbi Gamaliel's words."

"I understand that Abel ben Joktan also studies with the Rabbi."

"He does," Michael nodded. "He studies harder than I. It is a driving passion with him."

"I am certain Joktan ben Philemon is the driving force behind Abel. From my observation, he would allow no less than perfection." Nicodemus slanted his eyes towards his son. "I have also heard that Rabbi Gamaliel has a new student."

"Yes," Michael frowned. "Saul from Tarsus."

"Yes, that is the one. Gamaliel did not speak of this man's family."

"Perhaps that is because Saul does not discuss his family. He does not discuss anything but the Holy Scriptures, the Law Yahweh gave to Moses and the Tradition of the Elders."

After the fall of Israel as a sovereign kingdom, the Pharisees and teachers were concerned that the Law would become diluted and merge with beliefs of the pagan nations who ruled over them. As a result, the Pharisees and teachers expanded their interpretation of the Law to regulate every aspect of Jewish life. These interpretations—known as 'The Tradition of the Elders'—were considered by the Pharisees and teachers to be as binding as the Law itself.

"Saul's passion for his studies surpasses even that of Abel."

Nicodemus patted his son's arm. "Do not be concerned, Michael. While I do expect you to attend to your studies, I do not believe them to be the only consideration in a young man's life." He yawned. "I did not realize how tired I was."

"It has been a long day. Why don't you close your eyes and rest until we arrive home?"

"A wise suggestion." Nicodemus adjusted his clothes, smoothed his beard—heavier with white than black—and leaned back against the backrest of the carriage's seat as he closed his eyes. A few moments later, a heavy snore rose from the elderly man.

Michael glanced at his father and smiled before turning his attention back to the road where, up ahead, he saw two men walking. He pulled back gently on the reins, slowing the horses, allowing the men time to move off to the side of the road. As his carriage drew near, he looked over to make sure they had sufficient room. He was surprised when—instead of lifting a hand in acknowledgement of his kind gesture—both men turned away from him, but not before he caught sight of the shorter man's face. Judas Iscariot. He twisted around on the seat to look again, but they were hidden in the shadows.

I must have been mistaken. Michael shook his head. *Why would Judas be on the road to Jerusalem at this hour?*

Last year, when they celebrated Passover with Lazarus, Mary and Martha, it had been a wonderful surprise to see his childhood friend, Judas ben Shimon, among the guests. Like Lazarus, he had been shocked when he learned of the crucifixion of Judas' father, Shimon, for purportedly stealing from a Roman soldier. Judas had escaped Rome's habit of enslaving the family of criminals. Judas, along with his mother and sister—who had been visiting family in Galilee when Shimon had died—had altered the name of their family's home town of Kerioth and took it as their family name: Iscariot. Judas had explained that it was in Capernaum where he had met Jesus ben Joseph and had accepted the Teacher's invitation to be one of his disciples.

It didn't take long to see that Judas was different from the other eleven of Jesus' disciples. Michael had heard Judas suggest that Jesus ben Joseph was the *Messiah*, the one whom the prophets had foretold would become a King like David. Michael shook his head. Jesus might be a teacher and prophet of Yahweh—for how else could he perform the miracles he did—but the Teacher had never once spoken of raising an army. Even if he had such a thought in mind, that would require money, which—from the simple manner of Jesus' dress and life—he did not appear to have. Michael knew many people supported the Teacher with gifts of money and other valuable objects, such as Lazarus and Simon had done. He had learned from Judas—who kept oversight of the Teacher's money-bag—that Jesus would often give money to those in need.

Perhaps that *is why Judas was so angry over Mary's alabastron,* Michael frowned as he recalled Judas condemning Mary. His old friend was clearly shocked—they all were—but Judas' response was greater, as if Mary had stolen something from *him.*

Maybe he wanted more than money *from Mary,* he thought. Last summer, during their visit to Lazarus, Mary and Martha's home in Capernaum, Abigail had sent him out to the verandah where he found Judas alone with Ruth and Mary. Ruth told him later that she and Mary had gone outside to enjoy the cooling breezes off the lake and Judas had followed them. She explained she and Mary were both uncomfortable—it was improper for them to be alone with a man who was not family—but Mary could not dishonor a guest by pointing this out and Ruth refused to leave Mary alone with him. Ruth had blushed when she told him how

Judas' comments to them had been almost . . . intimate. After he sent the girls inside, Michael told Judas never to put his sister in that position again. His friend had apologized, stating that his intentions had not been disrespectful.

After that incident, whenever they were with Jesus and his disciples, Michael watched his sister closely. As for Mary, well, it was not his right to protect her and—as long as Judas was a guest in Lazarus' or Simon's house—he would not embarrass them by spreading a bad report.

The cessation of movement startled Michael. He looked around to see the horses had taken them up the road to Jerusalem, through the city's streets and had stopped in front of their stable.

Michael shook his head. He had been so focused on his musings about Judas and Mary that he wasn't even watching where they were going.

He jumped down from the carriage, "It's a good thing you wanted your stall and a manger filled with hay," he said, patting the horses' noses, "or I might not have noticed until we reached Rome."

He handed the reins to the groom and hurried around the carriage to help his father down.

The elderly man held on to his son's arm as they walked across the packed dirt and up the stone path that led to their home.

Torches burned brightly on either side of the arched entryway. Michael and Nicodemus greeted the servant who opened the door and handed them small oil lamps as they stepped inside.

Even by the light of their lamps, it was evident this was more palace than residence; yet to the family of Nicodemus ben Melech, it was home.

Intricate mosaics in gold, green and red tiled the long floor of the main corridor. Along the walls, marble tables trimmed in a pattern of egg and lotus flower and rosettes held vases filled with bouquets of fragrant spring flowers.

Michael escorted his father past several courtyards, public reception rooms, and *mikvahs*—the ceremonial baths—up narrow stairs, across a courtyard opened to the sky and down another corridor to a large bed chamber. Nicodemus waited while Michael walked around the room lighting the lamps on tall stands; the fragrance of the scented oil wafted above the flames.

The walls were covered in tapestries of lotus blossoms and pomegranates that his mother had woven. Along one wall were intricately carved chests for holding clothes and a wash-table holding a bowl, pitcher and several folded linen towels. The bed was on another wall: a thick pallet, covered in linens and placed on top of a wide wooden frame. A small table next to the bed held a cup and small *amphorae* filled with water.

On the far wall, beneath a long window stood a table on which rested a stack of blank parchment, writing implements and several scrolls. On one side of the table was something not seen in most homes: a chair. Made from polished ebony, it was a small bench with an upright piece of wood on one side for the person to lean their back against while sitting. As the owner of caravans, Lazarus had told Nicodemus about seeing these chairs on one of his journeys to Egypt. Intrigued, the elderly man had commissioned him to purchase several.

Michael took his father's lamp and set it on the table next to the scrolls; even though his father was tired, Michael knew he would wish to read before going to sleep. "Do you need anything, Father? Something more to eat? Shall I pour a cup of water?"

"No, thank you. I told the servants not to prepare food for us as we would sup at Simon and Martha's house." Nicodemus yawned. He slipped off his black head covering and outer robe, as he crossed the room and laid the garments on the edge of the table. "Even though Abigail, Martha and Mary claimed they had prepared a *light* meal, there was food enough to feed all the Sanhedrin." He laughed, running his fingers through thick white hair. "A year ago, no one would have expected food prepared by Mary bat Jacob to be edible." He sat on the chair, lifted the edge of his white tunic and reached down to untie his sandals. "Now Abigail tells me that Mary's cooking is so good that no one could tell the difference between her meals and those prepared by Martha."

"While I am happy that Abigail is married," Michael said, "I confess I miss her cooking." He ran a finger along the edge of the table, leaving a streak in the dust. "The house also misses her touch. With the number of servants we have, one would think it would be cleaner."

Nicodemus scratched his beard. "It doesn't matter how many servants you have, a house without a mistress lacks its heart. Your mother—may her memory be blessed—gave this house warmth, beauty and order. She trained our daughters well; after your mother died, Joanna and Abigail attended this house as carefully as she had."

"If I recall," Michael grinned, "you and Mother had *three* daughters."

Nicodemus sighed as he reached for a scroll. "Ah, yes…Ruth… well, she was young when your mother died and was still learning when Abigail and Lazarus married. She's acquiring the skills necessary to run a household; when it's time for her to marry, she'll be ready." He unrolled the scroll and lifted it close to his eyes. "As Mary will be."

"M-Mary?" Michael stuttered, beads of sweat stinging his forehead. "What do you mean?"

Nicodemus looked up, his beard spreading as he grinned. "Michael, the years might have affected my eyesight, but I can still see."

"But I have said—"

"—nothing about Mary," his father finished. "Perhaps not with words, but it is obvious that you are interested in her. Had you asked my opinion before Passover last year, I would have advised you to look elsewhere for a wife. Yes," he lifted a hand as Michael opened his mouth, "she is from an old, respected and wealthy family, but that means nothing to me. She appeared frivolous then and concerned only with her appearance and pleasure. However, in the last year she has left childish things behind. Now she is a godly young woman of an honored family and daughter of an old friend."

"Ruth tells me her change is because of Jesus ben Joseph." Michael paused. "Apparently something the Teacher said helped her to forgive—"

"Michael," his tone stopped the young man, "it is inappropriate for you and your sister to be discussing others, even if they are friends. However, you are right; it appears that Jesus has affected everyone's life." He lifted the scroll close to his eyes again.

Michael watched his father read for a moment. Then he quietly filled his lungs. "Father?"

Nicodemus' bushy eyebrows shifted as he glanced up at his son. "Yes?"

"What . . .what do you think Mary meant with the spikenard?"

"Nothing."

"Nothing?"

"Nothing." Nicodemus shook his head. "While her actions were— *unusual*, I saw nothing inappropriate in them. From what I can see, Jesus ben Joseph cares for Mary with the same level of compassion he has for everyone."

Michael's eyebrows arched a question.

"I do not think," Nicodemus said, "Jesus is interested in taking Mary—or any woman—as a wife."

Michael heaved a deep sigh and then grinned. "Would you speak to Lazarus for me?"

"Not now."

"What?"

"Passover is but days away. Once the festival is past, then I will speak to Lazarus."

"But, Father," Michael began, "how can I wait even a *few days* to tell her how I feel?"

Nicodemus grinned and laid the scroll on the table. "My son, from what I have observed, Mary knows how you feel.

"For the next several days, Mary will be helping Martha and your sisters prepare for the festival. From my years as a husband and father of three daughters, trust me when I tell you that most women want their betrothal to be a special moment, not something packed into an already busy schedule."

Seeing the downcast look on his son's face, he reached over to lay a wrinkled hand on a muscular arm. "Michael, if I have an opportunity tomorrow to speak to Lazarus, I will *mention* that we wish to talk with him. And if," he lifted a gnarled finger, "*if* over the next few days you find a moment when the timing is right and you wish to tell Mary of your affections and intentions then, yes, you have my blessing.

"However, I would advise that you keep your *feelings* to yourself." He picked up the scroll. "It's only a few days. What can happen in that length of time?"

CHAPTER THREE

The moon had fully ascended by the time Abel led Judas down the streets of Jerusalem and turned up the dirt path to his family's home. He opened the door and gestured for Judas to enter ahead of him. He lit a small lamp placed on a table, before escorting the disciple through the house.

It was modest in size and plain in furnishings. Judas recalled from his childhood that his father had commented that Joktan ben Philemon believed decorations to be a waste of money and only offered potential for idolatry. From the main room, the young men walked down a short corridor, turned left and entered the family courtyard.

Joktan was seated on a cushion near a low table placed in the center of the room. He held an unrolled scroll close to a lamp in order to read by the light of the flame. A cup and *amphorae* were by his elbow.

When they entered the room, Joktan carefully rolled up the scroll and set it aside before standing to face the two younger men.

Joktan ben Philemon was shorter than his son and Judas, yet his girth was twice as wide as either young man. Despite the late hour, he was still fully dressed in a white tunic and black robe and head covering. His beard—which was full and flowing onto his chest—had more streaks of white than black.

Abel bowed. "Father, I have brought Judas Iscariot to you."

"You have been gone many hours."

Judas froze in half-bow, shocked at being ignored. A quick glance at Abel confirmed that the other young man was embarrassed at his father's insult of not extending the traditional blessing of welcome and peace to a guest.

"I…uh…" Abel stammered, "had to wait for him to…uh…leave—"

"What Abel is attempting to say is that he had to wait for me to leave the home of Simon and your niece, *Martha*."

Judas' comment had the desired effect; Joktan's gaze swiveled from his son to him. *If his eyes were blades,* Judas thought, *my face would be frayed and bleeding. I don't care; if he refuses to show courtesy, why should I?* He lifted his chin, refusing to let the older priest intimidate him; he even smiled.

"You will *not* speak of that woman—or her family—to me," Joktan spat.

"I will speak of whomever and whatever I wish. Enough!" He did not pause when both Joktan and Abel opened their mouths in outrage. "Abel said you and the Temple Leaders want to speak with the Jesus ben Joseph. Is that correct?"

Joktan frowned and harrumphed, crossing his arms over his chest. He glared at Judas before giving a single, sharp nod.

"And you want me to…arrange…this meeting?"

Another nod.

"Abel also said that there would be…let us call it a *gift*…for arranging this meeting."

Another nod.

"How much?"

"That is not for me to decide."

"Then why waste my time? Take me to the person who makes this *decision*." Judas was enjoying the reactions his comments were causing in the other men; clear outrage that he would speak thus to a member of the Sanhedrin. *I don't care if I anger them. If I can get enough money, then our plans might not be a loss after all.*

The older man's eyebrows drew down. "How do I know that you are able to arrange such a meeting?"

"You don't. But, as you refuse to speak to La—" he paused, a slow smile spreading across his face, "—to *someone else* who knows Jesus, I am your only choice. So, if you wish to speak to the Teacher, stop wasting time and take me to someone who has more authority than *you*."

Joktan glared at Judas, his mouth turned down as if he had tasted a morsel of week-old fish. The disciple met his flat stare with one of his own. Abel looked at the floor as if he wished it would open up and swallow him.

After a moment, the older man harrumphed again and, unfolding his arms, nodded once more. He turned and walked out of the room. Abel gestured to Judas before hurrying after his father.

No one spoke as they left the house and walked through the moon-lit streets of Jerusalem to the center of the Jewish world; the Holy Temple.

Originally built by King Solomon, according to the instructions given by Yahweh to King David, the Temple stood for over 350 years before it was destroyed, pillaged and burned by King Nebuchadnezzar of Babylon. He had carried all its treasures—and the people of Judah—to Babylon. Later, under the supervision of the priest and scribe Ezra, and even later under Nehemiah—who had been appointed by the Persian King to be Governor over Jerusalem—the Temple was later rebuilt, although it did not have the grandeur of the original Temple.

About fifty years ago, Herod—who had been appointed by Rome to be King over Israel—restored the Temple. It took almost twenty years to complete the restoration. The new Temple was broader and taller than the original. Rising eleven stories, it was covered on all sides with massive plates of gold; during the day, gleaming in the sunlight, it could be seen from miles away.

One of King Herod's additions was a covered colonnade around the entire Temple area. On the eastern wall, the colonnade was called "Solomon's Porch." The three men walked through this colonnade, through the East Gate and the Court of Women, up fifteen steps to the Gate of Nicanor where parents would present their newborn children to be dedicated to Yahweh and into the Court of Israel, where only Jewish men were allowed.

Joktan stopped, holding out a hand to block Judas, but there was no need. Judas knew—as every Jewish man knew—that this was as far as those not trained in the priesthood could enter.

"You wait," Joktan told Judas. "I will let the others know you are here." He glanced at his son. "Abel, come with me."

Judas watched as the two men crossed the marbled floor to the Court of the Priests and turned to walk through a long arched doorway on one side. The golden plates accenting the hewn stone walls shimmered and glowed as though the walls had managed to capture the moonlight and hold it in safe-keeping.

He could see the ramp that led upwards to the altar of sacrifice and, on the other side, the Brazen Sea, a large basin filled with water. Priests whose turn it was to serve would wash their hands and feet here before walking through a curtain, embroidered with a map of the world, into the Holy Place.

During his childhood lessons, he had been taught that inside the Holy Place was the altar of incense, the seven-branched candelabrum and the table of shewbread. In the center was the Veil of the Temple. Stretching the height and width of the room and as thick as a man's hand, it was made of fine linen and blue, purple and scarlet yarn with figures of cherubim embroidered onto it.

The Veil prevented men from carelessly entering into the heart of the Temple, the Holy of Holies, where resided the holy presence of Yahweh. The Holy of Holies was covered in gold and the floors of a marble whose blue tinge gave it the impression of moving water. The High Priest would only enter it once a year, on the Day of Atonement, and not without careful preparation. After a ceremonial washing, he would don a simple, pristine white linen garments. Then, carrying burning incense to allow the smoke to cover his eyes from a direct view of Yahweh, he would bring the blood sacrifice, to pray and make atonement for his sins and for the sins of the whole nation of Israel.

The sound of voices approaching caught Judas' attention.

"Pilate said that, as so many foreigners would be coming to Jerusalem for Passover, it should be the Temple's responsibility—and not Rome's—to bury any stranger who dies while in Jerusalem."

"What arrogance! What did you tell the governor?"

"I told him that while we would of course bury one of our own, we didn't have money to buy land to bury *strangers*."

Two men, followed by Joktan and Abel, were walking towards him. Judas' eyes widened as a beam of moonlight caught their faces. Garbed in costly robes, the men who stopped before him were Caiaphas ben Joseph and his father-in-law, Annas ben Seth.

Judas' parents had raised their children to honor those who served Yahweh as priests, especially the High Priest. As he grew older, Judas learned these men were not chosen by Yahweh, but by Rome. He was a baby when Annas—a member of the Jewish nobility and a Sadducee—had been appointed as High Priest by the Roman Governor Quirinius. Annas had held that office for ten years until he was deposed by Valerius Gratus, who had been the Governor prior to Pilate. Although Caiaphas officially held the title of High Priest now, all knew that he gained this office through his father-in-law's suggestion and that he did not sneeze without permission from Annas.

Judas bit his lip to keep from sneering as he bowed from the waist. These men might be puppets of the Romans, but they wielded power. *But not for much longer. When* we *have power, what happens to the* Romans *will happen to* them. "The receiver of stolen goods is as bad as the thief," his father used to say.

"You are Judas ben Shimon?" Annas didn't even attempt to suggest that his son-in-law held precedence. The occasional streaks of black in the white of the priest's beard were reflected in his eyebrows which were pinched downward over a hawk-like nose.

"I am Judas *Iscariot*, Rabbi Annas."

The older man snorted. "Changing your name does not change who you are. 'A camel calling himself an eagle still cannot fly.' I remember when the Romans crucified your father as a thief."

"My father was not a *thief!*" Judas clenched his fists.

"According to the Roman soldier, he was."

"That Roman *pig* lied!"

"Perhaps, but the Romans crucified him nonetheless." Annas smiled; it was not pleasant. "If you wish to be called Judas *Iscariot*, it matters not. My son-in-law," he turned to acknowledge the High Priest with a slight nod, "and I, along with other Temple Leaders, are interested in Jesus ben Joseph."

"Why?"

Caiaphas stepped towards him. "It is not for you to question

Rabbi Annas or any Temple Leader! You—" he swallowed his words when Annas lifted a hand.

"It is alright, my son," Annas said. "I would expect a disciple to protect his teacher." He spread his hands—palms upward—in front of his waist. "Let me start again. We have *heard* much about this young man. He teaches the Holy Scriptures with wisdom and insight. He has even been rumored to perform...*miracles.*"

"They are not rumors," Judas folded his arms across his chest. "He *has* performed miracles. Healing people. Feeding thousands with just a few loaves of bread and fish." He glanced at Joktan and Abel. "Raising the dead. I was there. I saw them."

The older priest raised his eyebrows in slow motion, a gesture that managed to be sarcastic and arrogant all at once. "It matters not whether these acts were true," he dismissed Judas' eye-witness testimony with a wave of his hand; the Sadducees did not believe in an afterlife. "What matters is that many people *believe* them to be true. Jesus ben Joseph has many people following him, many people believing him to be...*more* than an ordinary carpenter and teacher. We have heard that many people believe him to be...the *Messiah.*"

Annas' mouth twisted as he spoke the last word. Judas noticed the other three priests echoed the older man's expression.

"We have long awaited the coming of God's Promised One," the older priest continued, "knowing that he will drive out the Romans from our land and return Israel to the glory of King David's reign.

"The Temple Leaders are obviously interested in anyone who might *be* the *Messiah.* We have heard that Jesus ben Joseph is in Jerusalem for the Passover festival."

"He is," Judas said.

"We would like to speak with him, to hear what—if any—are his plans. But this meeting needs to be in private. We would not want," Annas glanced side to side, as if searching the shadows, "*others* to be aware of our conversations."

He doesn't want the Romans to know that they are meeting with someone who might rebel against them, Judas thought. He smiled. It didn't matter what their reasons; if they wanted to help drive out the Roman pigs, so much the better. "Why do you need me?"

Annas nodded to Caiaphas, who stepped towards Judas. "Jesus ben Joseph is always surrounded by crowds of people. As my father-in-law explained, we would need to…get him alone…in order to speak with him. Would you help us do this?" When Judas hesitated, he added, "As Abel ben Joktan no doubt told you, we would offer you something for your…*assistance*." He looked towards his father-in-law, before reaching into the folds of his girdle to withdraw a heavy leather bag. It clinked as he extended it to Judas. "We thought perhaps thirty pieces of silver."

Judas gasped. Without even looking, he knew the coins would be tetradrachms. Of a purer silver than the Roman coin, the Tyrian shekels were used to pay the Temple Tax. Thirty of these coins would be the equivalent of four months' wages. *Not as valuable as the spikenard, but still….*

"Consider this…*gift*…as a sign of our appreciation for your efforts," Caiaphas continued. "Of course, if you do not wish it for your own use, you could give the money to help the poor."

Judas' hand—reaching for the leather bag—froze. His face darkened. Judas' gaze turned inward as the priest's comment brought back his earlier humiliation from the actions of *a woman*. He had not seen Mary leave the room at Simon and Martha's house, but he had noticed when she returned carrying the alabastron, which should have been kept as part of her dowry.

Mary was beautiful and her family wealthy. What more could a man want in a wife? Although Judas had nothing to offer her *now*, that wouldn't be for long. Once Jesus was anointed as King of Israel, all those who were close to him would have power and wealth. Several months before, during that meal to celebrate Simon's healing, he had tried to *suggest* this to Mary; after all, being the wife of a friend of the King would appeal to any woman.

He had not been prepared for her response. Instead of being flattered, Mary had *chastised* him—reminding him that it was inappropriate for him to talk to her of marriage before approaching Lazarus.

That was the first time it occurred to him that Mary might be looking higher for a husband.

Abel's position—standing beyond his father and the other two priests—allowed him a clear view of Judas. While he had expected the hesitation of being offered money—Abel had seen this teacher from Nazareth turn over the tables of the money changers in the Temple court and assumed his disciples would despise money—he was surprised at Judas freezing when the High Priest spoke of helping the poor. In the moonlight, Abel saw Judas' hand clench, his expression change, growing sharp as a knife's blade. After a long moment, he reached for the bag of coins.

"I'll take it," Judas said.

CHAPTER FOUR

11 Nisan 3793
Bethany/Jerusalem

Lazarus gently kissed the brow of his sleeping wife. Normally, Abigail would have been up before him, preparing the first meal of the day. But he and Simon had made arrangements to leave quite early to make the journey to the Temple. He had dressed quietly, pausing before leaving their bed chamber to smooth the linen sheet over her, to lay a hand on her swelling abdomen where their child grew.

Walking down the stairs, he turned down the back hall and stopped by the cooking area where thin tendrils of smoke wafted through the air, carrying the smell of baking bread. Located in a courtyard, the cooking area had cabinets for storing food, tables for preparing meals, and several open fire pits. Ruth was moving between the tables—where sat bowls of grapes and white cheese and pitchers of goat's milk—and the fire pits, where rounds of bread were baking on the hot stones. It always amazed him how women could co-ordinate the rhythm of food preparation so that all dishes were ready at the same time.

"Good morning, Ruth," he said, followed by the extra greeting for the coming holy week, "Time of gladness."

"Festivals and seasons of joy," Ruth added the traditional response. "Good morning, Lazarus. Do you have time to eat before you go?" She knelt by the fire pit to remove some bread to a platter and quickly placed more dough on the stone. "There is bread, cheese, grapes and a pitcher of milk."

"I do not. Simon and I must hurry to Jerusalem to present our lambs. However, I will take some food with me. If this is like all other festivals, no matter how early we arrive, we will have a long wait at the Temple." While Ruth wrapped some bread and cheese in a cloth, he crossed to the side table and poured a cup of milk. "Are you women still planning to go to our Jerusalem house today?"

"We are," she handed him the food.

To obey the Law Yahweh gave Moses—which, according to the Temple Leaders' interpretation—states the Passover meal had to be eaten within the walls of Jerusalem, Lazarus, Martha and Mary's father had purchased a building in the Upper City, the area between the Temple and the palace of King Herod.

During the year, this building was the place of business to store the goods the men purchased from the trips of their caravans. Several days before Passover, however, their family would move there to use it as their temporary home in order to celebrate the holy day.

"Once Abigail awakes, we will go to Simon and Martha's house. Father is sending a carriage and servant to drive the four of us to Jerusalem." She carried the platter of bread to the preparation table. "I baked extra bread to help Martha and Mary serve breakfast for Jesus and his disciples. What do you think?"

"That is a kind gesture, but I do not know whether the Teacher will still be there. After accepting Simon's offer of their guest chamber last night, Jesus told Simon and me that they would be leaving early today. I assume he is going to the Temple as well. After we finish at the Temple, Simon and I will meet you at the Jerusalem house."

"Good. We will need your help. With Passover only days away, there is much to do."

"Do?" Lazarus lifted his eyebrows in mock surprise. "Simon and I have already moved furniture, countless boxes of dishes, *amphorae*, spices and cooking tools, not to mention clothes, linens, soaps and oils for the lamps. I am glad we will be close to the marketplace to buy anything that might have been forgotten."

Ruth laughed, shaking her head. "I know it seems odd for men to understand, but women—"

"Go no further," Lazarus held up his free hand to interrupt her. "You are correct when you say men do not understand women. Besides my mother—may her memory be blessed—I grew up with two sisters. Even now that I am married, I still do not understand a woman's insistence on having everything be *just right* for a meal. As far as I am concerned, food tastes the same whether eaten from a cloth," he hefted the linen he was holding, "or from a golden platter."

"Ah, but you are accustomed to traveling long distances with your caravans," Ruth said. "You are used to eating around an open campfire or on the back of a camel. When I complained of all the extra work, my mother—may her memory be blessed—reminded me that this was Passover. 'To a peasant a basket; to a king a platter.' My mother explained that, as my father and brother chose a perfect lamb to present to Yahweh, we must wear our best clothes and serve the Passover meal on our best dishes."

Lazarus laughed. "My mother said the same thing. Then she would add," he pitched his voice higher, "'We must give Yahweh our best.'" He grinned. "When I was quite young, I thought she meant that Yahweh would be eating Passover with us and one time I asked if I could sit next to Him."

Ruth laughed. "What a delightful remembrance." She sniffed the air and crossed to the fire pit to flip the bread. "If you see Martha or Mary, please let them know I will bring the extra bread. If the Teacher and the Twelve do not eat it, then we can take it with us to Jerusalem."

"I will." He walked through the halls, into the front room of the house. Used to entertain family and frequent guests, it stretched the full width of the house. The walls were covered in smooth clay with bright frescos of pomegranates and flowers; the floor was tiled with an elaborate mosaic of alternating circles of purple, red and blue. Thick cushions were placed around a low table in the center of the room, where people would recline during a meal. Along one wall, several limestone pedestal tables held *terra sigillata* dishes. Large stone jars beneath the tables held water and wine.

Stepping out of their house, he walked the few streets to Simon and Martha's house. Simon answered his first knock.

"Peace be upon you, Si—"

"Shhh," Simon lifted a hand, cutting off Lazarus' greeting. He tilted his head and listened for a moment before letting out a soft breath. "Martha is still sleeping." He opened the door to allow Lazarus to step inside.

Lazarus' eyes widened. "Martha? My sister? Sleeping after the light of dawn?"

Simon nodded. "Although she tries to keep to her regular pace, pregnancy has affected her." He frowned. "I confess, I am concerned."

"Why?"

"Her stomach is quite tender and she is often unable to eat without being sick. I understand that is common for pregnant women in their early months, but there are days when she cannot keep down anything she eats and cannot stop vomiting." He sighed. "I have encouraged her to see a physician, but she insists that she is fine."

Lazarus shook his head. "That sounds like Martha. She was always the one to care for the sick, but never believed she could be ill." Noting the concern on his brother-in-law's face, he added, "Martha is a wise woman and would never do anything that might harm her or your child. Do you think it would help if I asked Abigail to talk with her? The two of them are always sharing their pregnancies."

Simon nodded. "That might work. But please ask Abigail not to tell Martha I said anything."

"I will." He clapped a hand on Simon's shoulder. "We must leave soon if we wish to reach the Temple before the crowds."

"We can leave now," Simon said. "Jesus and the disciples left about an hour ago. I am sorry that I have no food to offer you. With Martha and Mary not up, there was no breakfast. I found some bread and cheese in the cooking area; elsewise our guests would have gone hungry."

"That is alright." He lifted the cloth-wrapped food. "Ruth sent bread and cheese. I have plenty to share. We can also check the wild fig trees outside of Jerusalem. I noticed the other day that they are covered with leaves, so it should be near the time for their first crop."

"Good idea," Simon said. "I love figs."

The men left the house, walked through the town and turned

onto the road that would lead them to Jerusalem. Streaks of gold shot through the pink clouds, hinting at a hot day to come.

"Mary is not awake either?"

Simon shook his head. "Although I heard her stirring as I passed her room."

"A year ago, that would not have surprised me," Lazarus said. "But now…not to be up to prepare breakfast for guests…." He shook his head. "That is not like her."

"No, it is not. But, all the women were busy these last few days preparing for last night's feast. I am not surprised if they are tired." He snapped his fingers. "That reminds me; Martha and I will not be staying in Jerusalem for Passover. Before they left, Judas—"

"Judas?" Lazarus raised his eyebrows. "When did he come back?"

"Sometime before the break of day. The cock had not even crowed."

"Did he offer any explanations where he had gone?"

Simon shrugged his shoulders. "He didn't offer any explanation—at least none that I heard—he just showed up as Jesus and the others were about to leave. I did hear him ask the Teacher where they were going to be tonight. I guess, as the keeper of the money, it would be Judas' responsibility to secure lodgings."

"I would think so."

"Apparently, wherever Judas had gone last night, he did not make any arrangements for lodgings. I extended an invitation for Jesus and his disciples to stay here throughout the festival week."

"Did you extend an invitation to take Passover with us?"

"I did, as I felt sure you would wish me to do so. Jesus thanked me, but said that he wasn't sure yet where he was to eat the feast. That he had to talk with his, '*Father.*' I assume he means Yahweh. I know his earthly father is no longer living."

Lazarus nodded. "You are correct. Ah well, I would rather prepare as if they are coming than to not have enough food for guests. I know the women will agree with me." He smiled, "As you recall my mother—may her memory be blessed—used to say, 'Each person's portion of the Passover lamb may be as large as an olive, but their singing will break the roof.'"

Simon smiled. "I remember your mother quoting that old proverb.

Even if it meant smaller portions of food—although that was *never* the case—your mother was happiest when her house was filled will guests."

"No, we never ran out of food," Lazarus laughed. "I remember the many times she would send the girls—or me—to the market when Father brought home a guest at the last minute."

"It seems that the son is like unto his father," Simon grinned. "Martha told me how, last year, you surprised her by inviting the Teacher and his twelve disciples to supper the next night."

"I did," Lazarus shook his head laughing, "but did Martha tell you the whole story? I truly had no choice.

"It was the morning after we had celebrated my betrothal to Abigail. Her whole family was present, as was Uncle Joktan and Michael. Despite all of Martha's efforts, *that* had *not* been a pleasant evening. My uncle and cousin," he struggled to find the right words, "had been less than *hospitable*. Although I really didn't notice," he grinned, "as Abigail and I were seated in a far corner, spending a few quiet moments together under the supervision of our family." He unwrapped the cloth and offered bread and cheese to his brother-in-law.

"I found Martha in the family courtyard the next morning. Even though we had guests the night before, she was up before dawn preparing food. She was not…*excited*…to hear that we had more guests coming."

He and Simon ate the breakfast Ruth had prepared as he shared his remembrance of that day.

He had sat down for the first meal and suddenly remembered to tell her that he had invited guests for the evening supper.

"You invited *how* many people to supper tonight?" Martha had held the jug of goat's milk frozen above his cup.

"I am not certain; ten, twelve, maybe a few more." He had popped some white cheese into his mouth.

Martha had filled his cup. "I cannot believe you have done this to me," she fumed, setting the jug on the table with a thump; goat's milk sloshed over the edge. She sat down next to him and grabbed a cloth to wipe up the spill. "Especially after last night."

He had stared at her. 'What happened last night? I thought the evening went well."

"Of course you thought that," she had sputtered. She picked up a piece of flat bread and ripped it in half. "You were so engrossed talking to Abigail that you did not notice our uncle and cousin arguing with our guests." Instead of eating the bread, she kept ripping the pieces in half.

"That was wrong of him," he had said, but tried to soften his uncle's behavior by adding, "However, Rabbi Nicodemus knows our uncle and is familiar with his opinions."

Martha would have none of it. "But to *argue with a guest*, I would not have expected that, even of him." She frowned at the table for a moment and then turned to point a finger at him. "But do not think to distract me with talk of our uncle. When were you going to tell me you invited strangers for a meal?"

He had leaned over and kissed her forehead. 'I am sorry, Martha, please forgive me. I should have asked you before extending the invitation."

"You do not need my permission to invite guests to your house."

"*My* house?" he placed his palm on his chest, his smile wide. "Your hospitality is so well-known in Bethany that everyone calls this, '*Martha's* house.'"

She had rapped the back of his hand. "You exaggerate," she said, the corners of her mouth twitching a tiny smile. "Now, would you please tell me about these guests?"

"What guests?" Mary had walked into the courtyard to hear that last bit.

"It appears that our brother has extended the hospitality of *his house*," Martha smiled at him, "to strangers."

"Not all strangers," he had said. He asked Martha if she recalled a childhood friend, Judas ben Shimon.

She had remembered a rich banker named Shimon. His son Judas had been childhood friends of Lazarus, their cousin Abel and Michael ben Nicodemus.

Lazarus had told his sisters how he had seen Judas in the marketplace the day before. He asked Martha if she recalled that Judas' father had been killed by the Romans. It was the year when Lazarus was about ten years old. One day, Judas came to tell him that he—along with his mother and sister—were going to visit family in Galilee. They left the next day and a week later the Roman soldiers arrested his father. Later that night, Lazarus' father told the family that a Roman soldier had accused Shimon of stealing from him.

Not being a Roman citizen, Shimon was given a mock trial and crucified.

Although used by the Romans as their chief means of executing slaves and criminals, crucifixion had been developed by the Medes and Persians. It involved a tall stake—usually about five to six cubits tall—set into the ground, with a crossbeam either at the top of the stake or shortly beneath. The condemned person was often cruelly beaten before their hands were secured to the crossbeam by either ropes or nails; their feet were secured to the stake, sometimes on a small footrest.

Suspended by their arms, it cut off air to the victim and they had to pull up on their hands and feet in order to gasp a breath. This method of death was long and tortuous; it often took several days for the person to die. Once dead, the body was either thrown into a mass grave or, as a warning, left on the cross to rot.

As if death by crucifixion was not enough, the Romans would confiscate the victim's possessions and sell their family into slavery. While Judas and his family lost their home, they did escape slavery. Instead of going to his father's family in Kerioth, Judas' mother had taken the young boy and his sisters to Capernaum in Galilee, where she had family.

It was in Capernaum that Judas had met Jesus ben Joseph and became one of his disciples.

"When I saw Judas in the marketplace after so many years," Lazarus told Simon, "I invited him to supper. When he told me he was traveling with friends, I had no choice but to extend the invitation to them as well. To do less would have been rude."

"You are a brave man, Lazarus ben Jacob." Simon laughed. "I do not think I would have been able to do that were I in your position. Martha did tell me that the evening went well."

"It did," Lazarus nodded. "Martha and Mary prepared a wonderful meal and made our guests welcomed. And that night we met Jesus ben Joseph." He smiled. "And since meeting him, our lives have changed."

Simon nodded. "They have indeed. I recall when you introduced me to him. After having leprosy for seven years, I was ready to die." He smiled when Lazarus placed a hand on his forearm. "I still remember when Jesus touched me. It was the first time in seven years that I had felt the touch of another human." He filled his lungs and let the air out slowly. "And I was *healed*. Completely. My life was restored."

"And now you are not only healed, but my brother-in-law." He laughed. "You call me brave; you are the brave one. Even changed as she is by the Teacher's influence, Martha is still a *determined* woman. Rabbi Nicodemus told me that his mother—may her memory be blessed—used to say, 'Throw a stick into the air and it will land on its own end.' It is hard for my sister to break an old habit."

Simon nodded. "Martha and I were speaking about an old habit just the other day."

"Oh?" Lazarus offered his friend the last bite of cheese.

"Thank you." He indicated the cheese. "Actually, it was about food. Martha was telling me about the preparations for the feast we had last night. She mentioned something that Abigail did that was different from the way she had always done it."

"Uh oh," Lazarus said as he folded the cloth and tucked it into his girdle.

"You know your sister," Simon nodded. "She didn't say anything, as Abigail was a guest in our house; but she was concerned that Abigail might make changes for the Passover meal. I gently *reminded* her that Abigail was accustomed to running a larger house and, during this Passover meal, we would be the guests and Abigail the hostess."

Lazarus let out a slow whistle. "You are *brave*, my brother. Martha has always struggled over being a guest, to the point she had turned down many invitations. I believe she drew her strength from being known as a great hostess."

"I have come to realize that. I explained to Martha that I didn't want her to be embarrassed in front of the family or any guests which was why I mentioned it to her. It was an effort on her part but she finally agreed with me and promised to be a good *guest* and offer help *only* if Abigail asks for it."

"Abigail mentioned that same incident to me," Lazarus said, "and I might have accidentally made things worse."

"Oh?"

"I reminded Abigail that the transition from hostess to guest would be difficult to Martha and *suggested* she include Martha in the preparations."

Simon raised his eyebrows. "Call it cowardly, but I am glad that we are busy at the Temple today and will not be available to help the women prepare for Passover."

Lazarus nodded. "I can only imagine what the atmosphere will be like in other parts of Jerusalem."

CHAPTER FIVE

We will hurry Martha," Mary called back through the opened door, "but with so many people in Jerusalem for the festival, it might take longer than usual."

She closed the door to the family's Passover house and joined Ruth, who was waiting at the edge of the street. The girls turned to walk towards the Temple. After a few steps, Mary glanced back and then leaned towards her friend. "I do not think I have ever been more thankful to have to get water from the well in my entire life!" She adjusted the empty earthenware pitcher in her arms. "I have never *seen* Martha so *conciliating*."

"And I have never seen Abigail so *desperate* to ask for someone's advice," Ruth carried a pitcher similar to Mary's. She altered her voice, "'Martha, please tell me how you make the delicious bread.'"

Mary joined in, pitching her voice to imitate her sister. "'Abigail, how do you wish to arrange the table?'"

"'Oh, Martha, I wouldn't wish to change any of your family traditions.'"

"'But Abigail, we should honor *your* family traditions as well.'"

The girls dissolved into laughter. "Truthfully, we should not laugh at them," Ruth said. "They are trying."

Mary smiled. "I agree. They are trying. I do hope that when I marry, I do not face the same challenges with my husband's family."

"As do I." Ruth hefted the pitcher. "Do you recall that this time last year we were getting water and talking about husbands?"

Color bloomed in Mary's cheeks. "Please do not remind me of that. I cannot believe that I agreed to a wager that I could win any man's affections."

"Well, it was Leah who *suggested* that she could close her eyes, point out a stranger in the marketplace and you could make him want to marry you."

"No one forced me to do it. You were wise enough to suggest that we should not." Mary sighed. "I was so concerned with my appearance then."

"Now, Mary," Ruth touched her friend's arm, "you confided to me how your mother had made you feel that your beauty was all you had to offer a husband."

Mary smiled sadly. "Well, Mother tried to teach me, but I couldn't cook, I couldn't clean. I couldn't do anything a wife should do. I thought my looks—and my dowry—were all I had." Her cheeks reddened again. "And to think the man Leah pointed to turned out to be Jesus ben Joseph."

"It was a blessing that you were wearing a thick veil. Elsewise he would have recognized you when he and his disciples came to your house that evening."

"You speak truth," Mary agreed. Then her brow furrowed. "Although I am not certain whether he did recognize me and said nothing to avoid embarrassing me and my family."

"That sounds like something the Teacher would do," Ruth said. "He is a kind man."

Mary stepped to the side of the street to avoid a man leading a donkey carrying many bags and baskets. "You know; I was only suggesting our delay to Martha in order to give us time away from their *kindness;* but it looks like it might take a while to get the water. There are so many people today and Passover is still days away."

The center of the Jewish world, the streets of Jerusalem were always packed with local residents, Jewish leaders in their somber black robes, foreign diplomats dressed in rich raiment riding horses or camels, Roman soldiers in red tunics with body armor and weapons, or travelers from around the world, dressed in colorful and exotic attire.

The size of the crowds surged during festivals, especially Passover. A most holy feast for the Jewish people, Passover was the time when they remembered how Yahweh freed them from bondage in

Egypt. On the first Passover—and for many centuries following—the Jewish people celebrated the festival in their own hometown. However, after King Solomon built the first Temple, Jews began making the trip to Jerusalem to eat the festival meal within the walls of the City of David.

"You are right," Ruth said, nodding to several people she knew. "I have lived in Jerusalem all my life and I am always shocked at the number of people who travel here for Passover. Michael told me that he heard that as many as two hundred thousand people make the trip each year. My father said there were years when that number was many times that amount."

"I would agree with your father." Mary pointed to the base of a large tower. "Look at the crowd of people at the Pool Tower."

Jerusalem was one of the few cities in Israel that had access to their well from within the city walls. Built on a hill of hard limestone, beneath the city were caves created by underground water. The Gihon Spring emerged in a cave in the Kidron Valley, east of the city. The water from the springs followed a tunnel to the base of a shaft formed from a natural sinkhole. When Jerusalem was built, the sinkhole was widened and a tunnel developed to reach it from within the city's walls. To guard the city's water supply and allow citizens access to fresh water during times of siege, two towers—the Pool Tower and the Spring Tower—were built nearly two thousand years before.

Mary and Ruth joined the group of women entering the vaulted chamber. They gathered their robes—woven and constructed simply to be used for cleaning and cooking—in one hand to hold out of their way as they began walking down a steep, stepped tunnel. They had to descend a six-cubit drop by use of a ladder, walk a little further to the edge of a twenty-eight-cubit shaft over which a platform had been built. When it was their turn, the girls stepped onto the platform to lower a bucket on a rope to draw water.

"I am thankful that Father had a well dug in our family's cooking area," Ruth said as they began the trek back up the tunnel. "But, at least we do not have to go outside of the city to get water."

Mary agreed. "And the tunnel is pleasantly cool. If Nisan is so warm, I can only imagine how hot the month of Tammuz will be."

The girls stepped out of the chamber and moved to one side to allow other women to enter. They set their pitchers down, straightened their clothes and then carefully settled the heavy pitchers on their shoulders before turning to walk to the street towards their house.

"Mary," Ruth paused. "May I ask you something?"

"Of course."

"Last night…."

Oh no, Mary thought. "Yes?"

Ruth seemed to be searching for the right words. "After the supper…when you…."

Mary lifted her free hand to stop her friend. "You are wondering about why I poured the spikenard from my alabastron onto Jesus' head…and feet."

Ruth nodded. "Father would say that it is not my concern—"

"You are my closest friend and, because of Abigail and Lazarus' marriage, we are now family." She gave Ruth the same explanation she had given her sister. "As I told Martha, I felt *compelled*." Mary shook her head, careful not to jostle the pitcher.

Ruth smiled in relief. "I knew it was something like that. I realize that it is the custom to announce your betrothal, but from what I have seen, while the Teacher is concerned with Yahweh's words, he doesn't appear to concern himself with man's customs."

Mary laughed. "No, he does not. I believe *that* angers my uncle more than anything else Jesus does. But truthfully, Ruth, I would not keep my betrothal from you."

"I didn't think you would. It's just that the alabastron is…well…." Ruth's cheeks bloomed.

"I know." Mary's cheeks echoed her friend's blush. "I am thankful that only our family and friends were present to witness that. As it is, Martha said that Simon and Lazarus will speak with Jesus… " she shuddered, shaking the pitcher and sloshing a bit of water on her head, "and with Judas."

Ruth shuddered as well. "I know he is an old friend of our

brothers—and he follows the Teacher—but to be truthful, he scares me. There is something about his gaze. Ooof!" She gasped as a group of children ran past them, close enough to jostle Ruth, shouting something unintelligible.

Mary grasped Ruth's forearm to help steady her friend. "Are you alright?"

The other girl nodded. "I am fine." She reached up to steady the pitcher when Mary tightened her grasp and pulled her back.

"Watch out!"

Another group of children ran past, followed by men and women; some singly, others in groups. Some people stopped by palm trees to strip off the green fronds—other people removed their outer robes or headcloths—to wave as they started running again. Whether waving clothes or palm branches, everyone was running down the street, jumping, waving and shouting.

"Look! There he is!"

"Here he comes!"

Looking down the street, the girls saw people crowding around what appeared to be a man riding an animal.

As the throng reached them, they were forced to move back against a building and lower their pitchers. Mary was adjusting the edge of her head covering to protect the pitcher's opening when Ruth gasped.

"Mary, look!"

Mary's head shot up. In the middle of the crowd she could see Peter, Matthew, John, Judas—and the rest of the twelve—walking alongside a donkey. Seated on the animal was Jesus ben Joseph.

The people surrounding them were waving their palm branches or robes; some laid them down in the street for the donkey to walk over. Everyone was shouting.

"Hosanna! Hosanna to the Son of David!"

"Blessed is he who comes in the name of Yahweh!"

"Hosanna in the highest!"

Mary and Ruth—as did all Jews—recognized these proclamations. Taken from The Hallel—part of King David's psalms—and used during Passover, 'Hosanna' referred not only to Yahweh saving the people of Israel from Egyptian bondage; it was a promise of their future redemption by the *Messiah*.

It would have been impossible for Jesus to be unaware of the crowd. Although he smiled and nodded to those around him, he did not appear to be reveling in the crowd's adulation. As the donkey approached where they were standing, Jesus looked over and caught Mary's eye. He smiled gently and then turned a focused gaze towards the road that led to the Holy Temple.

The crowd followed Jesus, apparently unconcerned of either Temple Leaders or Romans hearing their cry, "Hosanna to the Son of David!"

"It looks like they are going towards the Temple. Do you think we should follow?" Mary asked.

"No," Ruth shook her head. "My father and brother are serving at the Temple. I do not think they would be pleased to see us in the midst of that crowd."

Mary sighed. "You are right. Simon and Lazarus are probably still there waiting to get our Passover lamb. If they saw us, they would want to know why we were not helping Abigail and Martha."

"Mary," Ruth grabbed her friend's sleeve and leaned in to whisper. "Look across the street. No! Do not make it *obvious*. Pretend to look at the crowd following Jesus and then *glance* back. At the edge of the building."

Mary followed her friend's instructions. As she swung her gaze casually towards the path of the people following Jesus, she saw a woman in the shadows of the building across the street. Ruth's grasp on her sleeve kept her from stepping closer.

"Do not stare!" Ruth whispered.

Mary looked down to swat at the dust that settled on her garments. "Then why do you wish me to look?" she whispered back

"Do you not know who that woman is?"

"No." She glanced at the woman again; all she saw was garments of fine yellow linen trimmed in gold.

"It is Claudia Procula." Ruth glanced over again. "You can relax. She's gone."

Mary's eyes widened. "The wife of Pontius Pilate?" she whispered. "Are you sure? I have never seen her."

Ruth began straightening her own garments. "I was at the marketplace with Joanna last week and a litter came down the street." She stopped whispering, but kept her voice low. "It was carried by four slaves and accompanied by four soldiers. At one point, the curtain was drawn back and she looked out. Joanna told me who she was."

Mary looked across the street. "Why would the wife of the Roman Governor be near our Temple?"

"I do not know," Ruth said. "She was watching the crowd following the Teacher."

The girls lifted their pitchers and settled them back on their shoulders before turning to walk away from the receding crowd and towards their home.

"That was all quite...*interesting*," Ruth said. "What do you think the Teacher was doing?"

Mary shrugged her free shoulder. "I do not know."

"Surely he was aware of what the crowd was yelling."

Mary shrugged again. "I am sure he was."

Ruth kept talking all the way to the house. While Mary responded automatically to her friend, a memory shot through her mind.

Last year during the Passover feast, Abel had *informed* Mary that, since they were going to become betrothed, he had the right and authority to oversee her present life. She smiled in grim satisfaction recalling the shock on her cousin's face when she had *informed* him that Lazarus was not going to force her into marriage to a man she did not care for. She blushed as she remembered saying, "'I do not know who I will marry, Abel ben Joktan, but you may be sure of one thing. Before I marry you, I will marry Michael ben Nicodemus, or Judas Iscariot or even Jesus ben Joseph!" only to realize she had been yelling and that everyone in the room—Lazarus, Martha, her Uncle Joktan, Aunt Naomi and Abel's sister Rebeca—had heard.

To cover the resulting embarrassment and avoid a confrontation from their uncle, Lazarus decided to move them to their summer home in Capernaum in the middle of the month of Sivan rather than in early Tammuz as was their custom. It proved to be a convenience, as the Teacher was traveling back to Capernaum. Lazarus offered the hospitality of their home on the lake to Jesus and those of his disciples who did not have family in the area.

Early one morning, soon after Jesus had left to take a solitary walk, Lazarus had asked his childhood friend, Judas Iscariot, about the Teacher.

"Some people say he is a simple teacher," Judas had said. "Others think he is a prophet like Elijah. Many people believe he is something more. Many people believe he will free Israel from Rome and restore the glory of King David's reign."

Mary's eyes had widened as had her brother's. "Restore Israel?" Lazarus repeated. "But surely you don't mean…that would mean Jesus is…that he is…."

"That he is the promised *Messiah*," Judas had finished.

Was Judas right? Mary thought as they turned up the path to their house. *Do the people in the crowd know? Is Jesus the promised Messiah? The next King of Israel?*

"Father, what did you say?" Michael yelled. "I can't hear you."

"I said," Nicodemus raised his voice, "watch out where you are stepping."

Michael shook his head. "I am sorry, Father," he yelled back. "I cannot hear—Ugh!" He looked down in time to sidestep a pile of sheep dung.

Nicodemus pulled in his lips to keep from laughing at his son. "I tried to warn you."

"You did," Michael grinned as he lifted the edge of his tunic to inspect his foot and sandal. "But the noise is so great, I could not hear you."

His father agreed. "That is to be expected with such a great crowd." He looked around the Court of the Gentiles, packed with people and lambs, and dotted here and there with piles of dung. "With Passover comes people and lambs."

Michael nodded. "Lots and lots of lambs." He inspected his foot one last time and lowered his garment. "In all my years, I do not remember a greater number of people in Jerusalem for Passover."

"*In all my years!*" Nicodemus laughed. "My son, you are so *old* for one so young!" He patted Michael's shoulder. "But you are right. This year does seem to have more people wishing to celebrate Passover in Jerusalem. Look at the courtyard."

During most days, the Temple was busy with people bringing various offerings—whether for expiation, consecration or communal. On the tenth day of Nissan, the grounds were packed with local residents and pilgrims.

Earlier that morning, the High Priest had gone through the Damascus Gate to the fields north of Jerusalem. There, he selected the most perfect lambs. These lambs were brought back to the Temple to be sold to those who either did not own sheep, to pilgrims who were unable to bring lambs with them, or to those whose own animal was not considered appropriate. Once selected, for the next four days, all lambs were left with the priests to examine them.

The Court of Gentiles, the only place within the entire Temple complex where Gentiles were allowed access, had been designated by the High Priest as the location for the presentation of the lambs.

Nicodemus regularly took his turn to serve in the Temple. However, due to the vast number of people descending on Jerusalem that day, he and Michael—along with as many other priests as were available—worked in the Temple. This year the father and son were assigned to the Court of Gentiles, in a spot shielded from the sun by the narrow roof of Solomon's Porch and near the steps that led down a tunnel to the city.

As many of the visitors to Jerusalem came from foreign lands, placed throughout the courtyard were tables for money changers. These men would exchange foreign currency for the Tyrian shekels used to pay the Temple tax. They also sold doves and pigeons for other blood sacrifices. To provide security, Temple guards carrying spears and shields stood around the court.

"Now, Michael, if you are ready to continue, there are people waiting. Good morning," Nicodemus turned to greet a man carrying a lamb. "Time of gladness."

"Good morning, Rabbi," the man responded. "Festivals and seasons of joy." He indicated the animal in his arms, "I am come to present my lamb for inspection."

Nicodemus stroked the lamb's soft curls. "And a handsome young ram he is. Michael, please take this lamb to be examined."

"Certainly, Father."

After making arrangements with the man to return in three days to get his lamb, Nicodemus greeted the next person. They continued the rhythm of greeting people and arranging for lambs to be purchased or examined. After several more people, Nicodemus looked up to see Lazarus and Simon standing in front of him.

"Good morning, Lazarus! Simon bar Hiram!" he smiled. "Time of gladness."

"Good morning, Rabbi," Lazarus and Simon returned the older man's greeting and nodded at Michael. "Festivals and seasons of joy."

"Ahhh, this is indeed a season of joy," Nicodemus' smile took in both young men. "Both newly married and awaiting the birth of your first child. How are the mothers today?"

"We left before they were awake," Simon said with a grin at Lazarus, "so we do not know *how* they are feeling. Mary and Ruth are helping them prepare our house here in the city. Once we have finished selecting a lamb, we are going to see whether they need anything from us."

"Once Father and I are finished here," Michael said, "I would be happy to see if Mary needs any more help." He squirmed under the knowing grins of the other three men. "Uh…I mean…if *any* of the women need help, of course."

"Of course," Lazarus said dryly. "But, I cannot understand what type of *help* you think you could offer…*any* of the women."

"Oh, uh…well…." Color bloomed on Michael's face.

"Stop," Simon jabbed an elbow into Lazarus' side. "You are being unkind. You know *exactly* the kind of help he means."

"Yes," Nicodemus said. "The *exact* kind of help *Lazarus* offered Abigail at this time last year." His glance slanted sideways towards his son. "Although I recall telling Michael it was best to wait until *after* the Festival to discuss this...*offer of help.*"

The other three men watched as the color in Michael's face deepened, before bursting out in laughter, slapping their knees and each other's backs.

"Forgive us, my brother," Lazarus said, grinning broadly. "We should not have made light of you. Your father is right; I know exactly how you feel." He glanced at his father-in-law. "Although I have known your honored father all my life, last year when he asked me why I wished to marry Abigail, I felt as if I were being examined as carefully as these Passover lambs. As your father said, there are traditions to be honored; but from what I have observed, Mary cares for you."

A grin split Michael's face. He glanced at his father, who lifted his shoulders in a shrug and nodded. "Lazarus, do I have your permission to speak with Mary," another glance at his father, "*if* the situation permits?"

"Yes," Lazarus echoed Michael's grin. "*If* the situation permits."

"Lazarus," Simon said, "would you care to wager on whether the situation *permits*?"

"No, Simon, I would not wish to *lose* that wager."

A man standing nearby pointed towards them and began whispering. "Leprosy." "Healed." "Dead." "Resurrected." Other people overheard and stared at them or pointed.

Lazarus and Simon turned slightly away from the uncomfortable attention. "I wish they would not do that," Lazarus said.

"You cannot fault them," Nicodemus said. "It is rare to see one miracle standing before you; but to see two..." he spread his hands out towards the two men.

"I would not mind if all they did was stare," Simon said. "But, many go beyond that."

"They stop us in the street or come to our place of business. While buying things, they begin asking questions, wanting to know all types of details," Lazarus said, "as if we have some...*power*...that will help them." He glanced at the crowd and softly groaned. "Here they come."

The people who had pointed them out were trying to wind their way through the crowd. Just as they were close enough to speak, a clamorous sound drew everyone's attention.

A group of men were climbing the stairs in the tunnel that led to up to the Court of Gentiles, with an even larger group of people following them.

"Look!" one of the people said. "It's Jesus ben Joseph!"

The crowd following Jesus and the twelve surged out of the tunnel and onto the marbled floor, waving palm branches and headcloths, startling the people and animals in the court. Over the bleats and cries, the crowd following Jesus called,

"Hosanna!"

"Blessed is he who comes in the name of Yahweh!"

"Hosanna to the Son of David!"

"Hosanna in the highest!"

As if by command, the crowd silenced. All watched as the Teacher walked around the marbled court, staring at the Temple built by Herod. It was common for visitors to Jerusalem to be awed by the beauty of the holy place. When the Teacher drew near, Lazarus opened his mouth to greet him, but was stopped by the touch of Nicodemus' hand and slight shake of his head. The older priest studied the young prophet as he walked towards a nearby table of a moneychanger.

Jesus reached out, laid a hand on the edge of the table and closed his eyes.

"Hey!" said a moneychanger, "remove your hand from—*iiieee!*" He screamed and jumped backwards as Jesus, drawing in a deep breath, squatted slightly and, grabbing the wooden edge, stood, overturning the table. Sunlight flashed on gold coins as they pinged and spun and skittered over the stone floors.

Before the moneychanger could recover from his shock, the Teacher stepped to the next table and turned it over. He moved from table to table, upending them, scattering bags and stacks of coins. He opened the cages of doves and pigeons, releasing the birds. Shocked by the Teacher's actions, the moneychangers scrambled around, trying to gather their coins or catch their birds.

As one, the crowd erupted into shouts as people dropped to their knees, grabbing coins from the marble floor and shoving them into the folds of their girdles. Fights broke out among people and moneychangers. The Temple guard tried to intervene; however, the crowd outnumbered them and kept them from reaching the Teacher.

From the hall leading to the Court of Israel, black-robed priests spilled out like ants whose hill had been disturbed. Joktan and Abel were among them, waving their arms, demanding silence, ordering the people to leave immediately and calling for the guards to *do something*. At the back of the group of priests, Caiaphas ben Joseph and his father-in-law, Annas ben Seth stepped out of the hall, wearing their dignity and authority as a robe.

Jesus, having upended the last table, crossed to the center of the court and stood, staring at the leaders of the Jewish people.

"Silence!" Caiaphas' voice echoed off the stone walls.

The cacophony stopped. People froze as they were—some standing, some kneeling, hands clutching coins or spears. All eyes swung between the High Priest and young prophet from Nazareth.

Caiaphas lifted a hand to point at Jesus. "What are you doing, Jesus ben Joseph?" He demanded. "You are disturbing the peace of Yahweh's Temple!"

Most people cringed when the gaze of the High Priest rested on them and trembled if he spoke to them. Jesus did neither.

"It is written," Jesus' voice resounded around the marbled courtyard. "'My house will be called a house of prayer,'" he lifted a hand to point at Caiaphas and Annas, "but you are making it a 'den of robbers.'"

A collective gasp rose. All Jews recognized that Jesus had quoted the prophet Isaiah:

"Their burnt offerings and sacrifices will be accepted on My altar; for My house will be called a house of prayer for all nations."

He had also quoted the prophet Jeremiah:

"Has this house, which bears My Name, become a den of robbers to you? But I have been watching! declares Yahweh."

As if dismissing the High Priest, Jesus turned and walked up to a man who was standing near the wall. His left foot, wrapped in dirty cloths, was lifted up and he used a tall stick to support his weight. Jesus placed his hands on the man's shoulders and closed his eyes. Then, opening his eyes, he knelt and, gently grasping the man's left foot, lowered it.

The man looked at Jesus and then at his foot. He gingerly shifted his balance and put weight on his wrapped foot. His eyes shot open. "It doesn't hurt." He moved his foot forward and put more weight on it. He dropped the stick and took a step. "I can walk." He walked in a large circle, blinking away the sheen of tears that gathered in his eyes. "I can walk! I can *walk!*" Then turning to Jesus, he dropped to his knees and grabbed the edge of the Teacher's tunic.

"You healed me! Thank you, Sir! Praise be to Yahweh!"

From the crowd, a woman hurried across the marble floor to Jesus leading a man with a bandage wrapped around his eyes. "Sir," she said. "My husband lost his sight last year. You have healed others," she glanced towards Lazarus and Simon. "Please heal him."

Jesus smiled at her before stepping up to her husband. He found the edge of the cloth on the man's face and unwrapped it; eyes, white and cloudy, did not flinch at the sunlight. Jesus placed his hands gently over the man's eyes and leaned in to whisper in his ear. Then he stepped away.

The man lifted a hand against the sunlight. His hand began to tremble as he lowered it, to stare at his palm. He lifted his face to his wife…and smiled. He held out a hand to her.

She threw herself against his chest, crying and laughing. The man looked around at the crowd; milky white eyes were now black as onyx.

"I can see," he said. "I can *see.*" The man looked at Jesus. "Thank you! Praise be to Yahweh! I can see!"

Pandemonium erupted as people cheered and danced. Young children jumped up and down, chanting, "Hosanna to the Son of David."

Caiaphas tried silencing the crowd, but to no avail. Gathering their robes, the High Priest and his father-in-law crossed to Jesus. Pointing to the group of children dancing and chanting around the Teacher, Caiaphas said, "Do you hear what these children are saying?"

Jesus reached down to ruffle the hair of a young boy before look-ing at the High Priest. "I hear them," he said. "Have you never read, 'From the lips of children and infants You have ordained praise?'"

Caiaphas' eyes widened. He opened his mouth but said nothing. He looked at his father-in-law.

Before the High Priest could speak, Jesus turned and walked to where Lazarus and Simon were standing with Nicodemus and Michael. He nodded respectfully to the older man. "Good day, Rabbi. Time of gladness."

With a glance at Caiaphas and Annas, who appeared furious, Nicodemus returned the greeting cautiously. "Festivals and seasons of joy."

Jesus looked at Simon. "If you do not mind, I would like to return to your home. I am fatigued and would like to rest."

"Certainly," Simon looked at Lazarus. "Lazarus, would you...."

"Go," Lazarus waved his hand towards his brother-in-law. "I will select a lamb for us, and then will go to the house to tell Martha. I know she and Mary will wish to return to Bethany."

"Thank you." He turned back to extend a hand for Jesus to precede him. "Shall we go, Teacher?"

With another nod to Nicodemus, Michael and Lazarus, Jesus and Simon crossed the courtyard near the tunnel where the twelve were waiting. Jesus and Simon descended the stairs, followed by the disciples. Judas, the last of the twelve, paused at the top of the stairs to glance back towards the Chief Priest, before hurrying after the others.

The crowd followed Jesus and the disciples down the stairs and out of the Temple. Their cheers rose from the city streets below.

"Blessed is he who comes in the name of Yahweh!"

"Hosanna to the Son of David!"

"Hosanna in the highest!"

"Hosanna!"

CHAPTER SIX

"Truthfully?" Ruth asked. "Jesus turned over the tables of the moneychangers?"

Lazarus nodded.

"I imagine it created quite a disturbance in the Temple," Abigail said.

"It did. If it had not been such a shock, I would have laughed." Lazarus smiled at the memory. "There was the Teacher, turning over table after table, opening the cages of doves and pigeons and everyone scrambling to grab the coins or the birds. The priests waving their arms and yelling at everyone and the guards too shocked to do anything. It was quite funny."

"I am certain Uncle Joktan and the other priests were not laughing," Mary said.

"No," Lazarus grinned. "But I have never seen him move so fast."

"Speaking of moving fast," Martha set a basket on a small table. "Mary and I need to leave quickly if we are to arrive in Bethany in time to prepare the evening meal for Jesus and the twelve." She lifted a length of cream linen from the top of the basket and draped it over her head and shoulders.

"Do not worry," Abigail helped her adjust the head covering. "Riding in Father's carriage, you will arrive in plenty of time."

"It was kind of Rabbi Nicodemus to send his carriage for our use. Please give him my thanks again." Martha checked the contents of the basket. "Bread, dates, cucumbers, cheese, figs and pomegranates. We can stop by the market on the way home and purchase a fish. That should be sufficient for tonight's meal."

"I will make more honey and date cakes," Mary wrapped a soft green linen around her hair. "We all know how much Jesus and Simon like those."

Martha smiled. "They do indeed."

They walked out of the house to the street where Nicodemus' servant, Daniel, was standing next to the carriage, holding the reins to a matched pair of chestnut stallions.

Martha turned to Abigail. "I do not know what the Teacher's plans are for tomorrow. If we can, Mary and I will return to help."

Abigail hugged Martha and Mary. "If you can, you can. The needs of guests come first." She draped an arm around Ruth's shoulders. "Besides, Ruth will be here to help."

Martha glanced up at the sun and turned to Mary. "If you are ready, we need to leave."

Lazarus helped his sisters into the carriage. As they drove away, Lazarus followed his wife and sister-in-law back inside.

"If I did not know the date, I would never realize that Passover was days away," he looked around and then grinned at his wife. "This room looks like where I would buy dishes and spices, not eat roasted lamb."

Simon and Lazarus were merchants, as was Lazarus' father, Jacob ben Philemon. But they were not simple merchants with a single booth in the marketplace. They owned many caravans that traveled to distant lands and returned with camels laden with costly perfumes and spices; flax and other textiles, including silk from the legendary lands of the far east; *terra sigilata* pottery; tall, slender Grecian *amphorae* to hold water or wine; precious and semi-precious stones; gold and silver fashioned into cups, bowls, plates and jewelry.

Each year, the women—with some help from the men—worked hard to transform this warehouse from a place of business into a temporary home.

Both floors of the building had a main room and several smaller rooms. The family used the smaller rooms on the second floor as bedchambers. The main room on the first floor was quite large, with walls of smooth clay and floors tiled in alternating squares of blue and white. Normally, this was where they celebrated Passover; last year in this room, they had hosted twenty-four people for the meal.

This Passover would be different.

Last week, Abigail had asked Lazarus if it would be alright to have the meal on the upper floor. She explained that—even at night—the heat seeping in from Jerusalem's streets was difficult for her tender stomach. "The upper room is so much cooler," she had said.

"Whatever is easier for you and our child," he had lain a hand on her abdomen, "is fine with me."

She had smiled. "Thank you, my love." Then her brows had lowered. "What about Martha?"

"Martha is experiencing the same discomforts from pregnancy as you are," Lazarus had said. "I am certain she will appreciate moving to a cooler area of the building."

"But Martha places great value on traditions," Abigail had said. "She might *say* it was fine, but I do not want her to think I am dishonoring the family."

As Lazarus followed Abigail and Ruth up the stairs, he wondered whether Martha really was alright with the changes. From her girlhood, Martha had placed all her focus on becoming the godly woman King Solomon wrote about in the last of his proverbs. She had worked diligently alongside their mother, learning how to cook and clean, weave and sew, barter and trade. After their mother's death, she had taken over running their home.

Up until last year, Lazarus hadn't realized just how much all of that meant to Martha. He cringed as he recalled the time he had even told her that after his marriage, Abigail—who was accustomed to running a larger home—would help ease Martha's work.

Reaching the top of the stairs, he looked around.

The central room on the upper floor was smaller than its counterpart downstairs. The room itself had no decorations, only lampstands placed between the latticed windows. Several days before, he and Simon had carried the two short and two long, low tables they had used for the previous Passover meal and arranged them to form a long box shape, so the diners could see each other. Placed beside the tables were thick cushions for the diners to recline on; a symbolic reminder that only free people had the luxury to recline while eating.

Two smaller tables were set against the back wall. One was to hold basins of water and towels for the guests to wash their hands and the other was for the bowls of side dishes that would be served as part of the meal.

Although subtle, the room showed evidence of Abigail's touch. Martha never added decorations to a dining table, feeling they would detract attention from the meal. Abigail had draped the dining tables with fine linen cloths and placed small vases along the centers. She explained to Lazarus that the afternoon before Passover, she would pick some flowers from her father's gardens to set in the vases.

He noticed his wife staring intently at him and, beyond her shoulder, he saw Ruth looking at him and nodding her head vigorously towards the table. *Ah, thank you, Ruth.* "Abigail, this room is beautiful."

She visibly relaxed. "I am glad you approve," she said, bending to smooth the linen table covering. "This is our first Passover as husband and wife. I want it to be perfect."

"It will be."

She glanced around the tables, counting the cushions. "This room is not so small. We could seat sixteen comfortably and, if needed, we could have twenty guests here. I wish Father and Michael were coming here instead of hosting Joanna's in-laws."

"I agree," Ruth said. "I don't know why Matthias' family is coming to Jerusalem now."

"Perhaps," Lazarus said, "they wish to celebrate Passover in the City of David as we do."

"Just as we do," Abigail repeated, smiling at Lazarus. "My husband is wise."

Ruth grinned. "Wouldn't it have been fun to hear little Deborah ask, 'Why is tonight different from other nights?'"

"It would be," Abigail laughed. "Maybe next year. Lazarus, do you know what the Teacher plans to do for Passover?"

"Simon told me that he asked Jesus."

"Did the Teacher accept the invitation?"

"Not exactly. Simon said that Jesus thanked him, but said he wasn't sure where he would celebrate Passover, as he had to talk with his 'Father.'"

"So, Jesus' family will be in Jerusalem for the feast?" Ruth asked.

Lazarus shook his head. "From what I understand, Jesus' father is dead."

"I don't understand." A frown creased Ruth's brow. "He mentioned his father."

"I assume that he means Yahweh. He has referred to Him as 'Father' on other occasions."

"Until we know for certain," Abigail said, "I would rather plan as if he and the twelve are coming."

"I told Simon that you and Martha would feel that way. I even mentioned something my mother—may her memory be blessed—used to say. 'Each person's portion of the Passover lamb may be as large as an olive—'"

"'—but their singing will break the roof.'" Abigail and Ruth finished in unison.

"Our mother—may her memory be blessed—said the same thing," Abigail said.

"It appears that *all* Jewish mothers quote that proverb," Lazarus smiled. "As you will to our children." He snapped his fingers. "Which reminds me. Did Martha seem alright to you?"

"Yes…" Abigail frowned. "Why?"

"Simon told me that she is experiencing some difficulties with this pregnancy."

Abigail placed a hand on her abdomen. "I know she and I both have tender stomachs."

"Apparently hers is worse than she is letting on. Martha was asleep when I reached her and Simon's house this morning."

Abigail's eyes widened. "Martha was asleep after dawn? That is not common for her."

Lazarus agreed. "Simon said that her stomach is quite tender to the point that there are days when she cannot keep down anything she eats and cannot stop vomiting. He wants her to see a physician, but she keeps insisting she is fine.

"I told Simon I would ask you to speak with Martha." He lifted a finger in caution. "Bring up the topic casually; just one pregnant mother to another."

"I will," Abigail said. "I am glad that Mary's cooking skills are improved. If Martha is as sick as Simon states she is, cooking will be a challenge for her."

"Hold your hand over the pan." Martha said. "Closer. There. Now, can you feel the heat?"

Mary nodded.

"Then it's ready for the fish. Grasp it by the tail and gently lower it into the pan." She watched her sister follow her instructions. "That's right. Now, fish cooks very fast. You watch it and I'll tell Simon that the evening meal will be ready in a few minutes." She smiled. "The last time I tried to serve fish to Jesus, it burnt. But, it was worth it."

Mary smiled as her sister left the cooking area. That 'time' was less than a year ago, shortly after the family had moved to Capernaum for the summer.

That was the morning that Jesus had left soon after the first meal to find a quiet place to pray.

"I have never known anyone to pray as much as he does," Judas had said of the Teacher.

Later that morning, the twelve had left to meet Jesus, inviting Lazarus to accompany them. Martha and Mary had left after the men; they needed items from the marketplace, including ingredients for the evening meal.

Mary loved the walk from their home to the village. On the one side was the Lake of Galilee, the cool, refreshing water reflecting the deep blue sky. She had seen mornings when a fine mist would hover over the lake, giving it a mysterious appearance. Opposite the lake were trees—palms and majestic cyprus—and colorful wildflowers dancing on the breezes. Beyond the village of Capernaum was the Plain of Gennesaret below the Arbel cliffs.

The marketplace was empty that morning. Old Cyrus, who sold fruits and olives, had told them that everyone had gone to hear Jesus ben Joseph talk.

Mary had suggested they go and listen to Jesus teach. They had walked to a level spot on the side of Mount Eremos, where the side of the mountain was teeming with people.

Soon after they arrived, a man in the crowd asked Jesus to tell them more about the new kingdom he frequently spoke of. She had noticed Judas standing with a group of rough-looking men. The disciple had nudged one of these men, who called out, "What must we do to make this new kingdom a reality?"

Jesus stared at Judas and then answered the man's question. "Yahweh's kingdom is not what you think and there is nothing you can *do* to bring this kingdom." He didn't have to raise his voice. The contours of the mountain's plains and slope allowed sound from the top of the mountain to be heard clearly at the bottom. "It is what's in your heart."

Jesus began talking about the different qualities in people that Yahweh blesses. But he never mentioned being rich and powerful as being one of these qualities. He said it was those who had no ability within themselves to please; those who recognized that Yahweh was their source; those who were humble and gentle. These people, he said, would inherit the earth, along with those who desired righteousness, showed mercy, sought peace and those who asked Yahweh's forgiveness.

Jesus spoke about being salt and light in the world, and when a man asked him to settle a dispute over an inheritance, he told the crowd that life was not measured by riches, clothes or food. Mary had re-lived that moment so much she could close her eyes and see it as if it were yesterday.

A flock of birds flew overhead. Jesus pointed to them. "Birds do not plant or harvest or store food, because Yahweh provides for them." He looked at the crowd. "Don't you realize you are worth much more to Him than birds?"

He pointed to a patch of yellow wildflowers growing nearby. "Look at how flowers grow. They do not work to make their own clothing and yet even Solomon—the richest king of all—did not own one garment that was as beautiful. If Yahweh clothes flowers that bloom for such a short time, don't you think He will also care for you?"

He sighed. "Is your faith in Yahweh so small?

"Don't worry about what food you will eat or drink or clothing; for Yahweh knows what you need.

"Do not desire treasures on this earth. What you should desire most is His kingdom and obeying His will, and then all these other things will be given to you."

She and Martha had left after that, in order to get back to the house. On the walk home, they discussed what Jesus had said. She had confessed that she placed too much value on her looks. She was surprised to hear Martha confess that she placed too much value on her cooking and keeping a clean and beautiful home.

That brought up sad memories of the only man who had ever thought Martha beautiful: Simon. Seven years ago, her betrothed husband had contracted leprosy and had left Bethany. No one had seen or heard from him and many considered him dead. Martha had resigned herself to remaining unmarried and unloved.

Little did she know what the coming hours would bring.

Martha had planned fish for the evening meal. Moments after she had placed the fish in the pan, Lazarus had come home and announced he had brought another guest.

Mary, who had been in the hall beyond the cooking area, grinned as she recalled Martha demanding who was the extra guest.

"It's me," Simon had replied.

Gasping, Martha had swung towards the door where next to Lazarus stood Simon, dressed in ragged clothes but completely healed of leprosy.

Simon had smiled at Martha.

Martha had clutched her stomach, whispered his name and fainted.

Mary had rushed past the men, to tend to her unconscious sister. When Martha came to, she had demanded to know what had happened. After telling her that Jesus had healed him, her sister had sat up and sniffed the air, only to realize that the fish had been left untended and was burnt.

She and Martha had scrambled to put together a meal for their guests.

Since that day, Martha had never had another opportunity to prepare fish for the Teacher.

Tonight was going to be the night. Martha had all the ingredients to re-create that meal exactly, including the large fish she had purchased at the marketplace in Bethany. While Jesus and his disciples rested, the sisters had worked together preparing the various parts of the meal. A bowl of roasted grain—which they would serve to whet their guests' appetites—sat cooling on the side table. Next to it were two platters covered with cloths; one with warm bread, the other honey and date cakes. There were also bowls of leeks, lentils, cucumbers, figs and pomegranates.

When Simon came in to tell them that the Teacher was awake, Martha turned her attention to the fish. Unwrapping the cloth covering the fish, Martha lifted the knife…and paused. Taking a deep breath, she lowered the knife and…paused again.

"Martha," Mary asked, "are you alright?"

"I'm fine!" she snapped. Taking another breath, she set the knife against the flesh of the fish…and dropped it. Snatching up a cloth, she lifted it to her mouth.

"Martha, don't!" Mary said. "That cloth was—"

Martha threw the cloth down and ran to the far corner to vomit in the slop bucket.

"—wrapped around the fish," Mary finished. She crossed to Martha. Wrapping an arm around her sister's waist, she held her as she retched and heaved. Mary looked away, biting her own lips and breathing deeply to keep from retching herself.

Several minutes later, she helped Martha to a bench, poured her a cup of cool water and handed her a fresh cloth dampened with water to wipe her face.

"Thank you," Martha said. "I do not know what happened."

"You are with child, that's what happened," Mary said. "You should lie down."

"I cannot. I must finish this meal." She set the cloth down and tried to stand, only to slump back to the bench. "I cannot ruin this meal again. I would be so embarrassed."

"I will do it," Mary said. "You sit here, away from the smell, and tell me how to prepare and cook the fish. I promise I will not tell the Teacher that I cooked it."

Martha smiled. "No, I will be pleased to tell Jesus who cooked it. Alright, it's not hard to prepare the fish."

Under Martha's eye, Mary cleaned and gutted the fish, filled the cavity with chopped olives, onions and garlic. After rubbing the flesh with olive oil, she placed the pan on the fire.

Leaving Mary to watch the fish, Martha went to tell Simon and their guests that the meal would be ready in a few minutes.

Mary lifted the edge of the sizzling fish to check its doneness. *Not quite ready to flip.* She looked around the room and smiled with satisfaction. A year before she was not able to cook anything. Now people would frequently confuse her cooking with Martha's. She took a deep breath. *I can cook. I can keep house. I am learning to weave cloth. I am almost prepared to be a wife.*

She frowned. But whose wife?

She did not need that little mirror she had lost in the wager to know that she was beautiful. She was accustomed to men's reactions when they looked upon her. Some would stare, jaws slack in awe as if they had made a rare find.

"…a rare find."

Mary smiled at the memory. That was what Michael ben Nicodemus had said about her last Passover, when she had said she was confused as to why their uncle was angry that Jesus ben Joseph had told a lame man his sins were forgiven—something only Yahweh could do—yet ignored the fact that the Teacher also healed that same man.

"Are not miracles from Yahweh?" she had commented.

Michael had smiled at her. "As my mother—may her memory be blessed—used to say, 'Two men look at the same bush; one man sees the thorns and calls it a weed, while the other man sees the flower and calls it a rose.' Wisdom and beauty…a rare find."

Not everyone's attention made her smile. Mary frowned as she flipped the fish. Her cousin, Abel—who appeared to desire only her dowry—made her furious. Other men's gaze—like Judas—made her feel as if scorpions were crawling on her.

Then there was Jesus.

Last year she had entered into that childish wager with Leah.

On pretext of buying a basket, she had contrived to speak to Jesus for the first time. It wasn't until Lazarus had brought him—along with Judas and the other eleven disciples—to their house, that she had officially met the Teacher. Even then, she was surprised when he did not react to her beauty.

From her childhood, she was convinced that it was her only asset. She had tried to learn to cook and keep house like her mother; but, despite her best efforts, she had failed. In frustration, her mother had given up trying to teach her. Mary could still hear her mother saying, "A goat is a better cook than you! It's a good thing you're so beautiful; otherwise, you will never find a husband."

Later, her father had found her crying. Mary never knew what he had said to her mother. From that day, whenever she asked for new clothes or jewels or any item she felt necessary to enhance her appearance, he had given it to her.

After their parents' death, Lazarus fell into their father's habit of buying whatever she wanted—money was not a problem for their family—yet he never knew her secret pain. Last summer, he had found her crying and she had confessed to him that she had been a disappointment to their mother.

Lazarus was shocked and had tried to convince her of their mother's love. But it was Jesus, who had overheard their conversation, who had said their mother had been wrong and stated that neither beauty nor skills were of true value. He had told her that her value was because she had been created and loved by Yahweh.

Jesus' words had opened her eyes and, for the first time, she had felt valued and loved just for being Mary bat Jacob. That was one of the reasons that, last night, she had poured the spikenard onto his feet. Because of the love she had for him. She felt loved. Loved by Yahweh; loved by her family; loved by her friends and yes, even loved by Jesus.

Last night she had felt warm and secure in that love. In the clear light of this morning's dawn, however, she had blushed as she recalled her actions. She had intended to prepare the first meal for Simon and their guests but, for some reason she could not identify, she could not bring herself to face Jesus.

What must he think of me? He had called my actions, 'beautiful.' But beautiful how?

When she thought of his reactions to her, she was certain Jesus loved her. But love from a brother or friend is not the same as love from a man who wishes to be her husband.

Which love does Jesus have for me?

CHAPTER SEVEN

12 Nisan 3793

T he clouds gathered in the afternoon sky like grey mountains. Abel shifted the fat jar he was carrying and looked around. *Where is Judas?*

He crossed to the rock wall and set the heavy jar on the ground. Removing the cover, he reached inside and lifted the brush—strips of cloth tied around a short staff. Turning to the wall, he swiped the brush against the rock wall, leaving swaths of white. He repeated the action, making the swath of white bigger. He got lost in the motions; dip, swirl, swipe, repeat. He had almost finished covering the wall, when a voice startled him.

"Whitewashing tombs?"

Abel dropped the brush—splattering the watered lime paint on his robe—and spun around. Judas was standing within arms' distance, grinning.

The valley north and east of Jerusalem held the tombs of the kings of Israel as well as tombs for people rich enough to be buried near royalty. Deep chambers cut out of the bedrock, they were lavishly decorated. The stones of one tomb were carved to look like grapes and acanthus leaves. Placed over the tomb of the prophet Zechariah was a square structure decorated with ornate columns and capped with a pyramid.

This valley was familiar to those who lived in or near Jerusalem. The Temple Leaders, however, did not feel these lavish monuments were sufficient to identify them as tombs to strangers. To prevent pilgrims from accidentally touching one—and thereby becoming ceremonially unclean—several days before Passover, they would send men out to apply whitewash to the tombs.

"You're late!" Abel snapped. He swiped at the splatters on his robe, cursing as his actions smeared the whitewash on his garment rather than remove it. "You were supposed to meet my father yesterday, yet you did not."

After Judas Iscariot had accepted the thirty silver coins, Caiaphas had insisted the young man send daily reports. Joktan, always anxious to bring himself and his son to the attention of the Temple Leaders—even if they were Sadducees and he a Pharisee—had volunteered himself and Abel to act as liaison.

Judas lifted his hands in front of him. "I could not help it. Due to the...*attention*...Jesus drew in the streets of Jerusalem and in the Court of Gentiles, everyone was watching the Teacher and those of us with him. It was impossible to slip away unnoticed."

"The High Priest and Rabbi Annas paid you well. They—and my father—do not care about your excuses."

"Caiaphas—"

"Rabbi Caiaphas!"

Judas shrugged. "*Rabbi* Caiaphas asked me to arrange a private meeting between him and the Teacher. During all the excitement of yesterday, if I had been seen approaching the High Priest, it would have drawn unwanted attention," he curled his lip. "Perhaps even *Roman* attention."

Abel paused and then nodded. "I will explain that situation to my father and the rabbis. Now, what information do you have? Where did Jesus ben Joseph go after he left the Temple yesterday?"

"He went back to Simon and Martha's house in Bethany."

Abel frowned at the mention of his cousin. "Did he discuss any plans? Did he meet with any zealots," he glanced at Judas' waist, where the shape of a dagger showed through the folds of his girdle, "any *Sicarii*?"

"No."

"He didn't?" Abel frowned. "What did he do?"

"He slept."

"What?"

Judas nodded. "He went to the guest chamber, laid down and fell asleep. After he woke up, he ate supper and then we went to the roof top and talked."

"You talked. About plans?"

"No," Judas shook his head. "About ordinary things. Favorite foods. Memories. Passover."

"Passover. What are his plans for the festival?"

Judas shrugged. "Who knows? Whenever anyone asks him, he comments that he has to ask his 'Father.'"

"His father? Is his father in Jerusalem?"

Judas laughed. "His father is dead. Jesus means Yahweh."

Abel's eyebrows crept upward. "What does he mean by calling Yahweh his *Father*?"

Judas shrugged his shoulders again. "I do not know. I do not understand most of the things the Teacher says."

"If he said that, then he must have meant—"

"Abel," Judas interrupted him, "I do not have time to discuss what Jesus *might have meant* by his words."

"Fine. What of today? What did he do today?"

"Nothing. He came to Jerusalem."

"Why?"

"To visit with his mother."

Abel refused to give Judas further opportunities to laugh at his ignorance. "Is his mother alive?"

"Yes. She lives in their hometown of Nazareth, near her other children. She sent word to Simon's house yesterday that she was in Jerusalem for Passover."

"Is she staying with Simon and Martha?"

Judas shook his head. "No. She is staying with a woman named Mary. Mary is from Magdala but met Jesus in Capernaum. I understand she was possessed by seven demons—"

"Seven demons?" Abel frowned "She must have been a sinner to have so many demons."

"I do not know; I think they were demons of sickness. Whatever they were, Jesus drove them out. Since that time, Mary has been a follower of Jesus. Like Simon and Lazarus, she is thankful for what the Teacher did for her. She also gives Jesus money to care for his—and his disciples'—needs."

"So, she is wealthy."

Judas nodded. "Jesus' mother sent word that she wanted to see him, and Mary offered to go to Nazareth and bring her here. They arrived yesterday."

"So tell me about this Mary from Magdala. Where are they staying? Tell me about anyone else in Jerusalem who follows Jesus in Jerusalem." Abel frowned.

"No."

Abel opened his mouth, but Judas continued before the other man could speak.

"The High Priest did not pay me to give you a list of all of Jesus' followers. He paid me to arrange a meeting with Jesus, which I have not *yet* had an opportunity to do. Now, I must go. Is there anything else you want to know?"

"Yes. Has Jesus done anything suspicious or *unusual?*"

"He frequently does *unusual* things." Judas grinned. "This morning he cursed a tree."

Abel's eyes widened. "What?"

Judas nodded. "Do you recall the wild fig trees on the road from Bethany to Jerusalem? Near the Mount of Olives?"

"I know which ones you mean."

"We were walking from Bethany and it had been a while since the morning meal. Peter saw the trees in the distance and mentioned that he loved figs. Jesus said he was hungry and went up to the nearest tree. Even though it was covered in leaves, there was not one fig on it."

"That is odd," Abel said. "Those trees produce several crops each season. I would have thought it was near time for the early harvest."

"That is what we thought, but there was not one fig to be found. I told Jesus that I would purchase some figs in the marketplace— which is what I am supposed to be doing *now*—but that's when he cursed the tree." He shook his head. "It was the strangest thing. He said, 'May no one ever eat fruit from you again!'"

Abel stared at him before shaking his head. "Jesus ben Joseph must be mad."

"I have known the Teacher for nearly three years. I do not think he is mad, but I doubt that even his mother truly understands him."

"Rabbi Nicodemus," Jesus said, "may I present my mother, Mary bat Eli."

"Peace on you, Mary bat Eli," Nicodemus bowed his head. "Time of gladness."

The diminutive woman standing next to Jesus bowed in response. "And on you peace, Rabbi Nicodemus ben Melech. Festivals and seasons of joy."

"I am honored to have the Teacher's mother in my home."

"The honor is mine, sir, to be welcomed in the home of an elder of our people."

The courtyard in Nicodemus' house was filled with family and friends. His oldest daughter Joanna stood by his side acting as hostess for the evening, while her husband Matthias divided his attention between talking to Lazarus and Michael and keeping an eye on David and Deborah who were listening wide-eyed to Aunt Abigail tell them stories. Simon and Martha were with Rabbi Joseph bar Neriah and Leah's parents, Susanna and Samuel ben Efraim. The men were discussing Samuel's newest foal—the rabbi from Arimathea had an interest in the young filly—and the two women were discussing housekeeping and pregnancies. After greeting Nicodemus, Leah had left her parents and crossed to where Ruth and Mary were standing—close enough to the door should Joanna need Ruth, yet far enough away for private conversation.

The three friends immediately began discussing the events of the previous day. Servants moved silently across the floor tiled in intricate mosaics patterns of gold, green and red, keeping the guests' cups filled and offering bowls of dates, almonds and roasted grain to hold everyone's appetite at bay until the meal was served.

All conversation stilled when Jesus arrived with his disciples and three women. Michael excused himself to his two friends and crossed the room to join his father and sister in greeting the newcomers.

Mary studied Jesus' mother. Much shorter than her son—her head reaching only his shoulder—she had thick black hair heavily salted with gray. It was obvious that Jesus had inherited his gentle smile and dark eyes from his mother.

The older lady turned to draw her companions forward. "Rabbi, may I present my sister, Salome bat Eli. You have already met her sons, James and John; they are disciples of my son."

Short like her sister, Salome had a sweet face and ready smile as she returned the rabbi's greeting.

"And this is my young friend, Mary bat Salathiel of Magdala," the Teacher's mother said.

Taller than the other two women, the younger Mary had almond-shaped eyes and long wavy hair.

"Three Marys," Leah whispered to her friends. "It won't be hard telling you apart. The Teacher's mother is obviously older than you and there is nothing exceptional about Mary bat Salathiel's features."

"She has pretty eyes," Ruth studied the other woman, "and she carries herself gracefully."

Mary agreed with her friend, adding, "You must admit there is something quiet and peaceful about her countenance which gives her a rare beauty." She slanted a glance at Jesus through lowered lashes. *That would attract many men. I wonder if he told his mother about my alabastron?*

"I agree with you Mary," Ruth grinned. "I have heard my brother frequently comment on your countenance *and* beauty."

Mary blushed as her friends chuckled quietly. *They think I was looking at Michael.*

"Peace on you, Mary bat Salathiel," Nicodemus greeted the younger woman. "Are you by chance related to Salathiel bar Pharez, who was the fish merchant in Magdala?"

Mary bowed her head. "He was my father," she said. "He joined our ancestors at Abraham's bosom two years ago."

"I heard of his death," Nicodemus said. "I am sorry for your loss. May your memories grant you peace."

"Thank you."

"Mary's parents were friends of my husband Zebedee's family,"

Salome slipped an arm around the other woman's shoulders. "When Salathiel died, Mary was left without family or a near-kinsman. She turned to us for comfort and wisdom."

"She prefers to be known as Mary Magdala," a voice whispered.

The three girls jumped and turned to see Judas standing behind them. His smile tightened into a grimace when, as one, they took a step away, Mary and Ruth each glancing towards their brothers. After an embarrassed pause, Ruth took up the responsibilities towards a guest of her father's house.

"Why would she not wish to be known as Mary bat Salathiel?"

Judas' smile returned. "Her father was not *just* a fish merchant. Magdala is known for their smoked fish."

Mary nodded. "It is delicious. Father would always buy large quantities of it when we moved to our summer home in Capernaum. Smoked fish from Magdala was one of my mother's favorite memories from her childhood,"

"Many people felt the same as you and your mother. Fish merchants in Magdala do quite well." Judas nodded towards the woman standing near the Teacher. "*Her* father was the most prosperous of them all. Mary's parents were older when she was born and she was their only child. As Mary bat Eli said, she was left without family or even a near-kinsman."

"How sad," Leah said.

"Without a male relation," Judas continued, "that not only left Mary the sole heir of her father's estate, but in complete control of her inheritance. As word of this spread, she was soon surrounded with men offering marriage. Realizing they cared only for her wealth, she moved from Magdala to Capernaum. She rarely uses her family name, preferring to be known as Mary Magdala. James and John's parents introduced her to the Teacher." His lips, spreading into a thin smile, reminded Mary of a predator. "Her commitment to the Teacher is most *fortunate*," he seemed to savor the word. "She is quite generous in her support of him."

Mary and the other two girls stared at the floor in an uncomfortable silence. They had been raised not to discuss money.

"There you are, Ruth."

The girls jumped a second time and looked up to see Michael standing at Judas' side.

"Oh, yes, Michael," Ruth replied. "Judas was...uh...telling us about Mary bat Salathiel."

"How *kind* of Judas." Michael looked from the three girls to the disciple; the smile on his face did not reach his eyes. His gaze returned to his sister. "Joanna asked me to fetch you. It is time for the meal to be served and she needs your help."

Ruth breathed a relieved sigh. "Yes, yes, of course. I will come now."

"Mary, Lazarus requested that I ask if you would help Abigail." He grinned. "She has run out of stories to tell young David and Deborah."

"Certainly," Mary smiled her thanks to Michael and turned to her friend. "Leah, why don't you come help me? You are good at telling stories."

As they walked towards Abigail and the children, Mary glanced back. Michael was talking with Judas; although the disciple was a guest, from Michael's demeanor, it did not appear to be a pleasant conversation.

Moments later, Nicodemus announced to his guests that the meal was ready. He and Joanna led the way from the courtyard, down several corridors, to the dining room. Perfumed smoke wafted from tall lamps. Limestone tables placed against each wall held *amphorae* of water and wine. In the center of the room were four low tables, set to form a rectangle with thick cushions placed on the floor beneath them.

"What beautiful tapestries," the Teacher's mother said.

"Thank you," Nicodemus said. "My wife—may her memory be blessed—wove these and many others throughout our home. Lotus blossoms and pomegranates were her favorite pattern."

"She was obviously quite skilled," Mary said.

"Your praise is kind. My wife would have been pleased." Nicodemus escorted them to one of the tables. "Now, if you will honor me by sitting with your son and companions here?"

While Joanna conferred with the servants, Nicodemus escorted his guests to their place at the table. His grace and kindness made each feel that their location at the meal was that of an honored guest.

Mary was placed with her brother and Abigail on one side. She knelt on the cushion, smoothed her garments—cream linen edged with green and gold thread—beneath her and looked up to Michael moving towards the empty cushion next to her.

"Ah, Michael," his father said, "I am certain you would wish to sit with the Teacher's disciples. Leah bat Samuel, I knew you would wish to be near Mary bat Jacob and your parents."

Michael, his dark eyes smiling at Mary, shrugged his shoulders. "Yes, Father; I do wish to sit with *the Teacher's disciples.*"

Leah grinned as Michael crossed to the other side of the room to sit between Peter and Matthew. She turned her head to whisper in Mary's ear. "When am I to wish you happy?"

Mary flushed as her eyebrows shot up. "What?"

Leah lifted a goblet from the table and held it to her mouth as if to drink. "As Michael does not hide his attraction to you," she said around the lip of the cup, "I am assuming he has approached Lazarus. When will your betrothal be announced? Unless, of course, you are still considering marriage to *another*?" She slanted her eyes towards the table where Jesus was talking with Rabbi Nicodemus.

Mary lifted her own goblet and took a sip of cool water. "I have no plans for marriage with *anyone.*" With quiet words—and frequent glances to see that none were listening—she explained about the alabastron. "I don't even know what Martha did with the empty jar."

Leah set her goblet down and lifted a square of linen to wipe her mouth. She spoke from behind the cloth. "I completely understand. My parents frequently tell me that I act without thought." Leah said. "I do not think that anyone present the other night would spread harmful stories about your actions…except perhaps…" her gaze slanted towards Judas. "He seemed quite *angry* about your actions."

"He was," Mary explained about Judas' marriage proposal. "Martha said she would ask Lazarus to speak with him. Since Judas approached us tonight, it would appear that my brother has not had that opportunity yet."

"This is a busy week. Once the festival is passed, I'm certain Lazarus will speak with him. After all, what can happen during Passover?"

Mary agreed and turned her attention to Rabbi Nicodemus as he spoke the blessing before the meal was served.

Abigail had told her that, even though her family had wealth, her father preferred simple foods. That changed, however, when guests were present for a meal. Servants brought in platters of roasted fish stuffed with garlic, onions and olives; bowls filled with lentils, leeks, cucumbers, various cheeses, figs, grapes, dates and pomegranates. And platters piled high with bread, still warm from the baking stones.

Nicodemus was a perfect host, encouraging his guests to try foods new to them or to take another helping of a favorite dish.

Although she did not intend to listen in on a conversation not her own, Mary was seated close enough to hear Rabbi Nicodemus' conversation with the elder Mary.

"While it is an honor to meet the Teacher's mother," he said, "I confess I am curious to learn more about your son. It is rare to meet a man of his age who is so knowledgeable in the Holy Scriptures. Who was his teacher? My son Michael," he smiled at his son who was talking to Peter, "is presently studying under Rabbi Gamaliel ben Simon."

"All of Israel has heard of Rabbi Gamaliel," Mary wiped the corner of her mouth with the linen napkin. "Growing up in Nazareth, my son did not have the opportunity to study with one as learned as Rabbi Gamaliel. But that did not lessen his desire." She smiled at Jesus. "He spent most of his days either working in his father's carpentry's shop or studying with our rabbi, Omir bar Reuel. The rabbi told us that our son asked endless questions."

"I did," Jesus laughed. "He was kind and patient to answer them."

"Patience is the sign of a good teacher," Nicodemus said. "I understand Jesus was your firstborn. Do you have other children?"

Mary smiled. "Yahweh blessed my husband Joseph—may his memory be blessed—and me with five sons and seven daughters."

"Do they live in Nazareth?"

She nodded. "They do." She laid a hand on Jesus' forearm. "Jesus comes to see me when he is able and often sends letters and small gifts." She smiled. "He was in Jerusalem for Passover last year and purchased a lovely basket for me."

Mary glanced at Leah, who grinned. They knew exactly which basket that was, as they had been present when Jesus purchased it.

Last year, just days before Passover, she—along with Leah and Ruth—were in the marketplace in Bethany, speaking—as girls their age frequently did—of the men they would someday marry. They had pointed out several men, discussing the possibility that their future husbands might be in that very marketplace.

"Mary can have anyone she wants," Leah had said. "Besides coming from a wealthy family, she is such a beautiful girl."

"I don't know about that," she had replied. Martha had accused her of being vain and she was trying to prove to herself that she was not.

"Nonsense" Ruth had said. "Everyone knows you're the most beautiful girl in Bethany; probably in all of Israel."

"All the unmarried men I know want to marry you," Leah had added.

"My brother Michael thinks you're beautiful," Ruth had said. "I heard him say as much."

"That is...kind...of him to say that," Mary remembered saying.

"Kind?" Leah had snorted. "Mary, I will wager that I could close my eyes, point out a stranger in the marketplace and you could make him want to marry you."

Mary still blushed as she recalled taking up Leah's wager, betting her new mirror against Leah's amber necklace.

Mary glanced across the room at Michael, who caught her eye and smiled. *If you knew what we had done last year,* she thought, *would you still be interested in me?*

The girls had found a solitary spot near the marketplace. Then Leah had closed her eyes, turned several times and had pointed out a young stranger standing near the booth of old Timeus the basket weaver. They then came up with a plan for Mary to meet the stranger. She remembered what happened next as clearly as if it were yesterday.

Walking slowly towards Timeus' booth, Mary had taken deep breaths and concentrated on slowing her racing pulse. By the time she had arrived at the booth, she felt a strange mixture of calm and excitement. She had picked up a small basket to study it while she waited for the opportune moment.

Timeus was showing the stranger a long narrow basket. "What about this one?"

"It's well-crafted," the stranger had said. Mary remembered noting that his voice was rich and well-modulated. "This is the right shape, but I need something larger." He had smiled. "I am sorry to be so particular, but it is a gift for a special lady."

"A gift for your wife?" Timeus had smiled.

Mary could still remember holding her breath. *Married?*

"No," the stranger had said. "I am not married. The basket is for my mother."

Mary had quietly released her breath.

"Ah," Timeus had smiled. "A good son always remembers his mother. If you will wait, I think I may have just the one. It is with my special baskets." He had turned to walk towards the back of his booth.

Mary recalled slanting her eyes in the stranger's direction. He was looking at a deep round basket, the type Martha used when harvesting vegetables from their garden. She had looked around. No one else was near the booth. *Now is my chance.*

Slipping her hand into her own basket, she had grasped the small bag of saffron she had just purchased. Bending over to inspect a small stack of baskets, she had gently tossed the bag a handbreadth from the stranger's feet.

Straightening, she had taken several steps away before gasping, "Oh no!" Lifting her basket, she had moved the cloth-wrapped jar of honey. "Where is my saffron?" She had unrolled the crock of honey, furrowing her brow in concern.

"Is this what you're looking for?"

Mary had looked up at the stranger extending the bag of saffron towards her. "Yes, that's it," she had taken the bag with a sigh of relief. "Thank you. I must have dropped it somehow." She had replaced the spice in the basket, rewrapped the honey and placed it on top of the bag of spice. "My sister needs this saffron for tonight's meal."

"Then I am happy I could help you," he had smiled.

Up close, Mary remember noting that his appearance was unremarkable; except for his eyes. They were like deep pools of onyx, fringed with thick, dark lashes.

"Mary!" Leah and Ruth had rushed over at that point. Leah had looked concerned while Ruth's expression was more fear than anxiety; of the three girls, pretense was hardest for her.

"We were walking through the marketplace when heard you cry out," Leah had hugged Mary. "Are you alright?"

Mary had reassured her friends that she was fine.

"What happened?" Ruth had asked.

"I had lost the saffron I had purchased for Martha, but this kind man," Mary had gestured toward the stranger, "found it for me."

Leah turn turned towards the young man. "Thank you, kind sir!" she gushed. Leah's reactions were always a bit too strong.

"I am glad I could help," the stranger had smiled. "Your name is Mary?" he had asked her.

She had nodded.

"That is my mother's name." The stranger had smiled, his eyes lighting up.

I've seen smiles like that before, Mary remembered thinking. *He's interested.* She had smiled at him, a dimple peaking at the corner of her mouth. "That's nice."

"Here's the basket," Timeus had returned at that moment, carrying a delicate basket. "What do you think?" He had handed the basket to the stranger and then turned towards the girls. "Greetings, Leah, Ruth and…" he had studied Mary for a second—she was wearing one of Martha's opaque veils which hid the lower half of her face—before smiling, "and Mary."

"Greetings, Timeus."

"Do you need a basket today?"

"No," Ruth had said at the same moment Leah spoke, "Yes."

"No," Mary had said, "uh…I mean…no." She had explained to Timeus about losing the saffron and how the stranger found it.

"Ahh…" the old man's expression had cleared. "Well, I am glad the saffron was found." He turned to the stranger. "Mary's sister Martha is known as the best cook in all of Bethany. Those who eat at her table consider themselves fortunate."

Another man had approached the booth at that moment and told the stranger that lodging had been secured for the night. The two left, leaving Mary to wonder how she was going to win the wager. The next morning, Lazarus had informed his sisters that he had invited Judas and the twelve men he traveled with—which included a popular new teacher—to their home. The teacher turned out to be Jesus ben Joseph.

After that evening, Lazarus extended the hospitality of their home to Jesus and his disciples. They even celebrated last Passover with them, which would have been pleasant if not for her Uncle Joktan, who clearly despised the Teacher, and her cousin Abel who—after their guests had left—reprimanded her for speaking to the men, as they were not family.

"You are my cousin, Abel," she had told him, "not my brother. You have no authority over me."

"When we marry you will be subject to me and—through me—to my father."

She had stopped him right there, informing him that she had never agreed to marry him. She enjoyed his surprise and confusion at her statement. He had stuttered that his father had spoken to Lazarus, informing her brother that it had been their fathers' wishes.

"Lazarus said it would be my choice," she had told him.

Abel's eyes had narrowed. "I see now," he had sneered. "You do not wish to honor our fathers. You wish for a husband who has more wealth, who has a family with a higher position and more power. Someone like Michael ben Nicodemus?"

Mary remembered grasping her robe to keep from slapping the smug expression off of Abel's face. Rage had seethed through her response. "I do not know who I will marry, Abel ben Joktan. But you may be sure of one thing; before I marry you, I will marry Michael ben Nicodemus, or Judas Iscariot or even Jesus ben Joseph!"

That was when she realized that everyone in the room—including her uncle—had heard her comment.

Lazarus and Martha had understood and agreed with her sentiments of that conversation. To avoid a confrontation with their uncle and cousin, they moved to their summer home in Capernaum several weeks early. It was convenient that Jesus had decided to travel back to the Lake of Galilee area at the same time; Lazarus told everyone their earlier move was to offer hospitality of their lakeside home to the Teacher.

It was there that, because of Jesus ben Joseph, many wonderful things happened. On the slopes of the mountain outside of Capernaum, Jesus healed Simon of leprosy. In her own mother's garden, Jesus had denounced her mother's hurtful words and revealed her true value found in being created and loved by Yahweh.

Those things alone had opened her eyes to the foolishness of the wager she had made with Leah, which she promptly ended. Not to mention Jesus raising Lazarus from the dead. The thankfulness she felt towards him had prompted her actions with the alabastron the other night. She glanced where he sat, listening to his mother and Rabbi Nicodemus discussing Jesus' childhood. Mary felt a love for the Teacher; but was it the love of a friend or was it something deeper?

"My son's desire for the Holy Scriptures has always reminded me of the thirst of one lost in the desert," the Teacher's mother said. "Sometimes, it consumed his attention before all else." She turned to her son, "May I tell the rabbi of that particular Passover?"

Jesus smiled at his mother and nodded.

"It was his twelfth year," she explained. "Our family had traveled with many others from Nazareth to Jerusalem for the feast. The trip itself was pleasant. The children ran and played with their friends all day and even around the evening campfires. It was not uncommon at night for me to cover a sleeping child who was not my own.

"After Passover ended, we gathered our things and started home. When Jesus did not appear for the meal that first evening, I was not concerned; I assumed he was with a friend or relative. The next morning, I began looking for him among our group, but couldn't find him."

"Oh no!" Nicodemus said. "As a father, I could imagine your fear."

"It was almost overwhelming. I prayed for Yahweh to protect him," she said. "We turned around and came back to Jerusalem. We retraced all our steps, going to the place we had stayed, looking in the marketplace. It wasn't until the third day that we found him."

"Where was he?" Nicodemus asked.

"In the courts of the Holy Temple, talking with the teachers."

"*Wait*! I believe Joseph and I were there that day," Nicodemus turned to call the attention of his friend. "Do you remember about twenty years ago when that young boy spent two days in the Temple, talking with the teachers?"

The rabbi from Arimathea rubbed his beard—which contained more grey than black—as he nodded. "Yes, I remember him. His understanding of the Holy Scriptures was remarkable for one his age."

Nicodemus gestured towards the Teacher. "That young boy was Jesus!"

"Truly?" Joseph asked.

"You both were there that day?" Mary asked.

Joseph nodded. "We were not numbered among the teachers, but I remember your young son carried on a profound discussion with them."

"I didn't know what they had been discussing," Mary said. "But I do remember that—while I was relieved to have found him unharmed—at the same time, I was astonished to see that he was not terrified nor truly lost. I asked him why he had treated us that way and told him that we had been anxiously searching for him."

Jesus smiled at his mother and reached over to cover her hand with his own. "I asked why you had been searching all over Jerusalem for me. Don't you know—then as now—that you can always find me in my Father's house, going about His business?"

CHAPTER EIGHT

13 Nisan 3793

"**M**ary," "Martha whispered.

Mary turned towards her sister. "Yes, Martha?"

Martha shook her head. "Shhhh." She looked ahead where Simon was walking with Jesus and his disciples. Then she gestured to her sister to draw closer. "I am hungry."

"What?" Mary's eyebrows crept towards her head covering. "You ate a huge meal not an hour ago. How could you be hungry so soon?"

"I *just* am," Martha frowned. "My stomach is unsettled. If I do not eat something soon, I'm afraid that—"

"Oh dear," Mary said. "We did not bring any food." She pointed to where the city walls of Jerusalem could be seen. "We're not that far from Jerusalem; can you wait?"

Martha shook her head. She pressed a hand against her mouth. She looked towards the men. "I would be shamed if I vomited before the Teacher and his disciples."

"I understand," Mary said. She glanced around and pointed towards some trees near the Mount of Olives. "Aren't those wild fig trees? Would that ease your stomach?"

"Yes," her sister said, "but please don't let the men know it's for me."

"I won't," Mary lifted her voice. "Simon? Would it be alright if we pick some of those wild figs? Martha and I need them for a dish for tonight's meal."

"Certainly." He smiled at his wife. "Shall I pick them for you?"

"No, thank you," Martha returned his smile. "We need to choose the right ones. If you don't mind waiting; Mary and I won't be long."

As they turned towards the stand of trees, Peter spoke up. "I'll come with you. I love figs."

Mary looked at her sister, who gave a slight shrug.

"I wanted to try some of the figs yesterday," the disciple said, "but we weren't able to get any."

"They are very good," Simon said. "We have been getting figs from these trees since our childhood."

"Look!" Mary said.

The other three looked where she was pointing. All the trees were covered in large leaves; except one. Its branches, reaching towards the azure sky, were covered with dried, curled or rotted leaves.

Simon walked up to the tree. Reaching up to grab one of the branches, he bent it; the branch snapped off. Instead of a healthy light green pith, it was black. He broke off several more from different areas of the tree; all were the same.

"It's rotted," he said. "The whole tree withered from the roots."

"I don't understand," Peter said. "This is the very tree I tried to find figs on yesterday."

"It's dead." They turned to see that Jesus and the others had followed.

"But, Teacher," Peter said, "isn't this the tree that yesterday you—"

"Cursed," Judas' eyes were wide.

All eyes turned towards Jesus. He was studying the tree. Then he turned to look at the others. "Have faith in Yahweh," he said.

Mary looked at Martha who shrugged slightly. She noticed that Simon and the disciples seemed confused as well.

Jesus pointed towards the nearby mountain where an orchard of olives grew. "If you say to this mountain, 'Go, throw yourself in the sea,'" he pointed to the Salt Sea in the distance, "and *truly* believe what you say will happen, it will be done."

"What did He mean by *that*?" Leah asked.

Mary shrugged. "I do not know. While most of what the Teacher says touches my heart, there are times when I do not understand what he means."

"So, yesterday he cursed a fig tree," Leah said. "Today the tree is dead and the only answer he gives is to *trust in Yahweh* and tell mountains to throw themselves into the sea?"

"I *think* he was talking about trusting Yahweh to answer prayers," Mary furrowed her brow. "He also said to not remain angry at someone, but before you pray, forgive them."

Leah's eyes widened. "Forgive them? How can you forgive someone who has done something horrible? That would take a miracle as great as killing the tree with a curse."

"It would be difficult." Mary's eyes flashed. "When I think of what my uncle did after Lazarus died, trying to take over my and Martha's life, trying to force me to marry Abel, and telling me I had to either stop following Jesus or lose everything or…" She clenched her fists, folding her lips into a thin line. "I do not know how I could ever forgive him."

Leah laid a hand on Mary's arm. "Let's not talk about your uncle or cousin. Let's talk about what we want to purchase in the *marketplace*. I am sorry that Martha doesn't feel well, but I am happy for the opportunity to spend time with you."

"I agree." She glanced up at the sun. "Let's hurry. Lazarus said I was to meet him at mid-day."

Earlier, after they had arrived at their Jerusalem house, Simon told Martha to lie down. The ease with which she agreed to her husband's suggestion gave evidence of how bad she felt. To take some of the burden off her sister, Mary offered to go to the market to purchase the things she needed.

Adjusting her plain linen head cloth and picking up a large basket, she had joined Lazarus in the main living area. Stepping outside, they turned towards the Xystus Market.

Larger than the one in Bethany, the Xystus was filled with numerous booths selling beautiful items—many obtained from Lazarus and Simon's caravans—including fish, spices, honey, wine, oil—both for cooking and lamps—vegetables and fruit, balms and other medicinal supplies, cooking pots, dishes, including the glossy red *terra sigillata*, linen and wool, costly apparel, ivory, ebony, gold, silver and precious stones. At the far end of the marketplace were pens for animals; chickens, pigeons and other birds, sheep or goats, camels and donkeys. Situated on the northeast corner of the Upper City, the Xystus Market was convenient to the Holy Temple, King Herod's palace and the homes of many wealthy people, including Rabbi Nicodemus.

Samuel ben Efraim had a small corral where he sold horses raised in his stables. Mary was pleased to learn that Leah had come to the market with her father; Leah got permission to go with Mary to do her shopping. Lazarus handed Mary a pouch filled with coins and Samuel gave Leah several coins, "In case you see something pretty."

Tucking the money into the folds of their girdles, the girls walked into the heart of the marketplace.

The market was always busy, but due to the holy feast, it was packed like fish in a net. Priests in their somber attire walking towards the Temple; foreign diplomats riding camels; Roman soldiers carrying weapons marching through the streets and travelers from all corners of the world dressed in colorful and exotic attire.

The sound from the market was a cacophony of animals clucking, barking, whinnying, bleating, screeching or braying and human voices in various dialects and languages. At some booths, merchants hawked the quality of their wares and customers pointed out supposed flaws. At others, merchant and customer were going through the rhythmic barter/offer, counter offer/arguing and offering again, until a price was agreed upon, coins and product exchanged and the transaction completed, followed by an exchanged blessing for the holy week.

Mary stopped at one booth to purchase an *amphora* filled with olive oil, a sack of dates and spices needed for the evening meal. She also purchased some herbs to settle Martha's stomach. At another booth, Leah found a length of yellow silk from the Far East, hand painted with flowers and birds. Mary waited as her friend bartered with the merchant, handed over two small coins and gently placed the material into her basket.

"This is so pretty," Leah smoothed the material. "I will ask Mother to make a new tunic for me."

"The yellow will look good on you," Mary said. "If it were not too late, you could wear it for the Feast."

"Maybe I will wear it for my betrothal ceremony." She smiled at her friend.

"Leah!" Mary grabbed her friend's arm. "You did not tell me! Who is it?"

Soft color washed Leah's cheeks. "Azariah bar Cleopas."

"The blacksmith's son? When did this happen?"

"His father spoke with my father last night. After Passover, we will have the betrothal ceremony."

"*Mazel tov*, Leah! Azariah is a good and honorable man; he will be a wonderful husband. I am so happy for you!"

"I want you and Ruth to be one of my bridal attendants."

"I would be *honored*." Mary hugged her friend. "You will be the first of our friends to marry."

"I never thought I would marry before you. You are so beautiful."

"Leah, you are beautiful as well." Taller than Ruth or herself, Leah had womanly curves and long, curly hair. Many considered her pretty, but frivolous. Now, as Mary looked at her, she noticed something more, something in her countenance that transformed her. *It's love. She loves Azariah.*

Leah smiled. "And when you marry—"

"Wait!" Mary laughed, holding up a hand. "No one has approached Lazarus."

Her friend waved off the lack of a suitor. "It's just a matter of time. You are the most beautiful girl in all of Bethany and, I would even say, Jerusalem. It is clear that many men are interested in you. Even without Ruth telling us, it is obvious that Michael ben Nicodemus is attracted to you." She paused. "There's the Teacher."

"*Leah*," Mary gasped, grabbing Leah's forearm. "What do you mean?"

"Just what I said." Her friend pointed over Mary's shoulder "There's the Teacher."

Mary turned to see Jesus and several of his disciples near the bee keeper's booth. As always, a crowd of people had gathered around him. He was talking to these people and, when he looked up and saw Mary and Leah, smiled at them. Mary was accustomed to men smiling at her, but she could not read the intent behind the Teacher's smile. *I wonder when Lazarus will speak with him about the other night?* Mary realized that, even if Jesus called what she did *beautiful*, with each passing day, the more uncertain she grew about her actions of that night.

"Come on," Leah grabbed her sleeve and drew closer to the Teacher. "I don't get to hear Jesus talk as often as you do."

Mary glanced around to see where Judas was—*I don't want to stand near him*—and breathed a small sigh of relief to see he was not in the crowd. She did see Philip—one of the Teacher's disciples—talking to a group of men standing nearby. The strangers were wearing a *chiton*—a tunic that reached their knees—draped by the *pallium*—an oblong piece of cloth worn over one shoulder—identifying them as Greek.

Philip turned from the foreigners and excused himself as he moved through the crowd around the Teacher to stop at Andrew and Peter's side. Shorter than the brothers, Philip leaned up to whisper something. Peter looked at Andrew, who nodded, before stepping aside to allow the other disciple to move closer to Jesus.

"Teacher," Philip pointed to the group of foreigners, "there are men from Greece who have come for the Feast. They would like to see you."

Jesus looked at Philip, to those around him and to the Greek men before speaking. "It is now time for the Son of Man to enter his glory." A young girl standing near Jesus was carrying a basket. Jesus reached into it and lifted a handful of wheat kernels. Letting them fall through his fingers, he continued, "You all understand that, unless a kernel of wheat is planted in the soil and dies, it remains alone. But only when it *dies* will it produce more kernels and a plentiful harvest."

Several people nodded their heads. He smiled briefly before continuing, "Anyone who loves their life in this world will lose it. However, those who do not love this life will keep it for eternity."

Many in the crowd frowned in confusion. Leah looked at Mary

and arched an eyebrow. Mary lifted a shoulder in mute reply. *I told you I often do not understand the Teacher.*

"Anyone who wants to be my disciple must follow me and be where I am." Jesus put a hand on Philip's and Peter's shoulders. "The Father will honor all who serve me."

He dropped his hands, closed his eyes and let out a long sigh. "Now I am deeply troubled in my soul. Should I pray, 'Father, save me from the coming hour,'?" He shook his head and opened his eyes, his gaze hard as marble. "For this is the very reason I came. No; instead I will say," he lifted his hands towards the cloudless sky, "'Father, bring glory to Your name.'"

"*I have already brought glory to My name,*" Mary and Leah—and those around Jesus—gasped as a voice rumbled and echoed around them, "*and I will do so again.*"

A babble rose from the crowd.

"It was a voice of an angel!" a woman standing near Jesus said.

"Silly woman!" a man sneered. "It was thunder."

"Thunder?" another woman asked. "Out of a cloudless sky? Who is silly now?"

"The voice," Jesus' voice silenced further arguments, "was for your benefit, not mine."

All eyes riveted on the Teacher as he continued. "The judgment of this world has come, when Satan, the ruler, will be cast out."

Leah leaned towards Mary. "Did Jesus just call Tiberius Caesar *Satan?*" A Roman centurion, wearing the ring-mail armor vest and carrying the *vitis latina*, a vine-stick cudgel—a measure of his rank—walked past the group. Leah dropped her voice to a whisper. "And did he just *suggest* a—" she dropped her voice even further, "rebellion against Rome?"

"Shhh!" Mary kept her eyes on the soldier, as did several other people in the crowd. The slightest breath of treason against Rome was handled swiftly and cruelly.

"When I am lifted up," Jesus said, "I will attract all peoples to myself."

Jesus' words drew the crowd's attention back to him. Every Jewish child learned the story of Moses 'lifting up' the bronze serpent in the wilderness after the people had sinned. However, the phrase was also used by many as a reference to execution, either by hanging or crucifixion.

The crowd erupted again.

"What are you talking about?" the woman near Jesus asked.

A man near Mary spoke up, "Are you saying you're going—" he glanced towards the street where the soldiers had turned onto, "to *die?*"

"Wait!" another man said. "The prophets and Holy Scriptures state that the *Messiah* will live forever. How can you say the Son of Man will *die?*"

"And who is this Son of Man, anyway?" a woman on the other side of the crowd demanded.

"*In my vision at night I looked, and there before me was one like a son of man, coming with the clouds of heaven.*"

As a voice nearby quoted Daniel's prophecy, Mary's head spun like the whorl of a spindle. Standing on the edge of the crowd was her cousin, Abel. He did not look at her or at anyone in the crowd; he glared at the Teacher.

"Jesus ben Joseph; are you claiming," he asked, "to be the one spoken of by the prophet Daniel?"

CHAPTER NINE

"**J**esus ben Joseph claimed to be the Son of Man? The *Messiah?*" Joktan's face darkened, a vein throbbing above his eye.

Too impatient to wait for Judas to come to give his report to the High Priest, Joktan had sent Abel to seek out the Teacher's disciple. The young man had planned to start his search in Bethany. As he had walked out of the Temple towards the Xystus Market, however, he noticed a crowd and, in the center, was Jesus. A quick glance told him that Judas was not with the Teacher; however, he did see his cousin, Mary.

After that day, four months ago, when his father disowned his cousins Martha and Mary, all contact had been cut off between their families. Whenever anyone mentioned Lazarus, Martha or Mary, Joktan would declare that they were dead. That changed many of Abel's—and his father's—plans. Years before, his father had told him of the agreement between himself and his brother Jacob. Abel had grown up believing that the beautiful Mary would one day be his wife. Her rich dowry would only enhance his father's and his position among the Temple Leaders.

After Lazarus' *supposed* death, Mary's refusal to obey her uncle and marry him humiliated and angered Abel. The fact that his cousins allowed people to believe the lie that Lazarus had been dead and resurrected was obviously a ploy to increase the popularity of Jesus ben Joseph.

The loss of their future plans—as well as their disgrace at the hands of *women*—could be laid squarely at the feet of the teacher from Nazareth. Rabbi Caiaphas' and Rabbi Annas' decision to learn more about Jesus was the perfect opportunity for Abel and his father. If they could find *something* that would reveal Jesus as something other than the pious teacher he pretended to be, his cousins would be publicly shamed and his, Abel's, humiliation would be revenged.

At the sight of Mary in the crowd around the Teacher, Abel had turned away, hoping to find a secluded spot where he could listen to Jesus unaware. But the Nazarene's words froze his foot in mid-stride.

In his studies under his father and recently under Rabbi Gamaliel, Abel had read the writings of the prophet Daniel. During his captivity in Babylon, the prophet had several dreams, including one of four beasts coming out of the sea. In this dream, a throne was set before the four beasts and the Ancient One sat upon it, with countless people attending him. Then the prophet said,

"In my vision at night I looked, and there before me was one like a Son of Man, coming with the clouds of heaven. He approached the Ancient One and was led into His presence.

He was given authority, glory and power so that all peoples, nations and men of every language would obey Him. His dominion is an eternal dominion that will not pass away, and His kingdom would never be destroyed."

Abel knew the 'Ancient One' was Yahweh. Rabbi Gamaliel and his students spent hours discussing who was the, "Son of Man," that Daniel mentioned. Throughout the Holy Scriptures, "son of man" is often used to refer to mankind as opposed to Yahweh, which would explain why the woman in the crowd asked Jesus who the 'Son of Man' was. In Daniel's dream, however, it appears that this "Son of Man" was something more. The one given authority, glory and an eternal kingdom was the *Messiah*.

Jesus referring to himself as the 'Son of Man' was what Abel reported to his father.

He found his father in the Court of Gentiles, overseeing the table where people would exchange their coins to pay the Temple tax. There were other priests in the court, as well as an increased number of Temple Guards; after the chaos Jesus had created the other day, the Temple Leaders wanted to be prepared.

"He did not plainly answer my question," Abel answered his father's question, "but he did not *deny* it."

Joktan gnashed his teeth. "What *did* he say?"

Abel paused, realizing that his father—and Rabbis Caiaphas and Annas—would want the Teacher's exact words. "He said that his light would shine for them just a little longer. He encouraged them to walk in that light, so that darkness would not overtake them. He explained that people who walk in the dark cannot see where they are going." Abel thought for a moment. "He said, 'Put your trust in the light while there is still time; then you will become children of the light.'"

"That's all he said?" Joktan demanded. "He said nothing more about casting out the Romans or trying to become a ruler?"

"No." Abel shook his head. "To speak truth, Father, the Teacher's words were confusing to me and—it appeared—to those in the crowd."

"What did Jesus do next?"

"He walked away."

"*Racha!*" Joktan growled. "You fool! This is not enough to take to the High Priest! You are worthless! You should have followed him; at least we would have known where he was going."

Under his father's tirade, Abel dropped his gaze. He was a man full grown, yet his father's words had the power to shred his soul and reduce him to a boy. He stared at the marble floor of the Temple, uncertain what to do, when his father hissed.

"What is *he* doing here?"

Abel looked up, following his father's gaze, to see Jesus ben Joseph entering the Court of Gentiles. The crowd that had surrounded him in the marketplace had grown. It took Abel only a second to see that Mary and her friend Leah bat Samuel were with them. Slanting a glance at his father—rage tightening his face like an old wine skin—was evidence that Joktan had seen his niece

The atmosphere in the Temple courtyard reminded Abel of the air before lightning strikes. The Temple Guards gripped their swords, their gaze never leaving the Teacher. The crowd in the courtyard shifted looking between Jesus and the High Priest, who had just entered the court, followed by his father-in-law and a group of elders. Rabbi Caiaphas and Rabbi Annas watched the Teacher as one would watch a cobra.

The only one apparently at ease was Jesus. He walked around the courtyard, smiling at a young child, respectfully greeting an elderly man who stopped him.

"Good morning, Sir," the elderly man said. "Time of gladness."

"Festivals and seasons of joy," Jesus responded.

"Are you Jesus ben Joseph, the Teacher?" the elderly man asked.

"I am," Jesus replied.

"I am Aaron bar Gershom. I live in Caesarea Philippi."

"You are a long way from home."

The elderly man shrugged. "My time on this earth is coming to an end and soon I will go to Abraham's bosom. I wanted to come to Jerusalem for Passover one more time. I have heard that you speak of good news about the coming Kingdom of Yahweh."

"I do."

The older man smiled. "If you have a moment, I would love to hear of this."

Jesus smiled in return. "Of course."

Abel echoed his father's gasp. *The coming kingdom? Jesus dares to talk of rebellion against Rome* here? *So close to the Antonia Fortress?*

As Jesus began speaking, others in the courtyard gathered around him.

Joktan grabbed his son's arm. "Come." They crossed to where the Chief Priest and elders were standing, arms crossed, ears straining to hear Jesus to speak the first word of treason. The tension among them grew palpable until finally Rabbi Caiaphas stepped towards Jesus only to be stopped by his father-in-law's lifted hand.

"Jesus ben Joseph," Rabbi Annas' voice echoed against the marble walls.

Jesus excused himself to the elderly Aaron, before turning towards the cluster of priests and Temple Leaders.

Annas, accustomed to his presence being sufficient to silence a room, appeared unsettled by the Teacher's calm demeanor. He *har-rumphed.* "Your words and," he spread his arms wide, encompassing the courtyard, "your actions two days ago. Who gave you the authority to teach these things and to do such things?"

Several of the elders—including Joktan—raised their chins in self-satisfied anticipation. His answer would sway the crowd one way or the other.

Jesus did not appear to be awed by the man standing in front of him. He looked at the former High Priest for a moment and then smiled.

"A fair question," Jesus said. "I will give you the answer you seek, *if*" he lifted a finger upward, "you answer my question. Tell me, John's baptism—was it from Heaven or was it from men?"

Abel did not need Jesus to add John's father's name; all those present were aware *who* the Teacher meant.

John was the only son of the elderly priest Zechariah ben Barach and his wife Elizabeth, both of whom were of the line of Aaron. Barren for many years, in their old age, Yahweh had blessed them with a son, whom they named John. Three years ago, John—now a young man a little older than Abel—showed up in the area beyond Bethany, but not to follow in the priestly tradition of his father. He began preaching of the soon-coming judgment of Yahweh on the world and declaring that all people needed to prepare by repenting of their sins and being baptized in the waters of the Jordan River.

John's message and appearance—he wore garments made of coarse camel hair and ate the pods from the wild honey locust trees—drew many people; none had ever been privileged to see a living prophet of Yahweh.

However, John also made many enemies. The High Priest and other Temple Leaders were obviously concerned when anyone claimed to be a prophet and they sent a group of priests—including Joktan—to hear the young man. Joktan came home that night, furious. He told his family that John had dared to call the priests, "a brood of snakes" and claimed that being a descendant of Abraham was insufficient to be pleasing in the eyes of Yahweh.

John also made political enemies, including Herod Antipas. After the death of Herod, known as the Great, nearly thirty years before, Caesar Augustus had appointed Herod's son, Antipas, to the position of Tetrarch. Although politically aligned with Rome, Herod Antipas was an Edomite and had been raised according to the Law given to Moses. The Law had little influence over the Tetrarch's life though; after an affair with Herodias—his brother's wife—Antipas and Herodias divorced their spouses and married.

While many were disgusted at this adulterous relationship, the Baptizer openly condemned Herod Antipas. In response, Herod had John arrested and thrown into prison.

During a feast in celebration of Herod's birthday, Salome—Herodias' daughter—danced for her step-father, which pleased the Tetrarch so much that he promised to give the girl whatever she asked, even up to half his kingdom. After conferring with her mother, who was known as a jealous, ambitious schemer, Salome asked for the head of the Baptizer on a platter.

Although John had not committed any crime deserving of death, for Herod to break an oath before his guests would have been embarrassing. He sent the executioner to the prison, who beheaded the Baptizer. John's head was brought to the girl and she gave it to her mother.

Jesus ben Joseph's present question concerning the Baptizer's authority created a difficulty. As horrendous as the event was, when John's death was announced, Abel knew that Joktan—along with the other Temple Leaders—were relieved that the Baptizer was no longer able to influence the people.

Everyone in the courtyard waited for the elderly priest's answer.

Annas stared at Jesus for a moment and then, lifting his chin, he turned away, gesturing for his son-in-law and the Temple Leaders to gather around him. Joktan, his hand still on his son's arm, moved closer. Glancing over his shoulder at the young man from Nazareth, Annas lowered his voice.

"How should we answer him?" he asked.

Caiaphas stroked his beard. "If we say, 'From Heaven,' then he will ask, 'Why did you not believe him?' But if we say, 'From men...'" his words died away as he glanced towards the crowd with Jesus.

"Yes," Annas said. "The people believe John was a prophet. If we say, 'From men,'" he dropped his voice, "the people will stone us." He looked at the priests gathered around him. "Do any of you have an answer?" When no one responded, he lifted his chin and turned back to the Teacher.

"We…do not know where John's authority was from."

Jesus looked at him for a moment and shook his head, smiling sadly. "Neither will I tell you by what authority I am doing these things." The Teacher lifted a hand towards the group of priests. "I need your thoughts," he said.

"There was a man who had two sons. He told his eldest son to work in their vineyard. The young man refused at first, but later he repented of his disobedience and went to the vineyard.

"The father told his younger son to work in the vineyard. The young man promptly said that he would, but he did not go."

Jesus glanced at Rabbi Annas. "Which of these two sons did as the father wanted?"

Abel was not surprised when Annas crossed his arms and slowly arched an eyebrow at Jesus; no one questioned the High Priest. The Teacher appeared unconcerned by the rabbi's displeasure; he stood watching the older man. After a long moment, Annas cleared his throat. "The first son," he responded.

"You are correct," Jesus said. "When thieves, tax collectors and prostitutes heard John's message, they repented of their sins. These people will enter Yahweh's Kingdom ahead of you because, even after all you heard him teach, you did not believe and repent."

A gasp rippled among the gathered priests.

How dare *he insult and condemn the priests and Temple Leaders!* Abel fumed. He noticed that the people around the Teacher, however, were obviously not shocked. Some of the men stroked their beards to cover their mouths while others openly grinned. He saw Mary look down, lifting a hand to apparently adjust her head covering, but he knew it was a ploy to hide her enjoyment of the Nazarene's ridicule of the priests and leaders.

Jesus walked back to the elderly man. "You asked about Yahweh's Kingdom. Let me tell you a parable." He turned towards the center of the Court of Gentiles; all eyes were on him.

"A king prepared a great wedding feast for his son. When all was ready, he sent his servants—bearing gifts of fine clothes for the guests to wear to the feast—to notify those who had been invited that the time for the wedding feast had come. But they refused to go."

Another gasp rippled around the courtyard. Once an invitation had been accepted, it was the height of discourtesy—and folly in the case of a royal invitation—to refuse to attend.

Jesus nodded. "Some of those invited just went about their business, but others seized the king's servants, insulted them and killed them."

The Teacher turned so all could see him, spreading his arms wide. "As you can imagine, the king was furious. He sent an army to destroy the murderers and burn their town.

"Then he said, 'My son's wedding feast is ready and the guests I invited are not worthy to attend.' He sent other servants, bearing more garments, and said, 'Go to the street corners and invite everyone you see.'

"The servants obeyed the king. They brought everyone they could find—no matter who they were—and the banquet hall was filled with guests.

"When the king went in to greet his guests, he noticed a man who was not wearing the clothes provided for the wedding guests."

Another collective gasp. It was as much folly for this man to attend a royal feast uninvited as it was for the first guests to ignore the invitation.

"'Friend,' the king asked," Jesus' voice took on a soft, dangerous timbre, "'how is it that you are here without the garments I provided for my guests?'"

Jesus shook his head. "The man had no answer.

"The king called his aides and said, 'Bind his hands and feet and throw him into the outer darkness, where there will be weeping and gnashing of teeth.' For many are invited," Jesus looked at the priests before turning towards the crowd, "but few are chosen."

Without looking back at the assembled priests, Jesus turned and left, with the crowd—now growing from those in the courtyard—following. After a moment, a cry, "There's Jesus ben Joseph," rose from the streets below.

The courtyard was empty save for the priests, Temple Guards and money changers. The only sounds were the bleats and coos of the sheep and doves. Abel—as did his father and the others present—stood still, studying the marbled floor. Only a foolish man would be the first to speak after the Teacher's obvious insults towards the High Priest and the priesthood.

Abel startled as a curse resounded around the courtyard. He looked up to see Annas—face suffused with blood—slapping a closed fist into his other hand, spittle flying from his mouth as he pronounced curse after curse on the Nazarene. Finally, he paused for breath. "How dare he, how *dare* he speak judgment on us! He must pay for this."

A Teacher of the Law spoke up. "What can we do? This man keeps on doing things. Healing people, feeding multitudes and—" he glanced at Abel and Joktan, "*other* miracles. If he is allowed to continue, soon everyone will believe in him and then—" he glanced towards the north, where stood the Antonia Fortress, which housed six hundred Roman soldiers. He lowered his voice before continuing, "—and then the Romans will come and remove what power and privilege we now have."

"What can we do?" Annas glared at the corridor where Jesus had walked through. "Kill him." The words echoed around the courtyard.

Abel stared at the elderly priest, thankful that he was considered too young to speak his opinions before the Temple Leaders.

"But Rabbi Annas, this is not proper." Rabbi Nicodemus stepped forward. His age, wealth and family position granted him a voice in the Sanhedrin that few had. "Does our Law condemn a man without summoning him before the Sanhedrin, without proper witnesses and without making any investigation of the man's words or actions?"

"Rabbi Nicodemus, you know nothing." Caiaphas said. Without even glancing at his father-in-law, the High Priest continued, "Can't you see that it is to our advantage that *one* man dies for the people rather than the *whole* nation be destroyed?"

Nicodemus stared intently at Caiaphas and Annas for a moment before turning and leaving the courts. Rabbi Joseph bar Neriah followed.

"We need to keep watch over what we say before those two," Annas said. "Nicodemus is kin to those known to be followers of Jesus ben Joseph." He glanced toward Joktan and Abel. "Killing a poor teacher from Nazareth is one thing; killing a rich and powerful man like Nicodemus ben Melech or Joseph bar Neriah would be impossible."

Death. From what Abel had heard over the past months, it was obvious that the leaders of their people might be leaning towards dealing with the Nazarene *permanently*. Now they had finally spoken of it.

"We must find something that will condemn him before Pilate."

With the exception of the times the Roman Governor turned his head when the people stoned someone—or when a foreigner entered the area of the Temple grounds designated only for Jews—Rome had stripped the Sanhedrin of the right to carry out an execution. As Jesus was not a Roman citizen, the fact that the High Priest wanted to hand the Nazarene over to the Romans meant one thing: crucifixion.

Annas tilted his head towards the sound of the echoes of praise for the Teacher floating up from the streets. "He is still near. We need to act quickly. David bar Mattan," the elderly priest nodded towards one of the Sadducees. He scanned the group, his gaze stopping on Abel and his father. "Joktan ben Philemon. Abel ben Joktan. You brought the Teacher's disciple Judas to us."

Abel glanced at his father. Joktan nodded, preening like a peacock.

"You are also family to Lazarus ben Jacob," Annas continued.

Joktan's preen turned to a barely contained grimace.

"The Teacher is obviously accustomed to seeing you at your kinsman's house. You can ask Jesus ben Joseph questions that will trap him." He nodded at his son-in-law, who gestured for David, Joktan and Abel to step closer.

"Here is what you are to ask him."

From the questions the High Priest listed for them to ask the Teacher, it was obvious to Abel that the Temple Leaders had been planning this trap for a while. *I told Judas the Temple Leaders wanted to talk with Jesus. What will he do when he realizes they want to kill the Nazarene?*

Abel felt uncomfortable having a hand in a man's death. His face darkened as the memory of the last Passover came, when his cousin Mary announced that she would marry anyone else rather than marry him. Or, several months later, when his father told him that she chose to be cast-off and penniless rather than stop following Jesus and become his wife.

He stepped closer to listen to the High Priest.

"There he is."

Abel didn't need his father's help in locating Jesus. He was in the Xystus, only a few streets from the Temple. The crowd surrounding the Teacher had grown even larger—Abel saw Judas standing near the edge of the group—and the people listened as if the Teacher spoke the words of Yahweh. *Even Mary.* Abel noted that his cousin was acting shamefully, trying to move closer to this man, smiling when he looked her way. *Your smiles will change,* cousin, *when the Guards arrest him.*

Joktan put a hand on his son's sleeve. "Rabbi David, this man knows I am not a friend to him and will wonder why I was asking him these questions. He only met my son once at Passover last year. I doubt that he even remembers Abel." His father's frown deepened. "I suggest that you two ask the questions Rabbi Caiaphas commanded." He pointed to the side of the herb seller's booth. "I will stand there in the shadow of the booth and listen. Together we will be the witnesses to his answers."

Abel nodded, understanding that his father was referencing the Law giving to Moses. To condemn a man to death, you had to have two or three witnesses.

When Rabbi David agreed, Joktan crossed to the booth and nodded to them. Abel gestured for the older priest to precede him as they walked to the edge of the crowd surrounding the Nazarene.

Rabbi David cleared his throat. "Teacher. We would speak with you."

Jesus was smiling at a youngster, ruffling his hair. He straightened and looked at David and Abel. His smile faded. "Yes?"

Abel had to control himself to keep from squirming under the Nazarene's penetrating gaze. He swallowed twice before speaking. "Teacher, we—" indicating Rabbi David and himself, "know that you are a man of integrity and that you teach the way of Yahweh in accordance with the truth. You are not influenced by men, because you pay no attention to who they are." He tried to speak casually, as if he wasn't reciting the question exactly as given by Rabbi Caiaphas. "Tell us your opinion. Is it right to pay taxes to Caesar or not?"

The people surrounding Jesus stilled, waiting to see how he answered. If he spoke against paying taxes, the people might like it but Pilate would consider it treasonous. If he spoke for paying taxes, the people might think he was aligning himself with Rome.

Jesus looked at Rabbi David and Abel and then shifted his gaze briefly to the booth where Joktan was hiding. He breathed a sigh, shaking his head. "You hypocrites," he said, "why are you trying to trap me?" He held out a hand, palm upwards. "Show me the coin used for paying the tax."

Abel gaped; this was not one of the responses they discussed. The older priest jabbed him with an elbow, gesturing his head towards the Teacher. Abel reached into the folds of his girdle and brought out his coin pouch. Untying the strings, he searched among the coins until he found a denarius. He extended the coin to Judas, who gave him a quizzical glance before taking the coin and handing it to Jesus.

Jesus held the silver coin, looking at Caesar Tiberius' profile on one side and then flipping it over to see Caesar seated on a throne, holding a spear. Then he lifted his gaze to Abel and Rabbi David. "Whose portrait is on this coin? Whose inscription is on it?"

Abel noted several Roman soldiers walking past. *This could not be more convenient,* he thought. He raised his voice. "Caesar's."

The soldiers heard him and stopped, turning towards the crowd, their hands moving to the hilts of the short swords at their sides.

Jesus looked at the soldiers and then turned to hand the coin back to Judas. "Give to Caesar what is Caesar's," he said, "and to Yahweh what is Yahweh's."

Abel's eyes widened. *His answer protected him either way.*

The crowd surrounding Jesus smiled and nodded at the wisdom of his response. The Roman soldiers shrugged, removed their hands from their sword hilts and continued walking.

Jesus looked from Abel and Rabbi David to the herb seller's booth before turning and walking down the street of the marketplace. The crowd and disciples followed him; except for Judas. He moved as if to tuck the coin into the folds of his girdle until Abel extended his hand.

"My coin?"

Judas flushed angrily and handed the coin to Abel. Abel grabbed the tips of the disciple's fingers and squeezed, glaring at him. "There are *people* who want to hear from you," he whispered. "Do not fail them."

Judas nodded slightly before jerking back his hand. "I will come soon," he said before turning to lose himself in the crowd in the marketplace.

CHAPTER TEN

14 Nisan 3793

Martha scowled at the dust on the table top. *Truly? I spend all this time preparing for the Teacher's mother to visit. I asked Mary to do one thing—one thing—dust the furniture. But, noooo...she can't even do that right. She had to go to Jerusalem with Simon to help Abigail. Well, I needed her help too.* Her stomach tightened around her meagre breakfast; nausea and stress over the coming visit of Jesus' mother had reduced her morning meal to a single piece of bread and a few sips of water.

She turned to find a cloth for cleaning when the sounds of an approaching carriage stopped her. Looking around, she lifted the hem of her robe and swiped at the table. Patting the dust off the green linen garment, she dropped it and crossed to the door. Taking a deep breath and holding it for a moment, she exhaled slowly, smiled and opened the door to her guest.

"Peace be on you, Mary bat Eli." Martha nodded her head to the older woman standing in the doorway. "Time of gladness."

"And on you peace, Martha bat Jacob. Festivals and seasons of joy."

Martha turned to the servant driving Rabbi Nicodemus' carriage. "Daniel, if you will drive to the back of the house, you will find water for your horses and food and drink for yourself." As the carriage moved away, she turned back to her guest. "Please come inside. It was kind of Rabbi Nicodemus to arrange for you to have use of his carriage."

"I am thankful for Rabbi Nicodemus' generosity." Mary shook the folds of her blue robe and cream tunic to remove the dust before touching her fingers to the *mezuzah*—the box on the doorpost that contained sacred scriptures—and stepping into the front room. "Thank you for inviting me to your home." She sat on a small bench placed near the door and, as all guests do upon entering a home, removed her sandals and set them in an empty basket.

"It is my honor to have you visit our humble home." Martha moved to the table next to Mary, where a small basin of water, a towel, an *amphora* and a cup were placed. Lifting the basin, she knelt and placed it on the floor in front of her guest to allow Mary to wash her feet. In homes of wealthy people, this task was done by a servant. Martha still refused to hire servants—despite Simon's encouragements—so their guests washed their own feet as they would do in a poorer home.

After Mary dried her feet with the towel, she retrieved her sandals, wiped the dust from them, and retied them on her feet. Martha picked up the *amphora* and poured a small amount of olive oil onto her guest's head, followed by offering her a cup of cool water. She helped the older woman stand and leaned forward to kiss her cheek.

Mary thanked Martha for the acts honoring a guest and then looked around. "This is a lovely room."

Simon's house was similar in design to Lazarus and Abigail's but touches of Martha's hand were evident throughout. Thick hand-hewn stone of the house's exterior kept the Judean heat at bay. The front room stretched the width of the house with a mosaic floor patterned in rosettes of red, white and yellow. Colorful frescos of palms and lotus blossoms decorated the smooth clay walls. Lamp stands filled with fragrant oil stood in the corners of the room and niches along the walls held delicate glassware and painted pottery. Two limestone tables were placed along the back wall to hold stone jars of water and wine during meals. Thick cushions in reds and yellows were placed around the low round table in the center of the room. On either side of the front door, white lattice shutters covered the windows.

"Thank you," Martha said. "Simon allowed me to alter the decorations as I wanted. I chose patterns and furnishings that reminded me of the home of my parents. As Simon had spent much of his youth in our house, he was pleased to honor them in such a way." She smiled at the Teacher's mother. "If you would please walk with me to our family courtyard, I have food and drink prepared."

Martha escorted Mary through the archway on the side of the room, down the hall, up the staircase and into the room set aside for family and special guests. Pomegranates and flowers were painted on three walls while the outside wall had three large windows with shutters opened to allow in cooling breezes. Tall lamps stood in each corner; even unlit, the fragrance from their oil perfumed the air. Several low tables with thick cushions were placed around the room. On one table close to the windows was a platter holding cheese, grapes and olives and another platter with date and honey cakes. There were also linen napkins, cups and two pitchers beading with condensation.

After settling onto the cushions, Martha offered Mary goat's milk or water. Handing her the cup, Mary moved the platters of food closer to her guest.

"Ah, these are the cakes my son has told me about." Mary selected one and bit into it. "Mmmm, they are as wonderful as Jesus described. Would you please share your recipe?"

"I am honored that you and the Teacher enjoy them and I would be happy to tell you how I make them." Martha smiled.

"Your sister is not joining us?"

Martha bit the inside of her cheek to keep from grimacing. "Mary is helping our sister-in-law Abigail prepare our Jerusalem house for Passover."

"How kind of her. I am certain Abigail bat Nicodemus is thankful for her help."

"I am certain she is," Martha said dryly. "I am sorry Salome bat Eli and Mary Magdala could not come with you."

"Ah well," the older woman took a sip of milk. "Salome had to purchase some things in the marketplace before we return home. With Passover almost upon us, this was her only opportunity and Mary offered to go with her. Both asked me to convey their sadness at not being able to accept your hospitality." She set her cup on the table and reached for a grape. "Although their absence gives me the opportunity to get to know you better."

"I am also thankful for this opportunity to get to know you as well. Jesus speaks highly of you."

Mary smiled. "He is a good and loving son."

"That is a blessing every mother prays for." Martha laid a hand on her abdomen.

"It is indeed. When are you and Simon to be blessed by Yahweh?"

"I am newly expecting. Our child will not be born for many months," Martha's eyes softened. "Sometime in Kislev or Tevet."

"Jesus was born in Tevet."

"Truly?"

Mary nodded. "It was a cold day." She shuddered and then laughed. "I confess I was so happy to be somewhere dry and warm, it did not matter that I gave birth in a stable."

"A stable?" Martha's eyes widened. "You did not give birth in your home?"

"No. Jesus was not born in Nazareth. Did he never tell the story of his birth?"

"Not in my hearing. I would be honored if you would share it."

"It was during the reign of Caesar Augustus, after the death of King Herod, he who had been named *Great* by Caesar Octavian. The news had come to Nazareth that Augustus had issued a decree for a census."

"In order to raise taxes, no doubt to build a new palace," Martha spat, "or to support the army or the governors or to pay for some public spectacle." Martha's mouth pulled down as if the milk in her cup was spoiled. "It angers me that Rome does not tax her own citizens, yet her taxes crush the peoples under her control. Roman grain is watered by the blood of her provinces." She paused and shook her head. "Forgive me. I should not have spoken harshly."

"You speak truth, Martha bat Jacob," Mary said. "Rome's taxes place a hardship on many people. Not only was this census included a tax to be levied to pay for Rome's needs, Caesar required that everyone return to the town of their ancestors." She paused. "Are you familiar with Nazareth?"

Martha shook her head. "Outside of the area surrounding Jerusalem, I have only traveled to Capernaum."

"Nazareth is about a three-day journey from Capernaum. It is a small, humble village, but we have a noble heritage. When I was a girl, we were taught that when the people of Israel returned from exile in Babylon, the ancestors of King David settled in the area that became Nazareth. That makes most of those in our village a descendant of King David. Not only that, but we were also taught that the prophet Isaiah said the *Messiah* would be the *netzer*—the branch—of Jesse, King David's father. That is where our village derived its name. Because of this prophecy, all the women of child-bearing age believed that anyone of us could," she laid a hand on her abdomen and smiled, "give birth to the *Messiah*."

"That is a noble heritage indeed."

Mary nodded. "When the census was announced, I was in the latter part of my pregnancy with Jesus. If the Romans had traveled to each village for the census, it would not have been so great a problem. However, because Rome required that everyone return to the town of their ancestors, that meant that Joseph and I—along with many from our village—had to travel to King David's birthplace: Bethlehem.

"It would take most of a week to travel that distance."

"Four days for most people; we knew it would take longer for us. Because of my pregnancy, it took extra days to prepare for the trip. I would not be able to walk to Bethlehem, so we had to find a means for me to travel; after several days, Joseph found a donkey. Joseph and my mother wanted to make sure I was as comfortable as possible; she sent extra blankets for me to sit on and packed extra food. By the time Joseph and I were ready, all the other people from our village had been gone for several days. It was likely that most had arrived in Bethlehem to be counted and were already returning home."

"The trip was not easy." She looked at Martha. "Has your pregnancy given you a delicate stomach?"

"Oh my yes," Martha laughed. "At times, it seems that I will never find anything that will agree with my stomach."

"I remember what that was like. Try drinking tea from mint leaves; it helped me," Mary said. "By the time of the census, the nausea of my early pregnancy was gone. However, even with the extra blankets to sit on, riding a donkey for long hours was difficult. Joseph would stop frequently to lift me down so I could stretch and walk around some.

"But the evenings made up for the long days." Mary's gaze softened; she stared through the opened window as if seeing through the years. "As the sun began setting, Joseph would find a spot that would shelter us; sometimes it was near a large rock or the trunk of an ancient tree. While I set out our meal, he would gather wood for a fire and tend to the needs of the donkey. After the sky grew dark, we would sit near the fire and gaze at the stars.

"I have looked at the stars all my life. My father taught us the word of the prophet Isaiah," her voice took on an awe-filled resonance, "*Look at the heavens: Who created all these? He who brings out the starry host one by one, and calls them each by name.*' My father would point out the different stars and tell us their names; *Tzedek*—" she looked at Martha. "Father said that the Romans called it by another name, but I do not recall what it was."

"Jupiter. The Romans named it after the father of their gods. I love that *Tzedek* means *justice* and *righteousness.*"

"I agree. What do the Romans call the star *Heilel?*"

"Um...." Martha thought for a moment. "Venus."

"And what about the *mazzaloth*—the arrangement of stars—of the Lion, the one we call *Labi?*"

"Leo."

"And *Zerah*, the virgin holding the wheat?"

"Virgo."

"What about *Taleh* the Ram?"

"Aries."

"My father told me that the brightest star in that *mazzaloth* is named *El Nath*, which means, *Elohim* and *broken or poured out.* I never understood that."

"My father spent many years traveling to distant lands," Martha said. "He told me that several years before I was born, *Tzedek* came near another star named *Sharu* by the Babylonians or *Rex* by the Romans. Both words mean *King*. He said that, when the two stars came together, they looked like one very bright star; the brightest he had ever seen."

Mary clapped her hands. "That was what Joseph and I saw! Before we left on our journey, everyone in Nazareth would watch these two stars as they drew closer together, certain it was some portentous sign. As we traveled to Bethlehem, Joseph and I would watch the stars each night and wonder at their appearance.

"On the morning of our sixth day," the older woman laid a hand on her abdomen, "I knew something was different. My stomach felt like a hand squeezing to make a fist. Then it would ease. My back ached as it had not done during all the months of my pregnancy. I assumed I was just fatigued from traveling. We were so close to our destination, I said nothing to Joseph, as he would have stopped.

"We reached Jerusalem by late afternoon. I had come to the City of David before—for Passover—and always marveled at the size of the city and the splendor of the Temple. This time, however, I barely glanced at them. The tightening," she squeezed her fist against her abdomen, "had continued all day. All I wanted to do was reach Bethlehem and find a place to lie down.

"We had turned down the road leading out of the city towards Bethlehem when the tightening was so bad that I gasped. It was then I realized that I was in labor." She shook her head, chuckling. "Having been raised around animals, I was certain that I would know when it was my time. I was wrong.

"I tried not to worry Joseph when I told him the child was coming." She grinned. "My poor husband; I can still remember his eyes growing wide. 'Are you sure?' he asked me, as if I would joke about such things.

"He jerked on the donkey's reins and began dragging that poor animal down the road.

"Those few miles between Jerusalem and Bethlehem felt like an eternity. I kept my eyes closed, trying to control my breathing. Daylight was fading by the time we arrived in that little town.

"Although we were of the lineage of David, neither of us had been to Bethlehem before. We didn't know where to find the inn. Joseph stopped at the first building we came to and banged on the door. After what seemed like forever, the door opened wide enough to reveal a very angry man. He demanded to know what we wanted.

"Joseph explained that I needed a place to be private.

"'Private?' the man bellowed. 'All of Bethlehem is filled with travelers coming for the census. This is not an inn and yet I have people I don't even know sleeping all over my floors. There's no room for anyone else, much less room for *privacy*.'

"Joseph didn't even wait for the man to shut the door. He turned and ran to the building across the road to bang on the door. The owner of that house told the same story; travelers took up all available space. Joseph dragged the donkey down the street of the small town, knocking at each door.

"All the while, the tightening continued to grow. It felt like a knife cutting through me. I tried not to cry out, but it finally hurt so much, I could only gasp one thing: his name. 'Joseph!'

"Dropping the donkey's reins, Joseph lifted me from the animal's back; but he didn't set me down. He held me and the donkey's reins as he continued walking. I remember him praying over and over again, asking Yahweh to help us. There was only one building left. Joseph carried me up the path and kicked on the bottom of the door.

"The door opened to reveal an elderly man holding a lamp. Beyond him, we could see what appeared to be a public room. He took one look at us and said, 'My inn is filled, but there is a small place out back where I keep a few animals. It's warm and private.'

"'Thank you,'" Joseph said, 'Anywhere is fine.'"

When Mary paused to take a sip of milk, Martha refilled her cup.

"Thank you. Are you certain you want to hear this?"

"I do, if you don't mind continuing. I want to hear other women's stories of giving birth. To help me know how to be ready for the birth of my own child."

"You can prepare, but no woman is ever truly *ready* for the birth of her child. I have had twelve children and each labor was different." Mary laughed. "However, I pray that no woman *ever* has to give birth as I did my first time." She took a deep breath and continued her story.

"The elderly man grabbed several blankets and a lamp and led the way around the inn to a small cave dug into a hill where a cow and her calf, some chickens and several sheep were sleeping.

"He set the lamp and blankets on the ground and then grabbed armloads of fresh hay. He threw them on the ground and covered them with the blankets. He apologized that I would have to give birth in a humble stable, but he offered to bring water and to care for our donkey.

"Joseph thanked him. After the innkeeper left, Joseph told me he was going to look for a midwife.

"I was in such pain; I couldn't think clearly. All I knew was that I didn't want Joseph to leave me." She laughed softly. "My poor husband. He had thought that when I gave birth, he would stand outside the room, wringing his hands and waiting for the cry of our child. Instead, he had to act as my midwife.

"By this time, my pains were coming in steady waves. In between the pains, I rested and gasped out instructions. Joseph plumped up the hay behind me to form a chair. He found two long pieces of rope and tied them from the rafters of the ceiling to dangle above my head. He knotted the ends of the ropes, so I could grasp them."

Martha was familiar with how women would give birth. With each pain, the mother would reach up, pull on the rope and straighten her body to allow the baby room to move downward. Between pains, she would collapse against the pillow—or hay, in Mary's case—to rest.

Mary told her how Joseph would wipe her face between the contractions and give her sips of water. When it came time for the baby to be born, Mary dropped the ropes and grabbed her knees. With each pain, she lowered her head and chest towards her knees, held her breath and pushed, working with the pains to birth her baby. Mary explained that she had to tell Joseph how to hold the babe when she pushed him out.

"I felt the babe slip from my body. He took his first breath and began wailing. Joseph lifted him and laid him on me," Mary placed a hand against her chest, "and covered us both with a blanket. The babe continued to cry—strong, healthy cries—until finally he settled down and began nursing.

"I looked at Joseph. He was covered in sweat—as was I—and he looked as exhausted as I felt. It was then I realized I could *see* Joseph. I could *see* my baby. It was long after the new moon had risen at the feet of *Zerah* the Virgin, yet the stable was bathed in a warm light. It was as if *Tzedek* and *Sharu*—and all the starry host of heaven—had come together and stopped over the stable to celebrate Jesus' birth with us." She closed her eyes and dropped her voice to a whisper. "It was the holiest moment I have ever experienced. Since that night, I have often thought of Jesus' birth and treasured those moments."

"Treasured?" Martha shook her head. "Forgive me, Mary bat Eli but you labored and gave birth under the most difficult circumstances. How can you *treasure* those moments?"

"Is there one part of the Holy Scriptures that you cherish above others? One that *resonates* with you?"

Martha was surprised by Mary's question. "Yes, I loved the proverb that King Solomon wrote about the godly woman. As a young girl, I read it over and over again, until I knew it from memory. All of my life, I wanted to become like that woman."

"'*Who can find a virtuous wife? She is worth more than rubies.*' I am certain your Simon feels that way about you."

"You are kind," Martha smiled.

"I have always been drawn to the scriptures that promised that Yahweh is with us. There are several, including the time that Moses commissioned Joshua and told him, '*The LORD goes before you and will be with you; He will never leave you nor forsake you.*'

"You spoke truth, Martha bat Jacob, when you said that Jesus' birth was difficult; indeed, the hardest of all twelve of my children. But in those moments between Joseph and me, when we worked together to bring forth this new life, I felt the presence of Yahweh in that humble stable. Since that time, whenever I am faced with a challenge," she drew a deep, shuddering breath, "as when my Joseph went to Abraham's bosom, I remember Jesus' birth and remind myself of the promise that Yahweh is always with me."

"Yahweh with us," Martha mused. "Isn't there a passage from the writings of the prophet—Isaiah, I think—that speaks of Yahweh being with us? '*Therefore the Lord Himself will give...*' I do not remember the rest of it."

"'*Therefore the Lord Himself with give you a sign; the virgin will be with child and will give birth to a son and will call Him Immanuel.*'"

"That's the one. While I do not understand what the prophet meant by a virgin giving birth, I did love the word, 'Immanuel.' 'Yahweh is with us.'"

"It is difficult to know what prophecies mean *before* they happen. But afterwards," Mary smiled again as she laid a hand on her abdomen, "seeing prophecies coming to pass is a reminder of Yahweh's love for us and His presence with us."

Prophecies coming to pass? Martha paused. *What can she mean?* Rather than question her guest, she chose to comment on what she did understand. "Yahweh's love. That is a new teaching for me. My uncle is a priest and I grew up hearing him talk about Yahweh's authority and wrath and judgment. Your son was the first person to ever speak of Yahweh's love. He told my sister Mary that our value is not found in our abilities or in our beauty, but in the fact that we are created and loved by Yahweh. His words healed wounds that had long festered in our hearts."

Mary smiled. "My son is a wise man."

CHAPTER ELEVEN

J esus ben Joseph is a trouble-maker!" Joktan fumed. "I wish an earthquake would split the ground beneath him and swallow him whole. If not for *this man,* we would have been finished with our Temple duties hours ago and would be home by now."

This day of Passover week was always busy for Joktan and Abel, along with the other priests and Temple Leaders on duty at the Temple. On this day each year, the Temple was packed with people retrieving the lambs they had presented for examination as their Passover sacrifice.

Whatever time of the year, the priests had other duties in the Temple and they were not set aside because of Passover.

Most duties surrounded the sacrifices. The Law Yahweh gave to Moses contained five different types of sacrificial offerings: the meal offering, the peace offering, the trespass offering, the sin offering and the burnt offering. In many of the sacrifices, after the priest presented, waved or sprinkled the item offered—whether grain, oil or animal—he would take a portion of the sacrifice. The rest was returned to the person who brought the sacrifice.

The sin offering paid for the worshippers' unintentional weaknesses and failures against Yahweh and His Law. The burnt offerings were to atone for the peoples' sins against Yahweh and was a continual dedication of one's life to Yahweh. These sin and burnt offerings were completely consumed by fire.

One daily burnt offering was the *Tamid,* the 'perpetual sacrifice.' Twice each day, at the third hour and again at the ninth hour, a male lamb—without blemish—was sacrificed in the Temple and was offered along with flour and wine.

For the Jewish people, the most holy of all days was the Day of Atonement, known as *Shabbat Shabbaton,* "a Sabbath of Sabbaths." On the tenth day of Tishri, the High Priest would enter the Holy of Holies to present a blood sacrifice for himself and for the people. The sacrifice was to avert Yahweh's wrath for the sins of the past year and reminded all Jewish people that—in spite of all of the other sacrifices presented throughout the year—sin was never fully atoned for.

The priests and Temple Leaders had developed a routine for handling the extra duties during Passover. This year, however, the Nazarene had showed up at the Temple each day. Instead of attending to their Temple obligations, Rabbi Annas and Rabbi Caiaphas—along with other priests and Temple Leaders—had spent most of the days questioning Jesus, hoping to catch him in something that they could use against him. When not challenging the Teacher, they met to plot their next move to trap him.

Despite their collective years as elders of Israel, teachers of the Holy Scriptures and priests of the Temple, they were unable to determine a question or argument that would trap this teacher from Nazareth.

Not only were they unable to catch him, Jesus ben Joseph appeared neither impressed nor intimidated by their position and authority. Just that morning, Abel had been tending the offering box and overheard Jesus commend the miniscule offering of a widow, declaring it of more value than the rich offerings of the wealthy Jews.

Since that first day he rode into Jerusalem to the cries of "Hosanna," Jesus had come daily to the Temple, to openly denounce the Jewish religious leaders. Earlier that very day, while people were waiting for their turns to be allowed in the courtyard while the Passover lambs were sacrificed, Jesus entered the Court of Gentiles. Spreading his arms wide, he said,

"The teachers of the Law and the Pharisees interpret the Law given to Moses. You must obey Yahweh's Law and do what it tells you." He pointed a finger towards Rabbi Annas, Rabbi Caiaphas and the group of priests who—hearing the people call Jesus' name—had stopped their duties and crowded into the Court of Gentiles, open disdain painting their features. "But do not do what *they* do," Jesus ben Joseph said, "for even they do not practice what they preach.

"They take the Law given to Moses and, by their interpretation, add to what Yahweh said and create heavy loads that they force men to bear, but they do not wish to help these men.

"Everything they do, including the clothes they wear, is for position and to gain men's respect. They love the place of honor at banquets and in the synagogues and love being revered as, 'Rabbi.'"

With each word the Nazarene spoke, the countenances of Rabbi Annas, Rabbi Caiaphas and the other priests—including Joktan—grew darker. After telling the crowd about Yahweh being the only Father, that all men were brothers and encouraging the people to humble themselves, Jesus turned back to the priests with a vengeance.

"Woe to you, teachers of the Law and Pharisees. You are hypocrites. By substituting the Law of Yahweh with your wretched *traditions,* you have shut the Kingdom of Heaven in men's faces. You do not wish to enter it and neither will you let those enter who wish to."

Rabbi Annas and Rabbi Caiaphas gaped at Jesus' words; before either could respond, he continued.

"You travel great distances to win a single convert to Judaism yet, after he becomes one, you make him twice the son of hell that you are.

"You are all blind guides. You say, 'It means nothing if anyone swears by the Temple. But, if they swear by the gold of the Temple,'" he swept a hand towards golden plates on the white marbled walls of the Court of Priests gleaming in the sunlight, "'he is bound by that oath.'"

Rabbi Caiaphas took a step towards Jesus, but stopped when the Teacher pointed a finger directly at him. "You blind fools! Which is greater: the gold, or the Temple that makes the gold sacred?"

Abel stared in shock. Jesus ben Joseph had openly called the High Priest a *fool?*

His father was furious. "Who does this man think he is," Joktan hissed, "that he addresses the leaders of the people thusly?"

Jesus continued criticizing the Tradition of the Elders, their tithes, their ceremonial washings, causing a gasp—mingled with quickly subdued laughter—to ripple around the courtyard when he likened them to the whitewashed tombs outside of the city. "These tombs look beautiful on the outside, but are full of dead men's bones and all manner of uncleanliness. In the same way, you appear righteous, but are full of hypocrisy and wickedness.

"You built and decorated the tombs of the righteous. You say, 'If *we* had lived in the days of our ancestors, *we* would have been on the side of the prophets and not on the side of those who killed them.' But, by your very words and actions, you prove that you are descendants of these murderers.

"Listen! I am sending you prophets and wise men and teachers. Some of them you will kill and crucify; others you will flog in your synagogues and pursue from town to town. As a result, the righteous blood of these people will fall on you.

"Oh Jerusalem, Jerusalem." Spreading his arms wide, Jesus turned in a wide circle, his voice echoing over the Temple's marbled walls to the city beyond. "You who kill the prophets and stone those sent to you, how often I have longed to gather your children together, as a hen gathers her chicks under her wings, but you were not willing. Your house is left to you desolate. For I tell you, you will not see me again," he stopped and—arms still wide—lifted his gaze upward, "until you say, 'Blessed is he who comes in the name of Yahweh.'"

Before the echo of his pronouncement died, Jesus ben Joseph turned and—without a glance at the High Priest—left the court-yard. A few moments later, the now familiar cry of, "There's Jesus ben Joseph!" and "Teacher!" rose from the streets beyond the Temple, and with them were mingled the cries of, "He's a prophet!" and "Jesus is the Son of David; the *Messiah!*"

Those left in the Temple courtyard held their breath. Rabbi Caiaphas' gaze was hot enough to burn the sacrificial animals to ashes. The High Priest turned to his father-in-law, who gestured to the priests standing nearby; after scanning the courtyard, the older priest located Joktan and gestured for him to approach.

Joktan straightened. He smoothed his robe and his beard, his hand hiding a smile. "Come with me," he said to Abel, "but say nothing."

Quickly straightening his own clothes, Abel hurried after his father, stepping so as not to create even one echo on the marbled floor. *You do not need to worry about my speaking, Father. I do not wish Rabbi Caiaphas or Rabbi Annas to even* glance *my way.*

Joktan and Abel joined the crowd of priests following Caiaphas. Leaving the Court of Gentiles, they walked through the Gate Beautiful, through the Court of Women, up the fifteen steps to the Gate of Nicanor, past the Court of Israel, to the Court of Priests. Stopping in front of the altar, the High Priest turned to the group of black-robed priests. He opened his mouth to speak, but closed it as his father-in-law stepped forward.

"Something must be done about Jesus ben Joseph. Now. Today." The older priest frowned, stroking his beard. "I had hoped to wait until after Passover, but with each passing day, his power over the people grows stronger. The people care nothing about the Temple Leaders, even laughing when *this man* dared insult us." He turned to Caiaphas. "What have we learned about him that we use for his arrest?"

The High Priest lowered his eyes under his father-in-law's gaze and cleared his throat. "We…uh…we have found nothing."

Annas' eyebrows drew down, cutting deep white furrows in his forehead. "What do you mean, you have found *nothing*? Did you not send priests and teachers of the Law to question him?"

"We did. But *this man* evaded their questions. His answers did not provide anything worthy of arrest."

"That matters not," Annas' hand sliced through the air. "How Jesus *answered* and what we *report* he answered are different matters. A handful of denarii will get the answers we want."

Several of the priests—including Joktan—nodded in agreement, but Abel's eyes widened. *Rabbi Annas is suggesting that we twist Jesus' words, that we pay people to lie about him?*

The elderly rabbi stroked his beard. "We need to deal not only with Jesus ben Joseph, but with his kin and any of his followers who might try to seek revenge." Annas' gaze turned towards Abel's direction. "Joktan ben Philemon, it is known that your own nephew and nieces are *close* to the Nazarene."

Joktan's gaze darkened. "My nephew and nieces are dead," he said flatly.

Annas peered at him for several moments before nodding. "Ah...I see. Well, their *deaths* would mean that, as their near kinsman, all of their property would come to you."

Joktan's face tightened in a smile, his eyes blazing. He nodded.

Annas continued. "You and your son brought one of this man's followers...uh, Judas ben Shimon...to us. He was to arrange a meeting between us and Jesus."

Joktan bowed his head, "That is correct, Rabbi Annas."

"The meeting needs to be soon. Even tomorrow."

"Tomorrow?" Joktan's eyebrows climbed towards his scalp. "Tomorrow is Passover."

"*Racha!* Fool!" Annas spat. "I know tomorrow is Passover."

Joktan's face reddened under the elder priest's insult.

"Once the Feast is over," Annas continued, "the people who came to the City of David for Passover will return to their homes. We cannot risk Jesus ben Joseph leaving Jerusalem. With his sway over the people, he could easily light the fire of rebellion. Joktan, make contact with Judas to arrange for the meeting tomorrow." He paused as a Temple Guard walked to the edge of the Court of the Priests. "Yes," he growled. "What do you want?"

"Rabbi Annas," the guard's knuckles whitened around the staff of the spear he set on the marbled floor, "a man wishes to speak with you."

"*Racha!*" Caiaphas spat, the muscles in his throat working. "Can you not see that we do not wish to be disturbed?"

"Pardon, High Priest; but this man said you and Rabbi Annas would wish to see him," the Guard paused, clearing his throat. "He said his name is Judas Iscariot."

Chapter Twelve

Your son is indeed wise," Martha smiled at the Teacher's mother. "His words—and his...*miraculous*...actions—changed my family's life." She shared the story of how she had thought Simon dead from leprosy and how Jesus' healing restored him to those who loved him. "For the last seven years, I had set aside the thought of marriage and having my own home, and had resigned myself to remaining as a maiden in my brother's house. Now, because of Jesus, I am a wife and," she smiled, laying a hand on her abdomen, "soon to be a mother."

"And also soon to be an aunt," Mary added. "Abigail bat Nicodemus is a sweet and godly young woman and I know she is a blessing to Lazarus as well to you and your sister."

Martha's hand clenched her tunic. "Abigail *is* a blessing," she said, "but to tell truth, it has also been *difficult* for me. I took over running our household after my mother's death. I had everything organized and a pattern to how things were done. I realize that it is now Abigail's home, as this," she swept a hand to indicate the room, "is now my home. Abigail has *done* nothing wrong...it's just..." She dropped her hand and let out a deep sigh. "I cannot explain."

Mary lifted the cup to her lips. "You do not like change."

Martha wiped at a spot on the table. "I never have. Change is uncomfortable to me. That is why I changed the decorations in this house to reflect those in Lazarus' house."

"Change makes the unknown a reality. Sometimes that is good, but sometimes that is painful. Not liking change allows you to control the pain."

"Avoiding pain is not bad."

"No, but sometimes the plans of Yahweh might bring pain." She set her cup down on the table. "Our forefathers experienced much pain. Abraham and Sarah were barren for many years. Joseph was sold into slavery by his brothers. Our people were slaves in Egypt. The prophet Daniel lived his life in captivity in Babylon and was even thrown into the lion's den. In each story, Yahweh was in control of those situations."

Martha nodded.

"You spent seven painful years believing Simon dead. Now, because of Yahweh's hand on his life, that pain is gone. Jesus healed Simon and the dreams you had of being a wife and mother fulfilled. Martha, you have heard Jesus speak of Yahweh's love. Do you trust that love?"

"The idea of Yahweh's love is *new*," Martha drew the word out. "I *think* I do. I know I want to trust His love."

"Learning to trust is like a child learning to walk. His first steps are hesitant and he frequently falls. Yet, he gets back up and keeps trying until walking becomes like breathing." Mary laid a hand on Martha's sleeve. "Martha, trust Yahweh's love. Trust His love for you in the change, even if the change brings pain."

Footsteps in the hall drew their attention. Martha looked up to see her sister standing in the doorway to the courtyard.

"Hello, Martha." She bowed her head towards the Teacher's mother. "Greetings, Mary bat Eli. Time of gladness. Welcome to our home."

"Festivals and seasons of joy," the older woman replied. "Thank you."

"I am sorry I was not here earlier."

"Martha explained that you were helping your sister-in-law prepare for Passover."

"Yes. I believe we are ready. Abigail sent Ruth and me to the marketplace for the last few items. Which reminds me, Martha; there is news. Leah bat Samuel is betrothed to Azariah bar Cleopas, the blacksmith's son."

"How wonderful. I will have to wish her *mazel tov*."

"She has asked Ruth and me to be her bridal attendants."

"How exciting for your friend," the Teacher's mother smiled. "Marriage is a blessing from Yahweh. I am sure it will not be long before you, Mary bat Jacob, will also be blessed with a betrothal."

"Uh…do not all young girls dream of marriage?" her eyes shifted from their guest to her sister. Martha, seated slightly behind the Teacher's mother, lifted her shoulders and shook her head. "Martha, if you and Mary bat Eli will excuse me, I must wash and change. There were so many people in the marketplace and on the road from Jerusalem; the city was covered in a dome of dust."

Mary walked down the hall, up the stairs to the guest room. The walls were a soft yellow with frescoes of golden roses edging the top. Situated under the shuttered windows was a wash-table that held a bowl and pitcher and a dressing table with her brush, combs and vase of fresh parsley. Nearby was a chest containing her clothing. The bed of thick cushions was covered with golden linens. In one corner of the room was a narrow wooden shelf; it held Mary's jewelry box and a plain wooden box.

She crossed to the shelf and lifted the latch on the box. It was empty, but the wool still had the shape of her alabastron. Even though it had been several days since she had broken the seal and poured its contents on Jesus ben Joseph, the heavy, sweet, musky perfume filled the room.

The fragrance of the spikenard brought back the memory of that night. No matter what Martha or Leah or Ruth said, she could not think of it without blushing. She knew her intentions had been pure—indeed, as she had told Martha, she felt *compelled* to anoint Jesus.

"Martha has always said I acted without thinking," she closed the box. "It got me in trouble in the past."

But that was before Jesus came into their lives. A smile touched her lips as she recalled all the times the Teacher had been a guest in their home, talking with them, laughing with them, telling them about Yahweh. Since that night last year, when he first came to their home, Jesus had changed their lives.

Did my actions change that friendship? she thought. *Judas said it had.*

After purchasing the final items they needed for the Feast, she and Ruth turned away from the marketplace and began walking towards their Jerusalem home.

"I cannot remember a Passover week like this one," Mary said, adjusting the basket, filled with fresh fruit and several *amphorae* of olive oil, to a more comfortable position on her arm.

Ruth agreed. "Much has happened and most of it is due to Jesus ben Joseph. Yet, he seems," she paused, searching for the right word, "*different* somehow."

Mary frowned. "What do you mean?"

"I haven't been around him that much this week but, when I have, he doesn't laugh as much as he used to and doesn't engage in lighthearted conversation. He seems...*focused*...on something other than what is going on in the room."

Mary considered Ruth's words before nodding. "I agree. When he is at Martha and Simon's house, his attention does seem to be elsewhere. After evening meals, he often excuses himself to find a solitary place to pray."

"I feel certain that Father is not telling us everything, but he concerned because Jesus openly criticizes the High Priest and the Sanhedrin. Not that the things he said are not true," she laid a hand on Mary's arm, "but these are powerful men."

"But Rabbi Nicodemus is an honored and important member of the Sanhedrin; surely he can convince the other priests of the truth of Jesus' words."

"They *listen* to my father but," Ruth's lips tightened, "I do not think Rabbi Annas and Rabbi Caiaphas will tolerate Jesus's insults much longer before they act."

"And Jesus will not tolerate them much longer before he acts."

The girls jumped and turned. Walking towards them from a shadowed side street was Judas Iscariot.

Mary looked over her shoulder towards the marketplace, noting thankfully that they were in full view of anyone looking their way, before turning her eyes back towards the disciple. Even though he was a childhood friend of Lazarus and Michael, there was something about Judas that always disturbed her. His bearing—arrogant and prideful—was at odds with Jesus' humble and kind demeanor and his predatory gaze always made Mary feel soiled.

"Good day, Mary bat Jacob, Ruth bat Nicodemus," he nodded his head. "Time of gladness."

Ruth glanced at Mary before responding. "Good day, Judas Iscariot," she said, cautiously adding the traditional response.

Mary echoed Ruth's greeting. "Is the Teacher nearby?" She glanced beyond the disciple.

"No," Judas' smile tightened into a grimace, "Jesus is not nearby. He and the other disciples are going back to Bethany. I have. . . errands…to do, so I stayed in the city." He looked at Ruth. "Your comments are very observant, Ruth bat Nicodemus. The Teacher's *focus* is shifting; those of us *near* him realize that the *time* is coming."

"The *time* is coming?" Mary repeated. "Time for what?"

Judas looked around before stepping closer; his grimace changed into a frown as the girls stepped away from him. "The time is coming," he lowered his voice to a whisper, "when those *in control* will be *removed*. As I mentioned to you before, Mary bat Jacob, the time is coming for Israel to be restored to the glory of King David's reign."

He is referring to the time months ago when he cornered me, Mary thought, *and spoke of marriage.*

Judas nodded. "Yes, you recall that day and our conversation. My…*offer*…still stands. When Jesus is," he glanced around before continuing, "crowned King of Israel, those who *helped* him gain his throne—as well as their *wives and families*—will receive power and wealth."

Mary's eyes widened in shock. *After everything that has happened, after everything I* have said *to him, he still suggests* marriage? *In front of Ruth?* She lifted her chin. *How* dare *he insult me thus.* Due to the healing words of Jesus ben Joseph, she was a different woman than she was a year ago, but she was *still* Mary bat Jacob, the daughter of a wealthy house. She would not be approached like a lowly servant girl.

"Yes, I do remember our conversation of that day. I *remember* telling you that it was improper for you to be talking to me first, as it is improper for you to be speaking to me now, in front of my friend.

"As you still do not care to observe the proprieties, I will speak to you plainly. As Lazarus has said nothing to me, I know you have not spoken to him." She bit back a smile at the shocked look on Judas' face. "Without my brother's permission and blessing, I will not agree to marry *anyone*, no matter what their *power*, their *position* or their *wealth*."

Before she could lower her chin, Judas seized her arm. Pulling her close, he hissed. "Your brother's permission and blessing will be of no value if no one else wants you as his wife." He smiled and not pleasantly. "Did you think that, after the other evening, it is certain you will become Jesus' wife? Jesus might have called what you did, 'beautiful,' but since that night, he has not mentioned you *once*. Has Lazarus told you of anyone else asking for his *blessing and permission*?" He scanned her shocked face. "I thought not. When the report of your *immodest actions* gets out, *no one* will approach Lazarus for his blessing."

Staring into Judas' eyes, Mary knew there was no need to ask how the story of her actions would be spread. Her heart was sinking as she realized that, once everyone heard about her actions, he would be the only man who would want to marry her. But she refused to let him have that satisfaction.

She jerked her arm free and stepped away from him. "Never touch me again, Judas *ben Shimon*." She let a small smile appear at the shocked look on his face. "Do you think I am so desperate for a husband that I would marry you? You are wrong." She lifted her chin proudly. "I am the daughter of Jacob ben Philemon. I am the daughter of Esther bat Abrahim. I come from a noble family. I am loved by my brother and my sister and by their spouses. I would be happy to live as a maiden in their houses than to marry you. And, guest or not, if you *ever* speak thusly with me again, I will go to Jesus with your accusations and threats."

When she finished, she laid a hand on Ruth's arm. "Come, Ruth. We are finished here." Turning, the girls walked away.

As she and Ruth walked away, she refused to look back, but she could feel the heat from his gaze searing her. She hated that she had to speak to him as she did—especially reminding him of his father—but maybe now he would believe her.

The other night, Martha had said that she didn't think Judas would do anything rash and had reminded her of something their father used to say, "'Empty vessels make the most noise.'" However, Mary remembered something else their father used to say, "'Beware of enmity, however insignificant; for the smallest insect has often caused the death of the greatest man.'"

Be prepared, Mary bat Jacob, for Judas to do something in retaliation for your insult.

Mary shook herself, telling herself to stop thinking about Judas, although in truth, there was more to her wanting to bathe than—as she had told Martha and Mary bat Eli—to remove the dust on the road.

Mary untied her sandals, before removing her garments and setting them aside to be laundered. Walking to the wash-table, she poured water from the pitcher into the bowl. Picking up a bar of oatmeal soap, she focused on washing and not on Judas' comments or the night she had poured the spikenard over Jesus.

"Jesus was a guest in our home," she told herself as she lifted a foot to wash it. "Obviously he would not openly criticize my actions."

Judas was correct; since that meal, she had not spoken to Jesus and she didn't know whether Lazarus had spoken to him in order to determine what the Teacher's feelings were towards her.

As she shifted to wash the other foot, a thought came unbidden, causing her to freeze.

Do I want Lazarus to speak to him? About the anointing, yes of course, she wanted Lazarus to talk to Jesus. *But to question him about* his *feelings towards me?*

Mary's eyes widened. From the first moment she saw Jesus, when she had foolishly agreed to Leah's wager, the thought of marriage to him had always been a possibility. *But do I* want *to marry him?*

She closed her eyes, calling back the dreams of her future wedding. Like many of her friends, she had dreamed of this day to the point that, by simply closing her eyes, she could see it clearly.

Beginning with her betrothal. After the young man's father and Lazarus had made appropriate arrangements for the *mohar*—the bride price—and the dowry, the young man would speak the words of the betrothal ceremony, which would bind them together in marriage in everything but the physical union.

Her bridegroom would then prepare for their future life together. According to custom only—and not the Law of Moses—this lasted about a year. For some couples, it meant the groom would build a room onto his parents' house. For the man who already owned a home—or whose parents' owned a large home—it meant setting his affairs in order and making arrangements for the wedding banquet. When her bridegroom was ready, he would come for her.

She would be going about her daily routine when Ruth and Leah—along with her other bridal attendants—would run into the house to announce that her bridegroom was coming.

She would drop whatever she was doing and rush to don her bridal garments—made from rich fabric—and adorned with jewels. She would wear her hair loose, her sister and attendants braiding jewels and gold into its lengths. Martha would drape a long beautiful veil over her face and place a gold crown on top.

Arrayed as a queen, her brother and sister—and accompanied by her attendants—would lead her out of the house where she would wait for the sight of her bridegroom.

He would be dressed like a king in flowing robes of colorful silk and wearing a crown. He would be accompanied by his friends who carried torches and tambourines and other instruments.

Before leaving her childhood home for the last time, Martha and Lazarus would speak a blessing over her. *"You are our sister; may you become the mother of countless thousands and may your children's children's children rule over the nations."*

Her bridegroom would escort her from Martha's or Lazarus' house to his home. Preceding them, her brother and sister would scatter parched grain along the path, while the groom's attendants played their instruments and danced. As they walked through the streets, their guests—all carrying torches—would join the procession.

Arriving at the bridegroom's home, Martha would take her aside and straighten her hair and garments. Making sure her face was covered by the veil, her sister would lead her to a canopy set outside, as Mary always dreamed of perfect weather under the stars for her wedding.

There her bridegroom would be waiting for her. Standing by his side, they would listen to the blessings given by his father and by Lazarus.

Then the wedding banquet would begin. Seated at the place of honor, she and her husband would reign as king and queen of the day. They would praise Yahweh for His many blessings and would laugh as the steward of the feast told riddles. She would graciously acknowledge the compliments paid to her and smile at the praise of her bridegroom.

In the midst of the wedding banquet, her groom would take her hand and escort her to the wedding chamber. While their guests continued to celebrate—Mary blushed—they would consummate their marriage.

Once they were physically joined as husband and wife, she would rise from their marriage bed and take the alabastron, which Martha and Lazarus had earlier arranged to be placed in the room. Kneeling before her bridegroom, she would break the seal and pour the spikenard over his feet, acknowledging him as her bridegroom, her husband and her beloved.

Her alabastron was gone, but that did not keep Mary from dreaming—as many young maidens did—of her wedding day. She knew every moment, every detail; except one.

The face of her bridegroom.

Over the last year, she had often wondered whether, at the moment she looked into her bridegroom's face, she would see eyes the shade of onyx, fringed with thick, dark lashes. Mary reached up to wipe away the tears that trickled down her face. Now, after Judas' open threat, she realized that she might never look into the eyes of her bridegroom.

"I cannot believe that the Sanhedrin met *without* you," Michael said.

He held on to his father's arm as they walked through the marketplace and turned down the street leading to the Upper City and home. The sun hung low in the darkening sky but, even at this late hour, the streets of Jerusalem were busy.

He and his father had been on the other side of the Temple that morning and had been unaware of Jesus' open condemnation of the priests and the Temple Leaders, nor of Caiaphas' hastily called meeting. Joseph bar Neriah had come upon the meeting as it was ending. He relayed the information to Nicodemus adding that, from the evasive answers given, it was obvious that the High Priest and his father-in-law had not wanted these two elders to be part of the meeting.

"Joseph said that the High Priest explained that, as it had not been *technically* a meeting of the Sanhedrin, there had been no need to call us away from our duties," Nicodemus said. "However, I do not think that I believe him."

Michael's eyebrows climbed towards his scalp. He realized that his father did not like Caiaphas, but to suggest that the High Priest *lied*?

"Joseph also mentioned that he saw one of Jesus' disciples leaving the Court of Priests."

"Which one?"

"He said it was the one who had been your childhood acquaintance."

"Judas Iscariot?"

"That is what he said."

"Why would Judas be meeting with the High Priest?"

His father lifted his shoulders. "I do not know. I am only repeating what Joseph told me."

"Perhaps Rabbi Joseph was mistaken. After all, he has only seen Judas a few times."

"Perhaps."

Michael recalled the other night, when he and his father were driving home from Bethany, that he thought he had seen Judas walking towards Jerusalem. He had since concluded that he had been mistaken and decided not to share the story with his father.

"Joseph also learned that Jesus had been at the Temple this morning and insulted Annas and Caiaphas. Even without my being present," his father continued, "I have no doubt that the meeting Caiaphas called had to do with the Teacher. The High Priest cannot speak of Jesus without getting angry."

"Father, do you think the High Priest and Rabbi Annas mean to harm Jesus?"

"I wouldn't be surprised. They are both Sadducees. They do not believe in the afterlife, and therefore are more concerned about their power and comfort in this life. They would wish to deal with anyone who might threaten that power." He raised bushy eyebrows to look up at his son's face. "They might also wish to deal with anyone *close* to Jesus."

"Father, the Temple Leaders do not know that Jesus' mother is in Jerusalem. *Wait.*" He stopped walking, his grip tightening on his father's arm. "You mean Lazarus and his *sisters.*"

"Ease your grasp, my son; piercing my skin will not change anything." He lifted a hand to pat his son's shoulder. "You are correct; I do mean Lazarus and his sisters. After he was raised from the dead, Lazarus' fame drew attention to himself and increased attention to Jesus. Several months ago, during a discussion about Jesus, I recall Caiaphas mentioned Lazarus."

"I will not allow *anything* to happen to Mary," Michael seethed and then added, "or to Lazarus, Martha or Simon.

A brief grin lit his father's face. "Your concern for *all of that family* does you credit. Do not worry. Those comments from Caiaphas took place before Lazarus' marriage to Abigail. Since their marriage, neither the High Priest nor his father-in-law would dare suggest harming Lazarus in my presence. I am sure our family's wealth and position will provide protection to Lazarus and…to his sisters. Ah…we are home." They turned up the path leading to their house. "Michael, I would not wish to disturb anyone. We will keep this conversation between us."

"But Father, doesn't Lazarus have the right to know, so he can protect himself and his family?"

"He does," the older man nodded his head, "and *if* it appears that he is in danger, then I will tell him. But I believe that, as my daughter, Abigail would be protected and so would her husband."

"Father, if someone did…harm…Lazarus, what would happen to his sisters?"

"Martha is married. She would be under the protection of her husband."

He stopped in front of the door to their home, where burning torches chased away the twilight. "Father, what about Mary?"

Nicodemus sighed. "She would fall under the control of her near kinsman."

"Joktan?" Michael hissed. "He hates her!"

"True, but he loves her money."

"If we were married, I could protect her."

"My son, powerful family or not, Joktan would never let you marry her. Lazarus told me that his uncle was furious when Mary refused to marry Abel. I do not think he would give up a second chance to control her wealthy dowry."

"What can we do? I will not allow anything to happen to her!" Michael grasped his father's sleeve. "Father, I know you said to wait until after Passover, but if Mary and I have to become betrothed *now* to protect her, I will."

"Patience my son," Nicodemus laid a wrinkled hand over his son's strong one. "Nothing has happened to Mary or her family yet. The Feast is a day away. I do not think that even Caiaphas and Annas would wish to disturb the holy day." He turned to touch his fingers to the *mezuzah* and opened the front door. "In the meantime, we will watch."

Chapter Thirteen

15 Nisan 3793

The Morning of Passover

L azarus ben Jacob! What did you just do?"

Lazarus was uncertain how to respond to his wife. Normally quiet and calm, Abigail bat Nicodemus stood, her hands on hips, spots of color burning her cheeks and her full, red lips folded tightly together. Normally he loved getting lost in her dark, almond-shaped eyes; now Abigail's gaze was sharp enough to peel away his skin.

She was standing in the middle of the room located on the upper floor of their Jerusalem home. Cool morning air blew through the opened lattices on the windows facing the street.

It was that coolness that had caused Abigail to approach Lazarus about having the Passover feast in the upper room rather than the larger room below where the family had traditionally held it.

A new bridegroom, Lazarus never even paused before agreeing with his young wife's wishes. It did not occur to him that his sister Martha might have other thoughts about this arrangement.

That decision—made with the best of intentions—created *challenges* between the two sisters-in-law. Prior to her marriage to Simon, Martha kept the room for the Passover meal—as well as their homes in Bethany and Capernaum—the same way their mother had. While Abigail wished to honor the memory of her husband's mother, she also wanted to bring some of her family's traditions and her own touches to her new home as well as to their feasts and celebrations.

He and Simon had each spoken privately to Abigail and Martha, supporting their own wife's wishes while pointing out their sister-in-law's position. It appeared to have worked—both women were courteous about preparing for the Feast. However, when Lazarus commented to Mary on the *success* of his and Simon's actions, she rolled her eyes.

"Only a *man* would think this issue is settled," she laughed. "Martha and Abigail are *particular* about how things are done in their homes. They are not going to change easily."

He had thought Mary didn't know what she was talking about. He knew Martha had strong opinions on how things should be done, but his Abigail was sweet and conciliatory and would happily oblige others.

Now, he wasn't sure.

"Uh...I..." *Allow yourself time to think.* "I'm not sure what you mean, my Beloved," he said, adding a smile.

Normally, the combination of a smile and his love name for her would spark a pleasant response in his wife. Now, she lifted her chin and crossed her arms in front of her. "*Beloved*," her word carried no softness, "I am referring to the announcement I *think* you just made. Would you please repeat it?"

"Well...I...uh, offered our house to the Teacher and his disciples for the Passover meal." With each word, his voice grew softer, until it ended just above a whisper.

"You offered our house to the Teacher and his disciples for the Passover meal." Abigail spoke each word slowly as if speaking a new language for the first time. "Don't you mean that you *invited* them to join *our* celebration?"

Lazarus filled his lungs and shook his head as he blew out the air. "Jesus did not want to be a guest. He wanted to celebrate the Feast privately with his twelve disciples."

"Privately." Abigail stared at him for a long moment before dropping her arms and shaking her head. "Lazarus, I still do not understand. Please tell me exactly what happened."

He reached out and took her hand; although married less than a year, he had already learned that gentle physical contact took the edge off of difficult situations. Leading Abigail to the table near the window, he helped her sit on a cushion. Crossing to one of the small tables, he filled a cup with cool water from the *amphora* and carried it back to Abigail.

She eyed his actions doubtfully, but thanked him. She took a sip of the water, set the cup on the table, smoothed her soft yellow tunic, folded her hands in her lap and looked up at him. And waited.

Lazarus lifted a hand to stroke his beard, pondering how to begin. "I know you have been busy preparing for Passover. I realize it has been harder than anyone expected." Because Jesus and his disciples were at Simon and Martha's house, there had been times when Martha needed to remain in Bethany to care for their guests' needs and was unable to help Abigail. "I understand you wanted everything to be perfect; after all, it is our first Passover as husband and wife." He swept a hand over the table where Abigail was sitting. "You have set the table with the dishes your father gave us at our wedding *and* with the goblets that belonged to my mother. I *honor* you for the consideration.

"I knew today would be especially difficult for you with last minute details. That's why, when you asked me to get water from the Pool Tower, because you needed Mary and Ruth to begin preparing the food, I said yes."

He chuckled. "You should have seen me. I was the only man in the Tower. I could feel the women's eyes on me. I tried to behave as if it were perfectly natural for me to be there, drawing water.

"I left the Tower and had reached the street leading towards our house. I was thanking Yahweh that no one we knew had seen me, when *someone called my name.* I kept walking, trying to pretend I didn't hear them, when they called my name again."

Lazarus took a deep breath. "I knew I had no choice. I had to turn around. Imagine my surprise when it turned out to be Peter bar Jonah and John ben Zebedee."

Abigail's eyes widened. "The Teacher's Peter and John?"

Lazarus nodded. "As they approached, I was certain they would laugh at me and make some comment about a man doing a woman's task. But they didn't. In fact, they behaved as if my carrying a jar filled with water were something amazing. Apparently, Jesus had sent them to find me."

"Why would that be amazing? The Teacher knows that your family always celebrates Passover inside the walls of Jerusalem."

He shook his head. "That's not what I meant. Peter and John told me that, earlier this morning, Jesus had sent them to make preparations for the Passover meal. They asked the Teacher where he wanted them to prepare it, thinking perhaps that he—or Judas, as he holds their money—had already made arrangements.

"Jesus told Peter and John that when they entered the city, they would see a *man* carrying a jar of water. They were to ask this man, 'Where is the guest room, where I may eat the Passover with my disciples?' Jesus said this man would show them a large upper room, furnished and ready for the Feast. Peter and John never thought that the man they would meet would be *me*."

He knelt in front of his wife and took her hands. "Abigail, if it were anyone else, I would have said, 'No.' But this is the Teacher, this is Jesus ben Joseph. I owe him—we owe him—so much. Martha and Mary are changed women. He healed Simon of leprosy. He restored my life."

Abigail looked into his eyes, but her gaze had lost its focus. Lazarus held his breath, knowing, from the emotions flickering across her face, that his wife was re-living his sickness, his death and his resurrection. After a long moment, her gaze focused back on him...and she smiled.

"Of course, you could not say, 'No.' It is true, we owe the Teacher much." She swept her hands wide, indicating the room. "Everything Jesus and his disciples need for Passover is ready. The table is large enough for thirteen men; we'll just need to adjust the number of dishes and goblets. All the disciple will have to do is bring the food from the cooking area up to this room. But, Lazarus, what will *we* do for Passover?"

"Do not worry, Beloved." This time, Abigail smiled at his love name. "Once Peter and John left to tell Jesus they would be celebrating Passover *at our house*, I went to your father's house. Joanna is already supervising your father's servants in preparing for extra guests.

"Abigail, I know it's not what you wanted, but your father's house has more than enough room for many guests. Beyond all of that, consider; he is growing older. We do not know how many more Passovers we will have to celebrate with him. Having all his children and grandchildren, in addition to extra guests, at his house will only bring him joy. My mother—may her memory be blessed—loved having a house full of guests for Passover. I remember her saying, 'Each person's portion of the Passover lamb may be as large as an olive, but their singing will break the roof.' From the things your father has said, I think he feels the same way."

She nodded. "Father has *suggested* that to me, but I was so absorbed with this being my first Passover as a wife, that I never understood what he was trying to say to me." Abigail smiled. "Yahweh has indeed blessed me with a wise and loving husband."

"Thank you, Beloved. Now come," Lazarus helped her to stand, "the day is fading. We must tell Ruth and Mary the news and then we must gather what we need and get to your father's house before sunset."

Mary had celebrated sixteen Passovers; yet, this was the first time she celebrated the Feast as a guest and not as a daughter of the house. If she was going to be a guest somewhere, she was convinced there was no place superior to the home of Rabbi Nicodemus.

They arrived about an hour before sundown. After greeting them, Joanna had asked Ruth to escort Mary to a guest bed chamber while she did the same for Martha and Simon; Abigail and Lazarus would occupy Abigail's former bed chamber.

"This is a beautiful room," Mary told her friend. Located on the upper floor, it was of a size with her own bed chamber in Bethany. The room had tapestries of roses and lilies on three walls; the fourth wall had a large latticed window that, when opened, overlooked a walled courtyard filled with containers of fragrant flowers.

Ruth pointed out the carved chests where Mary could store her clothing. Near these chests was a table with a bowl and pitcher of water, a bar of fragrant soap and several linen towels. The bed was covered in linens the color of roses. A small stool stood next to a dressing table where Mary could place her comb and perfumes. It held an *amphora* filled with water and a cup, as well as a small vase filled with fresh parsley.

"When we arrived, I sent a servant to place the parsley here," Ruth explained. "I remembered you telling me you like to chew the leaves to freshen your breath."

Mary thanked her friend. "That was kind of you, as are those," she pointed to a table next to the bed where stood a delicate container filled with a large bouquet of flowers.

"I would say, 'You're welcome,'" Ruth said with a curious frown, "but it would be lying to say that I arranged for them. It was probably Joanna; by the time we arrived, it was too late to pick flowers."

"Well, it was kind of whoever did it." Mary leaned over to smell the sweet, heady aroma of the blossoms. "I love flowers."

"I will mention it to Joanna," Ruth said, "I must go now; I'm sure she needs me to help with last minute details." She glanced out of the window, where the sun was hanging low in the sky. "You have time to wash and change before the Feast. I just hope I do."

After her friend left, Mary spent a few minutes laying out her clothes for the meal and moving the rest to the chests. After placing her combs, hair ties and a small bottle of perfume on the dressing table, she crossed to the window to close the lattices.

She removed the simple tunic and head covering she had worn for the morning's cleaning and preparation. After Lazarus had informed her and Ruth of the change of plans for the Feast, the girls didn't have time to freshen up; they quickly gathered their clothes. She lifted the pitcher and poured water into the bowl. The bar of soap smelled of flowers. *I must ask Joanna if she makes this soap.*

After bathing and toweling dry, she crossed the room to the bed, where she had laid out her best tunic. Made of silk the color of ripened wheat, it was edged in leaves sewn with golden thread. Both the silk and the golden thread were gifts Lazarus brought home from one of his journeys. She wore it only on special occasions. *In fact,* she smiled, *I wore it last year at Passover.*

Slipping on the tunic, she wrapped the girdle of dark golden silk around her waist. She combed through her hair and then deftly braided the lengths, securing the ends with a narrow golden ribbon. Her head covering was of the same color as her girdle, but of a fabric as delicate as butterfly wings and trimmed with tiny gold bells that dangled over her eyes. Mary did not wear jewelry much anymore—not since that day in Capernaum when the Teacher helped her see that her true value was not found in her appearance. She had planned to remove the bells from the veil, but the timing of Lazarus' announcement prevented her. Last year she had also worn a set of jewelry—earrings, necklace and bracelets made from beaten gold—with these clothes. Now, she left them in her jewelry box placed in the chest with her clothes.

Crossing to the dressing table, she twisted off several leaves of parsley and popped them in her mouth. After chewing and swallowing the herb, she poured a cup of water. Peering into the cup, she smiled at her reflection in the water. She might not have a mirror to check her appearance, but she could check her teeth for bits of parsley. Satisfied that her teeth were clean, she took a drink of water and then sat down on the stool to tie her sandals on her feet.

Straightening up, she lifted the small *amphora* of perfumed oil and paused, looking at the flowers next to her bed. Setting the *amphora* down, she crossed the room and picked blossoms from several flowers. Lifting them to her nose, she inhaled their fragrance before closing her fist and crushing the petals. Raising her chin she opened her hand and wiped the oils from the bruised petals along her neck and also along her wrists.

She left the petals on the table and crossed the room to open the door, the flowers' fragrance wafting after her.

She walked past several guest chambers, down the stairs and followed the sound of voices to the dining room. Beneath the windows were large planters filled—Mary noted—with bouquets of the same flowers as had been placed in her room.

There were fewer people than had been present the other day, but it was no less festive. Martha and Simon were talking with Lazarus and Abigail, no doubt, Mary thought, about the change

145

of location for their celebration. Rabbi Nicodemus was standing near the door with Matthias, Rabbi Joseph bar Neriah and an older couple.

"Ah, Mary bat Jacob," he smiled, "Peace be on you. Time of gladness."

"And on you peace, Rabbi Nicodemus," she replied, adding the traditional, "Festivals and seasons of joy. Thank you for having us for Passover."

"It is my pleasure. While I realize it created some *challenges* for the women of your family, I confess I was pleased that Jesus' request allowed me the delight of having you all for the Feast." He turned to the people standing near him, "I know you have met Rabbi bar Neriah, but have you met Matthias' parents?"

Mary bowed her head, greeting Rabbi Joseph before turning to the elderly couple. "I was much younger, but I had the pleasure of meeting Matthias' parents at his and Joanna's wedding feast." She exchanged the traditional greetings with Ithiel bar Lemuel and Ephrath bat Teman. Joanna's husband looked more like his father, with dark curly hair and broad chest, but he got his ready smile from his mother.

Mary grinned at Joanna and Matthias' children, David and Deborah. Laughing, the toddlers ran across the room's intricate mosaic floor, looking for the leavening their Aunt Ruth had hidden for them. As they peeked behind the tapestries and tall lampstands or under the long, low tables, the children announced, "No leavening here."

Ruth entered the room—Mary noticed that her friend *had* found time to freshen up—and whispered to her father. He nodded and announced that the Passover feast was ready and invited everyone to the banquet room.

On the tables were set goblets and *amphorae* filled with wine. Mary knew from her friend that the goblets and *amphorae* had belonged to Rabbi Nicodemus's mother. Bowls filled with bitter herbs and sauces were placed in the middle of the tables, along with platters of unleavened bread. On tables near the door Joanna and Ruth oversaw servants placing bowls of vegetables. Michael followed his sisters into the room, carrying the platter holding the lamb. Sacrificed and then roasted for the meal, Rabbi Nicodemus—as the head of each Jewish home would have done—had spread the lamb's blood on the door posts of their home, as part of the commemoration of the first Passover.

The elderly priest escorted Mary to the spot next to Martha and Simon. She thanked him, smoothed her garments and knelt on the thick cushion. There was an empty cushion next to her; she glanced at Michael under lowered lashes, wondering if, like last time, he would try to sit next to her. As he turned from arranging the platter with the lamb, his father called to him.

"My Son, would you please sit next to Matthias? With Joanna and Ruth serving the meal, I am certain your brother-in-law would be glad of help with David and Deborah."

Michael shot a glance at Mary before nodding and moving to the spot opposite Mary. He sat between Matthias and David, but his gaze never left Mary's face. *Just like last time*, Mary thought Only the last time, the smile he gave her held a promise; this time a frown creased his brow.

Why are you staring at me thus, Michael ben Nicodemus? Mary blushed as she caught herself lifting a hand to smooth her veil and then reminded herself, *Beauty has no value.*

The Teacher had told her that after he come upon her and Lazarus in their mother's flower garden at their Capernaum home. Weeping, Mary had just confessed to Lazarus that their mother had been disappointed in her; that Mother had told her it was a good thing she was beautiful and wealthy, otherwise she would never find a husband.

"Your mother was wrong," Jesus' words had startled them. "Beauty of face or form—or skills—are not of value." He had swept out his hands, indicating the lush garden. "Look at these flowers. They are beautiful, but they will soon die and then where will their value be?

"You, Mary bat Jacob, are worth so much more than these flowers. You have value because you are created by Yahweh and He loves you.

"What is true beauty? It is written in the Holy Scriptures that Abraham's wife Sarah was beautiful. She had a face and form that many men *desired, but that was not what made her beautiful. Sarah was beautiful because she was gentle and kind. She was beautiful because she loved and obeyed Yahweh and used that love to serve others.*

"*If you seek to love and obey Yahweh above everything else in your life,*" *Jesus had said,* "*if you love others as yourself, that will show in your actions and in your countenance. You will be beautiful; and that beauty will never fade.*"

The Teacher's words poured over her wounded spirit like a healing balm and, from that day, Mary's concern over her appearance diminished.

She lowered her hand, the fragrance from the flowers still lingering on her hand, determined to focus on the Feast and not think about what was behind Michael's frown.

The first of the four cups of wine were poured and Rabbi Nicodemus spoke the first prayer, "Blessed are you, Yahweh, Creator and King of the Universe, who has created the fruit of the vine… And you, Yahweh, have given us festival days for joy, this feast of the unleavened bread, the time to remember our deliverance from Egypt. Blessed are You, Yahweh, who has kept us alive, sustained us and helped us to enjoy this season.'

Ruth and Joanna rose to carry basins of water for their guests to wash their hands. When they took their places again, everyone dipped a small piece of bitter herbs and ate them to remember the suffering their ancestors had undergone. Following that was breaking and eating the unleavened bread.

It was at this point in the meal that the youngest person present asked the four traditional questions that centered on the reason for Passover. Being the youngest of her family, Mary had always been the one to ask these questions. Tonight, however, little Deborah, with whispered help from Matthias, asked, "Why is this night different from other nights?"

Nicodemus grinned at his granddaughter before reminding everyone of the four hundred years the Israelites had been in slavery to the Egyptians. How they had cried out for freedom and how Yahweh had answered them by sending Moses. Of how Moses had told Pharaoh to free the Israelites. How, when the king of Egypt had refused, Yahweh had sent ten plagues to torment the Egyptians until, at last, Pharaoh had set them free.

A second hand washing preceded the serving the Passover Lamb. More prayers and thanksgiving and then the meal, which was a relaxed time to visit with those at the table.

Up to this point, Mary had focused on the different aspects of the celebration. Now, as Ruth and Joanna set the food on the tables the memory of last year's Passover at their own house rushed back in

Mary remembered walking to the head table, to place a bowl of lentils between her uncle and Rabbi Nicodemus, who had been the guest at their meal.

"Forgive me, Rabbi Nicodemus," Uncle Joktan had said, "but how can he be a righteous man?" He was staring at Jesus ben Joseph who was talking with Lazarus at the opposite table. "I have heard reports from Teachers of the Law in Capernaum that he told a man that his sins were forgiven."

"I heard reports of this too," Nicodemus had responded. "I understand the man was paralyzed, yet Jesus healed him. Now the man can walk."

Mary remembered being amazed at the thought of someone being able to heal lame people, just like the prophets of old. But her uncle's focus had not been on the healing.

"That is the one. Who does this Jesus think he is? Only Yahweh can forgive sins."

She could still see her uncle's smug smile. *She had lowered her eyes to hide her anger, as she moved to place a bowl of lentils in front of Michael.*

"You do not agree with your uncle," he had whispered.

Even though her uncle's words had angered her, Mary had known it would have been inappropriate for her to criticize him to Michael. She had glanced back to her uncle, who was obviously pleased with finding fault with someone who was a guest. "I was not trained in the Temple," she had whispered, "and I do not wish to show disrespect, but I do not understand my uncle's anger."

Michael had nodded as he picked up a piece of roasted lamb. "You do not understand why your uncle focuses on what Jesus ben Joseph said and ignores the fact that a paralyzed man can now walk."

She had nodded. "Are not miracles from Yahweh?"

"As my mother—may her memory be blessed—used to say, 'Two men look at the same bush; one man sees the thorns and calls it a weed, while the other man sees the flower and calls it a rose.'" Michael had smiled at her. *"Wisdom and beauty…a rare find."*

Color washed Mary's cheeks at the remembrance of Michael's words. While she had grown up hearing people comment on her beauty, that was the first time in her life that anyone had called her, 'wise.'

Despite her attempts to hide it, her conversation with Michael had been seen by her cousin, Abel. At the end of the Feast, when their guests were leaving, he had approached, stating that he wished to speak with her.

Just days before, Lazarus had informed her that their uncle had told Lazarus that their late father had agreed to a betrothal between Mary and Abel. However, her brother had assured her that he would never force her to marry against her will. From the look on his face, Mary knew that Abel would not leave until he had spoken.

Instead of speaking of tender feelings and the desire to become betrothed to her, he had criticized her behavior of speaking to Michael—or any man who was not family—as inappropriate. He was also angry that she had spoken against his father.

"Spoken…" she had gaped at him, *"spoken against your father? I did not speak against my uncle. If you heard our conversation—which you obviously did—you know that all I said was that I did not understand my uncle's anger towards Jesus ben Joseph."*

Abel's frown had deepened. "My father's anger is none of your concern. You also had conversation with Judas Iscariot. What did you speak of?"

Mary had indeed spoken to Judas. Even though she had not understood his mystifying comments about who Jesus ben Joseph truly was, she was determined not to tell her cousin.

"My conversation with Judas Iscariot is none of your concern," she had told Abel.

Her reply had surprised him. "What?"

"You are my cousin, Abel, not my brother," she had told him. *"You have no authority over me."*

It was then that he informed her that, once they married, she would be subject to him and to his father. She had replied that her brother would allow her to choose a husband. Abel had accused her of wanting a husband with more wealth and power and position. *"Someone like Michael ben Nicodemus?"* he had suggested.

She looked from under the screen of curling lashes to the other side of the table. Michael was lifting little David up to reach the platter of honey cakes. Even now, a year later, she frequently re-lived that moment and her response.

"...before I marry you, I will marry Michael ben Nicodemus, or Judas Iscariot or even Jesus ben Joseph!"

Obviously, now the name, "Judas Iscariot" would definitely *not* be one of the men she would consider marrying. But what about the other two?

She clenched a fist, nails piercing her palm, to keep from looking at Michael again. Of the three men, she had known Michael ben Nicodemus all her life. She was close friends with his sister, respected his father and was now joined through Lazarus and Abigail's marriage. Their families held positions of honor in the City of David. And yes, their families were also known for their wealth.

A year ago, that wealth meant something to her. That changed after Lazarus' death, when her uncle demanded that she never again see or speak to Martha, who had just learned she was still betrothed to Simon. It changed when her uncle demanded that she marry her cousin, because *he* wanted control of her rich dowry.

And when Martha told her that Jesus was coming to Lazarus' tomb, her uncle—enraged—demanded, *"I forbid you to see him or even speak of him again. If the name of Jesus ever crosses your lips, you will lose everything. Do you hear? Everything. Your sister might marry Simon the* leper, *but you will not get one copper penny from me. Who will marry a penniless girl?*

"And even if you did find someone who would take you without money, they will never get my permission. Who will want you then? Not Michael ben Nicodemus. You will grow old and die a poor, unmarried wretch, begging for your food.

"So, choose," her uncle had folded his arms across his chest. *"Either a life as Abel's wife or a poor follower of Jesus ben Joseph."*

The choice had been easy. She had gone with Martha, leaving their uncle spewing curses.

Within the hour, Lazarus was raised from the dead and restored to them. Because of Jesus. Her life was renewed as she had never thought possible. Because of Jesus.

Now money and possessions and beauty did not mean as much as it had. But, Mary realized something; she still wanted to be a bride. She still wanted someone who would love her; someone who would care for her; someone who would set her above all others.

The question remained: who would be her bridegroom?

All of those thoughts flashed through her mind in the time it took to eat her meal.

The celebration continued with the third and fourth cups of wine, followed by eating the last of the unleavened bread. Rabbi Nicodemus spoke the final blessings over the meal and they all joined in singing the psalm written by King David. The fading of the final words, "*Give thanks to Yahweh, for He is good and His love endures forever,*" signaled the end of the Passover celebration.

Those gathered around the table began standing and stretching. Ever the gracious host, Nicodemus invited all to follow him to the rooftop, where they could enjoy the cool evening breezes.

The roofs of most homes in Jerusalem were made from clay packed over a thick mat of branches laid across wooden beams. But the home of the wealthy Nicodemus ben Melech was not like most homes. A stair from the family courtyard led to the roof which was made of the same cut stone as those that made up the outer walls of the house. Following a suggestion from Lazarus, Nicodemus had lattice screens—similar to the ones used on the windows—placed around the parapet edging to provide additional privacy and protection for his young grandchildren. The lamps around the edge of the roof were not lit; the full moon washed everything in a soft glow.

Thick cushions were placed around the rooftop for everyone to sit or recline on. Joanna and Ruth moved among their guests and family, offering cups of wine and a platter of honey cakes. Only

David and Deborah were interested in the cakes; everyone else shook their heads, declaring they could not eat another morsel.

Aside from the general comments of joy over Passover and praise to the women for the delicious meal, conversation on the rooftop wafted between the clusters of people. Joanna and Ephrath shared pregnancy and motherhood stories and advice with Abigail and Martha. The men discussed Temple issues and politics. Nicodemus and Rabbi Joseph entertained David and Deborah by pointing out the stars and the *mazzaloth* that covered the Passover sky: The Great Bear, the Hunter, the Bull and the Ram. Soon, the toddlers fell asleep, their heads lying on their grandfather's knee.

Ruth invited Mary to a spot away from the others. "Although I am sorry for the last minute changes," Ruth said, "like my father, I am glad you are here. This week has been so busy; now we can relax."

Mary agreed. "Passover is generally busy, but this one more than others. Thank you for making me welcome in your home. It is not often that I am a guest anywhere."

"You are welcome," Ruth smiled. "I must apologize. With all the hurried preparations for the meal, I forgot to give Joanna your thanks for the flowers in your room."

"That is alright," Mary said. "I will try to thank her myself."

The appearance of a servant on the top of the stairs drew everyone's attention; after the conclusion of the meal, Nicodemus had dismissed the servants to their beds.

"Pardon, Rabbi Nicodemus." The flame trembled above the small lamp the man held and he sounded nervous, which was unusual for a servant of this house.

"What is it, Baruch?"

"Sir," the servant cleared his throat, "there is…someone…here to see you."

Nicodemus frowned, "It is late. Who would want to see me during Passover?"

"I reminded him of the lateness of the hour and of the Feast, but he was insistent."

The sounds of footsteps hurrying up the stairs grew louder until a man appeared beside the servant.

"Rabbi Nicodemus." The man stepped beyond the servant into the moonlight. "Sir, you have to do something!" Fear etched his voice.

"James," Lazarus stood up. "James ben Zebedee. What are you doing here? What's the matter? Where are the others? Where is the Teacher? Where is Jesus?"

Simon and Michael stood as the disciple stumbled across the rooftop and clutched Lazarus' sleeve. "Lazarus. John is following them, but you must come. They have taken him!"

"What do you mean?" Lazarus asked.

"Who has taken whom?" Nicodemus asked.

"Jesus." James' voice cracked. "The Temple Guards have arrested Jesus."

Chapter Fourteen

abbi Joseph, where should we go?" Michael asked as they hurried down the path from his father's house and onto the streets of the City of David.

The older man shook his head. "I do not know yet."

Michael did not have to slow his pace for Joseph bar Neriah. Of an age with Nicodemus, the rabbi from Arimathea carried himself with the grace and strength of a man years younger. His face—with high cheekbones, strong nose and noble brow—looked carved from the trunk of a mulberry tree. Only his hair and beard—containing more white than black—betrayed his age.

Joseph and Nicodemus, along with the other men, had questioned the terrified James, while the women huddled nearby after putting the children in bed. The disciple provided little more information; he kept repeating that a large group of men carrying torches along with armed guards had come upon them in the garden and arrested Jesus.

Shortly before the second watch of the night, Lazarus announced he would go and determine what happened—even demand Jesus' release if need be—only to be stopped by his father-in-law.

"I appreciate your concern for the Teacher," Nicodemus said. "But only one person could send a detachment of Temple Guards to arrest Jesus."

"Caiaphas," Lazarus spat out the name, refusing to add the man's title. "Who else? He hates the Teacher."

"Yes," Nicodemus nodded. "And I am sure that Annas is also involved. If these two are indeed behind Jesus' arrest, nothing you say will change their minds. In fact," he laid a hand on Lazarus' shoulder and turned him, lowering his voice so that none of the women could hear. "it occurs to me that they might hope you would come."

"What?" Lazarus frowned. "Why?"

"Jesus' actions and teachings have stirred up the people. I have heard that some think he might be something *more* than a teacher or prophet. Of all the miracles Jesus has performed, your resurrection is one of the greatest.

"Some of the Temple Leadership are...concerned...that—with a single word—Jesus could raise an army to overthrow Rome. As the High Priest is appointed by Caesar, such a rebellion would affect his position and authority. For the Sadducees, this is of ultimate importance.

"I believe that something has been going on lately among some members of the Temple Leaders. From things I have heard and seen, it appears that Rabbi Joseph and I have not been informed of certain *meetings* of the Sanhedrin. Whenever I have come upon the High Priest and his father-in-law at the Temple recently, I have a suspicion that they have been talking about me...or someone close to me." He raised his eyebrows significantly.

Lazarus' eyes widened. "Do you mean," he glanced at Abigail, before lowering his voice, "you think they would arrest me because of my friendship with Jesus? What about my *sisters*? What about *Abigail*?"

"I think not Abigail, because of her relation to me. However, they might come for you and your sisters," Nicodemus shrugged his shoulders. "I cannot say any of this for sure. But I would not wish you to take that risk."

"For myself I do not care, but if they try to harm *Abigail or my sisters*—" Lazarus eyes narrowed as he clenched his hands into fists.

Nicodemus patted the air. "Peace, my son. As my mother—may her memory be blessed—used to say, 'When a kettle boils over, it overflows on its own sides.' The rash man harms only himself."

"I will not be rash, but what can I do? This is Jesus!"

"You can wait here with me for the other disciples. If James ben Zebedee came here, I am certain others of the Twelve will come as well. We will question them; perhaps one of them knows more than James. In the meantime, someone else will go to learn what has become of the Teacher."

"I will go," Joseph bar Neriah said. "If this is true, an arrest made at night and during the Feast go against our law. As a member of the Sanhedrin, there might be something I can do."

"Thank you, my friend," Nicodemus said. "Your position in the Council carries great weight. I will send Michael with you. If you must stay to add your voice to any proceeding, he can bring word back to us"

Michael and Rabbi Joseph left the other men to reassure the women. Michael walked silently down the moon-lit streets beside the older man, allowing Joseph time to ponder the situation. His father's words of his friend were not mere flattery. Rabbi Joseph's position and respect in the Sanhedrin was due to more than his family name and wealth; he was also revered for his wisdom and calm demeanor in the face of crisis.

The older man stopped at the crossroads of two streets. He stroked his beard, looking first down one street and then the other. "Which is closer to your father's house: the house of Rabbi Annas, the palace of the High Priest or the palace of Herod?"

"We are about the same distance between all three places." He pointed towards the north. "Herod's palace is several streets that way," he pointed towards the south, "and the palace of the High Priest is several streets in that direction." He nodded his head towards the street in front of them. "Rabbi Annas' house is several streets that way."

"I do not think they would involve the Tetrarch at this time of night," Joseph said. "Let us go to Annas' house first. Although Annas is no longer High Priest, I have never witnessed Caiaphas acting before his father-in-law has had his say first."

Joseph's comment proved correct. The facade of Annas' house was illuminated from brightly burning torches. Men dressed in priestly garments rushed in and out of the front door, while a Temple Guard stood next to a servant girl to verify those entering the house.

Michael followed the older priest to the door of the house. The servant girl and the Temple Guard bowed their heads acknowledging them—all of Jerusalem was familiar with Joseph bar Neriah and the family of Nicodemus ben Melech—before stepping aside to allow them to enter.

Although smaller than the palace of the High Priest, the grandeur throughout the house gave evidence of the power of Annas ben Seth. Built of dressed stone, the house was two storied and centered around a courtyard located on the ground floor and opened to the sky. Fire burned in several large braziers; people clustered near these, warming themselves against the growing night chill. Michael surmised, from the look of their garments, most were servants to those attending the meeting.

A low stone wall on the eastern side of the courtyard separated it from a large reception hall. The floor of the hall was a tiled mosaic in green, gold and cream and columns placed on top of the stone wall supported the hall's ceiling, which was covered with swirls of stucco. The hall was warmed from fires burning in braziers placed at intervals along the walls.

Two men entered from a side corridor, carrying a heavy marble bench, followed by another man carrying a small table. They placed the table and bench at the end of the hall, between two large braziers. Two servant girls entered the room to place cushions on the bench and a tray holding a cup and *amphora* on the table.

The reception hall was filling with men dressed in priestly garments, all of whom Michael recognized as members of the Sanhedrin. They gathered in small groups, whispering to each other.

He was surprised when Rabbi Joseph, instead of moving further into the hall, stopped near one of the large columns at the back of the room. "It would be best for us to assess the situation first without *certain people* knowing we are here," the older man whispered. "Look," he nodded his head towards a group of priests near the marble bench.

Michael followed the rabbi's gaze; in the midst of the group, stood Joktan and Abel. *Their presence does not bode well for the Teacher,* he thought.

A movement in the courtyard caught his eye. He turned to see a man standing in the shadows waving furtively in his direction. Frowning, Michael narrowed his eyes to study the man. *John!* He touched Joseph's sleeve. "John ben Zebedee is in the courtyard," he whispered.

Joseph followed his gaze. "Go to him. See what you can learn."

Michael glanced around the room before walking quietly out of the reception hall into the courtyard where the disciple was waiting. He looked around once more to see if anyone was looking in his direction before stepping into the shadows with John.

The disciple grabbed his forearm. "Michael ben Nicodemus," he whispered, his gaze darting around the courtyard, "why are you and Rabbi Joseph here?"

"Your brother came to my father's house," Michael whispered. "James told us that Jesus had been arrested by Temple Guards. Rabbi Joseph and I came to see what was happening, while Father and the others wait at our house in case any of the other disciples go there. Why are you here?" He looked around. "I do not believe it is safe for you."

"I had to come. When the Temple Guards arrested Jesus, we... the disciple's voice cracked, "*we all ran away.*" His hands trembled on Michael's arm.

Michael's eyes widened. "You...ran away? You mean, *you abandoned Jesus?*"

John nodded. "I was a coward. We all were. I ran out of Gethsemane—"

"Gethsemane? You were at the garden on the Mount of Olives? James mentioned a garden, but I thought I had misunderstood him. Weren't you at Lazarus' house for Passover? No," Michael shook his head. "This is not the time; you can tell us what happened later. I must get back to the hall. Rabbi Joseph and I are here to see what—if anything—can be done."

"That's why I signaled you," he said. "Jesus is my kinsman; I must hear what is happening. Can you get us into the reception hall?"

"Us?" Michael looked around, his brow furrowed in confusion.

"Simon Peter," John said. "He is outside. We found each other outside of the garden and followed the Guards who brought Jesus to this house. We saw you and Rabbi Joseph. The servant and Guard outside the door were not going let us in until I told them that we knew you. They made Peter wait outside but let me come speak to you."

"Alright, but we must hurry."

Michael followed John to the front door. The servant girl was still there, along with the Guard, his hand on his lance. They were both watching Simon Peter.

"Here he is, Peter," John said. "I found Michael."

"Pardon me, sir," the girl said to Michael. "These two men tried to enter the house. They said they know you." Her tone indicated that she thought they were lying.

"They do know me," Michael said. It was one of the few times when he was thankful that his family's name and wealth carried weight. Stepping up to the other disciple, he said, "Greetings, Simon Peter." He did not add the traditional Passover greeting. Who would wish to hear, "Festivals and seasons of joy," after their friend had been arrested? Instead, he asked, "John tells me that you have some...*problems*?"

Peter, who had been staring furtively around the streets, focused on his face. "Michael," he said. "Michael ben Nicodemus." His hand shot out to grab Michael's shoulder. "You must help—"

"It's alright," Michael interrupted Peter. He grabbed the disciple's arm and turned away from the curious gaze of the servant girl and the guard. *We cannot have him blurting out about Jesus' arrest.* "John told me about the problems your *family* is having," he said, slanting his eyes towards the guard. "Rabbi Joseph and I are here for a meeting. If you will come inside, we will help your family once we are finished."

Peter frowned at Michael for a moment; then his expression cleared as he understood Michael's veiled message. He nodded.

"Now, come," Michael said. "I must return to the reception hall; the meeting will be starting soon."

He nodded to the servant girl and the guard and escorted both disciples into the house. They got as far as the courtyard when Peter stopped.

"I cannot," he said.

"What do you mean?" Michael asked.

"I can't go in there," Peter said.

"Peter," John said, "we must."

"I can't, John," Peter repeated. "I can't face *him*. You go."

"It's alright. Look Peter," Michael pointed towards the reception hall. "There's Rabbi Joseph. We will be standing with him. If you stand here," he indicated one of the braziers, "you can see and hear everything that goes on in there. Will that be alright with you?"

Peter looked at Joseph and then back at Michael. He nodded.

"Good," Michael said. "You stay here. John, we must go now."

Michael led the disciple across the courtyard and into the reception hall. The disciple barely had time to exchange a whispered greeting with Rabbi Joseph when the sound of approaching footsteps drew everyone's attention to the opening of a corridor at the far end of the hall. Preceded by the Captain of the Temple Guard and followed by a servant, Rabbi Annas entered the room. Garbed in a heavy white linen tunic and ebony robe, he crossed to the marble bench and stood, looking over the assembly of priestly aristocracy, his eyebrows slanted downward over a hawk-like nose.

Michael and John followed Rabbi Joseph's lead and took a silent step backward into the shadow of the column. His father often said that Rabbi Annas' hair might have more white than black, but the years had not dulled his gaze.

After a moment, Annas nodded and sat. He extended an opened hand towards the servant, who poured wine from the *amphora* into the cup and handed it to the priest. After drinking deeply, Annas set the cup on the table, placed his hands on the bench's curved marble armrests and looked at the Captain of the Temple Guard who stood nearby. "Bring the prisoner in."

The captain bowed his head briefly before crossing to a position in front of Annas. He signaled to the guards near the entrance at the far end of the hall. "Bring the prisoner in," he repeated.

Several minutes later, Michael heard more footsteps, along with the grating sound of metal against marble. A dozen guards entered, each carrying a long spear. In the center of the guards, hands and feet bound with metal chains, was Jesus ben Joseph.

At the sight of the Teacher, John opened his mouth as if to call out but, as Rabbi Joseph laid a hand on his forearm, he closed his lips.

As the guards led Jesus across the room, Michael noticed the clumps of priests stepping away from him. *They behave as though he is a wild man who would break free of the chains and attack them.* Jesus did not respond to them. His gaze—calm and focused—was on the far side of the room where stood the Captain of the Temple Guard and, beyond him, Annas ben Seth.

The soldiers stopped when they reached their captain and moved to form a barrier on either side and behind Jesus.

Annas stared at Jesus. "Captain, leave two of your men here," he said, "and position the rest in the courtyard and around my house to keep watch in case the prisoner's followers attempt to free him." He continued staring at Jesus.

The Teacher returned the priest's gaze evenly. *As if their positions were reversed,* Michael thought, *and Annas were the one shackled and awaiting judgment.*

After the guards had marched into the courtyard and the hall quieted, Annas spoke.

"Jesus ben Joseph," disdain dripped from his voice, "you have created much trouble in the City of David. Without seeking our permission or blessing, you have taught things contrary to what we," he lifted a hand to include the men in the room, "the priests and elders of the people, teach. What have you to say?"

"I have always spoken openly," Jesus' voice was as composed as his words were direct. "I have taught in the synagogues and in the Temple, where everyone can hear me. I have not spoken in secret. Why question me? Ask those who have heard me teach. They will answer your question."

In quick strides, Joktan crossed to Jesus, to raise a hand and slap him across the face. "Is this how you answer the High Priest?" he hissed.

A gasp echoed around the room.

"Striking a man who has not been convicted," Joseph whispered

162

to Michael and John, "is as improper as it is for Annas to attempt to coerce Jesus into self-accusation."

Jesus straightened from the force of the blow, blood streaming from his mouth, and looked at Lazarus' uncle. "Joktan ben Philemon," Jesus said, "if I said something wrong, tell me what it was. If I spoke the truth, then why did you strike me?"

Joktan, hatred painting his face, raised his hand again.

"Enough," Annas said.

Studying the former high priest's expression, it was hard for Michael to tell whether he was shocked by Joktan's actions or bored by Jesus' reactions.

"Before we are finished with him," Annas continued, "there will be many opportunities for the prisoner to answer." He looked at Jesus once more before standing. "Take him to Caiaphas. He should be ready. Joktan ben Philemon," he glanced at the priest, "send word to the High Priest when you arrive; he is waiting to hear from you."

Annas stood and exited by the same corridor he had entered, followed by his entourage. As the guards moved to position themselves on either side of the Teacher, a curse rose from the courtyard.

Michael turned.

Simon Peter, feet planted and chest heaving, faced several men and a servant girl near the brazier. Raising clenched fists towards the night sky, the disciple yelled, "By the Temple and the throne of Yahweh!"

A gasp rippled from those who heard someone using strong language in the home of Annas. All eyes watched as the man called down curses on himself, ending with, *"I do not know the man."*

As the echo of Peter's curses died, a rooster crowed.

Michael heard John gasp softly. "A rooster," the disciple whispered, his voice heavy with tears. "Oh no, Peter."

The other disciple froze, listening as if the bird announced his doom. He turned, fists still raised, towards the reception hall.

Michael followed Peter's gaze to where Jesus stood between the Temple Guards. Jesus was staring straight at the big fisherman. The look he gave his disciple—betrayal mixed with a sad acceptance—pierced Michael's heart. He blinked away the sheen of tears gathering in his eyes. He turned back towards the courtyard where Peter stood staring at the Teacher.

As the rooster screeched a second time, Peter began trembling. On the third crow, Peter dropped his hands to cover his face and turning, stumbled from the courtyard.

No one moved for a long moment until the Captain of the Temple Guards broke the startled silence. "You heard Rabbi Annas," he barked to his men. "Take the prisoner to the High Priest."

As the guards led Jesus from the room, the priests moved to speak in hushed tones to each other.

"Come," Joseph whispered, "and say nothing."

Michael and John exchanged quick glances before following Rabbi Joseph out of the house, down the street and into a darkened alley before stopping. After looking to make sure no one was nearby, the older man spoke.

"This is worse than I expected." He shook his head. "It appears that Annas—and I'm sure Caiaphas—have already determined the outcome of Jesus' arrest."

"Worse?" Michael's eyes widened. "You mean...*death?*"

Joseph glanced at John before letting out a long breath. He nodded.

The disciple's gaze widened as he looked from Joseph to Michael, shaking his head. "*No! No! No! You must be wrong!*"

"Shhhhh," the older priest lifted a finger to his lips. "I do not know for sure. However, their obvious trespasses against our laws—an arrest made during the Feast, trials held at night, Joktan's actions—all point to a pre-planned outcome."

John grabbed Joseph's arm. "Rabbi, you and Rabbi Nicodemus are respected members of the Sanhedrin. Surely you can do something."

Joseph laid his hand over John's. "I do not know yet what can be done. I am going to Caiaphas' house now to learn more. Michael, you take John to your house and tell your father and the others all that has occurred."

"Rabbi, I must go with you!" John insisted. "Jesus is my kin."

"I understand your reasons," Joseph said, "but I do not think it wise. Thankfully, your presence at Annas' house went unnoticed. I feel certain, however, that Caiaphas will give particular attention to who is allowed to attend this next proceeding. I will go and judge the *testimony* they bring against Jesus." He drew his lips into a tight line, his gaze hardening. "I promise you one thing. Rabbi Nicodemus and I will not stand quietly by and allow Annas and Caiaphas to condemn an innocent man to death."

The palace of the High Priest was more than a residence. The outer walls were made from simple cut stone with turreted sentry watchtowers. A fortified dwelling, it included a barracks for the detachment of guards who protected the High Priest as well as underground interrogation chambers and prisoner cells. Once past the outer gate, there were courtyards, public rooms, gardens and ceremonial *mikvahs* for the tax collectors, officers and other attendants of the High Priest.

While the other priests followed the guards escorting Jesus through the outer gate into the palace of the High Priest, a servant met Joktan and Abel. He led them to a small garden where Caiaphas stood waiting. The dawn's light—peeking through the branches of the cypress and citron trees—illuminated small pools of water situated amidst flowering oleander and cascading roses.

Abel and his father bowed their heads. "Greetings, Rabbi Caiaphas," Joktan said, "Festiv—"

The High Priest wasted no time with greetings. "Where is Judas ben Shimon?"

Abel watched his father shrink under the iron gaze of the High Priest. "I do not know, sir."

"You. Do. Not. Know." Caiaphas spoke softly; his voice echoed off the stone walls of the garden.

Joktan flinched as if each word spoken by the High Priest were a whip shredding his skin.

Caiaphas lifted a hand to tick off each item on his fingers. "You brought Judas ben Shimon to us. You offered yourself—and your son—to act as go-between with this man. To bring us reports. You were with them tonight when Judas led the Temple Guards to the garden on the Mount of Olives to arrest Jesus ben Joseph. Yet, now you do not know where Judas is. The Council is gathering. Quickly! I need to know what happened."

"Judas did lead us to Jesus' location." In the dawn's light, Abel saw Joktan's knuckles whiten as he clasped his hands. "It was dark; even with our torches, it was hard to see. Malchus—your servant whom you sent—was with me and Abel," his eyes flicked towards his son.

"Before entering the garden, it was arranged that Judas would lead the way. As it was dark, Judas would identify which man was Jesus by greeting him as you would a friend; with a kiss on the cheek.

"At that point, the Temple Guards rushed in to arrest Jesus."

"What happened?" Caiaphas asked. "What did Jesus do? Did his followers do anything?"

Joktan shook his head. "We expected Jesus or his followers might resist or fight back." He smiled, but not pleasantly. "It was obvious they finally realized the folly of following this man. When the Captain of the Temple Guard stepped forward, the Nazarene's followers ran away."

"What about Jesus? What did he do?"

"Nothing," Joktan said. "He did nothing."

Abel's eyes widened at his father's carelessly tossed lies. The only truth his father spoke of the events in the garden was the means of identifying Jesus with a friend's kiss.

Abel had been near enough to see Judas greet Jesus. It was strange; the Teacher did not seem surprised at a group of men— along with a cohort of armed guards—coming upon them in the darkened garden. Jesus looked at each of them and then at his disciple.

"Judas, are you betraying the Son of Man with a kiss?" Jesus had spoken softly.

Abel saw Judas gasp and step back at Jesus' accusation. His eyes widened as he looked from Jesus, to the Temple Guards, back to Jesus, as if he were expecting…something to happen. As if expecting Jesus to *do* something.

When the guards moved to arrest Jesus, one of the disciples—the one named Peter bar Jonah—sprang forward. He lifted a sword and swung it at Malchus. Abel saw his father jump, barely missing being sprayed by blood as Peter cut off the servant's ear.

Abel stepped back, covering his mouth, trying not to vomit, when he saw Peter turn towards him, raising the bloody sword.

"Stop!"

Abel froze, as did everyone, at the authority in the single word spoken by Jesus. The only sound in the garden was Malchus screaming and moaning in pain.

Jesus pointed towards Peter. "Put your sword back in its scabbard," he said. "Am I not to drink the cup that the Father has given me?" He then bent to pick up the bloody ear and crossed to crouch next to Malchus who was lying on the ground, writhing in pain. While everyone watched, Jesus reached out—shushing and speaking to the injured man as one would to a terrified child—to touch the severed ear to the side of Malchus' head.

When Jesus removed his hand, Malchus stopped moaning. His eyes widened as he lifted a hand to cautiously touch the side of his head. "My ear," he said. "It's healed." He looked at Jesus. "*You healed me!*"

Abel heard his own gasp echoed among the men around him. The Nazarene *healed* a man who was sent to arrest him?

Jesus nodded at Malchus, then straightened and turned to face the guards. "Am I leading a rebellion, that you have come with swords and clubs to capture me? Every day this week, I have taught in the temple courts, and you did not arrest me." He paused—closing his eyes and letting out a deep breath—before continuing. "But the Scriptures must be fulfilled."

All eyes shifted between Jesus and the man he had just healed, until Abel heard his father hiss, "Captain! Arrest him!"

The Captain of the Temple Guard shook himself and, voice shaking, gave the command. Abel stepped away as the guards moved past him to grab Jesus. He almost felt sorry for the Teacher's disciples, who stared in shock before turning to run into the darkened garden. Abel saw Peter look at Jesus, who stood still as a statue while his hands were bound with chains, before dropping the bloodied sword and disappearing into the garden.

Within a few minutes it was done. When the captain was certain that Jesus was securely bound, he gave the order to leave.

"Wait!" Joktan said, turning around, peering through the trees. "Where is Judas ben Shimon?"

As Abel listened to his father's report what had happened in the garden, he was shocked to witness how easily his father lied. All his life, he had grown up with his father holding the Law given to Moses as a standard and threatened with Yahweh's swift retribution for breaking the least commandment. Yet, here was his father lying to the High Priest.

"So," Caiaphas said, "Jesus did not resist being arrested and his followers—the men who have followed him for the last three years—abandoned him and ran away?"

Joktan nodded.

"And Judas ben Shimon?"

Joktan licked his lips. "I…uh…think he followed them…perhaps to find out where they went, so he could bring us word."

"Pray that you are correct, Joktan ben Philemon." Caiaphas punched his closed fist into his other palm. "My father-in-law and I had planned to have Judas testify against Jesus. As one who has been a follower, his testimony would have carried weight. Now, we have nothing."

The High Priest started to turn away, but Joktan's words stopped him. "You have us, Rabbi Caiaphas. My son and I." He laid a hand on Abel's arm.

Abel bit back a gasp as his father's nails—sharp as an adder's fangs—dug into his flesh. He kept his gaze lowered, afraid the shock of hearing his father's continued lies would reflect in his eyes.

"We met Jesus ben Joseph at my nephew's house many times," Joktan said. "We often heard him speak rebellion and blasphemy."

Caiaphas studied them. "If Governor Pilate learned of this, he might consider *all* who were present in that house to be guilty of rebellion against Rome."

Abel glanced up to see the flicker of alarm in his father's gaze.

"*All* guilty? But I—" Joktan sputtered until Caiaphas' lifted hand silenced him.

"As you are obviously *not* a follower of this man, I will see that Pilate does not hear of your presence there. However, I cannot guarantee the safety of your nephew and nieces."

"My nephew and nieces—" his father began, but was cut off by Caiaphas.

"—are dead. As you have said before. Fine." The High Priest nodded his head once. "You and your son will provide the testimony we need." He gestured for them to step closer. "Here is what I want you to say—"

Chapter Fifteen

16 Nisan 3793

Daybreak

After repeating the words which Caiaphas had determined was to be their *testimony*, Abel and Joktan followed him through the main doors of the palace. They walked up a marbled stairway, down corridors decorated with columns whose sculpted beams supported ceilings made from cedar. Interspersed on the walls were tapestries and mosaics of wood, woven and carved with vines, flowers, grapes and lions. At the end of the corridor was the great reception hall.

Used for official functions and to receive dignitaries and other guests, the hall measured twenty-two cubits long and fourteen cubits wide. The floor was white marble. The walls, of white stucco, were patterned with broad panels, topped with alternating rectangles in various sizes. The ceiling, also of white stucco, had a broad band of hexagons surrounding central panels of octagons.

Abel shadowed his father and Rabbi Caiaphas to the far end of the hall, where an intricately carved bench sat on a marbled platform. A scribe sat next to the bench, holding a table and stylus for taking notes. On the other side of the bench stood the Captain of the Temple Guard.

Abel noted that—even though it was but moments after the rooster announced the day—most of the members of the Sanhedrin were present. It was to be expected; whatever the hour, no one would refuse a summons from the High Priest. Abel saw Rabbi

Joseph bar Neriah and wondered why someone of his position was standing at the back of the group of priests.

"Rabbi Joktan, you and your son stand here," Caiaphas pointed to a spot at the front of the Council members. "I will need you."

Joktan smiled—a rare occurrence to those who knew him—and bowed his head in acknowledgement.

Abel didn't even wait for his father's glance, but moved to stand behind him.

Caiaphas stepped on the marble platform, crossed to the bench and sat down. After a brief Passover greeting, Caiaphas announced, "We are here to judge the man, Jesus ben Joseph. Captain," he looked at the guard, "bring in the prisoner."

As the guard left, a voice spoke up from the back of the room. "This should not be happening."

Heads swiveled as Joseph bar Neriah stepped forward.

"Ah, Rabbi Joseph bar Neriah," Caiaphas' eyes widened. "Greetings. Time of gladness."

He is surprised to see him here, Abel thought. Why? He is a respected member of the Sanhedrin.

The elderly priest did not return the greeting. "This violates our law on many points," he said. "You cannot arrest a man after dark. You cannot arrest a man during Passover. You cannot hold a trial after dark."

"It is not night, Rabbi Joseph," Caiaphas said.

"No, daybreak was but a few minutes ago. However, a trial may not take place before the morning sacrifice, which does not occur for several hours," Joseph replied. "I also refer to the travesty that took place at the home of your father-in-law."

"You were not—" Caiaphas began, but Joseph finished for him,

"—there? Ahh, but I was." He smiled at the look of surprise on the High Priest's face. "It is true that I—along with Rabbi Nicodemus ben Melech—were not *invited* to the gathering at Rabbi Annas' house. But, when we learned of Jesus' arrest, I went to discover what was happening during our holy festival. During that *proceeding*, two other violations occurred. Your father-in-law attempted to coerce Jesus ben Joseph into incriminating himself."

171

No one questioned the elderly rabbi's accusations. Abel could tell from their expressions—eyes slanting between the High Priest and the elderly rabbi, their lips tightening into frowns—that many Council members agreed with Rabbi Joseph.

"And I was shocked," he spread his hands to include those standing around the room, "as I'm sure those present were also shocked," he pointed at Abel's father; his gaze was as direct as his words, "to see the shame of Joktan ben Philemon striking Jesus. As Rabbi Annas did not stop nor deal with this injustice," he swung his gaze back to the High Priest, "the responsibility is left up to you."

Caiaphas paused before filling his lungs and straightening his robes, as if to remind everyone of his position. "Rabbi Joseph," he said, "have you forgotten to *whom* you are speaking?"

"At no moment have I forgotten who you are, Rabbi Caiaphas. The question is; have you forgotten *Whose* Law you represent?" He ignored the gasps that rippled around the room. "There are more mockeries of our Law I could mention, but any of these are sufficient to end this trial *now*."

"No!" Abel heard his father hiss under his breath.

The sound of footsteps approaching drew everyone's attention.

"Rabbi Joseph," Caiaphas drew his lips into a thin line, "your words are respected by all who hear them. The...*escort*...with Jesus ben Joseph is approaching. Let us not consider this a *trial*, but rather an opportunity to *ask* the Nazarene a few questions."

All eyes shifted towards the door. A moment later—surrounded by the same guards that had led him from Annas' house—Jesus entered the great reception hall. Still bound by chains, he gave no notice to the august body of priests in the room, but kept his gaze fixed on the platform where sat the most powerful man of the Jewish people.

No one in the room spoke while the guards situated Jesus before Caiaphas, although many—like Abel—glanced towards Joseph bar Neriah. The older rabbi stood tall as the pinnacle of the Temple, arms crossed, his expression fixed and determined.

Caiaphas studied the Nazarene for a moment and then smiled. "Jesus ben Joseph. Certain accusations against you have come to our attention. Accusations of such a grievous nature that they must be addressed *now*. You have been," he glanced towards the rabbi from Arimathea, "*brought* before the Sanhedrin to allow you to answer these accusations." He looked at the assemblage. "Who will speak against this man?"

The silence in the room grew until Abel could feel it as an itch between his shoulders. The High Priest had told his father that their *testimony* would be reserved for the last. Caiaphas scanned the men—most who would not meet his gaze—until finally he said, "Rabbi David bar Mattan. You reported this man's words to me. Repeat what he said to you."

"Ah," the elderly man smoothed his robe and nodded towards Abel. "Abel ben Joktan and I asked Jesus ben Joseph about paying taxes to Caesar and the tithe to the Temple."

"How did he answer you?" Caiaphas asked.

Rabbi David glanced towards Abel and then back to the High Priest. "He said we should pay neither."

Shocked murmurs rumbled through the room.

Caiaphas must have spoken to him, Abel thought, *as he did to my father and me.* He recalled Jesus' response to their question of paying taxes to Caesar. *"Give to Caesar what is Caesar's,"* the Nazarene had said, *"and to Yahweh's what is Yahweh's."*

Caiaphas nodded briefly and looked at Rabbi Joseph with a lifted eyebrow.

Rabbi Joseph shook his head.

Caiaphas frowned. He continued calling forth other witnesses.

"I heard Jesus tell the people to not obey the Law given to Moses," one man said.

"I was present when the man protected a woman caught in the very act of adultery," said another.

"He encouraged a man to violate the Sabbath."

"He said that the people should not obey the Traditions of the Elders."

With each man's testimony, indignation grew among the members of the Council. Abel dismissed Rabbi David's testimony, knowing it had been sculpted by the High Priest; but he felt any last vestiges of pity wink out as each of the other men testified to Jesus' irreverence. *Who does this man think he is to say such things?* he thought. Next to him, his father cried out repeatedly in indignation and fury.

During their testimonies, Jesus ben Joseph never looked at the men accusing him, but kept his eyes fixed on a spot above the High Priest's head.

Finally, Rabbi Caiaphas' gaze swung towards Abel and his father.

"Joktan ben Philemon. I understand that you and your son, Abel, heard this man speak as well. Share what you heard him say."

Abel saw his father lift his chin, a grim smile spreading across his face. He stepped to a spot where he could be seen by all present. "I heard this fellow," he pointed to Jesus, "say, 'I am able to destroy the Temple of Yahweh and rebuild it in three days.'"

Outraged gasps echoed around the room, followed by murmurs of, "Who does this man think he is?" "Only Yahweh could rebuild the Temple in three days."

Abel saw his father preen under Caiaphas' approving nod. Then the High Priest turned to look at him. "Abel ben Joktan," he said "did you also hear Jesus ben Joseph proclaim this?"

Abel glanced at his father, who nodded approvingly, to Rabbi Joseph's stern countenance and then at Jesus ben Joseph.

This man had caused a division between his father's household and that of his cousins; but for this man, Mary would have become *his* wife. This man taught things that were contrary to the elders, filling the people with strange teachings. This man criticized his father, criticized the leaders of the people, even criticized the priests present in this room. If allowed to continue, this man would bring the wrath of Rome—and even the wrath of Yahweh—down upon their heads. It was his—Abel ben Joktan's—responsibility to protect the people from annihilation. As he remembered hearing Rabbi Caiaphas say to Rabbi Nicodemus, *"It is to our advantage that one man dies for the people rather than the whole nation be destroyed."*

Abel looked at the High Priest. "Rabbi Caiaphas, it is as my father said. This man," Abel pointed to Jesus, "said, 'I am able to destroy the Temple of Yahweh and rebuild it in three days.'"

Caiaphas nodded his and then looked towards the Nazarene. "Jesus ben Joseph," he said, "you have heard the testimonies of these men. What do you have to say?"

Jesus said nothing.

Caiaphas frowned. "Jesus ben Joseph," he repeated, "you have heard these testimonies. How do you respond?"

Jesus still said nothing. He did not appear to have heard the rabbi, but continued staring at a spot above the High Priest's head.

Caiaphas' frown deepened. He stood, stepped off the marble platform and crossed to stand in front of Jesus ben Joseph. "Are you not going to answer? What is this testimony that these men are bringing against you?"

Jesus still said nothing. He did not even look at the High Priest.

Caiaphas' face darkened. He filled his lungs. "Jesus ben Joseph, I will bring a charge against you myself. I have heard it said that you claim to be the Promised One."

At this, Jesus lowered his eyes to the High Priest.

Abel saw Caiaphas flinch under the Nazarene's penetrating gaze, before steeling himself and lifting his chin once more. "I charge you under oath by Yahweh—to tell us if you are the *Messiah*, the Son of Yahweh."

Jesus took in a deep breath and expelled it. "Yes, it is as you say." His words, spoken softly, echoed around the vast hall. He turned to look at the members of the Council, the leaders of the people, standing behind him. "But I say to all of you," his voice grew in intensity, "the day is coming when you will see," he tilted his head to look upward, "the Son of Man sitting at the right hand of the Mighty One and coming on the clouds of Heaven."

The room was silent until the echo of his words died.

Caiaphas' breathing grew deeper, harder, until finally he was blasting air through his nostrils like an enraged bull. Lifting both hands, he grasped the neck of his tunic and pulled. His knuckles blanched under the tension until finally the linen of his garment gave way and ripped, exposing the white hairs of the High Priest's chest.

"Blasphemy!" He said hoarsely and then filling his lungs, he

175

screamed in fury, "With his own lips he has spoken blasphemy!" He looked directly at Joseph bar Neriah. "Why do we need any more witnesses?" He spread his arms wide as he turned to include all the men present. "You have all heard this blasphemy. What say you to this?"

Before the echo of the High Priest's tirade hit the far wall, Joktan ripped his tunic from neckline to chest. "Death! He is worthy of death!"

"Death!" Abel ripped his garments. "He deserves death!"

The sound of ripping fabric and the cries of "Death!" ricocheted around the hall.

"*I* do not condemn him." All turned to look at Rabbi Joseph. He still stood, arms crossed, apparently unmoved by what he had seen and heard. "I will not be associated with this *travesty* of our law."

You heard the blasphemer yourself," Caiaphas retorted. "He claimed to be the *Messiah*, the Son of Yahweh. If you cannot defend the Law, then leave. Go."

Joseph looked at Caiaphas and the others before turning to cross the floor. As he reached the doorway, the High Priest called his name. "Take word back to Rabbi Nicodemus. You should be careful—you all should be careful—lest people think you are one of this man's followers."

CHAPTER SIXTEEN

C aiaphas said *that* to you?" Nicodemus eyebrows climbed towards the ceiling.

After arriving at Nicodemus' house, Joseph was met by Michael. The younger man explained that, after he had arrived less than an hour before, he—along with the other men—had tried to calm the women and finally encouraged them to go to bed.

"The men are awaiting your report," Michael said.

He led Rabbi Joseph down corridors, up narrow stairs, down a hall to a small sitting room adjacent to his father's bed chamber, where Nicodemus, Lazarus and Simon were gathered.

The lamps stood cold and unlit on their stands. Through the long window on the far wall, the dawn's pale light leaked between the torn flesh of the clouds. In the center of the room was a low table with pillows placed around it. On the table were trays piled with cheeses, figs, clusters of grapes and bread, along with *amphorae* and cups.

Nicodemus stood to embrace Joseph and invited him to sit before pouring a cup of milk for his friend. While his friend drank, he explained that while Joseph had been gone, the rest of Jesus' disciples—except Peter, John and Judas—had shown up at the house. Although distraught, their stories about what had happened in the garden varied only slightly. Exhausted, they were sleeping in guest chambers.

Joseph related the events at Caiaphas' house, ending with the High Priest's veiled threat.

"Pardon, Rabbi Joseph." Lazarus said, "Are you certain of what you heard?"

Joseph nodded. "It could not be clearer."

Nicodemus shook his head. "I have known Caiaphas ben Joseph for many years. I know he—and Annas—concern themselves only with what promotes the power and position of the Sadducees and brings them more wealth. But to *threaten* you, to threaten *me*—" he spread his hands to include the men in the room "—to threaten our *friends and families*." The corners of his mouth pulled down. "And to condemn Jesus."

"Father, how can they pronounce a…" Michael, swallowed, "… *death sentence* on Jesus? Rome allows the Sanhedrin the right to pronounce death for anyone trespassing the holy places in the Temple, but anything else is denied. From what we," he lifted a hand towards Joseph, "heard at Rabbi Annas' house, and from what Rabbi Joseph heard at the High Priest's house, they are not condemning Jesus for that."

"No, you are correct, my son," Nicodemus said. "Rome has turned its eye when, in righteous passion, someone is stoned. But this decision was deliberate. From what I can surmise, it appears that Caiaphas and Annas wish to rid themselves of Jesus openly in order to destroy his growing popularity and any suggestion of rebellion against them. To do that means they will have to go to the governor."

Joseph nodded. "I agree with you, my friend. If we can get to Pontius Pilate, we might be able to speak on Jesus' behalf."

"You have been awake all night, my friend," Nicodemus stood. "I rested while you were gone. Michael and I will go to the Antonia Fortress, which is where I am certain they will take Jesus."

"I know Governor Pilate," Joseph insisted. "He will listen to me."

Part of the governor's responsibilities involved dealing with the Temple and the High Priest. Nicodemus told his son that, even though the High Priest was appointed by Rome, Rabbi Annas and Rabbi Caiaphas would frequently come to verbal blows with the governor. As Rabbi Joseph bar Neriah was a natural-born arbitrator, the rabbi from Arimathea was often called on to speak with the governor on behalf of the Jewish nation.

"If we need you to speak to Pilate, I will send Michael for you," Nicodemus said. "In the meantime, you should rest."

"That is wise counsel, my friend," Joseph said. "Go by Herod's Palace on your way to the Antonia Fortress. It is still early; Pilate might not have left for the fortress yet."

"Wouldn't he be staying in his quarters at the fortress?" Lazarus asked.

"I know that Pilate's wife, Claudia Procula is presently in Jerusalem," Joseph explained. "I am certain that the governor would stay with her in his rooms in the Tower of David at the palace rather than his quarters in the fortress."

Michael and his father could discern no unusual activity at Herod's Palace, so they turned eastward to walk towards the Temple and, beyond it, the Antonia Fortress.

Some sixty years before, King Herod rebuilt the stronghold that protected the Temple area and named it the Fortress of Antonia after his friend Marc Antony. It rose nearly eighty cubits tall and was partially surrounded by a deep ravine nearly one hundred and twelve cubits wide. The fortress functioned as a palace for the Roman governors and a barracks for the soldiers.

The fortress was always busy through the hours of the day and the watches of the night, with soldiers coming and going and dignitaries seeking the judgment or aid of the governor. When Michael and his father turned at the corner of the southern end of the Temple, the furthest away from the fortress, they heard the sounds of voices raised in anger.

They walked up a wide ramp to the fortress. Over two stories tall and the width of the Temple, the fortress had upper ramps which connected turrets at each corner. At the gate—wide enough for four men to march through abreast—were over two dozen soldiers. Arrayed in full armor, each was armed with a short sword or a long, metal-tipped spear. There were also soldiers positioned in the turrets above. From the way they watched the streets, it appeared they expected an imminent attack.

As they approached the gate, Michael overheard the soldiers' conversation. "Keep watch. With Jesus Barabbas and two of his men in the prison, some of the *Sicarii* might slip in with this crowd to free them." The soldiers turned at their approach.

His father bowed his head in greeting. "I am Nicodemus ben Melech and this," he turned to indicate Michael, "is my son, Michael. We are here to see Governor Pilate."

One of the soldiers frowned. "Nicodemus ben Melech?" he said. "I've heard of you. You're a part of the Jewish Council?"

Nicodemus nodded. "I am honored to serve the people of Israel as a member of the Sanhedrin."

"You can go in, but you better hurry," the soldier jerked his head towards the area beyond the gate. "The other members of the Council arrived before you and sent for the governor. He should be there speaking to them now."

Michael looked at his father and, after thanking the soldier, they hurried through the gate and to the far end of the courtyard outside the hall of the praetorium. It was in this courtyard—with banners and standards of Rome fluttering around the walls and turrets—that Governor Pilate would hold his tribunals. When he pronounced his judgment, he would have a wooden bema—a *judgment seat*—brought out and placed on the *Gabbatha,* a mosaic pavement on a raised platform.

The angry voices they had heard were from the men gathered in the courtyard. Here, Michael saw most of the members of the Sanhedrin along with other Temple Leaders, priests and teachers of the Law. He also saw Saul, who—along with himself and Lazarus' cousin Abel—studied under Rabbi Gamaliel. The man from Tarsus stood in a group of priests which included Joktan ben Philemon and his son Abel. Fists raised, all were screaming curses and abuse, hate scalding their words and removing any sense of justice towards the man who stood—arms bound behind him—in their midst.

Michael didn't need the man to turn around to know it was Jesus ben Joseph. From the way he held himself—drooped shoulders, head lowered, struggling to stay upright—it was obvious that the Teacher was exhausted. When he lifted his head to look upwards, Michael caught his breath. Dark crescents cupped his eyes; there was dried blood on his mouth and bruises forming on his face. "Father," he whispered, "they *beat* Jesus."

Nicodemus nodded mutely and then touched his son's arm. "Look over there. By the wall."

Michael turned to follow his father's gaze to the courtyard's western wall, near the underground passage which led from the fortress to the inner court of the Temple. There, in the shadow of the doorway stood a man.

Michael's eyes widened. "*Judas Iscariot!*" he spat. "What is *he* doing here?"

As the Teacher's disciples had shown up at his home, each had shared what they remembered of the events in the garden. While their descriptions varied to some degree, without fail, all remembered one thing: Judas had betrayed Jesus.

A confused frown creasing the disciple's brow, his eyes never left the Teacher's face. While Michael watched, Judas' hand twitched towards something under his robe.

As if sensing someone's scrutiny, Judas turned to study the crowd and started when he caught Michael's eyes. He moved as if to cross to them, when the sound of footsteps and the clank of armor silenced the crowd and drew everyone's attention to the corridor leading from the praetorium.

Accompanied by two dozen soldiers and a scribe, Pontius Pilate stepped out of the praetorium and onto the raised platform. Dressed in a flowing white toga edged with scarlet thread, Pilate did not need armor nor weapon to express his power. Appointed by Emperor Tiberius, considered a *friend of Caesar*, Pilate was prefect of Judea, Samaria and Idumea. For eight years he had represented the authority of Rome in this region. His responsibilities included mundane tasks such as tax collection and overseeing construction projects, to maintaining law and order, which he did by whatever means necessary. It was known that whatever he couldn't accomplish through diplomacy and negotiation, he achieved through violence and brute force.

While the soldiers positioned themselves on either side of the governor, the scribe found a place on the other side of the corridor.

Pilate scanned the crowd—his eyes widening briefly at the sight of Jesus, standing bound and bloodied before him—and then moved on to Caiaphas and Annas.

"Greetings, Caiaphas ben Joseph," he said. "Greetings, Annas ben Seth. What brings you to the Antonia Fortress today and at such an early hour? I thought you would either be tending to the Temple or celebrating Passover."

Caiaphas looked at his father-in-law, who nodded impatiently, before returning Pilate's greeting. "You are correct, Governor Pilate; we would be celebrating Passover if it were not for this *man*," he indicated Jesus, his words exuding disgust, "Jesus ben Joseph of Nazareth."

Pilate glanced at Jesus and then back at Caiaphas, raising his eyebrows in slow motion, a gesture that managed to be sarcastic, arrogant and dismissive all at once. "What accusation do you bring against him?"

As one, the crowd in the courtyard erupted in an angry cacophony, throwing accusations at Jesus like stones.

"This man is a criminal!"

"This man has violated our law!"

"He does not respect the priesthood!"

"He teaches things contrary the Teachings of the Elders."

"He—"

Pilate's raised hand cut them off. "I asked this question of Caiaphas ben Joseph. I will listen to none other, except of course," with a slight nod towards Annas, "Annas ben Seth." Once certain that the crowd would remain quiet, he looked at the High Priest. "Now, Caiaphas ben Joseph, I repeat my question. What *accusations* do you bring against this man?" he said, sarcasm tinging his words.

The High Priest looked at Pilate. "If this man were not a *criminal*," his words echoed the governor's sarcasm, "we would not have brought him to you." He extended a hand towards Jesus. "He has subverted our nation."

Pilate smiled and not pleasantly. "Isn't that what every Jew believes Rome has done to Israel?"

Caiaphas *harrumphed*, drawing his eyebrows downward. "He was heard opposing payment of taxes to Caesar."

Pilate lifted a single brow. "This was reported to me." He looked at a soldier standing near him. "Centurion Flavius Maximus, you reported that you heard this man speak of taxes the other day near the Xystus Market. Repeat his words."

The soldier looked at Pilate, "Sir, I heard this man tell the people to pay what is owed to Caesar."

Pilate looked at Caiaphas, a bored expression on his face. "What else?"

Caiaphas opened his mouth, but was cut off by Annas. "He claims to be the *Messiah*, the king promised by Yahweh through His prophets."

"Indeed?" Pilate sighed. "Rome has numerous prophets for her gods and goddess. I want nothing to do with your Yahweh or His prophets and their promises." He waved a weary hand. "Take this man and judge him by your own laws."

"We have no right to execute him," Annas said, a sneer slashing his mouth. "Rome has seen to that."

Pilate's eyes widened. Since he had appeared in the courtyard, this was the first time Michael had seen the governor express anything other than disdain and boredom.

"Execute?" Pilate repeated. He looked at Jesus once again. "You want to kill him? For subverting the teachings of your Law?"

Annas' frown deepened. "As I said, this man claims to be the *Messiah*. The king prophesied to overthrow *our captors*," he nodded his head towards the Roman standard nearest him, "and return Israel to the glory of King David's reign."

Michael sucked in his breath. "Rabbi Annas *openly* supports Rome's rule over Israel?" he whispered. "This will not sit well with the people."

"Without Rome, neither Annas nor Caiaphas would have power," his father said. "It appears that Annas feels dealing with Jesus is more important than having the people's respect." He filled his lungs and released the air slowly. "If not for this accusation, the governor could have refused them. Annas realizes that any threat to Rome, no matter what size, must be investigated."

Pilate stroked his chin while he studied Jesus. Michael saw

Caiaphas open his mouth to speak but shut it again when Annas laid a hand on his forearm. Finally, the governor dropped his hand. "I will question him further. Maximus, bring him to the hall of the praetorium." He turned to walk away, but stopped when Caiaphas cried out.

"You cannot take him!"

Pilate turned and looked silently at the High Priest. "What do you mean, I *cannot* take him?"

Caiaphas squirmed under the governor's gaze. "Uhh…well…" he licked his lips, "we cannot go with you." He looked at his father-in-law, who spoke.

"What my son-in-law means, is that if we were to enter into a Gentile's house—or in this case, the hall of the praetorium—we would be considered unclean. We would not be able to finish celebrating Passover."

"I see…" Pilate drew the word out. "You wish me to condemn a man to death on your word alone. You might be the Jewish High Priests, but that is not how Roman justice is meted out. I wish to examine Jesus ben Joseph. If you don't want to come into the hall yourself, then send someone to represent you." He turned and left the courtyard.

"May Yahweh send Pontius Pilate and all Romans pigs to *Gehenna*," Caiaphas hissed.

Abel gaped at hearing the High Priest of the Jewish people condemning anyone to suffer the fires of eternal punishment.

"What can be done?" Caiaphas asked his father-in-law. "Pilate cannot question *this man* privately. Who knows how he would answer?"

"There is only one thing that can be done," Rabbi Annas replied. "Someone must go into the praetorium and observe the proceedings."

"But who?" Caiaphas asked.

"My son will."

Abel startled to hear his father speak his name. He watched in shocked silence as his father stepped up to the two elderly priests.

Bowing his head, his father turned to extend a hand towards him. "My son Abel will go."

"Father," he began but swallowed his protest at the unbridled fury in his father's eyes. He controlled his expression when Rabbi Caiaphas and Rabbi Annas flicked glances at him before turning back to his father.

"You understand that this will render Abel *unclean*," Rabbi Annas said, "and he will not be able to celebrate the remainder of Passover."

His father nodded. "Of course."

Abel's cheeks burned with shame. His father had raised him to keep the smallest iota of the Law and to avoid anyone he considered *unclean*, no matter what the reason, even to the point of lifting the edge of his garments or walking around them lest he come in contact with them. Now his father was consigning him to these people. *Unclean. I will be unclean. Like the leper Simon who Martha married.* Abel lowered his eyes, wishing the mosaic pavement would open under his feet and the earth would swallow him whole.

"Be it as you will," Rabbi Annas said to his father before turning to look at him again. "Abel ben Joktan, follow the Romans into the praetorium. Listen to what the governor asks Jesus ben Joseph and how the man answers. Then, report back to us. Now hurry."

Abel nodded mutely. As he lifted his head and turned, he caught sight of Rabbi Nicodemus ben Melech and his son, Michael. He was not surprised to see them there. His father had conjectured after Rabbi Joseph bar Neriah had left the palace of the High Priest that he would go to Rabbi Nicodemus' house. He believed they would attempt to bribe the governor to release Jesus ben Joseph.

Abel caught Michael's gaze. The other man smiled sadly at him. *He overheard*, Abel's face burned with shame. *He heard my father offer me up as a sacrifice, not caring that I will become unclean, and Michael feels sorry for me. Me! Does he think that because he is the son of a wealthy and powerful man that he can feel pity for me? More like condescension.* Abel's thoughts darkened as his shame twisted into jealousy. *Does he think that his father's wealth will buy whatever he wants? A palace for a home? Expensive clothes and horses? A beautiful wife?*

All of his life, Abel had heard his father rail against his father's brother, Jacob. Jacob chose not follow in the footsteps of their ancestors—as Joktan had—and become a priest. Instead, he joined relatives of his mother who owned several caravans. Jacob's skills in buying and selling had increased his relatives'—as well as his parents'—coffers.

Abel knew that his father never forgave his brother for abandoning the priesthood. It did not matter that Jacob later married the daughter of a Temple leader and had three children; Martha, Lazarus and Mary.

Joktan told Abel that no matter how hard he, Joktan, had tried—studying hard, obeying the Law to its smallest letter—their father loved his brother Jacob more. Joktan denounced the wealth that his brother accumulated and criticized the things he spent it on, including building a second home in Capernaum. As far as Joktan was concerned, his brother's money had stolen his father's love and approval from him.

When Jacob was dying, Joktan went to visit him. He came home to tell Abel that he and his brother had agreed that Abel would marry his youngest cousin, the beautiful Mary. Through this marriage, Joktan said, they would not only have wealth and power, but would finally prove that Abel's grandfather was wrong.

Abel was proud to be able to help his father achieve his dreams.

At last year's Passover, however, his cousin Mary shocked him. During the meal, she had acted shamefully, speaking with men who were not relatives. When he had chastised her for this, stating that when she became his wife more would be expected of her, she informed him that they would never marry. She shamed him further by announcing in front of all present, "…before I marry you, I will marry Michael ben Nicodemus, or Judas Iscariot or even Jesus ben Joseph!"

Joktan was furious at Mary's inappropriate behavior but, after that night, it seemed to Abel that his father blamed *him* for the loss of Mary's dowry. When Martha and Mary *announced* that Lazarus was dead, Joktan once again stated the money would come to him through a marriage between Abel and Mary. When Lazarus pretended to be resurrected—Joktan refused to allow any consideration that Jesus ben Joseph had *raised* Lazarus from the dead—once again the money from Mary's dowry was lost.

Abel's frown deepened. Her words, *"before I marry you, I will marry Michael ben Nicodemus, or Judas Iscariot or even Jesus ben Joseph!"* circled in his brain like vultures over a corpse.

He dismissed Judas as a rival. Vain and desiring a lavish lifestyle, Mary would never think of marrying a poor man. That left either Michael or Jesus. When he had accused his cousin of wishing for a husband with more wealth, with a higher position and more power, he thought that man was Michael ben Nicodemus. But the other day in the marketplace, he saw her in the crowd following Jesus. Her behavior proved that she was considering the Nazarene as a potential husband.

The man had no money and no family, true; yet earlier this week people had hailed him as the promised *Messiah*, the King of Israel.

What woman would not wish to become a queen?

Abel ground his teeth. It was Mary's fault that his father's plan had come to naught. It was Mary's fault that he, Abel, had lost value in the eyes of his father. It was Mary's fault that his father had consigned him to become *unclean.* Mary desired to marry Jesus ben Joseph. If Jesus died, he would never become the next King of Israel and Mary would never become queen.

All of that flashed through his mind in the time it took him to read the pity in Michael ben Nicodemus' eyes. *No, Michael. You, your father and Rabbi Joseph will not help Jesus. No one can help him. When Jesus is killed by the Romans, Mary and her family will be repaid for everything my father and I have suffered.*

Abel lifted his chin and steadily met Michael's eye, before turning to follow the soldiers who had already led Jesus up the stairs and into the heart of the praetorium.

The tall stone corridor blocked the heat of the Judean spring, but it also reduced the light. Flickering torches cast hulking shadows dancing along the walls. Abel hurried after the soldiers and caught up with them just as they turned into a large reception hall.

Spartan-plain, the room had no furnishings save for the Roman standards placed behind a simple wooden bench at the far end of the hall where Pontius Pilate sat, drinking from a cup. A servant stood next to the governor, holding a tray with an *amphora*. The scribe was seated on the floor behind Pilate, legs crossed, stylus poised above the tablet on his lap.

In front of the governor stood Jesus ben Joseph with soldiers on each side. The Nazarene's head was lowered, his eyes closed.

Pilate lowered the cup, placed it on the tray and dismissed the servant with a wave of his hand. Resting an elbow on his knee, he cupped his chin and studied the prisoner. "Annas ben Seth says you claim to be the *Messiah* and wish to overthrow Rome. Tell me; are you the King of the Jews?" Abel heard a tinge of sarcasm in the governor's voice, as if the idea of the man standing before him overthrowing the rule of Rome was ludicrous.

Jesus ben Joseph drew in a ragged breath and then lifted his head to look at the governor. "Is this your own idea," he asked, "or did someone else tell you about me?" He did not sound as if he were bound in chains before the representative of Rome.

Pilate's eyes widened briefly; then he sneered. "Am I a Jew? Who would be speaking of you to me? Your own people and the chief priests have brought you to me, demanding your death. What have you done? I repeat; are you the King of the Jews?"

Jesus studied Pilate for a moment before speaking. "My kingdom is not of this world."

Abel bit back a gasp. *He claims to have a kingdom?* He wrinkled his brow. *What does he mean by 'not of this world?'*

"If my kingdom were of this this world," the Nazarene continued, "my followers would fight to keep me from being captured by the Jews." He paused, before shaking his head. "My kingdom is not of this world."

It appeared to Abel that Pilate was also confused by Jesus' 'not of this world' comment and jumped on what he did understand. "So you are a king, then?" the governor asked.

"As you say, I am a king," Jesus said, his voice echoing around the room. "It was for this purpose that I was born into this world, that I should testify to the truth. Everyone who is on the side of truth listens to me."

"Truth?" Pilate snorted. "What is truth?" He paused before slashing the air with his hand. "Enough of this!" He stood and looked at the soldiers. "Bring the prisoner." He crossed the floor and left the room.

The soldiers turned Jesus around and followed the governor.

Abel gaped at being ignored by the Romans. He hurried out of the hall, down the corridor and out of the praetorium. He saw his father—standing near Rabbi Caiaphas and Rabbi Annas. He was able to do nothing more than shake his head before Pilate crossed to the edge of the raised platform.

The Roman Governor extended a hand towards Jesus ben Joseph and addressed the High Priest and the crowd waiting with him.

"I have questioned this man and found no fault in him."

The crowd—led by Caiaphas—erupted into screams.

"Do not believe this man's lies. He is a criminal!"

"He has violated the Law given to Moses!"

"He does not respect the priesthood and our traditions!"

"He plots to lead the people in a revolt against Rome!"

Pilate raised a hand, cutting off the barrage of accusations and turned to Jesus. "Do you hear what they are saying about you?"

Jesus said nothing. He didn't even look at the governor. He kept his eyes closed.

Pilate stepped closer to the prisoner and began speaking to him.

Abel looked at his father, who frantically waved a hand towards Pilate. He stepped closer and heard the governor, with lowered voice, ask the Nazarene,

"Are you not going to answer me? These people accuse you of many things."

"Do not trust this man!" Abel heard his father scream. "He stirs up the people all over Judea, from Galilee all the way to Jerusalem."

Pilate looked at Joktan, who shrunk under the gaze of the Roman governor.

"Wait," Pilate turned to look at Caiaphas and Annas, "This man is a Galilean?"

The High Priest and his father-in-law glanced at each other before nodding, eyeing the Roman hesitantly.

"You should have informed me of this before. This man is under Herod's jurisdiction. I would not wish to trod on his authority." Pilate's voice was heavy with sarcasm and his smile a carelessly tossed lie. All Jerusalem knew he and Herod Antipas were, at best, barely tolerant of each other. "Centurion," Pilate turned to the soldier standing guard over Jesus, "take the prisoner to the palace. Let the Tetrarch judge him."

Pilate barely waited for the soldier's salute before turning to go back into the praetorium.

Following behind the soldiers leading Jesus down the steps, Abel crossed to where his father was standing with Caiaphas and Annas. Although he knew entering the praetorium would render him unclean, his eyes widened when the three men stepped back, holding their garments against their bodies. *They're afraid I will touch them,* he thought.

"What happened in the praetorium?" Annas asked. "What did he ask the Nazarene? How did the man answer?"

Abel related what had occurred in the reception hall.

"So, he did confess to being a king," Caiaphas said. He turned to his father-in-law. "What do you think he meant by his kingdom not being of this world?"

Annas shrugged. "I do not know but, even though *this man* claims that his followers would not rally to free him, we need to keep a watch over all known to be his friends and disciples. That includes," he turned to Joktan, "your nieces and nephew. Yes, yes, I know they are dead," he said when Joktan opened his mouth. Then he sneered. "But you have personally experienced how a dead man can ruin your plans, have you not?"

He looked at Abel. "Abel ben Joktan, you are already *unclean*," the emphasis the elderly rabbi placed on the word made Abel feel as if no sacrifice—no amount of bathing in the ceremonial *mikvahs*—would ever be sufficient to render him clean again. "Follow the guards to Herod's Palace. Then come back and report to us."

Michael and his father watched as the soldiers led Jesus bound out of the Antonia Fortress.

"Father, what can be done?"

"At this point, nothing."

"Nothing?" Michael was incredulous. His father was one of the richest men in the country. While Nicodemus never used his wealth to gain power, it was rare that he did not get what he wanted. "Caiaphas is demanding Jesus' death. You can do nothing?" he repeated.

Nicodemus shook his head. "I have no dealings with the Tetrarch. Even if I gained entrance into the palace, nothing I said to him would make any difference." He turned to watch a small group of men—led by Caiaphas and Annas—cross the courtyard and enter the underground tunnel that led to the Temple. "But I can say something to them. Come."

Michael and his father hurried across the courtyard and entered the tunnel. At the far end, Joktan was holding a torch to light the way for Caiaphas and Annas.

"Caiaphas ben Joseph. Annas ben Seth," Nicodemus called out. "Stop."

Michael's face reflected the surprise of all those present. His father might dislike Rabbi Caiaphas, but he was always careful to show respect to the office of the High Priest.

The Temple leader turned and scowled. "Nicodemus ben Melech."

"What are you doing?" Nicodemus demanded.

"It should be obvious. It is drawing close to the second hour of the day. While we await Herod's judgment, we," he gestured to his father-in-law and the priests with him, "are attending to our Temple duties."

"That is not what I meant," Nicodemus spat.

"What do you mean?"

"Jesus ben Joseph is *not* a criminal."

Caiaphas lifted his chin and bushy eyebrows. "Of course *you* would say that."

"You cannot prove that he has done anything wrong."

"No proof is necessary. From his own lips *that man* spoke

blasphemy. Joseph bar Neriah heard it himself; or did he neglect to tell you of that atrocity?"

"The only atrocities Joseph reported were committed by you and the other members of the Sanhedrin who were present." Michael's father lifted a hand to tick off the offenses. "You arrested Jesus during a holy festival and at night. You coerced Jesus into speaking what you claim was *blasphemy*. You, Caiaphas, should not have been the accuser *and* the judge. You allowed Jesus to be struck!"

Nicodemus lowered his hand. "There are more violations of the Law I could mention, but any one of these is sufficient to set at naught a verdict of guilty."

The High Priest waved away the other priest's accusations. "Jesus ben Joseph condemned himself when he pronounced himself the son of Yahweh. Pilate and Herod are merely the means to his death."

"Death?!" The word, coming from behind them, echoed in the tunnel.

Michael—along with the rest of the men—turned. Judas Iscariot stood a short distance from them; the light from the torch cast bizarre shadows on his face.

Judas rushed towards the priests, but Caiaphas' servant Malchus jumped in-between the disciple and the High Priest, arms spread wide.

"Death?" the disciple choked on the word. He looked from Caiaphas to Annas. "You told me you only wanted to *speak* with the Teacher. You cannot do this! I *cannot* do this! Jesus ben Joseph is innocent!" He reached into the girdle at his waist and drew out a leather bag. It clinked as he extended it to Caiaphas. "Here! Take back your *blood money*. I have sinned! I have betrayed innocent blood!"

The High Priest glanced at the bag in Judas' hand. "What is your sin to us?" he asked. "That is your responsibility."

He turned and gestured to his father-in-law to precede him into the Temple.

"Aiiiieeeee!" Judas screamed as he lifted the bag to throw it at Caiaphas.

Chaos erupted in the tunnel. Shouts echoed against the stone walls. Caiaphas and Annas—as did those men near them—ducked, throwing their arms over their heads. Michael and his father jumped back against the tunnel's wall.

The bag missed the High Priest by a hands-breath and hit one of the marble columns. The cord around the neck of the bag loosened as it fell, sending coins skittering across the Temple floor.

Screaming curses at the priests and at himself, Judas turned and ran out of the tunnel.

"Malchus," Caiaphas straightened and gestured to his servant. "Follow Judas. See where he goes and what he does." After Malchus left, the High Priest looked at the coins scattered across the Temple floor. "Someone pick these up."

Joktan handed the torch to another priest. He scooped up the leather bag and began picking up the silver tetradrachms to drop them in the bag. After gathering the thirty coins, he tightened the cord around the bag. "What should we do with the money?" he asked the High Priest.

"Judas Iscariot was correct; it is blood money," Caiaphas frowned. "Pity. That amount of money would have been *useful* in the Temple treasury. However, nothing can be done about it." He turned to his father-in-law. "Do you have any suggestions, sir?"

"I care not," Rabbi lifted his shoulders unconcernedly, "as it cannot benefit us or the Temple."

"We have to do something with it," Caiaphas said. "Wait," he snapped his fingers. "What about the problem Pilate mentioned the other day; what to do with the bodies of dead foreigners? We can use this money to buy land as a burial place."

Annas nodded. "That would be a solution. I heard that Lehi Bar Mordecai, the potter, has stripped all the clay from his field. As it is good for nothing else, he is looking to sell it."

"After we deal with the matter of the Nazarene, I will speak to Lehi." Caiaphas took the bag from Joktan. "This money should cover the cost."

"That was settled easily enough," Annas said. "Any moment now, Pilate's soldiers will deliver the prisoner to Antipas." He looked at Nicodemus and Michael and smiled; it reminded Michael of a hyena. "If all goes well, the matter of the Nazarene will be settled as easily."

Considered the second most important building in Jerusalem after the Temple, the Palace of Herod was situated in the northwest corner of the Upper City near the Jaffa Gate. It was one of three palaces of the Herods—the others located at Masada, Herodium and Caesarea Maritima.

The palace in Jerusalem had been built by Antipas' father, Herod the Great, three decades before. As he had done with the Temple, Herod constructed the palace on an elevated platform six hundred and seventy-seven cubits by one hundred and twenty-one cubits. The palace itself had three towers which Herod named after his brother Phasael, his friend Hippicus and his favorite wife, Mariamne, whom he had executed. This tower was considered the most beautiful of the three, which Herod proclaimed as appropriate since a tower named after a woman should surpass the beauty of towers named after men.

Built from white marble, the palace consisted of two main complexes—named Agrippa and Caesar—with banquet halls, baths, sleeping quarters and reception rooms, and would accommodate hundreds of guests. Situated between the two complexes were gardens, groves, canals and bronze fountains.

The palace was surrounded by a citadel, which included a massive tower, known as the Tower of David after a line from the song written by David's son and heir, Solomon, *"Your neck is like the Tower of David, built with turrets, on which hangs a thousand shields and all the armor of the mighty men."*

Abel was relieved when the Roman soldier Maximus did not comment when he joined the soldiers at the top step leading to the palace. He didn't know how he would have convinced the door keepers at the palace to grant him entrance.

They followed one of Herod's servants through several corridors to a large banquet hall. Pillared in marble, on one side the hall opened onto a sheltered garden, fragrant with flowers and herbs.

Clusters of tables and reclining couches covered in fine linen were placed around the room for the comfort of the Tetrarch's guests. As most of these guests would still be sleeping, the only person in the room this morning was Antipas himself.

Of an age with Abel, the Tetrarch was short of stature and slightly built, with curly black hair and beard. He wore a short, white linen tunic with a deep purple robe trimmed in gold thread thrown over it. He was seated on a reclining couch, surrounded by half a dozen guards armed with long spears. A servant was placing a tray of bread, cheese and grapes—along with a golden goblet and *amphora*—on the table in front of Antipas. A scribe sat nearby, preparing a stylus, ink and parchment to write at the Tetrarch's command.

Although Herod the Great had died three decades before, the stories of his atrocities were still told. The worst was the time—about thirty-three years ago—when he sent his soldiers to the small village of Bethlehem to kill all the boys who were two years old and younger. It was whispered behind closed doors that Herod had not been sane and—looking at his son—Abel wondered whether Antipas had inherited his father's insanity.

When they drew near, the centurion saluted the Tetrarch before explaining their mission. "When Governor Pilate heard that this man was from Galilee, he commanded that we bring him to you for judgment," he finished.

"Please *thank* the governor for me, Centurion Flavius Maximus." The Tetrarch's smile was oily.

The soldier nodded and gestured to his men to follow him from the hall.

As the echoes of the soldiers' sandals died, Antipas turned to look at Abel. "Who are you?"

Abel squirmed under the Tetrarch's stare. "Uh…sir…I am Abel ben Joktan. My father is a priest in the Temple. Rabbi Annas and High Priest Caiaphas sent me to inform you that *this* man is—" but was cut off by Antipas' raised hand.

"I know *who* this man is and what people claim him to be—the *Messiah*, the promised King." The Tetrarch studied Jesus ben Joseph before speaking to him. "But, it is also said that you are more than a *king*. I have heard reports that you perform miraculous deeds. Healing the sick, feeding multitudes, raising those who were dead."

Abel bit back a grimace.

"I have seen many kings, but I have never seen a miracle. I would see some of these deeds." Antipas lifted the goblet from the table and leaned back against the cushions of the couch. "You can perform them for me. You could even perform them later for my guests, for their entertainment. Perhaps, if your *magical arts* are truly amazing, I might set you free and keep you as a magus."

"You cannot!" Abel cried.

"Cannot?" The Tetrarch looked him, eyebrows lifted. "You dare to tell me, Tetrarch of Galilee, that I *cannot?* You would be wise to hold your tongue, Abel ben Joktan, lest someone *cuts it out.* Pontius Pilate sent this man to me to do with as I please. I *please* to see him perform a miracle." He looked back at Jesus. "Well?"

Jesus ben Joseph did nothing. He stood, head down, eyes closed.

Antipas frowned. "Perhaps you did not understand me. I *said* I wish to see a miracle."

Jesus was as still as one of the marbled columns.

"Ahhh," the Tetrarch said, "I understand. You cannot perform a miracle with your hands bound." He turned to one of his guards. "Nahor, unbind his arms."

Abel made as if to step forward but stopped when he realized what he was doing. The Tetrarch saw the move and smiled. Abel shivered; the other man's gaze reminded him of a crocodile he had seen in the Jordan River.

Antipas turned his attention back to watch the guard remove the chains from Jesus' wrists. "Your hands are free. Now, perform some of your miracles." He drained his goblet and set it on the table in front of him. "I'm still thirsty. Refill my goblet without touching the *amphora.*"

Jesus did not move.

Antipas lowered his eyebrows. "Did you not hear me? Refill my goblet."

Jesus was still.

"I said, '*Fill. My. Goblet.*'" The Tetrarch infused each word with venom.

Nothing.

"Perhaps you need some *encouragement*." Antipas gestured to the guard who had removed the chains. "Nahor, *help* the man."

The guard lifted a hand and struck Jesus across the face. The Nazarene staggered and fell.

"Now, this will not do," Antipas said in mock sympathy. "The *Messiah* should not be kneeling on the floor. Nahor, help him *up*.'

The guard grabbed Jesus' arm and jerked it upwards and behind the man, pulling Jesus up so that he was bent in a parody of a bow.

"You should not be *bowing* to me, *Messiah*." Antipas laughed. "Careful, Nahor; you would not wish to *trip* the next King of Israel.'

The guard gestured to one of his men, who stepped towards Jesus. While the one called Nahor still held up the Nazarene's arm, the other guard stuck his long spear out and swept Jesus' feet from under him.

Antipas erupted in laughter. "Oh, no, *Your Majesty*," he cried. "You *fell* again. Please allow my guards to help you."

The guards moved to surround Jesus.

One guard grabbed the prisoner's other arm, wrenching it up and away from his body, saying, "Here, *Your Majesty*, allow me to help you."

A third guard kicked his knee, causing Jesus to crumble to the ground, arms still held by the other two guards. "Excuse me, *Your Majesty*."

One lifted his spear and spun, knocking the butt against Jesus' temple. "My pardons, *Your Majesty*. I didn't see you."

Antipas sat up. "Wait!" He laughed. "I understand why no one recognizes this man as a *king*." He waved a hand towards Jesus. "Look at his clothing. They're not royal." Standing, he removed the purple robe he wore and tossed it towards the guards. "Here, put this on *His Majesty*."

Nahor caught the robe, and signaled to his men to stop. He slipped the robe onto the prisoner's arms and then, lifting a foot, kicked Jesus' side.

The guards continued picking Jesus up and knocking him down.

Antipas threw himself back against the couch, holding his stomach, laughing.

Abel's mouth was spread in a grim smile as he watched the Nazarene struggle between being wrenched up and knocked down. *Mary, I wish you could see your precious Jesus ben Joseph now.*

Finally, Antipas lifted a hand. "Enough. I grow *bored.*"

The guards stopped and stepped back from Jesus who stood head down, eyes closed.

Antipas extended his hand. The servant refilled the goblet and placed it in his hand. Lifting it to his mouth, the Tetrarch drained it before handing it back to the servant. "Nahor, bind the prisoner and send him back to Pilate." He stood. "I'm returning to my bed chamber."

He started crossing the floor. As he reached the door, Abel called out. "Tetrarch. Please…what should I tell the High Priest about?"

Antipas stopped and turned to look at Abel. "I care not what you tell Caiaphas." He stared at Jesus one last time. "Scribe, write a note to send to Pilate."

The scribe lifted the stylus above his tablet.

"Write this: 'Greetings to Governor Pontius Pilate from Herod Antipas, Tetrarch of Galilee and Perea. I have *examined* the prisoner, Jesus ben Joseph, and am sending him back to you. He *said* nothing. He *did* nothing. As far as my judgment is concerned, he *is* nothing.'"

CHAPTER SEVENTEEN

H e is *my* son!" the Teacher's mother said. "Surely Yahweh will not allow anything to happen to him."

Shortly after sunrise, Mary and Martha had found Joanna, Ruth and Abigail in the large banquet hall. The daughters of Nicodemus were busy overseeing the serving of the morning meal. Lazarus and Simon were seated at a table with Peter, James and several of the Teacher's disciples, discussing what had happened the night before and trying to determine how to help Jesus.

Mary and Martha greeted the disciples before turning to Joanna to offer their help. "I know your father has a large staff of servants," Martha said, "but I know from experience how a number of unexpected guests create extra work. To be truthful, I am unaccustomed to doing nothing."

Joanna laid a hand on Martha's sleeve. "I appreciate and understand your offer, my friend; but truthfully, everything is under control. I left David and Deborah with Matthias and his parents while my sisters and I tended to our morning duties. Samuel ben Efraim and Susanna and Leah are still in their bed chambers. They have sent word that they plan to return to their home after the morning meal."

She looked beyond Martha's shoulder and lowered her voice. "Mary bat Eli and Rabbi Joseph just entered the room. Come; I'm certain he has informed her of what has happened."

The younger women crossed the tiled floor to where the Teacher's mother was standing with the elderly priest. Lazarus, Simon and the disciples left their meal and crossed the room to join them.

"Good morning, Mary bat Eli. Good morning, Rabbi Joseph." Joanna nodded her head. "I hope you were able to rest."

The priest from Arimathea returned her greeting. "I did sleep some," he added.

"Good morning," the older Mary nodded to the younger women and to her son's disciples before speaking to Joanna. "Although your father's bed chambers are most comfortable, sleep was elusive."

"I can understand," Joanna replied. "The morning meal is ready. Perhaps after you eat, you could try again to rest. If not in your bed chamber, Father has several lovely gardens with benches and reclining couches."

Mary waved away Joanna's offer. "I thank you, but I could not eat nor can I rest. I *must* go to my son."

"You should try to eat something," Rabbi Joseph said. He turned to the others. "I was explaining to Mary bat Eli that Rabbi Nicodemus and Michael are seeing what they can do to *help* Jesus."

"I appreciate their help," Mary said. "Since James arrived last night," she nodded her head towards her nephew, "with the news of my son's arrest, I have been worried. I prayed all night. I had to remind myself repeatedly that Yahweh gave Jesus to *me*. He is...." she paused for a second, "*my* son! Surely Yahweh will not allow anything to happen to him."

Joseph opened his mouth to reply, but the sound of a door slamming in a distant part of the house followed by footsteps running drew everyone's attention. The footsteps grew louder until Michael appeared in the doorway of the banquet hall.

He stopped and bent over, hands on his knees, trying to catch his breath. "Rabbi Joseph," he panted.

"Michael!" Lazarus rushed to his brother-in-law. "What's happening?"

"No time to explain," he said. Straightening, he looked at the older man. "Rabbi Joseph. Father has sent me to get you. Jesus is at the Antonia Fortress, on trial before Pilate." He slanted a look at the women in the room before stepping closer to whisper to the rabbi and the other men.

"No!" The older Mary demanded, stark fear suffusing her face. "*Tell me* what is happening to my son."

Michael looked at the Teacher's mother and then at Rabbi

Joseph—who nodded—before taking a huge breath and expelling it. "Caiaphas is demanding his death."

Michael drove the carriage that took him, Rabbi Joseph and Daniel, one of Nicodemus' servants, back to the Antonia Fortress. For an unsettling moment, it had appeared as if the Teacher's disciples, his own sisters, along with Lazarus' sisters and Jesus' mother would accompany them. It took all of the persuasive skills of the older rabbi to convince them how ill-advised this idea was.

"If Jesus is on trial for treason—which would be the only accusation the governor would be interested in—then those who arrested him would be interested in his family and friends as well."

Mary bat Eli brushed the threat away as if it were a gnat. "I do not care what they do to me. Jesus is my son."

"I want to go," John said.

"He is our kin," James added.

"He is our Teacher," Andrew said. The other disciples echoed this statement, Peter more vehemently than the rest.

This went on for several minutes, until finally Rabbi Joseph said. "Mary bat Eli, if you were arrested—" he looked at the others, "if any of you were arrested—it would not help the Teacher. Not only would it only cause him great sorrow, it would be exactly what Caiaphas and Annas want."

"What can we do?" The Teacher's mother clasped her hands, whitening her knuckles. "Something must be done."

"What you can do is stay here," Joseph said. "Eat and rest. You *must*," he insisted when the older woman vehemently shook her head. "If you are needed, it will not aid your son if you are weak from hunger and lack of sleep."

The older Mary stared at him for a long moment before heaving a heavy sigh. "You are wise, Rabbi Joseph. I will stay—*we* will stay," she said with a look at the others. "But I must send word to my sister and Mary Magdala."

"We will continue discussing things we can do," Lazarus looked at the disciples. "Rabbi Joseph and Michael will send word as soon as they are able." He looked at his sister, who crossed the room to stand next to him.

"Rabbi Joseph, Michael," she said, "please let us know soon as you know anything!" Tears pooled in her dark eyes. "*Please* help Jesus."

"We will," Michael nodded. "I promise you."

"Now, Michael," Rabbi Joseph said, "you are a young man. Unlike you, I will not be able to run back to the fortress."

"I called for the servant to bring our carriage the moment I arrived," Michael said. "Daniel should have it waiting for us even now." He extended a hand for the elder man to precede him. As the two men reached the door, Michael glanced back to see Mary lift the lower edge of her head covering to wipe away tears. *She cares about the Teacher. No*, he thought, *it's more than caring. She loves Jesus.* His heart ached for her; and for himself. *Can I consider marrying a woman who loves someone else?*

"Ah, Joseph, Michael," Nicodemus said. "Thank Yahweh you are here at last."

"Your son drives his horses swiftly and with enough skill to compete in the Circus Maximus in Rome." Joseph stepped down from the carriage and patted the dust from his garments.

"One moment, my friend," Nicodemus turned to his servant. "Daniel, move the carriage to the shade of that sycamore tree, in case we have need of it soon." As the servant drove off, he turned back to his son and friend. "Come, both of you; we must get back to the courtyard immediately." He led them up the ramp leading to the Roman fortress.

"What is happening?" Joseph asked. "Did the Tetrarch make a judgment concerning Jesus?"

Nicodemus shook his head. "He did not. Antipas returned Jesus to Pilate. That is why I sent Michael to bring you. Pontius Pilate has called for the Judgment Seat."

Abel backed up against the wall as two soldiers carried the *bema*, a large wooden chair, out of the praetorium and set it on the raised platform. Two other soldiers led Jesus ben Joseph, still bound, to stand on one side of it.

The crowd in the courtyard had—from the members of the Sanhedrin who had demanded Jesus' death earlier that morning—grown to include priests, scribes and Temple leaders, as well as merchants and ordinary people in Jerusalem for the Feast.

"They're here to ask Pilate to honor the Passover custom of releasing a prisoner," Abel's father had told him after he had returned from Herod's Palace. "Rabbi Caiaphas has already spoken to those associated with the Temple; but, he wants to make sure the other people in the crowd don't ask for *that man's* release. As you are already *unclean*," he infused with word with disdain, "he wants you to stand near the prisoner, in case the governor takes the Nazarene back into the praetorium."

Abel climbed the stairs to the platform to wait. He saw his father—along with other priests—moving through the crowd, whispering to both men and women, pointing to Jesus and—in some cases—pressing coins into hands. Abel also saw some men that, although dressed in ordinary garments, had the hardened look of warriors.

The crowd's attention turned to the platform as Pontius Pilate stepped out of the praetorium and crossed to sit down on the Judgment Seat. He looked at the prisoner and then the crowd, before turning to address the High Priest and Rabbi Annas.

"High Priest Caiaphas ben Joseph. Rabbi Annas ben Seth. You brought this man," he extended a hand to the prisoner, "Jesus ben Joseph, to me. You accused him of matters relating to *your* religion claiming he attempted to persuade people to not follow the teachings of your Law and the Temple Leaders. You *also* suggested that he was trying to stir up a rebellion against Rome.

"I care not about defending the Jewish faith, but I examined him and found nothing to support your accusations of sedition. Wait." His raised hand stopped Caiaphas from speaking. "When I learned he was a Galilean, I sent him to Herod Antipas. The Tetrarch sent him back to me, along with a communication that he had examined this man and also found nothing to condemn him.

"I agree with Antipas. I find that this man has done nothing deserving of death."

A roar exploded in the courtyard, led by the priests. Both men and women surged forward, denouncing the governor's judgment.

Pilate stood and crossed to the edge of the platform, raised both hands and yelled, "Silence! Silence!" When the crowd continued screaming, he turned to the centurion, who stood on the platform near Abel. "Silence this rabble."

The centurion signaled other soldiers who followed him down the stairs and into the crowd, knocking some people down, butting heads here and there. Abel saw his own father threatened with a raised sword. After several minutes, the noise in the courtyard subsided.

The governor glared at the crowd, "You think to sway the judgment of Rome with curses and threats?"

The High Priest stepped forward, sputtering as he addressed Pilate. "Governor Pilate, we," he swept a hand to include those present in the courtyard, "are outraged that *this man*," he pointed to Jesus, "has attempted to pervert the people and lead them away from the true worship of Yahweh. I *insist* that something be done."

Pilate frowned. "You insist?" He stroked his chin before spreading his lips in a thin smile. "Very well; I will do something." Turning, he crooked a finger to Maximus.

Abel glanced at his father, who jerked his head towards the governor. He slid a foot across the stone platform, careful not to draw attention to himself. He was only able to hear Pilate say,

"—and bring Barabbas."

As the soldier saluted and turned to enter the praetorium, Abel stepped back hurriedly. He looked at his father and shook his head slightly as Pilate turned back to the High Priest.

"As you wish *something* to be done, I will have the man flogged and then released."

"No!" Caiaphas' mouth twisted as if he wanted to spit. "Flogging is not sufficient."

"Not sufficient?" The governor raised his eyebrows. "Not sufficient?" he repeated. "From what you have told me, your own

Temple Leaders use flogging as a punishment for many violations
of your Law. Didn't you explain that—to reflect the *mercy* of your
Yahweh—you limit the number of blows to thirty-nine, to keep
the violator from dying?

"Do not worry, Caiaphas ben Joseph, if you do not wish to show
this man mercy." His smile dripped sarcasm. "We Romans are quite
skilled at flogging."

"A Roman flogging!" Michael gasped.

Nicodemus placed a hand on Michael's forearm. "Calm, my son."
He drew Michael away from the crowd and to the eastern wall.

"Your father is right. We must proceed cautiously," Rabbi Joseph
said.

"Cautiously! Father! Rabbi Joseph!" Michael's eyes widened as he
looked between the two older men. "What are you saying? I don't
understand this *caution*. Rome places no limit on the number of
blows in their floggings; it could be thirty-nine or it could be one
hundred and thirty-nine! No one can survive that!" He paced several
steps away from them and then turned back. "And the Romans
don't just use a whip; they use instruments of torture."

"I have seen them when I traveled to Rome," Rabbi Joseph
frowned. "Some whips have multiple leather ropes tied to the
handle. The *flagrum taxillatum* has pellets or bones or metal tied
along each strand and a hook at the end."

"And yet you wish to proceed *cautiously?*"

His father grabbed Michael's upper arms and shook him slightly.
"Michael, listen to me. Of course, Rabbi Joseph and I do not wish to
see Jesus flogged. But *think*. You heard Pontius Pilate say that *after*
Jesus was flogged, he would be released. Obviously, the governor is
trying to free Jesus *and* satisfy Caiaphas and Annas."

"Michael," Joseph said, "Pontius Pilate told me that the Roman
soldiers are trained how to place their blows if they wish the prisoner to survive the flogging."

"It will surely be excruciating," his father said, "but Jesus will *live*.
And where there is life, there is hope."

205

"Rabbi Joseph bar Neriah?"

The men turned to see a young woman standing nearby.

"Lady Claudia Procula," Joseph crossed to her.

Of an age with Joanna, Governor Pilate's wife was dressed simply for her status as a Roman aristocrat. She wore a linen cream tunic with a dark green girdle wrapped around her waist. A matching green *palla*, an oblong shawl, was draped over her hair— which was styled in intricate braids—and fell softly around her shoulders and arms.

"Lady," Joseph said, "you should not be here."

Michael glanced over his shoulder and then stepped sideways to block the woman's view of her husband's soldiers leading Jesus to a large pole in the center of the courtyard.

She noticed his action and smiled sadly. "I appreciate your consideration, young man, but unfortunately, I have seen a man flogged before." She nodded towards the courtyard beyond Michael. "Rabbi Joseph, is my husband passing judgment on a young Jewish man?"

Joseph's eyes widened as he looked to Nicodemus and Michael and then back to her. "Yes he is, Lady. The man is our friend, Jesus ben Joseph, the Teacher from Nazareth. Perhaps you have heard of him?"

She nodded. "All in Jerusalem have heard of your friend. I was in the marketplace earlier this week when the crowds heralded his arrival to the city." A frown creased her brow as she chewed her bottom lip. "Last night...I *dreamt* about him." She shook her head as if to rid herself of a bad memory. "I must warn my husband, before he passes his final judgment. He must *not* condemn this man. He's *innocent*."

"We are grateful for any help you could give Jesus," Joseph said. "Your word would carry great weight with your husband."

"I wrote a note as soon as I awoke this morning, while the effects of the dream were still upon me." She reached into the folds of her girdle and pulled out a small, sealed scroll, "If I cannot speak directly with my husband, I will send this message to him."

206

Abel had attempted to follow the soldiers leading Jesus down the stairs, but stopped when his father shook his head and nodded slightly towards the governor. He jumped when Pontius Pilate spoke behind him.

"Your father is not skilled in the art of subtlety. He wishes you to stay near me. Perhaps he thinks you can *influence* me." His mouth spread in a sarcastic smile. "I am sorry to disappoint your father, but you *can't*." He turned his head as the centurion approached. "What is it, Maximus?"

"Sir, the Lady Claudia is here."

"What? My wife?" Pilate frowned as he looked to where the soldier pointed out a lady on the edge of the crowd, waving furiously at the governor. "What is she doing here?"

"She wanted to talk to you," the soldier said. "When I explained that you were not able to speak with her at this moment, she instructed me to give you this message."

The governor took the proffered scroll, broke the wax seal and unrolled it.

Abel slanted a glance and then turned his head as if he hadn't seen his father jerking his head furiously towards Pilate. *Father is not only unconcerned with me becoming unclean,* he ground his teeth, *but he also doesn't care that I would be arrested for attempting to read the scroll over the governor's shoulder.*

Pontius Pilate frowned as he scanned the message and then rolled the scroll up and tucked it into his girdle.

"Shall I bring Lady Claudia to you?" the centurion asked.

"No. Tell her that I will do what I can. Send an escort with her to Herod's Palace with my *request* that she remain there until I arrive." He grabbed the centurion's elbow. "Increase the soldiers guarding our rooms at the Tower of David."

Abel watched Pilate meet his wife's gaze, lifting his shoulders in a slight shrug. She turned as the centurion approached her and delivered his message. Looking at her husband, she nodded in reply before following an escort of four soldiers.

"Unlike you, Abel ben Joktan," Pilate spoke to him while watching Lady Claudia leave, "my wife *has* influence over me. I will do everything I can not to disappoint her." The governor turned his attention to the courtyard where the soldiers were securing Jesus ben Joseph to a post. "Have you ever seen a man flogged?" he asked.

Abel nodded.

When no specific punishment was stipulated by the Law given by Yahweh, the Temple Leaders generally administered flogging. As far back as Abel could remember, his father had taken him—and later him and his sister Rebeca—to witness these floggings.

The offender's clothing was removed from their upper body and their hands tied to a post. The Law specified that, no matter what the violation, flogging could not go beyond thirty-nine lashes. The one doing the flogging would stand above the violator and, using a whip with multiple leather strands, would beat the bare skin of the person—thirteen lashes on their breast and the remainder on their back. With each blow, the one administering the punishment would recite scriptures to admonish and comfort the violator.

No matter how distressed it made them, Joktan never let Abel or Rebeca turn away—not even when they were young children—but insisted they watch each lash. "This will happen to you," he had warned, "should you *ever* disobey the Law of Yahweh." From his father's inflection, it was clear that he considered also any violation of his *own* rigid set of rules as a violation of the Law of Yahweh.

"I have seen many floggings for violators of Yahweh's Law," Abel answered the governor.

Pilate waved his hand dismissively. "I'm not speaking of those *punishments* the Temple Leaders administer as if to a child," he sneered. "Have you ever seen a Roman flogging?"

"No, sir."

"We take great care with our punishments, to inflict as much pain as possible." Pilate spoke lightly, almost pleasantly. "We not only use them to punish the violator, but also to warn the populace." He pointed towards the pavement. "Observe."

The soldiers had stripped all clothing from Jesus ben Joseph. Two soldiers—one tall and lean, the other large as a small mountain—had brought out different whips. The air whistled and cracked as both men tested them before each selected one. Jesus was bent over a low post, his hands tied to an iron ring; the governor explained to Abel that securing the prisoner this way would stretch the skin, making the lacerations from the whips even deeper.

The two soldiers positioned themselves several steps back on either side of him. They looked towards the governor.

Pilate raised his hand. Dropped it.

The tall soldier rushed towards Jesus while raising the whip and lashing the prisoner's back, ripping a gash from his shoulders to his waist.

Jesus collapsed against the post, moaning as blood spurted from the opened wound.

Caiaphas and Annas—along with Joktan and those around the High Priest—cheered.

Before Jesus could stand, the large soldier's lash caught his shoulder and tore across his upper back.

Jesus fell to the ground, his arms raised over his head. That did not stop the flogging. The second blow from the tall soldier caught the side of his neck, leaving a rivulet of blood running down to his chest.

"Get up, *Messiah!*" Annas laughed. "Throw off the bonds of the Romans and lead the people to freedom!"

"Where are your followers now, *King of the Jews?*" Caiaphas yelled.

"Strike him again!" Joktan screamed; his cry was echoed by the priests interspersed in the crowd.

The large soldier laid his whip across Jesus' legs, ripping gashes into his thighs.

The two soldiers fell into a grisly rhythm, alternating their lashes, leaving Jesus with bare moments between the blows to scream, to moan or to collapse.

With each whip of the lash, the crowd around the High Priest grew louder, screaming for more blood. Abel, accustomed to witnessing flogging at the Temple, struggled to not vomit at the sight of the Romans' whips flaying the Nazarene's body.

"These soldiers are trained in the art of flagellation," Pilate spoke as if he were teaching a child a simple task. "If the flogging is to be a punishment and not death, they know how to deliver the blows with mathematical precision to avoid killing the prisoner." He lifted a hand; the centurion called to the soldiers to stay their whips.

Jesus laid against the post, his arms held in a grotesque position above his head. Blood poured from his wounds. He did not move.

"Is he dead?" Caiaphas called out.

"Check the prisoner," Pilate commanded.

The tall soldier handed his whip to the large soldier and approached Jesus ben Joseph. Leaning over, he thumbed open the Nazarene's eye and then laid his hand on the bloodied chest. He closed his eyes for a long moment and then looked up at the governor.

"He lives."

At Pilate's nod, the soldier stood and moved to release Jesus' hands.

"No!" Annas shrieked, fists raised.

"Finish him! Caiaphas screamed.

"Death!" Abel couldn't tell who screamed the loudest; his father or the High Priest. From the edge of the crowd, he heard Joseph bar Neriah, Nicodemus ben Melech and his son Michael cry, "No! Let him live!"

Caiaphas shrieked. "He must die!"

"Why?" Pilate demanded. "He has committed no crime worthy of death. Did the flogging not satisfy your *blood lust*?"

The sound of footsteps and chains in the corridor to the praetorium stilled the screams and drew everyone's attention. Four soldiers, armed with lances and short swords, stepped out onto the platform. Behind them, bound in chains, was Jesus Barabbas.

Pilate pointed to a spot on the left side of the Judgment Seat. "Put him there." Then he turned and looked at the soldiers with Jesus ben Joseph. He pointed to a spot on his right side. "Bring the prisoner here."

Chapter Eighteen

What is Pilate doing?" Michael asked as they watched the soldiers lead Jesus—swaying and stumbling from exhaustion, pain and the loss of blood— up the stairs to the platform in front of the praetorium. "Why did he bring that *murderer*, Barabbas, here?"

Nicodemus was studying the scene, eyes squinted against the bright sunlight. "It appears that he is going to offer the crowd a choice of amnesty."

Rabbi Joseph nodded. "I think you are correct."

"A choice?" Michael asked. "Is this like the custom of releasing a prisoner during the Passover?"

"In a sense," Joseph said. "It appears that the governor is going to offer the crowd a choice between what the Romans call the *indulgentia*," he pointed to Barabbas, "where he pardons a condemned prisoner, or offer them the *abolition*," he pointed to the Teacher. "where they acquit a person before judgment is passed. I have heard that during Roman feasts, this is one method the Caesars used to placate the populace. Sometimes, the Roman governors use this custom in the provinces over which they rule."

"If he is using this custom, shouldn't we try to get closer, in order to sway the crowds to ask for the Teacher?" Michael asked.

"We should get closer," Nicodemus nodded, "but, we must be careful," he added as they moved towards the front of the courtyard. "This crowd could turn against Jesus."

"Turn against him?" Michael stopped.

"Shhh…" Nicodemus and Joseph patted the air, slanting their eyes towards those around them. Michael lowered his voice before he continued walking. "How could they choose a rebel and murderer like Barabbas over Jesus? Father, you and I were in the Temple when many of these people followed Jesus into the Temple courtyard. You saw how they listened to his every word." He looked around and lowered his voice even more. "Some even declared him *Messiah* and claimed he was like King David."

"My son, these people don't want a *Messiah* who will be like the shepherd-poet David," Nicodemus paused as they passed a group of priests. "They saw Jesus overturn the tables of the money-changers in the Temple. *That* is the type of *Messiah* they want; a warrior-king like David, who will overcome Israel's enemies. Not someone who is weak and bloodied from Rome's lash."

By the time they reached a spot beneath where Pilate stood, Jesus was standing between two soldiers on the right side of the Judgment Seat.

Looking at the Teacher, Michael understood what his father meant. Jesus could barely stand from the lack of sleep, from being dragged all over Jerusalem, from beatings and now from floggings. *He does not look like the man who would defy those who hold Israel captive.* Michael shifted his gaze towards Barabbas. Tall and muscular—even bound in chains—the man exuded strength, nodding to the crowd, sneering at Pilate and cursing the soldiers on either side of him. *That is the type of man many would believe could stand against Rome.*

The crowd was buzzing but stopped when the governor stood and raised a hand.

"You have a custom," he said, "that I—as the governor—should release a prisoner to you today. There are several prisoners held in the Antonia Fortress, so I will give you a choice." He extended his left hand. "Should I release the *Sicarii* murderer, Jesus Barabbas, or," he extended his right hand, "should I release the King of the Jews, Jesus ben Joseph? Whom do you wish? Barabbas the murderer or Jesus," he looked towards Caiaphas and Annas, "who is called the *Messiah?*"

Michael opened his mouth but, before he could speak, Joktan stepped forward. "Not *this man!*" he screamed, pointing at Jesus. The other priests in the crowd joined him; soon the crowd surged forward, screaming.

"Do not release *this man*!"

"Release Barabbas!"

"Take this man away!"

"Give us Barabbas!"

Pilate stepped back as if the barrage of screams were arrows. The soldiers in the courtyard moved in, shoving, punching, even lifting a sword, to force the crowd to move back. When they complied, the governor spoke again.

"If I release Barabbas—this *murderer*—to you, what shall I do with Jesus, the one you called the *Messiah*, the King of the Jews?"

"He cannot be the *Messiah*!" Joktan screamed. "When the *Messiah* comes, he will be strong. He will never allow himself to be captured." He pointed at Jesus. "He *lied* by claiming to be the *Messiah*! He *lied* to us! He *lied* to us! Release Barabbas!"

"He's not the *Messiah*!" one man yelled.

"That's right!" another called. "He lied to us!"

The crowd echoed their cries.

"He's not the *Messiah*!"

"He lied to us!"

Pilate lifted his hands again; this time the crowd silenced without the soldiers' threat. "But what should I do with Jesus?" he asked.

In the lull, Joktan spoke.

"Crucify him."

A gasp rippled through the crowd. Many of those standing near the priest turned to look at him.

Although developed by the Medes and Persians, it was Rome who had taken crucifixion as their own particular method of executing slaves and criminals. Although an Israelite—in a moment of righteous anger—might pick up a stone to throw at someone, no one who considered themself a 'Child of Abraham' would ever consider crucifixion.

Joktan ignored the stares of those around him. His eyes burned and his mouth twisted with hate. "*Crucify* him."

Abel saw the High Priest nod at the other priests that were interspersed in the crowd.

"Crucify him," Rabbi David bar Mattan shouted.

"Crucify him!" a priest by the west wall yelled.

Out of the corner of Abel's eye, he saw Barabbas motion towards a man near the stairs. The man nodded and cupped his mouth to yell, "Crucify him!"

"No!" Rabbi Nicodemus cried out. "Do not crucify him!" His plea was echoed by Rabbi Joseph. Abel smiled when he saw Michael frantically echoing his father. *Your money and wealth cannot help your friend now, Michael ben Nicodemus. How does it feel to be powerless?* Abel stretched his mouth in a grim smile as he filled his lungs and joined the crowd's scream.

"Crucify him! Crucify him!"

Pilate silenced the crowd again. "Why? What crime, what evil, has *this man* done?" He slashed the air with his hand. "No. I find no cause in him for death."

Without hesitation, the crowd resumed its chant. "Crucify him! Crucify him!"

The governor turned and gestured to the centurion. "I don't understand this." Pilate had to yell to be heard over the deafening crowd. "Just days ago, they called him a *king*, and now they want him crucified. I don't know what to do."

"I have an idea." The soldier said. He leaned in to Pilate and spoke one word. "Basilicus."

Pilate's eyes narrowed as he considered Maximus' suggestion. Finally, he nodded. "Take him."

Once again, Abel found himself following the centurion and a dozen soldiers as they led Jesus through the corridors of the praetorium to a private courtyard. In the center was a large brazier for warmth and meal preparation; stacked next to it was wood for burning and twigs and dried vines for kindling. The only furnishings were low tables for the soldiers to eat on and several narrow limestone tables which held *amphorae*, an array of cups and several carved wooden boxes.

This time, the centurion did not ignore Abel. "This courtyard is where the soldiers relax," he explained. "We eat. We drink. We also play games. Let me show you one of our favorites." He picked up one of the wooden boxes; something inside of it rattled. "Come."

He led Abel across the courtyard to a spot near the wall, where the soldiers had taken Jesus ben Joseph and were unbinding his wrists. Lying on the pavement in a crumbled heap was the robe Herod had draped over the Nazarene.

His wrists freed, Jesus slumped against the stone wall, moaning where the stones' sharp edges rubbed against his opened wounds.

Maximus drew Abel's attention to a series of squares and circles that had been carved into the floor; in the center, was a word written in Latin.

"Do you read Latin?" the centurion asked and continued when Abel shook his head. "That is the word *Basilicus*; it means, "The Game of the King." It is part of the festival of Saturn, but we," he swept a hand to include the soldiers who were dropping to one knee next to the etchings, "have altered it slightly for our amusement.' He handed the box to one of the soldiers.

The man opened it and turned out dice made from sheep knuckles into his palm. Cupping the dice in his fist, he shook it and opened his hand.

The bones skittered across the floor and stopped on several of the circles. "*Septem!*" he laughed. He gathered the dice and handed them to the soldier next to him. "You can't beat that!"

The soldier tossed the dice. "*Octo!*" he cried. "I win the round. I get to select the *king*. Hmmm…" he rubbed his chin, looking at the men in the room, before stopping on Jesus. "You!" Standing, he crossed to grab Jesus' hand and jerk him up. "I choose *you* to be our *king*." He drew his sword from its scabbard—the blade made a musical ring, the melody of death—and brought it to his chest in a salute. "Your Majesty."

Jesus didn't respond, but stood, eyes closed, breathing deeply.

"My turn," another soldier said. He rolled the dice. "*Tres!*" he handed the dice to the one next to him.

The soldier rolled. "*Duo!* You win the round."

The other soldier stood and walked to where Herod's robe lay in a pile of purple silk. "A king needs a royal robe." He picked it up and carried it to Jesus. "Here, Your Majesty, allow me to help you." He slipped the robe over Jesus' arms and onto his shoulders. "Oh, I'm so sorry, Your Majesty," the soldier said when the prisoner winced as the fabric touched the gashes in his skin. "Does that hurt?"

Like his comrade, he drew his sword and saluted.

The game continued. "A king needs a scepter," said the next winner. He crossed to the brazier and picked up a large reed from the pile of wood. "This will do." He walked back and slapped it in Jesus' hand before saluting. "Your Majesty."

The winner of the next round spread his arms wide. "What is a king without a crown?" He crossed to the brazier and, reaching into the kindling, grabbed a large vine. He cursed as he shook his hand, blood dripping from his thumb. "The *nabk* vine has thick thorns."

Grasping the ends of the vine, he twisted it into a large circle. He walked back to the others and held the thorny wreath over Jesus' head. "I crown you...*King of the Jews!*" he set the wreath on the Nazarene's head. "Hmmm...it doesn't seem to fit well, Your Majesty; let me *help*," he said and *shoved* the crown of thorns down onto the prisoner's head.

Abel flinched instinctively as Jesus cried out, pulling his head away in pain as the thorns dug deeply into his scalp, blood running down into his eyes.

The soldiers cheered and, as if by silent command, stood to circle the prisoner.

One took the reed out of Jesus' hand. "Hail, King of the Jews!" he cried, hitting him over the head.

Another grabbed the Nazarene's beard and jerked, pulling out a handful of hair.

The centurion laughed when a soldier used the hilt of his sword as a hammer and pounded on the *nabk* wreath, forcing the thorns further into the Nazarene's brow.

Abel forced himself to watch the soldiers' abuse through slitted eyes, struggling to fight the rising nausea.

"What's the matter?" Maximus asked. "Are your bowels too weak to witness this?"

Another soldier lifted his sword to his chest in a mock salute,

"Hail, King of the Jews!" and then struck Jesus' face with the hilt. Blood spurted from Jesus' nose.

"Hey, watch the blood!" Maximus shouted. "That robe is from Herod. I will be wagering for that.

"You see," the centurion told Abel in a conversational tone, "we used to play The Game of the King with new recruits. We'd start the game early in the day. One man would select the 'king,' another would give him a robe; another, a scepter; another, a crown.

"The game continued throughout the day, but changed as the hours passed. With each toss of the dice, we began gambling for all of the *king's* possessions: his clothes, his horse, his home back in Rome, even his wife.

"The final toss of the dice—the winning toss—was to choose who got to *kill* the king.

"Caesar Augustus heard about our *game* and, for some reason, he didn't like it." Maximus stroked his chin in a mockery of musing. "He claimed it 'hurt morale' and 'caused the Empire to lose good soldiers.'" He shrugged his shoulders, "Don't understand *why* he should think that. Anyhow, the emperor didn't *outlaw* the game, but commanded that—instead of using our new recruits—we should play The Game of the King," he pointed to where the soldiers were torturing Jesus, "with *condemned prisoners.*"

"Mary, I do not understand why you are still here," Salome said, "and not at the Antonia Fortress."

Moments after Michael and the rabbi from Arimathea had left for the Roman fortress, Joanna had offered to send a messenger to Mary Magdala's home. After requesting a servant to bring light refreshments, she escorted her father's guests to the family courtyard. Joanna invited the disciples and the Teacher's mother to sit at one of the low tables. Ruth sent a servant to bring her father's chairs for the two expectant mothers and placed in a shady spot near the opened windows.

"It is difficult to believe," Martha whispered to Simon as she accepted a small pillow from Ruth to place behind her back, "that, only a few days ago, we were all gathered in this very courtyard, meeting the Teacher's mother, his aunt Salome and his friend Mary Magdala for the first time."

It wasn't long before the other two women arrived. They thanked Joanna for her father's hospitality to Mary bat Eli, but waved aside the offer of food and drink. After hearing what had happened since the previous night, Salome bat Eli shook her head and wondered aloud why her sister was still there and not at the Roman barracks. She looked at her sons, "I do not know why my sons are here either and not trying to help their cousin."

"I agree with Salome," Mary Magdala said.

"Rabbi Joseph bar Neriah said we should wait here," the Teacher's mother wrung her hands in dismay. "He said that going to the fortress might be dangerous to us and that it wouldn't help Jesus."

"Mary," Salome took her sister's hands, "you are known to only a handful of people in Jerusalem. Those seeking to harm Jesus do not know who you are. That is protection enough. I say we go to the Antonia Fortress *now*."

"We are going," John ben Zebedee extended his hands to include the other disciples in the room.

"What? But Rabbi Joseph said—" Lazarus began when Peter bar Jonah interrupted.

"The Teacher needs us," he said. "Jesus needs to *see* that we are *still* his followers."

"Then I am going too," Mary bat Eli stood.

Joanna opened her mouth, but the Teacher's mother stopped her. "Joanna bat Nicodemus, I appreciate your concern and your desire to follow the advice of Rabbi Joseph and your father. However, Jesus is *my* son. I cannot stay here when he might need me, even if it's nothing more I can do than let him know I am there."

For the second time that morning, the sound of a distant door opening and running feet drew their attention. Moments later, the servant Daniel appeared in the courtyard.

"Daniel!" Joanna crossed to him. "What is it?"

He bowed his head briefly. "Joanna bat Nicodemus, your father has sent word." He scanned the room. "You are all needed at the Antonia Fortress. Now."

"What are they doing to Jesus?" Michael tried to ignore the soldiers guarding Barabbas and stared into the darkened corridor of the praetorium, as if his gaze could pierce its depths.

"I do not know, my son, but you need to stop pacing."

Michael paused in mid-stride and looked at his father, eyebrows lifted in a surprised question.

Nicodemus lowered his voice. "You are drawing unwanted attention to us."

Michael followed his father's slanted eyes to see Caiaphas and Annas—as well as the priests standing nearby—staring at them Hatred blazed in Joktan ben Philemon's gaze and his mouth was twisted into a snarl.

After the soldiers had led Jesus from the platform and into the praetorium a second time, Pilate had announced that he was going to examine the prisoner further and left the platform.

"My friend," Nicodemus had said to Joseph, "as Jesus Barabbas is still on the platform, it appears that Pontius Pilate might plan to give the people another opportunity to choose between the murderer and Jesus."

"I think you're right."

"It also appears that those in this crowd who are against Jesus are greater those who are for him."

Rabbi Joseph looked over the crowd and nodded. "Again, I agree."

"I think it might be best to bring those waiting at my house."

"Father!" Michael said. "You saw the flogging. There is no telling what the soldiers are doing to Jesus or will do when they bring him back. Do you want the women, his mother, my sisters and," he paused before continuing, "Lazarus' sisters, to *see* that?"

"No, I don't," Nicodemus said. "I am hoping that the sight of the Teacher's mother screaming for her son's life will sway the crowd. If it does not, if Annas and Caiaphas have their way," his beard drooped in a frown, "Mary bat Eli has the right to be with her son in his final hours. Now, please send Daniel with the carriage to our house."

Michael nodded and turned. He saw Annas and Caiaphas put their heads together, whispering and shooting darkened glances at the *bema* and at him, his father and Rabbi Joseph.

He shook his head as he hurried through the courtyard. He had grown up in the home of a priest and realized that they were just men, they had flaws. When he first began studying for the priesthood, his father cautioned him to live a life worthy of that calling. "Priests set the standard for others on how Yahweh wishes all to live," Nicodemus had said. "As my father—may his memory be blessed—used to say, 'If a priest robs, who will then bring a sacrifice to Yahweh?'"

All his life, Michael had watched his father dedicate his life to keeping the Law given to Moses. While Nicodemus did not care for Caiaphas or Annas as *men*, he set the example in his household of respecting those who served as priests of Yahweh, especially the position of the High Priest.

Now, the two men who held the highest position in the Jewish faith were not only clamoring for Jesus' death without a valid reason, it appeared they were willing to take down any who stood with the Nazarene.

This is a travesty! *No*, Michael's mind raged, *that's not strong enough. It is a* mockery; *it is a* perversion *of our faith.*

And now Mary will see the horrors of what has been done to the Teacher. How can I protect her from that? He shook his head, reminding himself that Mary was not yet his wife to protect. If Jesus survived all of this, she might not ever be his wife.

His frown deepened.

Within a short time, Michael found Daniel and sent him on his way. He rejoined his father and Rabbi Nicodemus with a nod. "It is done."

"Pray Yahweh that Daniel brings them in time," Nicodemus said.

The three men waited in grim silence.

After what felt to Michael like the day when the sun stood still for the patriarch Joshua, Pontius Pilate stepped out of the praetorium, shadowed by his scribe.

The governor walked to the edge of the platform; he studied the crowd, face as grim as the grave, before turning to one of the soldiers guarding Barabbas. "Send word to Centurion Maximus to bring the prisoner," he said and resumed studying the crowd.

No one—not even Annas or Caiaphas—spoke or moved.

The sound of footsteps and chains drew everyone's eye to the corridor. The centurion appeared first, followed by ten soldiers; they spread out on the platform, swords drawn. Abel ben Joktan stepped out and moved to a spot against the wall. Lastly, two more soldiers appeared, leading Jesus ben Joseph to a spot on the governor's right

A gasp rose from the courtyard at the sight of the Teacher, garbed in a purple robe, bruised from beatings and blood dripping down his face from the wreath of ugly thorns piercing his brow.

Michael, a growl rising deep in his throat, took a step towards the stairs, only to be stopped by his father's outstretched arm.

"Do not move," Nicodemus said, his countenance as hard as his words.

"Father!" Michael seethed. "Look what they've done to him!"

"And how will getting yourself arrested help Jesus?"

Michael released a frustrated sigh. "But, Father," he clenched his fists, "you don't intend for us to just stand here and do *nothing*"

Nicodemus' gaze softened. "Of course not, my son. Trust me; when I know we can do something to *help* the Teacher, we will no longer *just stand here and do nothing*. Now, watch and listen."

They turned back as Pilate extended a hand towards Jesus. "Behold the man! I have brought him out to you, so that you may all know that I find no fault in him."

"No!" Caiaphas yelled.

"Crucify him!" Annas' scream was echoed by Joktan, "Crucify him!"

"No!" Pilate shook his head. "He has done nothing worthy of death!"

"According to our law, he should die," Annas shouted, "because he claims to be the Son of Yahweh!"

Abel saw Pilate startle at Rabbi Annas' accusation. The governor

lifted a hand to silence the crowd. "What did you say?" The Roman asked the elderly rabbi.

"I said," Annas replied, "*this man* claimed to be the *Son of Yahweh!*"

The governor's eyes widened as he turned to stare at the Nazarene. He turned back to the elderly priest. "You told me that he claimed to be your *Messiah.* You said nothing of him claiming to be the son of your god."

"Why should I think that would matter to you?" Annas replied.

Pilate looked from Annas to the centurion. "Bring the prisoner," he said and turned to enter the praetorium once again, the scribe following. The centurion crooked his finger to the soldiers holding Jesus up before following Pilate into the darkened corridor.

Abel didn't need to glance at his father to know he was expected to go. Pilate had gone only far enough into the corridor to be out of the sight of the courtyard. He was talking to the centurion. The other two soldiers continued holding Jesus by the forearms. From the way the prisoner slumped, he would have crumpled to the floor if not for the soldiers' grasp.

As Abel reached them, Pilate turned to him. "Abel ben Joktan, I know little about your religion. Tell me—has your god ever taken on human form?"

Abel's eyebrows shot upward. "What?"

"Rome has many gods and goddesses," the governor glanced over his shoulder at the prisoner and lowered his voice, "and some have been known to take on human form and walk among humans."

"How *dare* you suggest such a thing!" Abel spat. He was surprised at his own vehemence, but he did not stop. "Our Yahweh is *not* like your pagan gods!"

Pilate glanced at Jesus ben Joseph again and then turned to the centurion. "Maximus, what do you think?"

"I am a soldier," the centurion replied. "I offer sacrifices to Mars, the god of war, on his feast days. Beyond that, I do not concern myself with the gods and goddesses, whatever form they take."

Despite the centurion's brave words, Abel noticed that he, too, slanted his eyes towards the Nazarene. *He's frightened,* Abel realized.

He knows that he was responsible for allowing his men to beat Jesus ben Joseph.

Pilate followed the soldier's glance and then looked back at Abel. "What if *this man* really is the Son of your Yahweh, but in human form?" He studied the floor for a moment before shaking his head. "No. I won't be responsible for the blood of a god." He turned to walk over to the Nazarene. "Annas ben Seth said you claim to be…" he licked his lips, "the Son of Yahweh?"

Abel noted that the governor's tone was diffident and cautious. *He truly believes* this man *might be a god.*

Jesus said nothing, but stood with his eyes closed. Pilate flicked a glance at Maximus and then back to the prisoner. He took a deep breath.

"*Where* are you from?"

Nothing.

The governor frowned. "Why don't you say anything? Don't you know that I have the power to *release* you and the power to *crucify* you?"

Jesus ben Joseph opened his eyes and looked at the Roman. He filled his lungs with a ragged breath. "You have no power over *me*," although he spoke softly—painfully—his voice echoed in the stone corridor, "that was not given to you from *above*. For this reason, he who brought me to you," he looked at Abel and then back at Pilate, "is guilty of greater sin."

Abel stepped back as if the Nazarene had broken his chains and attacked him. *Are you saying that I am guilty? How* dare *you! I never had* any *choice; my father* made *me go to Judas. He* made *me follow you in the crowds, question you, help arrange your arrest. My father* made *me lie about you. Now* I *am guilty of a greater sin? How* dare *you!*

Pilate studied the prisoner for a second longer before turning to his scribe. "Arrange for a bowl of water." He looked at the soldiers. "Bring him."

The scribe scurried away while the soldiers with Jesus followed Pilate and the centurion back to the platform.

Abel, only steps behind them, found his spot on the platform. He kept his gaze on Pilate to avoid looking where his father, Rabbi Caiaphas and Rabbi Annas stood.

The Roman governor crossed to the edge of the platform. "I have examined this…*man*," he swallowed, "and to appease *your desire* for his blood, I had him flogged. I will release him as I find no basis for a charge against him."

"No!" The crowd surrounding the Chief Priest screamed. "Death!"

"Yes!" Michael tried to out-scream the crowd. "Release him!"

"Kill him!" Caiaphas yelled.

"Crucify him!" Joktan shrieked.

Pilate raised his hands to silence the crowd. "He has done *nothing* wrong!"

"If you release *this man*," Annas said, "you are no *friend of Caesar*. Anyone who claims to be a *king* opposes Caesar."

Abel watched as the crowd erupted again, screaming for Jesus' blood and repeating Annas' words. It didn't take one skilled in the art of subtlety to recognize the veiled threat in the rabbi's statement. Unless Pilate killed Jesus, Annas would see that word reached Tiberius that Pontius Pilate, prefect of Judea, Samaria and Idumea, had released a man who was plotting to overthrow the Emperor.

Looking at Pilate, Abel saw that the governor understood Annas' warning.

Turning, the Roman crossed to the center of the platform and sat down upon the *bema*. He extended his hand towards Jesus ben Joseph. "Behold!" he said. "Here is your *king*."

"No!" Caiaphas screamed. "He is *not* my king!"

"Away with him!" Joktan shrieked. "Crucify him!"

"Shall I crucify your *king?*" Pilate asked.

"He is not our *king*," Annas said. "We have no king but *Caesar*."

The cacophony of the crowd continued to rise. The centurion stepped to the edge of the platform, directing his men in trying to control the crowd.

The scribe, followed by a servant carrying a towel and a large bowl, stepped out of the corridor. The scribe directed the servant to the governor's side.

The High Priest lifted his hands to silence the crowd and then turned to watch.

Pontius Pilate dipped his hands into the bowl and brought them up, dripping with water. He rubbed his hands together and dipped them back into the bowl. "I am innocent of this man's blood. It is your responsibility."

Abel bit back a gasp. *Pilate told me that he wasn't familiar with our religion, yet he is using the law concerning innocent blood!* According to the Law, if someone was found murdered, the man who owned the land was to offer a sacrifice and wash his hands over the sacrifice, while declaring, *"Our hands did not shed this blood."*

The crowd understood the governor's reference. "Let his blood be on us," they screamed, "and on our children."

Taking the towel from the servant, Pilate dried his hands. He turned to face the courtyard. "Centurion; release Jesus Barabbas," his voice carried over the crowd, "and crucify Jesus ben Joseph."

"Noooo!" A scream echoed around the walls of the fortress.

Michael turned to see the Teacher's mother at the back of the courtyard, falling to her knees. Standing next to her was Mary.

"No!" the older woman screamed again. "You cannot! You *cannot!*" Grabbing the neck of her tunic, she pulled, ripping the cloth. "My son! My *Son!*"

Michael ran to the back of the courtyard, his father and Rabbi Joseph moments behind him.

Mary had dropped to her knees next to the Teacher's mother and was cradling the woman's head against her shoulder as if she were a child and not nearly three decades older. "Shhhh," she crooned. "Don't cry. Something can be done." She looked up at Michael, lifting an eyebrow in a pleading question.

Michael didn't even look to his father for an answer; Pontius Pilate's pronouncement of judgment doused any flames of hope for Jesus. He shook his head.

Tears drenched Mary's amber eyes and trembled on her long lashes. She dropped her head on Mary bat Eli's shoulder and began sobbing.

The sound of the two women's grief constricted his throat and left his chest aching. He ran his hands over his head covering and looked upward, his mouth stretched in a silent scream. *Yahweh! Help us! Help Jesus! Help me! This was the first time Mary asked me to do something and I have* failed *her!*

225

"So that is the Nazarene's mother," Caiaphas said.

After Pilate's pronouncement, Abel hurried down the stairs to join his father and the priests who were following the High Priest and his father-in-law across the courtyard to the tunnel leading to the Temple. A woman's screams stopped the group. Abel turned to see an older woman screaming and rending her clothes before collapsing into the arms of his cousin, Mary.

"And there," the High Priest pointed to the group of people entering the courtyard and gathering around the grieving woman. "Joktan ben Philemon; are not those men his disciples and, among them, your kin?" At Joktan's nod, he continued. "We will need to watch these people, to be sure they do not attempt to free *that man* or create any future problems. Perhaps," he smiled snake-like, "your family's wealth will come to you at last."

"Rabbi Caiaphas!" The servant, Malchus, pushed through the crowd and approached the High Priest. He bent over, one hand on his knee, the other on his stomach, gasping in air. "The…man…Judas."

"Malchus, what is it?" The High Priest demanded. "Where is Judas Iscariot?"

"Dead."

"Dead?" Are you sure?" Caiaphas asked. "What happened"

"He hanged himself!"

"What?" The men in the group stepped away from the servant, as if the word itself would defile them.

Malchus nodded as he straightened. "I saw it. At the field outside of town. The one with the cliff? He tied a rope to the branch of a tree and tied the other end to his neck." He swallowed. "And stepped off the cliff." His mouth twisted. "He…*didn't die* right away. His…*writhing* caused the tree branch to break. He fell on the rocks beneath the cliffs. His…" He dashed the back of his hand across his mouth, "body *burst* open."

"What should we do with the body?" Joktan asked. "As Iscariot was a Jew, Pontius Pilate will expect us to bury it. To touch a dead body will render that person unclean."

"Leave it for now," Caiaphas said. "As your son is already unclean, he can deal with the body once the Nazarene is dead." He stroked his beard. "Iscariot's self-murder has reduced the number of *that man's* followers we will have to deal with.

"Sir," he turned to his father-in-law. "The field we are going to purchase from the potter, the one to bury strangers. Since we will be using Iscariot's money to purchase the field, let's bury him there."

"That is a good suggestion," Annas said. He noted the position of the sun. "We must go to the Temple now; it is nearing the third hour and it will soon be time for the *Tamid*, the 'perpetual sacrifice.'

"Joktan, you and," the elderly rabbi flicked a disdainful glance towards Abel, "your son, follow the soldiers to Golgotha. Make sure *that man* is nailed to the cross. Then report back to us.

"If all goes according to our plans," he straightened his head covering and smoothed his garments, "within a few days, the memory of Jesus ben Joseph will be forgotten."

CHAPTER NINETEEN

T he Antonia's main courtyard was empty. Abel and his father
followed the screams and cries until they found people gathered outside a small courtyard near the gate of the fortress.
As they pushed their way through the crowd, Abel recognized
some of the people as those his father and the other priests had
gathered to call for Jesus ben Joseph's death. He saw his cousins
Mary and Lazarus with the Nazarene's disciples and his mother,
who was still wailing. Rabbi Nicodemus and Rabbi Joseph had
joined them. He noted Michael standing near Mary. Abel felt a
dark satisfaction at their looks of helpless grief.

Leaning against the outer wall of the courtyard were tall, rough-
hewn wooden stakes of different heights; some had a crossbeam
at the top and others shortly below it. Several of the crosses had a
block driven into the upright stack, to serve as a seat. A few had
a small footrest.

"It appears *that man* is not the only one to be crucified today."
Joktan pointed to where soldiers were measuring Jesus ben Joseph
and two other men against the different crosses. The Nazarene
could barely stand and slumped against the crosses. The other two
struggled against their chains, spitting and cursing, until their curses
turned to screams at the sting of a *flagrum taxillatum* wielded by
one of the Romans.

"Your *King of the Jews* will have company today," the centurion
walked up to them. He nodded towards the other prisoners. "Those
two are Joses bar Abidan and his brother Jachin. Those *brigands*
were part of Barabbas' rebellion last month." He snarled. "Barabbas killed six of my men before we captured him and nearly two

dozen of his rebels. We have been crucifying several each week as a warning against those who would defy Rome's authority.

"Barabbas was supposed to join them today; but now, because of your *hatred* for this Jesus ben Joseph, Governor Pilate had to release that—" he spat out a curse that made Abel blink, "and crucify your king."

"*That man* is not *our king!*" Joktan seethed.

"That's right," the centurion's snarl twisted into a cruel smile. "Tiberius Caesar is your king. Ahh…it appears that my men are ready. Excuse me," he bowed in a parody of respect, "but I have to see to the crucifixion of *your king.*"

Mary stared at the rocky soil, her heart heavy in her chest. She felt Michael's presence—Rabbi Joseph had suggested that the men place themselves in a protective circle around the women—but she could not bring herself to look at him. *He* promised *me he would help Jesus. But he didn't.* She stepped closer to the Teacher's mother.

When Daniel had arrived with Nicodemus' summons, she had jumped up. Martha—along with Ruth, Abigail and Joanna—had also stated they too were going to the fortress.

"No," Matthias had silenced Joanna. "You *and* I will remain here at your father's house with David and Deborah. Yes, I know, my parents could watch the children," he had said when she started to speak, "but consider. We do not know what the outcome of this day will be. I am certain your father would wish his home to be ready should any of Jesus' followers seek shelter here."

Lazarus and Simon were also adamant that their pregnant wives should remain there as well.

"Daniel told us some of what has happened," Lazarus had told Abigail. "If things have gotten so bad that your father is calling for Mary bat Eli, I do *not* wish you to see it."

"But Lazarus," she had said, blinking back tears, "this is the Teacher, this is *Jesus.* We owe him so much. If not for him, you would still be dead."

"I know, my beloved," he had said, smoothing away a tear before leaning over to kiss her forehead. "But, you are carrying our child, and risking this precious life will not help Jesus."

Simon also had used his and Martha's child as a reason for her not to accompany them. Mary was only a little surprised at how quickly her sister had acquiesced. Martha might be a strong-willed woman, but she loved her husband and respected his wisdom.

"I will stay here, too," Ruth had told Mary, "to help Joanna."

"Mary will stay—" Martha had begun only to be cut off by Mary.

"No. I *cannot* stay." She had turned to her brother. "I don't know whether I can do *anything* to help him, but I need to see Jesus, I need to…" she had trailed off, uncertain how to frame her thoughts, not really sure what her intentions were.

"I understand." Lazarus had laid his hand on her shoulder. "You may come, but stay close. Now, we must go."

The eleven remaining disciples were standing near the carriage where the Teacher's mother, his aunt and Mary Magdala sat waiting. Daniel had lingered long enough for Lazarus to help Mary into the carriage before slapping the reins against the horses' rumps. The four women had held on to the benches and each other as the carriage careened through the streets of Jerusalem, but no one had urged the servant to slow down.

When they arrived at the Antonia, Mary bat Eli did not even wait for the horses to come to a complete stop before jumping out of the carriage and rushing up the ramp.

Mary had followed the older woman. She wasn't even sure whether they could get past the soldiers at the gate. *Martha will say I am acting without thinking, but I don't care. I have to get to Jesus.*

She had come up short when she heard the Teacher's mother scream. She saw the reason for Mary's cry; Jesus, bound, bloodied and bruised, wearing a purple robe and a wreath of thorns piercing his forehead.

The disciples and other men had gathered as Mary took the older woman in her arms, trying to reassure her that they had misunderstood, that something could still be done. *Michael* promised *me.*

But Michael had shaken his head.

Mary had gasped as a great pressure squeezed her lungs. She had lowered her head onto Mary bat Eli's shoulder and began sobbing.

She lost all sense of time and even now could only remember what followed as fragments of a nightmare from which she could never awaken.

Jesus, bloodied and bruised beyond recognition, staggering as the Romans dropped the cross onto his shoulders and directed him out of the Antonia Fortress onto the streets of Jerusalem.

Jesus, falling to the ground, the cross striking the back of his head and forcing the thorny crown deeper into his brow. A soldier jumping off his horse to pull a large man from the crowd to carry the cross for the Teacher.

Jesus, stumbling through the City of David. The streets lined with crowds of people who, only days before, had welcomed him with cries of "Hosanna" announcing him as the promised Messiah. Now only a few people pled for his release; the rest spat upon him, threw rocks at him and screamed for his blood.

Jesus' mother had never been more than a few steps away from her son as he had stumbled painfully along the streets of Jerusalem. Salome and Mary Magdala had been on either side of the older woman, arms wrapped around her waist to provide support. When Jesus had fallen to the ground, his mother had run to him dropping to her knees to wipe his face with the edge of her robe. When the crowds had screamed for his death, she had begged Yahweh to help her son.

They had followed as Jesus had dragged himself out of the city gate to a barren rocky hill, one the local people called *Golgotha*, the Place of the Skull. Close enough to the main road to Jerusalem, the Romans chose this spot for crucifixions so that people coming and going from the City of David would be reminded of the penalty for crimes against the empire.

Most of the crowd had dispersed at the bottom of the hill. Hatred might have been the impetus of their cries for Jesus' death, but only a few—like Mary's uncle and cousin—would actually want to witness his crucifixion.

The Roman centurion had directed the man who carried Jesus' cross to a spot where holes dug into the hilltop gave evidence of previous crucifixions. The large man had dropped Jesus' cross and turned towards the Teacher.

Mary saw Jesus draw a ragged breath. "Thank you," he had said.

The large man had shaken his head, sweat pouring down his face, mingling with tears. "I am…so sorry," he had said.

"No! No! Noooo!"

Mary had spun around as piercing screams echoed across the hill.

The soldiers were forcing the other two prisoners—who had been stripped of their garments—down onto the crosses.

An older soldier had untied a basket from a horse and dropped it near the crosses. He had pulled out several ropes and tossed them to the soldiers near the prisoners, before lifting an *amphora*. "Should we give them the myrrh wine?" he asked the centurion.

The oil from myrrh was known to ease pain. Sometimes, the Romans would offer a condemned man a drink of myrrh mixed with wine to dull the pain of execution.

The centurion had looked at the prisoners. "No."

The two brigands had kicked and twisted, trying to jerk their hands and feet out of the soldiers' grasps; but several lashes from the *flagrum taxillatum* had left them bloodied, whimpering and still. Two soldiers had stretched the prisoners' arms out and tied their hands to the crossbeams, while another tied the legs—placing one foot on top of the other—to the base of the cross.

Reaching into the basket, the soldiers had pulled out hammers and long, tapered iron spikes. Moving to the first prisoner, one soldier had dropped down, placing his knee on top of the man's forearm to immobilize it, while the other had placed the tip of a spike in the center of the man's palm, angling it towards the forearm. Raising the hammer over his shoulder, the soldier had said, "This is for our brothers," and swung the hammer down, slamming it onto the head of the spike.

The prisoner's body had arched, straining against the ropes, screaming as the spike was driven into his palm, through his wrist and into the cross. He had fainted after his second hand was nailed to the cross, only to awake screaming as a spike was driven through his feet.

The soldiers had moved to the second prisoner, nailing him to the cross.

Then they turned to Jesus.

"No, no, no, no, no!" Mary bat Eli had pushed past the men and threw herself at her son, wrapping her arms around his bloodied body. "No, no, no!" she screamed. "Not my *son!* Not my *Jesus!*" Wails ripped from her throat carried on the wind. "Oh, Yahweh; *help him.*"

A soldier had raised the *flagrum taxillatum*, but stayed his arm by the sharp retort from the centurion. The Roman officer looked towards those who had been gathered around Jesus' mother. "Get her."

John ben Zebedee had crossed to the Teacher and gently placed his hands on the woman's shoulders. "Aunt. Come."

Mary had shaken off his hands and tightened her grasp on her son, leaning into his bloodied chest, whimpering.

Jesus had raised his head upward, tears streaming down his face. He lowered his gaze to John and nodded.

John's throat constricted with tears as he reached for Mary again. "Aunt. Please. You must."

Mary had looked at her nephew and then her son. She shook her head.

Jesus had lowered his head in a single nod.

Mary had lifted a trembling hand to his cheek. "I love you," her voice caught on the words.

Jesus had turned to kiss her palm. "I love you," he whispered.

The Teacher's mother released her hold on her son and had walked with John back to the others, her gaze never leaving Jesus' face.

Once certain that Salome and the other Mary were comforting Jesus' mother, Mary had stepped towards Lazarus. Her brother wrapped his arm around her shoulders, drawing her close as they watched the soldiers, carrying ropes, hammers and nails approach Jesus a second time.

Mary had caught her breath when she saw Jesus remove the purple robe and turn to lay down on the cross, stretching out his arms and legs.

"Lazarus, what is he doing?" she had whispered.

Her brother had shaken his head. "I don't know."

Everyone on the hilltop, Romans and Jews, had stopped to stare at the sight of Jesus lying down on top of his cross, neither fighting nor resisting. Finally, the centurion shook his head and looked at the old soldier. "Give him the drink."

The older soldier had carried the *amphora* to Jesus. Kneeling by the cross, he lifted the Teacher's head and put the jar to his bloodied lips. After one taste, Jesus closed his mouth and turned his head away.

"Eh! What's this? You don't want it? Fine," the soldier had shrugged his shoulders. "If you want to suffer, then suffer."

As with the other two prisoners, one of the soldiers had knelt on Jesus' arm while the other drove the spike through Jesus' hand. Too weakened to scream, Jesus moaned and writhed as the hammer drove the iron into his hands and feet.

The centurion had handed two flat pieces of wood to the soldiers. "Here's the *titulus*, the charge against the brigands."

"What about this one?" the soldier had indicated Jesus.

"Pilate said he is preparing a *titulus* for him and will send it soon. Now, nail these to the brigands' crosses and then finish this."

After nailing the wood above the heads of the condemned men, the soldiers had wrapped lengths of rope around the crossbeam above Jesus. Looping the ends of the ropes around the saddles of a horse, a soldier pulled on the horse's reins while the others guided the base of the cross, pulling it upright. Only then did Mary turn her face into Lazarus' shoulder as the cross bearing Jesus ben Joseph dropped into the hole with a flesh-ripping jolt.

Abel unconsciously squeezed his hands into fists when the Romans drove the nails into the Nazarene's flesh. He didn't care about the man, but he had seen enough blood for one day. However, he didn't look away; his father had already instructed him to watch each moment of the Nazarene's crucifixion. "We have to watch for anyone trying to free him."

"Father, do you truly think that Jesus ben Joseph's followers could over-power the Romans?"

"Not *them*," his father smirked at the group of people standing beneath the prisoner's cross. "But you told me that Judas Iscariot was *Sicarii*. If *that man* was also a part of them, they could easily raise forces to attack the soldiers. Come."

Abel followed Joktan as he strode across the hill to the Nazarene's cross. His father ignored the cluster of people weeping beneath the dying man—which included their kin, Lazarus and Mary—but looked up at the man dying above them.

"Look at you now, Jesus ben Joseph! You *claimed* you would destroy the Temple and rebuild it in three days. Save yourself if you are going to do that; you can't do it from a cross, can you?"

Joktan turned to look at the people gathered on Golgotha. Pointing to the Nazarene, he sneered, "He saved others, but he can't save himself." He looked up at the man on the cross. "You claim to be the *Messiah*, the *King of Israel*; you claimed to be the *Son of Yahweh!* If you are, then you have no need of rescue from the cross. Come down; nay, call upon Yahweh to deliver you. Then we will believe."

Lazarus stepped up to Joktan. "Uncle, have you no compassion?" He leaned in and lowered his voice. "That *woman* is his mother," he nodded towards the older women beneath Jesus' cross, "and the other is his aunt."

Joktan snorted. "I have no compassion for *this man* nor *his family* nor," his glance flayed his nephew, "*his followers*. If that woman had raised her son to respect the Law of Yahweh and the Temple Leaders, he would not be dying on that cross."

A soldier arrived on horseback and approached the centurion. He reached into a bag attached to his saddle and pulled out a flat piece of wood as well as a small scroll. He handed both to the centurion. "From Governor Pilate."

The centurion's eyebrows arched as he glanced at the wood. Breaking the wax seal with his thumbnail, he unrolled the scroll and read its contents. The corner of his mouth twitched as he rolled the scroll up and handed the piece of wood back to the soldier on horseback. "Nail the *titulus* to the prisoner's cross, so that all may see the charge against him."

Abel's father smoothed his beard over his tunic, before crossing his arms and lifting his chin as he watched the soldier maneuver his horse next to the Nazarene's cross to nail the piece of wood above the man's head. When the soldier pulled his horse away from the cross, Joktan scanned the wording and choked.

Written in Latin, Aramaic and Greek, the *titulus* read:

JESUS OF NAZARETH
THE KING OF THE JEWS

Spewing out a curse, Joktan stomped to the centurion. "What is that?" he demanded, pointing at the plaque. "The charge is wrong! You should not write, 'The King of the Jews,' but the charge should be, 'This man *claimed* to be king of the Jews.' I *demand* that you change that immediately!"

The centurion frowned indifferently. "No."

Joktan filled his lungs. "I'll take it up with Pontius Pilate," he shook his fist in the air.

"The governor thought you—or the High Priest—might say that," the centurion handed the scroll to Joktan, "so he sent this note for you."

Joktan looked at the scroll as if it were made from the hide of a pig, before taking it from the centurion and unrolling it. His eyebrows lowered as he read it. Cursing, he ripped the scroll in half, threw the pieces down, stepped on them and twisted his sandal, grinding them into the dirt. Without speaking—or even looking—at the centurion, he turned and stomped off.

The centurion's laughter followed Abel as he hurried to catch up with his father. "What did the scroll from Governor Pilate say?"

His father spewed out curses as he turned to look at the Romans laughing at him. "It said, '*What I have written, I have written.*'" He spat. "Roman *pigs!*" He glanced up at the sun. "Rabbi Caiaphas should be finished with the morning sacrifice by now. I am going to the Temple to report what has happened." He looked at his son. "You stay here and keep watch. I'll be back later." Without even waiting for his son's nod, he started down the rocky path.

Abel turned. *I'm not sure what Father thinks I can do,* he thought as he gazed over the people scattered across Golgotha.

The soldiers saw to their horses' needs and stacked their lances in a circle before settling beneath the crosses. One soldier brought out several skins of wine, another gathered the condemned men's clothing, including the purple robe worn by the Nazarene. The centurion poured out dice from a leather bag while another carved the squares and circles for the Game of the King into the hard earth beneath the crosses.

With the exception of a few priests, the crowd that the Temple Leaders had encouraged to call for the release of Barabbas and the crucifixion of Jesus had dwindled. It took hours—and sometimes days—for a man to die on a cross. While it was one thing to call for a man's death, it was another to actually watch it through to the end. In fact, had it not been for his father's command that he remain, Abel would have left with those people.

The rest on the hilltop were those who cared for the condemned men. That the only people beneath the three crosses were the Nazarene's family and followers gave evidence that no one cared about the men on the other two crosses.

The woman standing directly beneath the cross—the one Lazarus identified as Jesus bar Joseph's mother—was sobbing inconsolably, as were his aunt and another woman. Abel noticed that his cousin Mary had dropped her face into her hands, her shoulders shaking and then lifted her gaze to the Nazarene, weeping as if her heart was breaking.

Abel frowned. *I would expect his mother and aunt to grieve,* he thought, *but Mary is acting improperly. She is not this man's family; she is* nothing *to him.*

"Father."

All on the hilltop turned to look as Jesus ben Joseph spoke.

The Nazarene's face was lifted towards the sky. He groaned as he pressed on his nailed feet and pulled on his arms to lift himself up high enough to fill his lungs. "Father," he rasped, "forgive each of these people." He pulled up again. "They do not know," another breath, "what they are doing."

Jesus slumped down with a moan. He was still for a moment, his chest barely rising; then he opened his eyes and looked directly at Abel.

Abel started, unable to break his gaze away. He couldn't identify what he saw in the man's eyes. Not hatred. Not condemnation. Pain, yes; sadness, definitely; but there was something more. Something he had never experienced before. Whatever it was, he couldn't bear what he saw in Jesus' gaze; Abel lowered his eyes and turned away.

Mary covered her face with her hands. She couldn't bear to see what the soldiers, what the people—what their own priests—had done to the Teacher. Jesus, who had taught everyone about the love of Yahweh, had been beaten and tortured beyond recognition.

But these were the last hours she would have with him.

Never again would she have the opportunity to talk with him. Lazarus had told her that he had not been able to speak with Jesus about her actions of the other evening. *Was that really less than a week ago?* Now Jesus would die never knowing that her pouring the spikenard out was an act of thankfulness and not meant to be anything intimate. But that did not matter now. She forced herself to look up.

Jesus' face was covered in blood and bruises, his beard torn out by handfuls, his hair a bloodied mat where the crown of thorns was forced down over his brow.

Mary startled when he opened his eyes and looked at her.

In his gaze, Mary saw pain and sadness, but she also saw the expression he had when he told her that she was worth so much more. When he told her that she was beloved of Yahweh. When he had told her that what she had done for him was *beautiful.*

Tears streaming down her face, she tried to return that gaze, to let him know how she felt about him. That she was thankful for the day he had come into her life. That she was grateful for all he had done for her and for her family. That she was a new person because of his words and his teachings. That she would never forget him.

Staring into her eyes, Jesus nodded his head slowly, the hint of a smile quivering at the corner of his mouth.

Michael couldn't remember a night and day lasting so long. From the position of the molten sun—standing almost directly overhead—he guessed that Jesus had been on the cross for nearly three hours. Three horrendous hours in a day that wouldn't end.

All last night and into this morning, he kept hope that he—along with his father and Rabbi Joseph—would be able to secure Jesus' release. Even when he had heard the Teacher lied about, he thought he would be freed; after all, Jesus was innocent of all the charges Caiaphas and Annas brought against him. When Jesus was tortured by the lash of the Roman whip, Michael had believed his father's statement that there was hope; after all, Pontius Pilate obviously wanted to release him. Even when the crowd in the fortress had chosen the murderer Barabbas over Jesus, even then he thought that something would happen. After all, it had been only days since the people had run through the city streets, joyfully proclaiming Jesus as the promised *Messiah.*

All last night and into this morning, Michael was certain that he would be able to keep his promise to Mary and somehow free Jesus.

But he failed.

He had failed her; he remembered the look she had given him before she laid her head on Mary bat Eli's shoulder and wept. He ached when she moved away from him and refused to look at him.

He had failed the Teacher; he had failed Jesus. Now the one who had restored his friend Simon, the one who had resurrected his brother-in-law Lazarus, the one who had healed the hurts in Mary's heart—was hanging on a cross, dying.

Michael wanted to do something, but he was helpless. He couldn't hit Joktan ben Jacob's pompous face for fear such an action would draw unwanted Roman attention to those standing near him. He couldn't block out the laughter and comments of the soldiers as they callously played some game, tossing dice and claiming the possessions of the men hanging on the cross. He couldn't block out the sound of the heart-rending grief of the women as they clung to each other. He couldn't block out the sight of the Teacher pushing himself up on the spikes driven through his hands and feet, so he could draw a ragged breath.

Michael raged at the utter helplessness he felt.

"Hey!" the brigand on the left side of Jesus—the one called Jachin bar Abidan—groaned as he pushed against the spikes in his feet. "Was that priest right?" he asked Jesus. "Are you the promised *Messiah*?" He paused to draw another painful breath. "If you are, then *prove* it. Save yourself and save us too!"

Michael stepped towards the cross, ready to do something—*any-thing*—to shut this man's mouth, when Joses, the other brigand, spoke.

"Jachin! My brother," he gagged, gasping for air. Pausing to push up and fill his lungs, he continued. "Even now, even at death, don't you fear Yahweh?" Another pause. "We committed the crimes for which we are dying." Pause. "But this man," he nodded weakly towards Jesus, "he is innocent." Moaning, he pushed up to fill his lungs and fell back to look towards the Teacher. "Jesus ben Joseph," he wheezed, "please remember me when you come into your kingdom."

Jesus turned towards the man on his right, his eyes softening. "Joses bar Abidan," he said, "I promise you. On this day, you will be *with me* in paradise."

Michael startled when the Teacher turned to look at him.

Michael's throat tightened against tears as he looked at his friend. In Jesus' gaze, Michael saw sadness; he saw pain, but he didn't see the sadness and pain of betrayal. He saw something more; he saw *acceptance*, he saw *strength*, he saw *determination*, he saw...*trust*. Michael filled his lungs and lifted his head, trying to imitate what he saw in the Teacher's expression.

Jesus bowed his head slightly and turned to look at Mary bat Eli. "Mother."

The older woman gently pushed away Salome's and Mary Mag-dala's hands to walk to the base of the cross. Her eyes were red and she drew a ragged breath. "My son," she whimpered.

Jesus grimaced as he pulled up on the spikes to fill his lungs. Drop-ping back down, he looked towards his disciples. "John," he rasped.

John ben Zebedee glanced at his brother James and his mother—who nodded—and then stepped towards the cross. He looked up at his kinsman and friend, the muscles in his throat working as Jesus pulled up for another breath.

"Mother," the Teacher wheezed, "consider John as you would a son."

Mary bat Eli put her hand over her mouth as she looked from her son to her nephew and back to her son. She blinked away tears as she lowered her head in a single nod.

Jesus drew another painful breath. "John, care for her as you do your own mother."

John dashed a hand across his eyes and, looking at Jesus, he nodded. He stepped towards his aunt and slipped an arm around her waist. "Come...*mother*," he said and turned her to walk back to the outstretched arms of Salome and Mary Magdala.

"Michael."

He turned to see his father and Rabbi Joseph beckoning him. Stepping gently past the women, he crossed to his father. He lowered his voice. "Yes, sir?"

"Rabbi Joseph and I have been talking." Nicodemus glanced up at the cross. "I do not know how long...*this* will take, but we do not believe Jesus can last much longer."

"To be truthful," whispered Rabbi Joseph, "I am surprised he has survived this long." He cleared his throat. "Rome does not grant condemned men an honorable burial. Most of the time, they throw the bodies into a mass grave."

Michael frowned. "Or they leave the bodies on their crosses to rot.'

Nicodemus lowered his eyebrows. "We cannot allow that to happen. I am still convinced that Governor Pilate did not wish it to come to...*this*," he nodded towards Jesus' cross, "and only gave in due to the threat from Caiaphas."

"I am going to the governor now," Joseph said, "to request..." he blinked away tears, "Jesus' body. Between your father and myself, we will see that all that is proper is done for the Teacher. I hope to be back before..." he shook his head. "Michael, would you be so kind as to help me down this hill? The path is rocky."

"Certainly, sir." Michael escorted the older rabbi down the path.

At the base of the hill, Joseph paused. "This is a sad day. Sadder than I can ever remember." He turned to look back up where Jesus hung dying. "In my lifetime, I have had the sorrow to see Rome flog and crucify many men. Yet, never once have I seen a condemned man behave as Jesus did. He did not resist. Not once." He shook his head and glanced at the sky. "It's nearly the sixth hour. If I hurry, I'll be back soon."

Michael rejoined his father. "Rabbi Joseph is on his way."

"Good," his father said. "Joseph is a persuasive man. I am certain he will convince Pilate to allow us to bury Jesus." He let out a deep sigh. "I think we have...*what? Michael? Michael!*"

"*Father? Father! Where are you?*" Terrified, Michael reached out, swinging his hands, unable to see his father or anything at all.

Terror clutched Golgotha as darkness shrouded the earth.

CHAPTER TWENTY

Abel had never felt so terrified or so alone.

After that glance from the Nazarene, he had moved to a spot that was as far away from the crosses as he could be on Golgotha. He was there, on the edge of the hill, when darkness had descended like death.

Chaos reigned as the hilltop echoed with a cacophony of women's shrieks, men's cries, soldiers' curses and horses' screams, mingled with the sounds of footsteps crunching as people stumbled in the blackness to find others to cower near. After a time, other soldiers from the Antonia Fortress brought torches for the centurion and his men, and servants from Rabbi Nicodemus' house brought torches for the Nazarene's followers.

The people huddled around their torches, drawing sparse comfort from the flickering light. After calming the horses, the soldiers began passing around the skins of wine and muttering to themselves as they continued the Game of the King.

And carried on the winds were the moans of the three dying men on the crosses.

Abel never even considered moving near the soldiers and was certain that his cousins would not welcome him into their group. He knew his father would never think to send a torch for him; he also knew his father would expect him to remain on Golgotha until the Nazarene was dead. He dropped to the ground and wrapped his arms around himself and rocked back and forth, praying that Yahweh would save him from this darkness. It didn't matter whether his eyes were opened or closed for his prayers; there was no difference in the darkness.

He had no idea how long it had been since the night had fallen in the middle of the day. It could have been only minutes; it seemed like days.

The darkness left as quickly as it had come. One minute, the sky was black; the next, everyone on the hilltop was blinking against the pale light.

The Nazarene's followers embraced each other, inquiring whether everyone was alright. Romans shrugged, laughing shakily, before resuming their game.

Abel stood. From the sun's position in the sky—hanging halfway between the horizon and its zenith—he gauged it was nearing the ninth hour, the time when the perpetual sacrifice was offered daily in the Temple.

The sound of footsteps approaching drew everyone's attention as Rabbi Joseph bar Neriah and Rabbi David bar Mattan appeared at the edge of Golgotha. It was obvious from the way they avoided each other's gaze that their arrival was a coincidence.

The priest from Arimathea joined the Nazarene's followers, who gathered around to hear something he was saying.

Rabbi David glanced at Abel, before crossing to the Roman officer. Abel followed him.

"Centurion Maximus," Rabbi David said. "Rabbi Caiaphas went to speak with Governor Pilate before," he shrugged uncomfortably, "the sky went dark. I have been sent with a message for you." He handed the officer a scroll.

Maximus frowned as he took the scroll and broke the wax seal. Glancing at the message, he *harrumphed* and tossed the scroll into the middle of the crudely-drawn game at the foot of the crosses. "It appears that our game is going to be interrupted."

He looked at Abel. "Your High Priest does not want the crucified men to linger until tomorrow. Something about," he pointed to the scroll, "not desecrating your Passover week by leaving their bodies on the crosses. He asked Pilate that we break the prisoners' legs. Since they will not be able to push up on their feet to draw a breath, they will die faster." He looked at the game board. "Marcus Lucius, it looks like you are about to win; you get to kill them."

"*Eloi!*"

The soldier named Lucius froze in half crouch. They all turned towards the central cross.

Jesus ben Joseph pushed up on the spike in his feet, to drag in a ragged breath. "*Eloi!*" His voice was hoarse. "*Lama sabachthani?*"

The centurion glanced at Abel. "That's Hebrew?"

Abel nodded.

"What did he say?"

Abel licked his lips. "He called on Elijah."

"No, he did not," Rabbi Nicodemus approached the Roman. "Jesus was not calling on Elijah. He was calling on *Elohim*, our Yahweh." He turned to look at the Nazarene. "Jesus said, his voice softened, "'My God, My God, why have You forsaken me?'"

"Well, I agree that your God has abandoned him," the centurion turned back to his men. "Lucius, Pilate wants the prisoners to die quickly. Since you won the Game of the King, you get the honor of carrying out the governor's order."

The soldier Lucius walked to the basket to grab the hammer and then moved to the cross where Jachin bar Abidan was hanging.

"No, no, no!" the brigand pleaded weakly.

Holding the hammer shoulder high, the soldier announced, "This is for my brothers," and swung his arms in an arc, slamming the hammer against the man's knees.

The soldiers laughed as the brigand screamed and collapsed as the bones in his knees broke. Jachin died as the soldier Lucius walked to the cross on the other side of Jesus.

The Nazarene moaned as he pulled up for another breath. "I thirst."

Rabbi Nicodemus crossed to the group of soldiers. "Please!" he said. "Give him something to drink."

"Why?" the centurion sneered. "He's going to be dead in a few minutes."

"And how much time will it take to give him one last drink?" Nicodemus glanced over his shoulder and then stepped closer to the officer. "That woman is his mother. Please."

The centurion looked at the women gathered beneath the cross and then shrugged. "Why not?" He leaned over to pick up a wine skin and lifted it to his nose to sniff. He shivered. "I think this wine has turned to vinegar, but if he's *really* thirsty, he won't mind." He handed the wine skin to Nicodemus. "There's a sponge in the basket. Pour the wine over it and put it on a long stick. You can hold it up to your *King of the Jews*."

Lucius positioned the hammer in front of the brigand Joses bar Abidan.

Abel saw Jesus push up for air and then turned to nod his head at the man on his right.

The younger brigand nodded at the Nazarene and then closed his eyes as the hammer slammed into his knees.

The soldiers cheered and laughed—clapping each other on the back—as Joses died.

Abel watched Rabbi Nicodemus hurry to get the sponge, gesturing for Michael to pick up a large stick. The rabbi upended the wine skin, saturating the sponge. Michael stuck the sponge on the stick and then walked to the cross and lifted it to Jesus' lips.

The Nazarene's throat worked as he drank the wine vinegar.

Lucius shoved Michael aside. "*His Majesty* has had enough to drink. I won the game, so now I get to *kill the King*."

The other soldiers cheered as Lucius jumped around, holding the hammer over his head as an athlete would after winning a contest.

Jesus lifted himself once more to fill his lungs. "It. Is. Finished." His voice was strong, ringing across the hilltop of Golgotha, echoing to the City of David below. "Father, into *Your* hands I commit my spirit."

Jesus ben Joseph bowed his head. With a sigh, a final breath left his body.

"No!" the Nazarene's mother slumped to her knees with a heart-rending moan. "No. No. No. No!" Lifting her hands to the edge of her tunic, she pulled, ripping the neckline further. She spread her arms wide and looked upwards. "Noooooooooo!"

"What?" Lucius stopped jumping and looked at the Nazarene. "No, no. no! You can't die on your own! *I won!* I get to *kill* the King of the Jews!" He dropped the hammer and ran to where the soldiers' spears were stacked. Grabbing one, he rushed to the center cross and *thrust* it into Jesus ben Joseph's side.

Abel watched as blood and water gushed from the wound.

As the first drop of blood hit the ground, he heard a sound—like a deep murmur—beneath his feet. The sound began swelling, growing as if a massive arrow were shooting towards him. He noticed movement out of the corner of his eye and turned to see the trees and buildings in Jerusalem swaying violently. A pain in his foot forced his attention downward; pebbles and rocks were bouncing over his sandals. Suddenly, Abel felt a rush as the murmur changed to a roar and the earth beneath him exploded.

CHAPTER TWENTY-ONE

A bel examined the fissure in the street in front of the Palace of Herod. Wide as a man's arm span, it was deep enough to swallow a horse. The palace had suffered damage from the earthquake. The Phasael and Hippicus Towers were leaning drunkenly against each other and part of the Mariamne Tower was lying in a crumpled heap of stones.

Stepping around the gaping hole, Abel turned eastward towards the Temple. He focused on where he was walking; side-stepping debris, going around groups of people who were surveying the quake's damage, testing the street gingerly before putting his weight on it. Anything to forget what he had experienced on that hilltop.

The quake's initial shock made the ground of Golgotha heave as a wave on a stormy sea. Rocks—from pebbles to stones larger than a man's head—bounced up in the air, some breaking from the force of the earthquake. Cries and screams of terrified people and horses were carried on the dusty haze.

Abel had pushed himself up and tried to stand, only to be thrown to his knees as the shaking continued. He had tried a second time and jerked himself to one side as the Romans' hammer flew across the hill and thudded into the ground where he had fallen.

After what seemed like an eternity, the quake stopped. The Nazarene's followers helped each other up, asking if anyone had been injured. Maximus told his men to look after the horses.

Abel stood, planting his feet wide to regain balance and shook his head, trying to clear the pressure that had built up inside his ears. He helped Rabbi David—who was wiping blood from a cut on his brow—to stand.

"Great Mars, protect us!"

Abel turned to see the soldier Lucius pointing, his hand trembling towards the crosses.

The earthquake had shifted the two outer crosses; they were lying at drunken angles towards each other. The bodies of Jachin bar Abidan and his brother Joses were hanging face down—heads dangling as if in a bizarre obeisance—towards the center cross.

The central cross was untouched by the earthquake. It stood upright, the body of Jesus ben Joseph as it had been when he bowed his head and died.

As one, the Roman soldiers stepped away from the crosses, eyeing the center cross warily.

The centurion licked his lips. "Truly," he rasped, "this man was the Son of God."

Abel looked up at Jesus and then turned and ran down the hill of Golgotha.

Because of the earthquake's devastation, the sun was nearing the tenth hour by the time Abel reached the Temple.

The Temple complex had not escaped the quake's hand. Stones from the walls were in crumbled heaps on the marbled floor where, here and there, fissures split their white beauty. All around gold flakes from the glided walls drifted down, giving the air a golden sheen.

He ran through the Court of Women, past the Court of Priests and stopped at the entrance to the Holy Place. He gasped, his eyes widening.

Two priests were replacing the shewbread back on the table, while two more were wiping up oil from the overturned menorah, the seven-branched candelabrum. That these holy items had been toppled by the earthquake was not what shocked Abel.

It wasn't even the sight of his father—along with several other priests—at the far end of the Holy Place, holding up the edges of a heap of material. Abel didn't need to get closer to know that the material was fine linen, as thick as a man's hand, the height and width of the room, in shades of purple, blue and scarlet with images of winged cherubim embroidered into it.

What shocked Abel was the jagged rip from the top of the Veil of the Temple—which shielded the Holy of Holies—going through the material to the floor.

"Abel!" his father shouted. Handing his section of the Veil to another priest, Joktan rushed across the marbled floors to stop in front of his son. "Get out!" He pointed over Abel's shoulder. "You should not be here. You are *unclean!*"

His father stormed past him, leaving the Holy Place. Abel followed; they didn't stop until they had reached the top of the stairs at the Gate Beautiful, which led down into the Court of Gentiles. There Joktan turned to him.

"Since you are here," he frowned, "I assume that *the Nazarene* is dead?"

Abel nodded. "He is."

"Good." Joktan's stretched his mouth in a grim smile.

"Joktan? Is that Abel?"

Father and son turned to see the High Priest and Rabbi Annas approaching. Rabbi Caiaphas opened his mouth, but his father-in-law spoke first.

"Is *that man* dead?"

Abel glanced at the High Priest before nodding. "Yes, Rabbi Annas. Jesus ben Joseph is dead."

Annas' white eyebrows drew down. "Are you certain? Did you *examine* the body? Did you see the Romans break his legs?"

"N-n-no," Abel stuttered. "The Romans broke the legs of the other two men, but Jesus died before they got to him." He described the Roman piercing his side.

"I would rejoice over his death," Annas frowned, "but it appears we are not yet finished with *that man*. Caiaphas," he indicated his son-in-law, "just received word that Joseph bar Neriah went to Governor Pilate to request the Nazarene's body, in order to give him a *proper* burial.

"We all remember that, while he was living, we heard rumors of *that man* saying, 'After three days I will rise again.'" Annas turned to his son-in-law. "It has been a long day for all of us. Caiaphas, tomorrow you will go to Pilate and *request* that he put the seal of Rome on *that man's* tomb. To break a Roman seal without the governor's permission is a crime."

The High Priest nodded. "I'll also *request* that he assign soldiers to guard the tomb."

"That is a good idea. I think we will need to deal with all of *that* man's followers."

"All of them?" Caiaphas raised his eyebrows. "From what Rabbi Joktan says," he glanced at Joktan, who preened, "many of *that* man's followers—including Joseph bar Neriah—are staying at the home of Nicodemus ben Melech. He and Joseph are powerful and wealthy men. We cannot *deal* with them."

"You are correct." Annas cupped his chin and tapped a finger against his nose, thinking. "However, we can *deal* with the others."

"Do not forget my nephew and nieces," Joktan interjected. "By aligning themselves with *that man*, they have turned against the Law of Yahweh and His Temple. They deserve to be punished."

"Joktan ben Jacob, your *devotion* to the Law and the Temple never ceases to amaze me." Annas' smile did not reach his eyes. "Fine. Arrange to have Temple guards watch the homes of your nephew and nieces. Once we have dealt with the Nazarene's disciples, all of their possessions will be yours."

Abel saw his father's eyes gleam at the mention of his cousins' wealth.

Annas filled his lungs. "Now, we must see about repairing the Veil of the Temple." With a nod towards Joktan and a slight glance at Abel, Rabbi Annas and Rabbi Caiaphas turned to walk back into the Temple.

Abel waited until the two priests were out of listening distance. "Father," he gestured towards the inner courts of the Temple, "what happened?"

His father hunched his shoulders as he shot a quick glance around. "I...do not know." Fear etched Joktan's voice. "It was the *earthquake*."

Abel's heart skipped a beat. "The *earthquake* caused *that*?"

His father nodded. "I was in the Holy Place, with Rabbi Caiaphas and Rabbi Annas. At the ninth hour, just as we offered the perpetual sacrifice, the earthquake started.

"The tremors knocked over the menorah and the table for the shewbread. That table is heavy; it's made of pure marble. As we were trying to lift them, we heard a terrible rending sound." He

251

licked his lips. "The pillars supporting the Veil of the Temple were still standing, but in the middle of the upper edge of the Veil there was a...*tear*. As we watched," he paused, "it ripped from the top to the bottom."

CHAPTER TWENTY-TWO

A day of no sleep. A day of endless nightmares. It was the longest day Mary could remember and all she wanted to do was forget it; but it was burnt into her memory.

The earthquake throwing Mary to the ground as chaos erupted on Golgotha. Screaming as explosions shot rocks into the air to fall back and shatter as thousands of arrows.

The crosses of the brigands angled towards the cross of Jesus. Mary felt a bizarre relief that his body was not damaged from the quake, thankful that at least something had not caused Jesus further pain that day.

The Teacher's mother breaking loose from her sister's grasp to stumble to the foot of Jesus' cross. Reaching up to touch her son's bloodied body, she moaned, "Get him off! Get him off! Get him oooofffff!"

A soldier approached the older woman, but stopped when Rabbi Joseph rushed over to hand the centurion a scroll. While the officer read the message from the governor, the Teacher's followers gathered around her.

"Mary bat Eli," Rabbi Joseph spoke her name softly, as if to a child

"Rabbi Joseph," her gaze was wild, "don't let them touch Jesus' body."

"I won't."

"Don't let them leave his body on the cross."

"They won't. I spoke to Pontius Pilate; he is giving Jesus' body to us."

"Promise me," the Teacher's mother clutched his sleeve, "promise me that my son will receive a proper burial."

"I promise you." He nodded towards Rabbi Nicodemus. "Rabbi Nicodemus and I will do all that is needed."

"It is late. Where will you get the spices and precious oils and the linen to…" she stopped, her throat constricting.

"Lazarus ben Jacob," he said. *"He and Simon bar Hiram are merchants. They will go to their warehouse to get what is needed."*

"What about a tomb?" the older woman grew frantic. *"Our family does not have a tomb in Jerusalem. Where will we lay his body?"*

"Aunt," John crossed to her. *"Do not worry. I promise you that all will be done for Jesus. Now, Michael and I will take you, my mother and the other women back to Rabbi Nicodemus' house—"*

She shook her head. *"I can't. I have to help prepare his body. To wash it and anoint it."*

"Aunt…Mother." He took a deep breath. *"I promised Jesus that I would care for you as I care for my mother, remember?"*

She nodded, her eyes filling. *"And I promised to treat you as I would my son."*

"If my mother were weary, as you are, I would want her to eat and rest. Soon, you can go to the tomb."

Salome bat Eli stepped up, clasping her hands. *"Sister, I will stay here and help prepare his body."*

"As will I," Mary Magdala said. *"Tomorrow is the Sabbath; the day after that, we will take you to his tomb."*

When it looked as if the Teacher's mother would resist, Mary stepped up to her. *"Mary bat Eli, I will go with you to Rabbi Nicodemus' house. Come,"* she slipped an arm around the older woman's waist, *"let us leave this place."*

She kept her arm around the older Mary's waist, helping her step over fissures in the streets, guiding her around heaps of stone and other debris, until they reached Rabbi Nicodemus' house.

As they reached the path leading to Michael's home, the door opened; Joanna welcomed them, adding that food was prepared and waiting.

Without a word, Martha walked over to enfold the Teacher's mother in an embrace. *"May Yahweh console you among the other mourners of Zion and Jerusalem."*

A tremor ran through the older woman as Martha spoke the traditional expression of condolence to one who is newly bereaved. Mary bat Eli slumped against Martha, sobs rising from deep within.

Joanna escorted the Teacher's mother to her room and Michael excused himself to make sure the house was secure. "Father is concerned that there might be repercussions against Jesus' followers," he explained.

Mary followed Martha, Abigail and Ruth to the family courtyard where a simple meal of bread, cheese and dates was waiting. Mary ate a piece of bread and several dates, not because she was hungry, but because the other women had stayed behind to prepare the food for them.

When Mary set the cup of wine down on the table and pushed her plate away, Martha spoke. "Tell us what happened."

Dashing a hand across her eyes, she told the story as simply as she could. Some things she avoided, being aware of the delicate stomachs of the two pregnant women. Some things she could not bring herself to share.

When she finished, Joanna encouraged her to go to her bed chamber, a suggestion that was endorsed by Martha. "I know that it is only a short time since the sun has set, but you—" Martha looked towards the opened window and gasped.

Turning, Mary—along with Ruth and Abigail—echoed her sister's gasp.

The sky had not yet surrendered to the night; here and there, stars were beginning to prick the expanse. Hanging low in the eastern sky was the moon, as red as blood.

Mary was grateful when Martha escorted her to the bed chamber, but thankful that her sister did not linger. Wearied by far more than what had been the longest day of her entire life, Mary paused long enough to remove her soiled garments—*tomorrow I will burn them*—and wash off Golgotha's dirt, before lying down.

She threw an arm over her eyes and drew in a ragged breath, trying to will away the pain hammering behind her eyes. *Don't think about hammers!* But no matter how deep her exhaustion or how comfortable the bed's thick pallet, she could not elude the nightmares that waited just beyond the edge of sleep. She woke up screaming several times.

Finally, she sat up and lit the small lamp on the table next to her bed. She filled her lungs, taking in the fragrance of the delicate flowers that had been left in her room only days before. Flowers always had the ability to calm her. She knew that Rabbi Nicodemus' house had a courtyard with a flower garden. Mary remembered playing there with Ruth when they were children, hiding behind the tall ferns when their older siblings would come looking for them.

Standing, she crossed to the chests that held her clothing and pulled out the tunic and robe that were on top. The light from the lamp was not strong enough to identify the garments' colors, but she shrugged. *I do not care if they match.* She draped a covering over her head to avoid having to comb and braid her hair. Tying on her sandals, she picked up the lamp and left her room.

Mary walked down the corridor, the flame dancing above the oil lamp, to a small courtyard. It was positioned on the east side of the house to shield the room from the afternoon sun; a long window allowed in the night's cool air. The moon's creamy light—*thank Yahweh it is no longer crimson*—cast a soft light over the floors and walls of white marble. The only furnishings were a few low tables with thick pillows beneath. In the center was a small ornamental pool with water lilies; around the room were pots of tall ferns, lavender, dove's tail, jasmine and still more lilies.

She set the lamp on a table and moved among the plants, greeting each as old friends; pausing to touch a delicate petal here, bending to smell one there. Her own mother—*may her memory be blessed*—loved flowers; she had planted a garden in their Capernaum home just for flowers. It was in that garden last summer, when Lazarus had found her weeping and when Jesus had told her where her true value lay. When he had spoken of the fleeting beauty of the blossoms in the garden.

"*You, Mary bat Jacob, are worth so much more than these flowers,*" he had said. "*You have value because you are created by Yahweh and He loves you.*"

She smiled at the memory. *Yahweh loves me.* And so had Jesus. *No one will ever love me like he did.* Her brow wrinkled. *But not like the love of a husband.* It had been a year since she had first met Jesus and, for a time, even considered him as a potential husband. Now she realized that she thought of him as …she wasn't sure exactly what he had been to her. *Teacher.* Definitely a teacher, but she would always remember him as a friend.

How can life change so quickly? Just a few days ago, we were thanking Jesus for Lazarus' resurrection; now we're mourning his death. She realized she would never be able to walk through the streets of Jerusalem and not think about him, not remember the horrors of these past few days.

I can't believe he's dead. A sob caught in her chest. *Why couldn't we have done something?* Being raised in a wealthy family, she knew the power of money and position. *If Father were still alive, he would have rescued Jesus.* She discarded that thought as quickly it came. She realized that there are times when no amount of money, no amount of position, can make a difference.

Yet you blamed Michael for not being able to save Jesus.

She sighed. *Yes, I did. I was wrong to do that.* She knew she would have to apologize to him. Michael, along with Rabbi Nicodemus and Rabbi Joseph, did everything they could to secure Jesus' release. Michael and his father even opened their home to provide shelter to Jesus' followers.

Home.

I want to go home. I want to sleep in my bed, in my room. No; I don't want to go there. It was only a few days ago that we had the feast to thank Jesus for resurrecting Lazarus. Tears flowed down her cheeks as she remembered pouring the spikenard from her alabastron onto his feet.

Capernaum. Maybe I can convince Lazarus to go to Capernaum sooner this year, just like we did last year.

No. Her mouth drooped. *Jesus and the twelve spent last summer with us there.*

Bethany. Jerusalem. Capernaum. No matter where she went, memories of Jesus would be there. *That's alright.* She lifted her chin, dashing a hand across her wet eyes. *I never want to forget him.*

"Thank you, Jesus ben Joseph," she whispered. She felt sadness like a great pressure from above. "For everything you did for my family and for me. No matter how long I live—every day for the rest of my life—I will remember you."

The sound of footsteps caught her attention. Mary froze, listening. Someone was walking down the corridor.

She didn't want to have to explain her presence nor share her grief. She stood, picking up the lamp and looked around before crossing to slip behind a large fern near the window. She blew out the lamp and waited.

The echo of sandals against marble in the corridor grew louder and louder and then paused; whoever it was had stopped at the doorway to the courtyard. Mary held her breath, silently willing them to keep going. After a moment, the footsteps began again, but not down the corridor; they entered the courtyard.

She stepped further behind the plant, easing her sandals down carefully. *Why did I have to come here? Why did I think this garden would soothe me?* She focused on staying as still as possible and prayed that whoever it was would soon leave the enclosed garden.

Mary's eyes widened when she heard the soft intake of breath, followed by heart-rending sobs. Setting the lamp silently on the marble ledge of the window, she turned to move the fronds of the fern apart to peer through. Someone—a woman from the size of her body—was kneeling next to one of the pots of lilies not three cubits from her.

The woman's face was cupped in her hands. Her body shook as her sobs increased. Spreading her arms wide, she lifted her head to the ceiling. Her head covering fell back; the moonlight outlined the delicate features of Mary bat Eli.

"Why?" the older woman cried. "Why? *You* gave him to me. He was *my* son! Why did You let Jesus die?"

Mary's heart went out to the Teacher's mother. In her own life, she had experienced grief. She had lost her parents and—for four terrible days—she had lost her brother. While their deaths were sad—and in Lazarus' case, painful—they died in their homes, surrounded by people who loved them.

But not Mary bat Eli. She had lost her husband and now her first-born son. She didn't get to comfort and hold Jesus in his final hours. She had to stand helplessly by while he was lied about, arrested on false charges, beaten, subjected to unjust trials, tortured, mocked, humiliated and finally nailed to a cross to die a slow, painful death gasping for breath.

While Mary knew that everyone's grief was different, she realized that her sadness over Jesus did not match what Mary bat Eli was going through.

She stepped out from behind the fern to cross the floor and kneel by the Teacher's mother. Laying a hand on the other woman's shoulder, she whispered her name.

The Teacher's mother gasped softly and, without hesitation, turned to lay her head on Mary's shoulder.

Mary wrapped her arms around the older woman, rocking her, cooing and shushing as she would a babe. She listened as the Teacher's mother poured out her grief, poured out her love for her son. It was painful to hear her talk about him, but Mary remembered how comforting it had been, when she herself was bereaved, to speak of those she had lost, to bless their memories.

"Tell me more about Jesus," she encouraged the older woman.

The Teacher's mother clutched Mary's robe, digging her face further into Mary's shoulder and poured out more memories of his life.

It was sweet; it was painful. But then Mary caught her breath, her eyes widening, when the grieving mother's stories changed from moments of Jesus' life and childhood to announcements and songs of angels, and visits from magi and shepherds.

Dawn was spreading its pale, grey light over the horizon by the time Mary silently closed the door to Mary bat Eli's guest chamber.

Once she had begun speaking of Jesus, his mother had poured out memory after memory of him, each one more astounding than the last. Finally, she began slowing down, deep, shuddering yawns interspersing her tears, as exhaustion won out over grief, and she finally agreed to Mary's suggestion to lie down.

Mary escorted the older woman to the guest room set aside for her. She encouraged her to drink a cup of wine, before lying down on the thick pallet. Her breathing was soft and even by the time Mary crossed to the door and stepped into the hall.

"Mary," Ruth asked, "why are you here?"

Mary pivoted, a finger to her lips. She glanced at the door to the bed chamber and then gestured silently for her friend to follow. She led Ruth to her own guest chamber, and closed the door behind them, before speaking.

"Ruth, I think Mary bat Eli might be...." she paused, choosing her words cautiously, "losing her sanity." She told Ruth all the Teacher's mother had said.

Her friend frowned. "Are you certain you heard her correctly? An angel told her she would conceive even though she," color washed Ruth's cheeks, "had never been with a man?"

Mary nodded. "And that Yahweh's Holy Spirit would—what did she say...." Mary frowned, "*overshadow* her and she would conceive. And that the child—that Jesus—would be the *Son of Yahweh*."

"I have heard of grief causing people to do and say wild things," Ruth said. "When my mother died—may her memory be blessed— my father was not himself for several days."

"That was the same with my father," Mary said. "But to speak of Jesus as the Son of the Most High..." She shook her head. "What should we do?"

"I do not know," Ruth said, "but I am certain that Father will. He is in the family courtyard with Rabbi Joseph and Michael. I just took food and drink for them. Come. We will speak with them."

Mary blushed when Ruth mentioned her brother. She knew she would have to see him at some point, in order to apologize, but she wasn't ready for that moment to be today. She had no choice; their concern for Mary bat Eli outweighed her own embarrassment.

Without thinking, she looked down to smooth her garments, only to realize that she was wearing a green silk robe over a simple tunic of cream linen. The tunic was one she had brought from home to wear while cleaning the warehouse for Passover; there were still spots and stains on it. *A few hours ago, it didn't matter to me whether my tunic and robe matched.* She drew her mouth into a thin smile. *Now it does?*

She followed Ruth to the room set aside for family and a few of their guests. Frescos of palm trees and pomegranates decorated the walls and, around the room, were niches displaying antiques, delicate glassware edged with gold or silver and *amphorae* filled with expensive fragrant oils. Should anyone wish to read, a shelf in one corner held scrolls.

Rabbi Nicodemus, Rabbi Joseph and Michael were seated at a table in the center of the room. In front of them were bowls filled with white cheese, grapes and dates and a platter of bread. Rabbi Nicodemus was pouring cups of goat's milk.

The three men looked up as she and Ruth entered the room; Michael jumped up, eyeing her warily. Mary noted that his wavy black hair clung damply around his head and he wore fresh garments. *He found time to bathe,* she thought and immediately chided herself when she noticed the dark crescents shadowing his eyes. *He has had less sleep than the rest of us.*

"Ah, Ruth. Good morning, Mary bat Jacob," Rabbi Nicodemus had a sad smile, "although I do not think it appropriate to add 'time of gladness.'"

"Good morning, Rabbi Nicodemus, Rabbi Joseph," Mary said. She glanced at Michael under thick lashes, "Good morning, Michael."

Michael nodded his head. "Good morning, Mary." He lingered over her name.

"Sir," Mary said, "I have just come from Jesus' mother."

"That poor woman," Rabbi Nicodemus' mouth turned further down. "She will find some comfort in knowing that her son was buried with honor. Salome bat Eli and Mary Magdala said they will take her to his tomb as soon after Sabbath as is appropriate."

"Father," Ruth said, "Mary told me about something about Mary bat Eli that has us concerned."

"What has happened?"

Mary was silent for a moment or two, not from embarrassment, but from consideration of how best to share the story. As simply as she could, she told them about what had transpired in the garden courtyard.

"Rabbi Nicodemus, Rabbi Joseph," she ended, "I think Mary's grief over Jesus has shaken her sanity."

"This is serious indeed," Ruth's father said. "What do you think, Joseph?"

Heavy brows lowered as the two elderly rabbis turned towards one another, arms folded, hands stroking their beards.

"I have seen grief affect people's reasoning," Rabbi Joseph said, "making it difficult to make decisions or sending someone into a deep depression."

"As have I."

"But I have never seen grief cause someone who is known to be upright to have...*delusions* that could be considered by some to be *blasphemous*."

"To claim to have conceived by the power of Yahweh's Holy Spirit," Rabbi Nicodemus said. "That can only be from a loss of sanity, for where else would she get that idea?"

"The prophet Isaiah spoke of something like this to King Ahaz," Rabbi Joseph closed his eyes in concentration. "He said, '*Yahweh Himself will give you a sign: The virgin will be with child and will give birth to a son, and will call him Immanuel.*'"

"So, my friend, are you saying that Mary bat Eli, in her grief, believes that she is the fulfillment of this prophecy?"

"I do not know what is in that poor woman's mind," Rabbi Joseph replied. "I am saying that the idea of a virgin conceiving does not necessarily come as a result of insanity."

"You are correct. Thank you, Mary," Rabbi Nicodemus turned to her, "for bringing this to our attention. We will discuss this further and take it up with John ben Zebedee when he awakens. Speaking of sleep, you look exhausted, my child. Ruth, take Mary back to her chamber so she can sleep."

As she followed Ruth across the marbled floor, the two elderly rabbis continued their discussion, offering medical examples, discussing scriptures and possible aid for the Teacher's mother.

Stepping out of the room into the corridor, she glanced back and caught Michael watching her. He met her gaze, his expression never changing, never revealing his thoughts.

Mary finally pulled her eyes away and hurried after Ruth. Her insides felt like a beehive shaken and tossed away.

"Mary. Mary!" She heard her name as if from a distance. "*Mary!*" Something shook her shoulder. "Wake up!"

She woke and sat up in one fluid, disoriented movement. "Huh? What?" She turned, trying to shake off the dregs of sleep, to see Martha kneeling by her bed. The look on her sister's face—alarm mixed with anger—doused Mary like a bucket of water from a cold mountain spring. "Martha!" She grabbed her arm. "What is it? Are you alright? Is the baby alright?"

"I am alright, as is my babe," she laid a hand on the swell beneath the black linen of her robe. Mary wondered idly where her sister had found clothing for mourning. "You must get dressed and go to the family courtyard. Simon and Lazarus are waiting."

"What is wrong?"

"They won't say anything until we are all gathered." She crossed to the door and opened it. "Now, hurry!"

Mary hurried to the table holding a bowl and *amphora* of water. She twisted her hair in a knot and poured water into the bowl to splash her face, thankful that she had taken time to bathe before falling back into bed.

Stepping to the chest that held her clothes, she riffled through the garments. She had not packed anything in black, but surely there was something that would be appropriate for mourning. She finally found a dove-grey robe and tunic. Slipping them on, she wrapped a dark blue girdle around her waist and a matching covering over her hair. Tying on her sandals, she rushed out of her room and hurried through the corridor and up a flight of stairs to the family courtyard.

It was here that, less than a week before, they had first met Jesus' mother, his aunt and Mary Magdala.

She found many of the same people present as had been there that night. Rabbi Nicodemus, Rabbi Joseph; Joanna and Matthias; Ruth stood next to Michael; Abigail leaned on Lazarus while Martha crossed to link her arm with Simon's. Whereas the atmosphere of the previous time had been jubilant, on this morning, tension permeated the room.

Michael saw her the moment she entered; his gaze held hers, still as inscrutable as it had been just hours before.

She looked away and crossed to stand next to her sister.

"Mary is here now," Martha said. "Now, please tell us what has happened."

Lazarus looked at Simon, who nodded. "We won't be able to go to our homes."

"What?" "Why not?" Mary and Martha said on top of one another.

"Because," Lazarus filled his lungs, "there are guards stationed around our houses."

Questions echoed around the room until Rabbi Nicodemus lifted a hand. "Please. Please. Let them tell us what happened and then we can ask questions. Now Lazarus," he turned to his son-in-law, "please continue."

Lazarus nodded before turning to the assembled group. "Samuel ben Efraim came to see Simon and me this morning. He said he had been to Bethany, to take a foal to Lamech, the inn keeper. Knowing that—because of what *happened*—" he swallowed, "we were still here, he decided to check on our house for us. He rode down the street and saw men—Temple guards—in the front of our house. He said they were armed with swords and lances.

"He rode past, trying not to draw attention to himself, and then rode over to Martha and Simon's house. There were guards stationed around their house as well."

"I don't understand." Mary said, "Who would order Temple guards to watch our houses?"

"I do not know for sure," Lazarus said, "but I suspect that our uncle arranged for it."

"Joktan?" Mary shook her head. "But why?"

"Is it not clear?" Martha's color was high, her nostrils flaring. "He wants our possessions. Our wealth. He has wanted them for years. When Lazarus—" she glanced at her brother.

"—when I died," he added.

Martha nodded. "Uncle told Mary and me that, as our near kinsman, he had control of our inheritance. It was then Rabbi Joseph," she smiled at the elderly man, "told Simon that he and I were still betrothed. That took my inheritance out of our uncle's control."

"And our uncle *informed* me that I would marry our cousin Abel—" Mary slanted a glance towards Michael; his face could have been carved from stone. "I refused, of course, but under the law, he still had control of my inheritance. He declared I would not receive a single copper penny. When…," she swallowed, "when *Jesus* raised Lazarus from the dead, that ruined all of our uncle's plans."

"I suspected on that day that Joktan ben Philemon hated the Teacher," Rabbi Joseph said. "It was obvious from the moment Jesus was arrested that Joktan has been working hand in fist with Caiaphas and Annas to find a way to deal with the Teacher. Nicodemus," he nodded towards his friend, "and I discussed this and we believe that Caiaphas and Annas—and those who stand with them—are not going to stop with just killing Jesus. We think they are going to *deal with* his followers."

"And once *we*, as followers of Jesus, are *dealt with*," Lazarus frowned, "our uncle inherits our possessions and wealth."

Mary ground her teeth. "What can we do?"

Lazarus shrugged, shaking his head. "Nothing."

"What?" Her eyes widened. "First he helps to *kill* Jesus and now he gets *our* houses, *our* things, *our* wealth? And we will do *nothing*?"

"What can we do?" Lazarus put his hands on her shoulders. "The Temple guards have swords, they have lances. We do not. Even if we did have weapons, would you want us to attack them because of *things*, because of *money*? If Jesus taught us nothing else, we learned that people—not things—have value."

Mary stared into her brother's eyes; after a moment, she nodded. "When you died, our uncle commanded that I stop following Jesus or lose everything that was mine. I realized at that moment that following the Teacher was worth more than any*thing*." She swallowed, her eyes misting. "Even though Jesus is gone, I will never forget what he taught. Fine!" She sliced the air with her hand. "Let our uncle have our things. What we have is of greater value."

Lazarus smiled. "That is my wise girl."

"What will we do?" Abigail asked.

"Simon and I have been talking. We agree that we have to leave Jerusalem. Leave Bethany."

"We also spoke of this last night," John ben Zebedee indicated the other ten disciples. "Tomorrow we are going back to our families in Capernaum. I will take my aunt—" he smiled sadly, "I should say my *second mother*—back to my house. Now, if you will excuse us, I need to inform her of our plans."

"Although Michael and I wish you would stay with us longer," Nicodemus said, "we understand. Abigail will arrange a special meal for your last evening with us."

After the eleven disciples left the room, Martha turned to Simon. "Will we go to Capernaum?"

Simon shook his head. "That is not safe either. I do not think your uncle will stop with taking our houses *here*."

"But uncle hated our house in Capernaum," Martha said. "He always refused to stay in a dwelling he felt had been influenced by Gentiles."

"That would be reason enough to sell it."

"You are right, my husband," Martha said. "Wealth and power are all that ever mattered to our uncle." She lifted her chin. "So, where will we all go?"

"There are many places we can choose from," Lazarus said. "Through our travels, Simon and I have established business connections in many cities. Personally, I was drawn to Kition in Cyprus." He smiled at Abigail. "It is a beautiful place; I think you will like it."

"As long as we are together, Beloved," she laid her head on his shoulder, "any place will be wonderful."

"What about us, Simon?" Martha asked. "Will we go to Kition?"

"While I agree with Lazarus that Kition is beautiful, I am drawn to northern regions. I have often wanted to expand our business to Gaul."

"I might journey with you, should you decide to go there," Joseph said. "I have heard that Gaul has cooler climes. I would like to experience it."

"Well, our destinations are settled," Lazarus said.

"And Mary?" Martha asked. "As you are her brother, will she go with you or will she come with us?"

Lazarus turned to look at Mary. "She has shown great wisdom today. I think she should choose."

Mary's eyebrows climbed. "I *choose?*"

Lazarus smiled. "Yes. You choose."

She looked at Martha, who smiled and nodded.

"I do not know," Mary shook her head. "I have always lived with you *and* with Martha. Even after you both married and Martha moved to Simon's house, we were only a few streets apart. I had not thought we would ever be separated. I will have to think about this."

"Well, your decision does not have to be made today," Martha slipped an arm around her shoulders. "In the meantime, we must prepare." She harrumphed. "Although our uncle has seen to it that we do not have many things left to us to gather."

"He might have guards around our houses," Lazarus said, "but as of yesterday, when Simon and I went to the warehouse to get the," he swallowed, "*oils and spices for the Teacher's body*, there were no guards there. Beyond that, Simon and I have monies in banks in the different places where we conduct business. While we won't be able to take our clothes and other things from our houses, we can gather other items from our warehouse. Once we arrive at our destinations, we can purchase whatever we need."

"I don't want to have to pack many *things*," Martha said, "but I do want our mother's goblets. We took them to use for Passover, they are still at the warehouse."

"Simon and I are going there now. I will be sure to get them," Lazarus said. "Now come; there is much to do."

Mary turned to leave the room, her mind in a swirl. *We're leaving. Good. But why does my heart feel heavy? I care not that I am leaving things behind. But we are not going to be together and I have to choose who I will be with.* Her heart ached. *I might never see the rest of them again.*

"No. Mary. Stop."

Mary froze. As Michael spoke her name, awareness shot through her like a wandering star in a dark night sky. She turned, her heart beating wildly.

Michael had reached out to her. "You can't." The muscles in his throat worked. "Please. I can't."

"Michael," Rabbi Nicodemus started, but his son interrupted. "Father, I must."

Must? Mary thought. She glanced at her siblings. Martha's eyebrows were arched in confusion. Lazarus and Simon were exchanging grins in that irritating way men had.

In quick steps, Michael strode across the room to stop in front of her. "I can't let you leave, without telling you, without allowing me...to ask." He licked his lips. "I have spoken to my father, to your brother...no," he shook his head, "that's not how I wished to begin."

"Take a deep breath, my son," Rabbi Nicodemus was grinning, "and begin again."

Michael filled his lungs and lifted his face to blow air towards the ceiling, before looking at her. "I have known you since you were born. For years I considered you as I would a sister. However, since last year, my...*views*...changed. Many men would want you for your beauty alone; but I saw more in you."

Mary's thick lashes dropped over her eyes. *Wisdom and beauty,* he had said to her, *a rare find.*

Michael shook his head, "I am stumbling over my words as a horse treading on a rocky path. Mary, I spoke with my father and with your brother. They advised me to wait, stating that a woman would not wish for such an important event to be crowded into a festival week.

"But with everything that has happened, I cannot wait any longer. Mary bat Jacob, I care for you—no, I *love* you—and want to become your husband."

Mary's eyes misted. "Michael, I...don't...know what to say."

"I understand," his eyes grew sad. "Recently, I came to think that perhaps you *cared* for...*Jesus ben Joseph* as more than a teacher. I honor him and what he did for *you* and your family, but...I mean..." Michael filled his lungs and finished in a rush, "I promise I will never be jealous of his memory."

"No," Mary shook her head quickly. "That's *not* what I meant," she said as despair washed over Michael's expression. "I did care for the Teacher and I confess that, for a brief time, even wondered about..." she blushed and stared at the floor. "But I soon realized that what I felt for Jesus ben Joseph, *what I still feel for him*, were not the affections that a woman feels for," she looked up at Michael, a shy smile touching her lips, "a *husband*."

Michael blinked, as if uncertain of what he had heard. Then his gaze cleared, and he smiled. "Truly?"

She smiled, joy rushing through her. "Truly," she whispered.

"What is happening here?"

Mary turned to see Martha's mouth opened, her expression outraged. "This can't happen!" She looked at her brother's grinning face, "I mean, this is not proper," she looked at her husband's grinning face. "I mean, this is not how," she looked at Rabbi Nicodemus— who was also grinning, "we do things," she finished in a small voice.

"I am sorry, Martha bat Jacob," Nicodemus said, "that my son felt the need to express himself *now*." He grinned at Michael before looking back at her. "You are correct; this is not how we have done things. But things are changing. Jesus ben Joseph—may his memory be blessed—brought *much* change."

Lazarus crossed to Mary and took her hands in his. "As I told you once before, although the Law gives me the right to choose a husband for you, I would never give you away as a possession." He looked at Michael. "Michael ben Nicodemus is a good man. He honors our people and obeys the Laws of Yahweh. While we have not yet discussed the conditions of the *mohar*," he drew his eyebrows down in a mock frown, "I am certain that I will be more than satisfied that you will be cared for *should you choose to accept him*." He looked at Mary but jerked his head towards Michael.

"Oh! Did I not make myself clear?" Mary looked at Michael, her eyes soft. "My father and mother—may their memories be blessed—always spoke highly of you. Ruth," she grinned at her friend, "considers you the best brother in the world. As you said, I have known you since my birth and you are one of the few people who saw value in *me*, Mary bat Jacob, not just my appearance nor my wealth. What I feel for you, I have felt for *no other man*." She smiled. "Yes, I will become your wife."

Michael released a deep breath. He turned to his father. "Please join us." As Nicodemus moved to stand near them, Michael reached into his girdle and drew out a soft leather pouch. Untying the strings, he drew out a small gold band. "My father gave this to my mother—may her memory be blessed—" he looked at his father, who was blinking back tears, "on the day they became betrothed. After her death, Father gave it to me, to one day give to my betrothed. I have carried it with me since the other day when I spoke with Father and Lazarus. If the ring does not fit, I will have the goldsmith adjust it."

Mary removed her left hand from Lazarus' grasp and extended it to Michael. He slid the ring onto her second finger as he repeated the phrase that would join them, "Behold, you are consecrated unto me with this ring, according to the Laws of Moses and Israel."

Mary lifted her hand to look at the ring. "It's a perfect fit, just as you are," she lifted her gaze to Michael, "*my husband.*" She realized she named him truthfully for, according to the Law, they were now considered husband and wife.

"Mazel tov my children!" Nicodemus wrapped his arms around both of their shoulders and squeezed. "May Yahweh bless you with many years of happiness and with many children."

"Mazel tov!" Lazarus hugged them, repeated Nicodemus' blessing of years and children.

"Wait! What are you doing?" Martha shook her head. "How can they become betrothed? We have to leave. Mary is coming with one of us," she looked at Lazarus. "You said so."

"She will go with you," Michael said. He looked at Martha. "I honor the traditions of our people and would not wish to offend the family of my *betrothed wife.*" He smiled at Mary. "I understand that you must go with your brother or sister. But I wanted you to know, before you left, that you were *betrothed to me.*" He took her hands and turned her to face him, "No matter where you go, no matter where you are, I will find you. Be waiting for me, for this I vow: I will come for you."

CHAPTER TWENTY-THREE

18 Nisan 3793

Mary squeezed her eyes against the sunlight streaming through the latticed windows. She turned onto her left side, pulled the sheet over her shoulder and tucked her hand beneath her cheek. She smiled sleepily at the feel of the gold ring against her skin. Breathing deeply, she *willed* herself to drift back to her dream of where Ruth and Leah rushed into the house to announce, "He's coming!"

She moaned...*no wait, that wasn't me. Who was moaning?*

Suddenly the floor beneath her bed *jumped*, tossing her off the thick pallet. Sprawling onto the floor, it took Mary only seconds to identify it.

Earthquake. But its force was not that of a true earthquake; it felt more like the earth was having second thoughts.

The small table near her tottered over, the bowl and *amphora* shattering as they hit the floor. Mary grabbed the pallet and pulled it over her body. Holding onto the bedding with one hand, she scooted into the center of the room away from any other furnishings that might be tossed from the quake.

Before the tremors subsided completely, she heard footsteps running down the corridor to stop at her chamber. "Mary!" Michael pounded on the door. "Are you alright?"

"I am fine. Wait a moment."

Pulling herself to her knees, she paused, giving the earth a chance to settle, before standing. She stepped around the shards of glass, to open the chest holding her clothes. Pulling out a thick blue robe,

271

she slipped it over her night garment and tied it with a girdle. She draped a soft blue covering over her hair; lifting the fabric, she draped it across her nose to tuck behind her right ear. *The room might be in shambles,* she thought, *but I will* not *be unveiled in the presence of my betrothed husband.* She smiled at that last word, savoring it as she would one of Martha's date cakes.

She crossed the room and opened the door to Michael. She smiled to see that he was wearing the same tunic he had worn to the feast that Joanna and Ruth had hurriedly arranged last night to celebrate their betrothal. Woven of the finest linen in the color of beaten gold, the garment had silver threads edging the hem, sleeves and neckline. He had worn a wide silver girdle and a golden turban and sleeveless robe for the feast; those last items were missing this morning. His was barefoot and hair stood out from his head in wild curls.

"Mary! Are you alright?" he repeated.

She smiled. "I am fine; although a bit unsettled."

She blushed when she noticed that he was staring at her lips hidden behind the veil. "We…uh, should check on the others."

"What?" Michael shook himself, spots of color on his cheeks. "Oh, uh…yes…we should." He stepped to the side to allow her to leave the room.

Following Michael, it took them a short time to determine that everyone was alright. At Nicodemus' suggestion, they all gathered in the dining room while servants prepared a light meal. "Perhaps some bread and cheese and fruit. I'm certain no one would wish for a heavy meal after the quake." Little David and Deborah were frightened by the earthquake. Nicodemus calmed his grandchildren by re-enacting how the quake had thrown him off the bed. Soon, everyone was laughing—and even Mary bat Eli smiled—as the toddlers giggled and rolled on the floor, yelling, "Earthquake! Earthquake!"

"Wait! Listen," Joanna said. She tilted her head. "Is that someone knocking at the door?"

In a heartbeat, Michael jumped up and moved to stand between Mary and the archway to the corridor. Lazarus moved to shield

Abigail and Simon stepped in front of Martha. Matthias and Joanna picked up their children and turned to hold them between their bodies. Ruth ran to stand by her father and Rabbi Joseph and the eleven disciples encircled Mary bat Eli.

A moment later, they heard the sound of footsteps hurrying to the room. Baruch entered. "Rabbi Nicodemus," was all he said before Mary Magdala rushed passed him.

"Rabbi Nicodemus," she said, her eyes darting around the room, "where is Peter—" she stopped as she located Peter bar Jonah. Rushing up to the big fisherman, she grabbed his sleeves. "Peter! Peter!" she cried. "You must come!"

Everyone gathered around Mary and Peter. Their voices rose as they demanded to know what had happened, what was wrong, what did they need to do? Finally, Peter bellowed, "Silence!"

They stopped.

"Pardon, Rabbi Nicodemus," Peter waited for the rabbi's nod before turning to Mary. "What is it Mary?"

"You must come!" she repeated. "You and John."

"Come?" John stepped up to her. "Come where? Why?"

Mary noticed the Teacher's mother and ran up to embrace her. "Mary bat Eli. I have seen him!" Her eyes misted. "I have seen *Jesus*."

The older woman shook her head. "I don't understand."

"What?" John ran over to her. "What do you mean, you have seen *Jesus*?"

"You couldn't have seen him," Thomas cried. "He's—" he glanced at the Teacher's mother and softened his voice, "he's *dead*."

"No," Mary Magdala shook her head. "No, he's not. He's *alive*."

Nicodemus crossed to the other two Marys. "Mary Magdala," he spoke softly, "I am afraid we do not understand. Would you please explain what has happened?"

Mary nodded, "Certainly, Rabbi Nicodemus," she said. She drew a deep breath. "I had gone to the tomb this morning, to anoint Jesus' body with more oils. I was nearing the tomb when the earthquake hit. It threw me to the ground. When the quake stopped, I got up and went on to the tomb. When I arrived, the stone that had been in front of the tomb was rolled to one side."

"It had been rolled to one side?" Peter repeated. "How? It took most of us to roll it in place."

"I don't know how," she said. "I ran up and looked inside the tomb and saw two men."

"Two men?" John asked.

Mary nodded. "They were *huge*—taller than any man I have ever seen—and their garments *glowed* like the morning sun. They were sitting on the stone where we had laid Jesus' body, one at the head and one at the foot."

"They were seated near Jesus' body?" James asked.

"No," Mary shook her head. "They were not. Jesus' body was *not there.*"

"These men took it?" Peter growled.

"They were not *men*," Mary said. "Don't you understand? They *glowed!* The men were *angels!*"

"Angels?" Thomas sneered. "You are mistaken."

"I am not!" she insisted. "They were *angels!* I was so terrified, I fell to my knees and began crying. Then I heard a voice; no, it sounded like many voices. *'Why are you looking for the living among the dead?'*

"I looked up and saw that the two angels were talking to me, but it did not sound like two voices; it sounded like a *multitude* of voices. *'He is not here; He has risen,'* they said. *'Remember what He told you when He was still with you, "The Son of Yahweh will be killed and after three days, I will come back to life."'*

"They looked *beyond* me and bowed their heads. I turned to see what they were looking at and saw a man." She looked at Rabbi Nicodemus, "I thought that perhaps you had sent a servant to care for the tomb. I ran up to the man.

"He said, 'Woman, why are you crying? Who is it you are looking for?'

"I said, 'Sir, if you have carried his body away, please tell me and I will get it.'

"Then he said, 'Mary.'" She lifted her head, her eyes glistening. "I *knew* that voice; I *knew* it was *Jesus!* I cried 'Teacher!' and reached to embrace him.

"He told me not to hold on to him, because he had not returned to his Father. He told me to find you all and tell you, 'I am returning to my Father and your Father, to my God and your God.'

"Peter," she grabbed his forearms. "John, James, *Mary!*" She turned to embrace the older woman. "I have *seen* him! Jesus is *alive!*"

Abel reached out as his father stumbled over a newly formed fissure.

"*Racha!* You fool!" His father growled, jerking his arm away. "Do not *touch* me! You are still *unclean!*" He straightened his garments. "Come! We must hurry. Once we finish at the Temple, I must go to Bethany to inspect our new houses."

Abel flushed that his father would shame him in front of a servant. Malchus had arrived at their home less than an hour after the earthquake, with a summons from the High Priest for both of them.

Grinding his teeth, Abel hurried after his father and the servant. When they reached the Temple, Malchus led them to the Court of Gentiles where the High Priest and Rabbi Annas were speaking with four Roman soldiers. As they drew near, Abel recognized one as Marcus Lucius, the solider who had been on Golgotha.

It was the same man, yet he was not the same. Gone was the swaggering solider who had laughed as he won the Game of the Kings, who had rejoiced as he broke the knees of the two brigands, who had rushed to thrust a spear into the side of Jesus ben Joseph.

Lucius and the other soldiers were trembling, their eyes wide. The Romans startled when Abel walked up with his father and Malchus.

"Greetings, Rabbi Caiaphas, Rabbi Annas," his father bowed his head. "Time of gladness."

Abel repeated his father's greetings.

"There is nothing to be *glad* about, Joktan ben Philemon," Rabbi Annas snarled.

Abel bit his lips to keep from smiling at the shocked expression on his father's face.

"I do not understand," his father looked between the two older priests. "Has something happened?"

"Yes, something has *happened,*" Caiaphas pointed to the soldiers.

"These men were supposed to be guarding the Nazarene's tomb; instead, they got *drunk*."

Lucius' eyes flashed. "We were not *drunk*!"

"Oh really?" the High Priest sneered. "Then how else would you explain what you *claimed* happened?"

"What we told you *happened*," one of the other soldiers said. "Two *angels* came down out of the sky. When they touched the stone in front of the tomb, an earthquake shook the ground."

"That's right," said the third soldier. "The earthquake knocked us all down. While we watched, these angels touched the stone and it rolled away like it was no heavier than a leaf."

"The stone covering the tomb was moved?" Abel's father asked. "The stone that had the seal of Rome on it?"

Lucius nodded his head.

"Tell him what happened then," Rabbi Caiaphas said.

As one, the Romans stared at the marbled floor. And said nothing.

"I'll tell you what they *claimed* happened," Rabbi Annas said. "They *claim* that after the *angels* appeared, after they touched the stone, after the earthquake shook the ground, knocking everyone down, these men," he pointed to the soldiers, "these war-trained soldiers of Rome, *fainted*."

"What?" Abel laughed.

"Silence!" His father glared at him before turning back to the soldiers. "You fainted? What happened when you woke up?"

Lucius filled his lungs. "The *angels*," he glared at the High Priest and Rabbi Annas, "were gone. We checked the tomb."

"And the tomb? The body?"

"The body of the King of the Jews was gone."

"*Gone!?*" Joktan screamed. "*Racha!* You fools!" He shook his fists. "Wait until Pilate hears this!"

"No!" Rabbi Annas spoke softly. "I think not."

"What?"

"No one—not even Pontius Pilate—must hear this story," Rabbi Annas said. "If word gets out that *that man's* body is gone, his followers will claim he was raised from the dead, just as he claimed he would."

"How can we *hide* the fact that the Nazarene's body is missing?" Joktan asked.

"We won't," Rabbi Caiaphas said. Turning to Malchus he said. "Bring a bag of gold." He glanced at the soldiers. "Bring four bags." After his servant left, the High Priest continued. "*We* don't want people to think that something *miraculous* happened at the tomb of Jesus ben Joseph, and *you* don't want the governor to hear that you allowed something to happen to the body you were guarding.

"Here is what will we will do. You are to say that you got drunk and fell asleep—"

"But we didn't!" Lucius clenched his fists.

"—and while you were asleep," Rabbi Caiaphas continued, "the Nazarene's disciples came, broke the seal of Rome, moved the stone and stole his body."

"We will be the *laughing stock* of the Antonia Fortress!" Lucius snarled.

Malchus returned at that moment, carrying four heavy bags. At Caiaphas' nod, he handed one to each of the soldiers.

"This should make up for any *embarrassment* you might experience."

"What about Pilate? What if he hears?"

"If this report gets to the governor," Rabbi Annas said, "we will make up something to satisfy him and keep you out of trouble."

Lucius looked at his men and then hefted the bag in his hand. "Fine," he nodded. "We will follow your suggestion."

Turning, the soldiers left the Temple courts.

Looking at his father-in-law, Rabbi Caiaphas said, "What do you think? Will it work?"

"I think it is as good a plan as we could have come up with. Breaking the seal of Rome to open the tomb is a crime against the empire. Whoever did it is a criminal. If it is the Nazarene's followers, then the governor will have them arrested."

Abel heard his father growl.

"When they are arrested," Joktan said, "I will personally nail them to their crosses!" He spewed curses that even Abel had never heard from him, finishing with, "May Yahweh send Jesus ben Joseph and all of his followers to *Gehenna*."

Abel gasped; not that his father would—in the presence of the High Priest and Rabbi Annas—curse someone to eternal punishment. He gasped because he had heard a sound—like a deep moan—beneath their feet. He knew what was coming.

Grabbing his father's tunic, he pulled him away from the columns of the Temple as the earth erupted. Abel fell, arms covering his head, as debris fell around them.

When the ground stopped heaving and the dust settled, Abel lowered his arms and looked around. Rabbi Caiaphas was helping Rabbi Annas to stand; both priests had cuts on their faces and long gashes in their dust-covered garments.

"Abel!" he heard his father scream. "Help me!"

Abel saw his father, lying face down, his head covering was pinned down around his head by several large rocks. No matter how hard his father kicked or squirmed, he could not free himself.

Abel ran over to lift the stones off his father's garments. He put a hand beneath his father's arm, helping him to stand.

Joktan shook the dust from his head and then reached up to straighten his head cloth, but stiffened when Abel screamed.

"What is it?" Joktan asked. "Am I bleeding?" He lifted a hand to his face and froze.

His hand, white as a maggot, was covered in rotting sores.

"Father," Abel stepped back. He licked his lips. "It's.... you're—"

"A *leper*!" Rabbi Annas screamed. "You're a *leper*! Get away! Go away! Get out of the Temple! You're unclean. You're *unclean! Unclean leper!*"

CHAPTER TWENTY-FOUR

21 Nisan 3793

"I cannot believe that, one week ago, Jesus ben Joseph died on a cross." Mary wrapped the goblet and placed it carefully in the chest next to the others.

"And a few days later, he was raised from the dead." Martha laid several layers of folded linens on top of the goblets and lowered the lid of the chest. "Lazarus, this chest is ready. Be careful; not only are these Mother's goblets—may her memory be blessed—but these were the same ones that Jesus and the Twelve used for Passover."

Lazarus hefted the chest to his shoulder. "How does the fact that they *drank* from these make the goblets special?"

Martha placed her fists on her hips. "It just *does*!"

Lazarus looked from his older sister, to his younger—who looked at him as if he were deliberately being thick-headed—to his wife—who smiled sadly at him—and shrugged his shoulders. "I will *never* understand women."

"And the sooner you realize that, my brother," Simon lifted another chest, "the smoother your life will be."

The men grinned and ducked to avoid the wet cloths Martha threw at them.

"Out! Out of my cooking area!" She called after them as they exited the room, "Be careful packing those chests. I better not see a *single* chip on one of those goblets!"

"I cannot believe that Simon and Lazarus are still talking about leaving Bethany." Mary lifted an empty chest to the table. "Our uncle is no longer a threat to us."

"Simply because our uncle no longer is not a threat to us, does not mean that we are not in danger anymore." Martha began sorting through her mixing bowls.

"Martha is correct," Abigail said. "My father and Rabbi Joseph said that while Rabbi Caiaphas and Annas are spreading the *lie* that Jesus was *not* resurrected, it appears that they are still *watching* all of the Teacher's followers. Lazarus said that it will be best if we are away from Jerusalem for a while."

"But for how long?" Mary asked.

"At least for the duration of our pregnancies," Martha said. "Possibly longer." She saw the droop of Mary's lips and crossed to her sister to drape an arm around her shoulders. "Do not worry; you will not be separated from Michael forever. Remember his promise that, no matter where you were, he would come for you."

"I know my brother," Abigail smiled. "If you were in the far reaches of the world, he will still find you." She lowered her brow in mock contemplation. "As we will be married to each other's brothers, will that make us *double* sisters-in-law?"

The three women laughed and returned to packing the kitchen.

The molten sun was arching overhead when Martha decided to end their work. "Let us have a simple meal—there's cheese and bread and grapes. After we eat, I suggest we bathe—packing has made me feel hot and sweaty. Then, I wish to lie down for the rest of the *day!*"

Mary agreed, thankful that her sister's pregnancy gave them all more time; Martha would *never* think of asking anyone to do work while she rested. *I wonder what she's going to do when the babe arrives?*

After washing the few dishes, Mary walked down the hall and up the stairs to her bed chamber. *My* own *bed chamber,* she smiled.

The walls were covered in tapestries that her mother—*may her memory be blessed*—and later Martha, had woven. Along one wall was her bed, a thick pallet on top of a wooden frame. Along another wall were carved chests that held her clothing; Lazarus had brought several chests like these from Egypt for her and for

Martha. Beneath the window was a wash-table with a bowl and pitcher and, next to it, the dressing table for her combs, bottles of perfume and the small vase filled with fresh parsley. The niche built into the corner of the room had two shelves; the lower one held her jewelry box.

Mary touched the shelf above the jewelry box, where stood the empty box that had held her delicate white alabastron. She didn't regret pouring the spikenard over Jesus' feet, but that was before her betrothal. Now, she had *nothing* to use to anoint Michael's feet.

"Stop it, Mary bat Jacob!" she said. "You have *much* to be thankful for. I am betrothed to the man I love." She kissed the gold band on her finger. "Uncle cannot threaten us anymore." *Although I do feel sorry for Aunt Naomi and my cousin Rebeca. And* even *my cousin Abel. May Yahweh bless them.* "And the greatest blessing of all; Jesus ben Joseph is *alive.*"

After Mary Magdala's amazing announcement, Peter and John had run out of the house to return with the news that the tomb was empty. John ben Zebedee was convinced that Mary bat Salathiel had indeed seen Jesus alive, but Peter was hesitant.

Then, several days later, she and Ruth had returned from visiting Leah, to hear that Jesus had just *appeared*—he had not walked—into the room where the disciples, as well as Lazarus, Simon, Michael, Rabbi Nicodemus and Rabbi Joseph, were gathered.

Later, Mary had cornered her brother.

"Lazarus, you spoke to Jesus. Did he explain what happened?"

"What?"

"I mean, Jesus resurrected you; who resurrected him? How was he resurrected?"

"He was resurrected; I didn't need to ask *how.*"

"Oh…how did he look?"

"Look? He looked like Jesus."

"That is not what I meant. I mean…did he look…*oh,* I don't know how to say what I mean."

Lazarus put a hand on her arm. "If you mean, was he covered in scars from the beatings, I don't know. He was dressed; I could not see his back."

I hope I can see him before we leave Bethany.

Lazarus and Abigail planned to leave town as soon as they could. Simon and Martha were waiting for Rabbi Joseph. The elderly priest had decided to journey with them to Gaul, but he had several important things he had to attend to first. He assured them that their departure would be no longer than two months.

Mary had thought at first to go with Lazarus and Abigail, as Cyprus is closer than to Jerusalem—and Michael—than Gaul was. But, she realized that Martha would be further away from family and would need her more when it came time to deliver her baby.

She turned away from the niche with a sigh. Removing her tunic, she crossed to the wash-table to pour water into the bowl. She lifted the bar of perfumed soap to her nose and smiled. During their betrothal feast, Michael had told her that he had been the one to arrange for flowers to be placed in her bed chamber. "I know how much you love them," he had said.

After bathing, she leaned her hair over the bowl to wash it. She knew Martha would say that she should go to their bath room to wash her hair properly, but she was tired; she didn't want to put her robe back on to leave her bed chamber. She rubbed her hair with a linen towel to remove excess water and then picked up the comb and began working it through her dark tresses.

I wonder whether our children will have wavy hair like ours. She blushed and then chided herself. She was betrothed; one day, she would bear Michael's children. She braided her hair before slipping on a light-weight night garment and laid down on her bed.

She dreamt of sons and daughters with black, wavy hair.

The sound of someone pounding on her door startled her awake. "Mary! Mary!"

"What?" She sat up. "Martha, is it another earthquake?"

"No, it is not. Let me in!"

"Mary stumbled across the room to open the door. Martha stood in the corridor and, behind her, was Ruth and Leah.

"Ruth? Leah? Why are you here?" She noticed idly that they were all wearing festive garments.

Leah stepped in front of Martha. "He's coming, Mary!"

"What?" Mary scratched her head, yawning. "Who's coming?"

"Michael," Ruth reached out to grab her arm. "He's coming for you!"

Mary stared at Ruth and Leah, then glanced at Martha. Her sister was smiling and blinking back tears. Her eyes shot open as realization washed over her.

Michael was coming to take her home as his bride.

Today was her wedding day!

"He's coming? Now? Today?"

Martha grinned and drew her into an embrace. "Yes, my dear sister. Your bridegroom is coming *now, today,* for you." She held her at arm's length. "However, Jerusalem is a short distance from Bethany. You must hurry if you wish to be ready when he arrives."

"Yes, yes, I need to get ready." Laying a hand across her forehead, Mary turned to look at her room, not quite certain what she was looking for. "Martha?"

"Yes?"

Mary turned back to her sister. "I do not have any wedding garments."

Martha threw back her head and laughed. She took Mary's hand. "Come."

Martha led Mary—followed by Leah and Ruth—to the bed chamber she shared with Simon. Crossing the room, she pointed towards the bed where some garments were laid.

The tunic was made from rose-colored silk trimmed with gold and silver threads. The girdle and robe were of a deeper rose. Next to it was a soft veil of rose silk edged with tiny gold bells, a golden crown and an opened box filled with jewels.

"Martha," Mary blinked back tears and looked at her sister. "Is this…are these…?"

Martha nodded, her eyes misting. "They are. These are the garments our mother wore on her wedding day and I wore on mine."

Leah broke the moment, "This is all very sweet, but you need to get *dressed.*"

Mary laughed and turned to her friends—her bridesmaids—and extended her arms to each side. "Help me get ready."

In a short time, she was dressed. Thankful that she had already bathed—although she suspected Martha had suggested that she bathe for a reason—Ruth and Leah slipped the silken garments over her head. Martha had her sit at a small table that held the stand mirror Mary had given her. "Don't look yet," Martha said, and turned her so that she could not see her image in the mirror.

Undoing Mary's braid, Martha combed her long, dark waves, before opening the box of their mother's jewels and weaving some into her sister's hair. While Leah and Ruth tied sandals on her feet, Martha draped the veil over her head and on top of that she placed the golden crown.

"Now you can look," Martha said, pointing to the mirror.

Mary swiveled on the bench and looked at her reflection.

"Mary," Leah breathed, "you look like a *queen*."

"No, Leah," Ruth smiled. "She looks like a *bride*."

"She does indeed. Now come," Martha took her hands and helped her stand, "let's go await your bridegroom."

Martha led Mary across the floor while Ruth and Leah rushed over to open the door. Mary saw Lazarus waiting in the corridor for her. He was dressed in a cream-colored linen tunic with a blue linen girdle and tunic.

He smiled when he saw her. "Ah, Mary," he embraced her. "You look beautiful. How do you feel?"

"I confess I feel a little bemused. I had not thought this would happen for years yet, not days."

He laughed. "Well, it is the bridegroom's responsibility to prepare for his bride. It is the bride's responsibility to be ready for him *whenever he comes*." He stepped to her side and slipped her hand through his arm. "Now, come."

He and Martha led Mary down the stairs, through the hall and main room and out the front door. Placed next to the door was a bench under an arch decorated with flowers.

Abigail was smoothing a gold linen cloth over the bench. She stopped to hug Mary before moving to stand with Lazarus. Ruth and Leah straightened Mary's garments, so she could sit. Then they all arranged themselves around her and waited.

Soon, Mary heard the faint sound of music and the plod of

horse hooves. Looking down the street, she saw a carriage draped in colorful ribbons and flowers. It was driven by Rabbi Nicodemus' servant Daniel and seated behind him was Michael. He was dressed like a king, in flowing garments of gold silk and wearing a golden crown. Behind him in another carriage were his attendants; her brother-in-law Simon and Peter bar Jonah.

The carriage stopped in front of their house. Michael smiled when he saw her, his eyes radiating love and passion.

Color washed over Mary's face as she shyly returned his smile.

Stepping down from the carriage, Michael walked up the path to their house and stopped next to Lazarus, his eyes never leaving hers.

Martha helped Mary to stand, while Ruth and Leah straightened her garments. Then Martha and Lazarus moved to stand between her and Michael. Lazarus lifted Mary's hand and Martha placed hers on top. Together, they spoke the traditional blessing over Mary—

"You are our sister; may you become the mother of countless thousands and may your children's children's children rule over the nations."

Martha and Lazarus stepped away, leaving Mary to gaze into Michael's eyes. Looking into those onyx depths, she felt *beautiful*; she felt *loved*; she felt *valued*.

Michael's chest swelled as he extended his hand to her. "I have come for you, my bride."

The rest of the day floated by like a dream from which Mary never wanted to awaken. Michael helped her into the carriage. Ruth and Leah joined them while Lazarus, Abigail and Martha climbed into the carriage with Simon and Peter. Ruth and Leah giggled the entire trip to Jerusalem, waving and calling as friends joined in the bridal procession. But Mary drank in the gaze of her bridegroom.

"Were you surprised?" he asked.

"Yes," she smiled. "I thought we would have to wait years before our wedding."

He threw back his head and laughed. The sound washed over her like a balm. "Well, I confess, this was my father's idea. He said that he grew tired of seeing me wander around the house, *moaning* and *sighing* and behaving as if all light had gone out of my life. After talking it over with Lazarus, who then spoke to Martha—"

"I *knew* she knew something." Mary laughed. "All her talk about wishing to lie down *in the middle of the day!*"

"You should thank her. I wanted this day to be perfect for you and knew you had not had the time to gather your bridal garments. Martha told me that she still had the garments your mother had worn and knew you would not want any other bridal garments."

"I wouldn't. These are perfect."

He smiled at her. "As are you, my bride."

The sun had set by the time they arrived at Michael's home. Martha and Abigail escorted her to a room in the house where they straightened her garments and hair. Making sure her face was covered by the veil, they led her through the house to a walled garden. Stars were scattered across the black expanse of the sky. Friends were gathered around the garden, their smiles illuminated by the soft light from the moon.

Martha and Abigail led her to the center of the garden where, beneath a canopy, Michael waited with his father and her brother.

Mary moved to stand by Michael. She smiled at him before turning to listen to the blessings given by Rabbi Nicodemus and Lazarus, the words that finally completed their wedding.

The feast was everything she had ever dreamt it would be. The touch of Joanna's skilled hand was evident in the banquet hall. The fragrant oil from countless lamps competed with the myriads of flowers set in large urns. "I do not think there is a single flower left in Jerusalem," Mary hugged her new sister-in-law.

"I do not think there is," Joanna laughed. "Michael insisted that the room be a flower garden for you."

Rabbi Nicodemus escorted them to the place of honor, where, seated side by side, they reigned as king and queen of the day. They listened as Rabbi Joseph praised Yahweh for his blessings and laughed as John ben Zebedee, acting as the steward of the feast, told riddles. She smiled when Rabbi Nicodemus—*no, he is now my Father*—praised Michael.

Mary startled when someone said, "I wish to speak of the bride."

She recognized that rich, well-modulated voice and turned to see Jesus ben Joseph walking towards them.

A gasp rippled around the room at Jesus' sudden appearance; then all grew silent and turned to the Teacher. He looked at Michael. "You are a blessed man, Michael ben Nicodemus. Yahweh has given you a beautiful bride; but her beauty goes beyond face and form." He turned to smile at Mary. "Mary is gentle and kind. She loves Yahweh and seeks to use that love to serve others. This is the beauty I speak of and this beauty is eternal."

"Thank you, Teacher," Michael said. He turned to Mary and grinned. "I agree with you."

The room erupted into laughter. Jesus stepped closer to the couple. "May Yahweh bless you with many years of joy in each other and in your children."

"Thank you," Mary blinked away tears. "Thank you for coming to our wedding feast. I hope someday to attend your wedding."

"I promise you, Mary," Jesus smiled, "you will."

Jesus turned as people gathered around him. Mary was thankful for a moment when the attention was not on her. She smiled as she looked around the room, seeing all the people she loved, laughing, singing, rejoicing as they gathered to celebrate this special day.

"Mary?" she heard Michael whisper her name.

She turned to see him smiling at her. He stood and extended his hand. "Come away with me, my beloved."

She stared at him, wondering why he was reciting from the love poem of King Solomon. Then she flushed, realizing what he meant. It was time to consummate their marriage.

She looked up into his face and smiled. She slipped her hand into his and stood. "I belong to my lover," she whispered the Beloved's response, "and his desire is for me."

She was thankful that the guests' attention was still on Jesus, as she and Michael slipped out of the banquet hall. He drew her hand through his arm as he led her through the corridors, up the stairs and down another corridor before stopping to open a door.

He extended his hand for her to enter.

The room was larger than the guest chamber she had used.

Flames dancing over lamp stands placed around the room gave off the scent of perfumed oil. The walls were covered in tapestries of lotus blossoms and pomegranates; Mary knew that Michael's mother had woven them. There were several carved chests along one wall and a wash-table with a bowl and pitcher and a small stack of folded linen. The bed was against another wall; a thick pallet, covered in fine linens, with a small table next to it holding two cups and an *amphorae* beading with condensation.

But what drew Mary's attention was the large urn holding deep-red roses. Crossing to them, she bent to smell their sweet fragrance.

"I asked Abigail to bring them in here for you," Michael said.

"I will have to thank her," Mary said.

"There is another gift for you."

Mary's heart began beating when he lifted a small, wooden box. Mary looked at Michael and then at the box. Her hands trembled as she took it, holding it as if it held something quite valuable. Slipping a finger under the latch, she opened the lid. Padded by thick wool was a slender white stone jar. Lifting it, she heard the *slosh* of liquid beneath the seal.

"My *alabastron*," she whispered. "What? Who?." she looked at him. "How did this *come* here?"

"Martha."

"Ma-martha?" she stuttered.

He nodded and picked up a small scroll. "She asked me to give this to you."

Mary set her alabastron on the table and took the scroll. Unrolling it, she read:

My Sweet Mary,

Over the last year, Lazarus and I have seen you grow from a wounded child into a loving young woman. The night we celebrated Lazarus' resurrection—when you anointed Jesus—you poured out the one thing that, for you, represented love.

I kept the jar and, after your betrothal, had Lazarus fill it with spikenard that he and Simon keep at their warehouse. We set it aside for the day you would become a bride.

That day is today.

CHAPTER TWENTY-FIVE

28 Ivar 3793

Bethany

"I love the Mount of Olives," Mary said. "The trees provide cool shade during the warm months."

"Not to mention all the delicious olives," Michael laughed, popping a large green olive in his mouth. "There's Abigail." He lifted a hand and waved.

His sister waved and walked over to them.

"Hello, Abigail." Michael jumped up to help her sit on the ground near Martha. "You look well."

"I look big, Michael, I look *big*." She fanned her face with her hand. "At least the wind is pleasant."

He laughed. "Where is Lazarus?"

"Over there with John ben Zebedee," she wiggled her fingers towards the upper slope of the mount. "Greetings, Mary bat Eli. Salome bat Eli, Mary Magdala."

The three women returned her greeting.

"How are you feeling?" the Teacher's mother asked.

"Better, now that my stomach is not tender anymore. I understand from Martha," she grinned at her sister-in-law, "that I have you to thank for the suggestion of the mint tea."

"I am glad to hear it helped," the older Mary said. "I used it during all of my pregnancies." She shaded her eyes with her flattened hand and looked around. "Have you seen my son—" she glanced at her sister, "I mean, have you seen Jesus?" She laughed, "To confess, it is still difficult to remember that, although Jesus *is* my son, he wants me to treat *John* as my son."

"We all understand that you would wish to forget what happened on *that* day," Mary Magdala said. Her eyes misted. "I still cannot walk past Golgotha without crying."

"Do not cry," Salome said. "Think of happier things. It has been over five weeks since Jesus rose from the dead and we have all seen him many times."

"And that brings me back to my question," Mary bat Eli said. "Does anyone know where Jesus is? There are so many people here, I cannot see—oh wait; there he is. Over by your brother Lazarus."

Jesus stood at the top of the mount. The white of his garments stood out against the grey clouds, some which seemed so low as to touch the ground. He gestured for everyone to gather around him.

Mary and Michael helped their own sisters stand and followed the crowd up the ridge. When they drew near to the Teacher, Lazarus joined them.

Jesus ben Joseph looked over the group, pausing to smile at his mother.

"Sir," Mary heard someone ask, "I believe—" the man nodded to those around him, "we *all* believe that you are the promised *Messiah*. Are you *now* going to restore the kingdom to Israel?"

"Do not worry about times and dates," Jesus smiled. "Those are already set by my Father by His own authority."

"Authority?" the man repeated. "What do you mean?"

Jesus extended his hands. "All authority in Heaven and on Earth has been given to me."

"If you have the authority," the first man asked, "what about us?"

"What should we do?" asked Peter bar Jonah.

"Wait." Jesus smiled at the confused look on the big disciple's face. "Do not leave Jerusalem, but *wait* for the gift my Father promised, the one you heard me speak about."

"Gift?" Mary heard a woman ask. "What *gift* are you talking about, Teacher?"

"You will know the gift when you receive it," Jesus answered.

"John baptized with water, but soon you will be baptized with my Father's Holy Spirit.

"When the Holy Spirit comes, He will give you power; power that you will use to be my witnesses in Jerusalem, in Judea and Samaria and to the ends of the earth. And know this," his voice grew louder, echoing across the Mount of Olives, "I will be with you always, to the very end of time."

Mary noticed the clouds behind the Teacher begin to shimmer and glow as if they had managed to capture the sun. The wind picked up, whipping up the hill, stripping leaves from the trees. She lifted a hand to shield her eyes; then she saw rays of light shining around her palm. She spread her fingers and peeked through.

The wind had parted the clouds, forcing them down to the very spot where Jesus ben Joseph stood. The brilliant sun shone down on him, his garments reflecting the light until they glowed. The sun and wind did not appear to affect Jesus; he turned his face upwards, smiling, his hair whipping wildly around his head.

As she watched, the clouds began to lift and Jesus rose with them.

Mary gasped, dropping to her knees. Michael dropped to his knees beside her, as did Lazarus and Abigail, Martha and Simon. All those on the Mount of Olives were on their knees, looking up as Jesus ben Joseph rose into the sky, lighting flashing in the clouds all around him.

"Do you hear them?" Mary bat Eli said.

Mary looked at the Teacher's mother. The older woman was staring upwards, her countenance radiant.

"Isn't it glorious?" Jesus' mother smiled. "It's the same song they sang at his birth."

Mary bat Jacob closed her eyes and listened. Yes, she heard something…no, she heard someone…many voices…*singing*. Their words were beyond her understanding, but it was glorious.

Opening her eyes, she meets Jesus' gaze. He is looking at her, just as he did from the cross. Only this time, there is no pain, there is no sadness. His death on the cross is behind him. Now, in his eyes, she saw peace. Now she saw joy. And something more…*Glory*. She saw victorious *glory*!

The clouds, still glittering with lightning, enfolded Jesus, hiding him from their view.

Mary craned her neck, trying to locate him, when voices echoed around the mountain top.

"Men of Galilee."

Mary lowered her face to see two men standing where Jesus had stood moments before. Dressed in luminous robes, they were taller and broader than any man she had ever seen before. From their hair whipping wildly around their faces to the skin of their massive bodies, every part of them was as white as their garments.

"Why do you stand here looking into the sky?" they spoke as one, their voices resounding. *"Jesus has been taken from you into Heaven."* The angels—for what else could they be—lifted their arms. *"But He will return in the same way you have seen Him go into Heaven."*

The angels vanished.

Mary did not gasp. How else should this moment end? *But it will not truly end,* she raised her face to look at the sky, revelation exploding in her mind as the lightning flashed across the clouds. *I will remember* this *moment. Every day, for the rest of my life, I will remember when Jesus ben Joseph was revealed in glory as the promised Messiah, as the Son of Yahweh.*

ABOUT THE AUTHOR

Early training in music and theater led Paula K. Parker to a life-long love for the arts. This passion eventually brought her to Nashville, Tennessee, where she—along with her writer husband, Mike—helped establish local community theaters Carpenter's Playhouse and Springhouse Theatre Company.

Paula co-authored *YHWH: The Flood, The Fish & The Giant* and *YESHUA: The King, The Demon & The Traitor* with New York Times Best-selling novelist, GP Taylor, before penning her own bestselling novel, *Sisters of Lazarus: Beauty Unveiled*, and its sequel, *Glory Revealed: Sisters of Lazarus Book 2*.

An internationally acclaimed playwright, Paula has written numerous short sketches, one-acts and full-length plays, including *The Sam Jones Story*, a historical play commissioned by Nashville's Summer Lights Foundation, and her popular adaptations of the classics, *Jane Austen's Pride and Prejudice*, *Jane Austen's Sense & Sensibility* and *Jane Austen's EMMA*.

To learn more about Paula and her writing, visit her online at

www.PaulaKParker.com

AUTHOR'S NOTE

When I read stories in the Bible, I wonder about how or why the people said or did certain things. How did Noah gather the animals into the ark? Why would Rebekah and Isaac favor one son over the other? Why did Balak not run screaming in terror when the donkey spoke to him? What did Peter think when he was walking on the water? Who could afford perfume that cost a year's wages?

Perhaps because of their "moment in time" nature, the people in these Bible stories are often viewed as iconic figures on a stained glass window. David was a courageous young boy. Solomon was the wisest of all. Peter was brash and impulsive. Judas was a traitor. Martha fretted over a meal while Mary sat peacefully at Jesus' feet. People misunderstood Who Jesus of Nazareth truly was.

But these people were more than a boy with five stones, a man with a floating zoo, parents who played favorites, a disciple who acted before thinking, a woman with an expensive bottle of cologne or people following the teacher from Nazareth. They had flaws and strengths, likes and dislikes, favorite foods, hopes and fears, pride and insecurities.

Just like us.

One reason I like writing biblical novels is that, for me, when I view these people as simple humans—when I research their time period and culture—the Bible stories come alive and I glimpse possible answers to some of my questions.

My original plan was to take *Sisters of Lazarus: Beauty Unveiled* through Passion Week. After all, I thought, you can't write a book about people mentioned in the Gospels without including the central story of the Bible. However, when I finished writing the scene of Mary anointing Jesus, I realized that was where the book needed to end. *Sisters of Lazarus; Beauty Unveiled* was about Mary and Martha and their struggles with issues of self-worth.

After *Beauty Unveiled* was released, I frequently received comments from people who had read the book, wanting to know what happened to 'this' character or 'that' character. When I realized that these readers were invested in the lives of those characters, I knew I needed to finish their story. Although I had never planned to write a series, this is what precisely what happened and *Glory Revealed: Sisters of Lazarus, Book 2* was born.

Glory Revealed picks up minutes after the final scene in *Beauty Unveiled* and follows the events of Passion Week through to the Ascension of Jesus Christ. All of the characters you loved, and those that you hated, from Beauty Unveiled are in it.

Just as *Beauty Unveiled* had an underlying message of our value being found in the fact that we are created and loved by God, *Glory Revealed* also has an underlying message based upon my own—and what I assume other people's—experiences.

By nature, I am more like Martha. I like order in my life. I create and live by my lists. I prefer to think things through before acting. I will even write down points before making an important phone call.

Occasionally, however, I act spontaneously like Mary did when she poured the spikenard over Jesus' feet. During those moments I feel wonderful, I feel exuberant. Once I walk away, or wake up the next morning, however, I begin to question the motives behind my actions. I sometimes wonder, "What does this person or that person think about what I did?"

When it is ordinary, everyday life, it is not a bad thing to question our motives. When that spontaneity is an act of worship, it is not uncommon for the enemy of our soul—Satan—to whisper in our ears, suggesting that people will not understand what we did and our value in their eyes will diminish. While it's sad that some people might think less of us, our Savior will never think less of us for acts of worship directed towards Him. And Jesus Christ's opinion of us is all that truly matters.

Selah.

If you would like to learn more about the research I used for different aspects of this book, visit my website: www.paulakparker. com and click on the link for Useful Information, Glossary, and Research.

Finally (and this is a big request), if you liked this story, would you consider leaving a review wherever you bought this book, or on your favorite social media platform? I love this story and want as many readers as possible to discover it, and your voice can help do that. Leave a review and tell a friend! Word-of-mouth is the best way to introduce this story to other readers.

Thank you, dear reader, for giving your time to read this book. Stories need an audience. It means a lot that you trusted me to entertain, and hopefully excite, you with this story.

Thank you.

And now a Sneak Peak at
Sisters of Lazarus: Book 3

GRACE EXTENDED

When Jesus told Peter and the rest of those on the Mount of Olives to, *"Wait,"* He had added, *"Do not leave Jerusalem."* Rabbi Nicodemus—and those believers who had homes in Jerusalem—welcomed those who did not, which included all the Eleven.

Not knowing what to do while they waited for the *comforter,* several days after Jesus' ascension, Peter and the other disciples showed up at Lazarus and Simon's warehouse. Lazarus relayed the story later that night, when he and Abigail were having supper with the family at Rabbi Nicodemus' home.

"Peter asked permission to use our upper room as a place for them to be together and pray. They explained it was the room where they had celebrated the last Passover with the Lord Jesus, may His name be blessed. Of course, we said 'Yes.' They are in the upper room, praying even now."

At first it was the Eleven—along with Jesus' mother, His aunt, and Mary Magdala—who gathered to pray. A few days later, other followers of the Lord Jesus heard about it and asked to join them. Soon, the upper room was filled throughout the day, and all the watches of the night, with people praying and sharing remembrances of what the Lord Jesus had done and said. During one of these times of prayer, the disciples, led by Peter, selected Matthias bar Esdras to replace Judas Iscariot as one of the Twelve.

Shortly after the believers began gathering, Martha had told Mary and Abigail she planned to bake bread to take to those people. "The warehouse belongs to our family," she said. "That makes them our guests."

Mary and Abigail offered to do the same. Elisheba, always interested in feeding anyone associated with the family of her beloved Mistress Hannah, put the servant girls to work, preparing bread and cheese to take to those praying.

There," Mary set the last basket on the table. "I hope it is enough. Let us join our husbands in prayer before the men go to the Temple."

Both floors of the building had a main room and several smaller rooms. The central room on the upper floor was smaller than its counterpart downstairs. The room itself had no decorations, only lampstands placed between the latticed windows.

Not that decorations would make any difference. The central room, as well as the smaller side rooms, were packed with people. Some were kneeling, others standing, and some sitting, their voices filling the air with a hum as they prayed.

"Do you see our husbands?" Mary whispered, scanning the room, "Wait, there they are; by the window, with Lazarus and Abigail."

"Praise Yahweh, a spot by the window," Martha whispered, lifting her tunic away from her body with a little shake. "The room is already stuffy. I cannot remember Sivan being so hot before."

"You have never been pregnant before."

"You speak truth."

They waited as Peter led the believers in the *Shemah*: "Hear O Israel, the LORD is our God, the LORD is one!" After speaking the first line of the *Shemah*, Mary repeated the second line silently, as every Jewish child had been taught: *Blessed be the name of His glorious kingdom for ever and ever.*

In the silence after the prayer, she and Martha stepped quietly to where Michael and Simon stood with Rabbi Nicodemus, Lazarus, Abigail, and Ruth. She smiled a greeting at Rabbi Joseph bar Neriah, who stood near her father-in-law. Mary glanced out of the window—which faced the street—and noticed a man standing behind the old sycamore fig tree across the street. She frowned. Normally someone standing beneath the shade of a tree would not be unusual, but the poor man was clasping his head as if in pain.

She started to draw Michael's attention to the man, but Peter began the prayer the Lord Jesus had taught them. She closed her eyes and joined in:

> *Our Father, Who art in heaven,*
> *hallowed be Your Name,*
> *Your kingdom come,*
> *Your will be done,*
> *on earth as it is in heaven.*
> *Give us this day our daily bread.*
> *And forgive us our trespasses,*
> *as we forgive those*
> *who trespass against us.*
> *And lead us not into temptation,*
> *but deliver us from evil.*
> *For Thine is the kingdom,*
> *and the power, and the glory,*
> *for ever and ever.*

The room resonated with the "Amen," and the voices grew quiet.

Mary loved this prayer, but it brought up many questions. She was beginning to understand the impact of the Lord Jesus' death. She still wept when she thought of that day on Golgotha, that He was to be the sacrifice for her—for everyone's—trespasses. But He was the Son of Yahweh; He had strength beyond hers. *How do I forgive others as He forgave me?*

Then there was the *kingdom.* Mary had been raised to believe the kingdom would be restored when the Messiah came, drove out the Romans, and returned Israel to the glory it had known under King David. Now, with the revelation that the Lord Jesus was the Messiah, but not as everyone expected, she had begun to wonder what else she had misunderstood. Not just about Yahweh's kingdom, but *everything* she had been taught. The problem was, no matter who she asked—even her beloved father-in-law or the esteemed Rabbi Joseph—no one could answer her questions.

Maybe this counselor *the Lord Jesus spoke of will have the answers.* Drawing a deep breath, she prayed, *Lord Jesus, I want to do what You commanded. I want to be the godly wife to Michael that King Solomon wrote about. I want to be as You described Sarah. I want to be the gentle, kind, and loving woman You spoke of during our wedding feast. On that last day—on the Mount of Olives—You said You would be with us always, but I do not understand what that means. How can You be with us when You are gone? I have so many questions, and no one has the answers.*

Mary heard a gentle breeze but did not feel its brush on her cheek. She heard another gust whistle around the room but did not feel its touch. She frowned when she heard a third blast that sounded as if a giant was trying to yank the shutters off the window.

Then she heard a gasp rippling from those around her. Looking up to see if someone was hurt, her eyes widened, her jaw dropped.

The sound of the wind was whipping around the room, yet not a single head cloth nor garment of clothing was disturbed. What caused the gasping, and drew every eye, was the massive flame in the center of the room above their heads. It flickered and danced, sending showers of red and yellow into the air.

Suddenly the flame *divided*—that was the only way Mary could describe it—into countless smaller flames. Mesmerized, she watched the flames floating toward each person in the room, to hover over their heads.

She sensed the flame dancing over her own head, saw its illumination around her. She felt the flame's warmth but not, as she would expect, from above. The warmth began in her chest and radiated outwards, from her stomach to her legs; from her arms to her fingertips, from her neck to her head. As the warmth rose, Mary felt a bubble forming in her throat. When the bubble reached her mouth, she opened her lips.

"Θα τραγουδήσω στον Κύριο, γιατί είναι πολύ έντιμος. Το άλογο και ο αναβάτης του έχουν πετάξει στη θάλασσα."

She had heard Greek spoken by Stephen ben Chariton and by other Greeks in the marketplace, but she did not know it. Nevertheless, she knew she was speaking the praise of Moses after Yahweh parted the Red Sea. "*I will sing to the LORD, for He is highly exalted. The horse and its rider He has hurled into the sea.*"

"*Vineam de Aegypto eiecisti gentes et plantasti eam,*" Martha spoke the language of the Romans—a language neither she nor Martha knew—yet Mary understood what her sister said. "*You brought a vine out of Egypt; you drove out the nations and planted it.*"

People around the room were speaking languages Mary had heard in the marketplace but could not identify; yet she understood them as they spoke praises from the Holy Scriptures.

"*You laid the earth's foundation!*" Michael called out, "*You marked off its dimensions! You stretched a measuring line across it and laid its cornerstone, while the morning stars sang together and the angels shouted for joy!*"

"*Who among the gods is like You, O LORD? Who is like You—majestic in holiness, awesome in glory, working wonders?*" from Rabbi Nicodemus

"*Give thanks to the LORD, call on His name,*" Lazarus cried. "*Make known among the nations what He has done. Sing to Him, sing praise to Him; tell of all His wonderful acts. Glory in His holy name; let the hearts of those who seek the LORD rejoice!*"

Abigail sang, "*Like Your name, O God, Your praise reaches to the ends of the earth; Your right hand is filled with righteousness.*"

"*You were in the blazing furnace with Your servants: Shadrach, Meshach, and Abednego,*" Rabbi Joseph shouted. "*When they came forth, all saw that the fire had not harmed their bodies, nor was a hair of their heads singed; their robes were not scorched, and there was no smell of fire on them. Because they trusted in You and were willing to give up their lives rather than serve or worship any god but You.*"

The unseen wind blew the flames; they pulsed and shimmered around the room, illuminating it as though they were standing under the midday sun. Mary felt each pulse from the flames as if they were coursing through her veins. The voices of the people raised in praise of Yahweh sounded to Mary like that of a mighty waterfall.